Additional Praise for *The Hammer of God*

"At last the splendid concluding chapter of Bishop Bo Giertz's *The Hammer of God* is available for English readers, and the symbolic shape of the book is complete: three parts, each divided into three chapters. This powerful historical and theological novel, set in one parish in Sweden in the years around 1810, 1870, and 1941, examines convincingly the continuing struggle against those persistent forces that would undermine and destroy the authentic faith of the Church. Large theological doctrines are here given a local habitation in memorable individuals, each with distinctive strengths and limitations. Read this book to learn theology, to be reminded of the strength of the historical Church, to be led more deeply into prayer and devotion."

—*Philip H. Pfatteicher*
Associate Pastor, First Lutheran Church, Pittsburgh
Adjunct Professor of Sacred Music, Duquesne University

"Giertz's themes are unabashedly Lutheran. God shapes us hammer-like on the anvil of experience. But God's Law is an alien Word. Authentic faith and discipleship are evoked only by the Gospel, God's proper Word. The novel's new chapter brings satisfying closure to the final story. Giertz makes his stories interesting and edifying, equally instructive for clergy and laity, a fine confessional resource for parish discussion groups."

—*Walter R. Bouman*
Edward C. Fendt Emeritus Professor of Systematic Theology
Trinity Lutheran Seminary, Columbus, Ohio

THE
HAMMER
OF
GOD

Bo Giertz

Revised Edition

A novel about the cure
of souls

Original English translation
of chapters 1-8 by
CLIFFORD ANSGAR NELSON
(1960)

Revised edition translation
of chapter 9 by
HANS ANDRAE (2005)

Augsburg Books

MINNEAPOLIS

THE HAMMER OF GOD

Copyright © 1960 Augustana Book Concern
Augsburg paperback, 1973
Revised edition copyright © 2005 Augsburg Fortress. All rights reserved.
Except for brief quotations in critical articles or reviews, no part of this book
may be reproduced in any manner without prior written permission from the
publisher. Write to: Permissions, Augsburg Fortress, Publishers, P. O. Box 1209,
Minneapolis, MN 55440-1209.

Large-quantity purchases or custom editions of this book are available at a
discount from the publisher. For more information, contact the sales depart-
ment at Augsburg Fortress, Publishers, 1-800-328-4648, or write to: Sales
Director, Augsburg Fortress, Publishers, P. O. Box 1209, Minneapolis, MN
55440-1209.

Library of Congress Cataloging-in-Publication Data
Giertz, Bo, 1905-
  [Stengrunden. English]
  The hammer of God / by Bo Giertz.—Rev. ed.
     p. cm.
  "Original English translation of Chapters 1-8 by Clifford Ansgar Nelson
(1960); Revised edition translation of Chapter 9 by Hans Andrae (2005)."
  ISBN 978-0-8066-5130-9
  I. Nelson, Clifford Ansgar. II. Andrae, Hans. III. Title.

  PT9875.G53S7413 2005
  833'.914—dc22   2004025013

Cover design by Laurie Ingram; cover art from PhotoDisc
Book design by Michelle L. N. Cook

The paper used in this publication meets the minimum requirements of
American National Standard for Information Sciences-Permanence of Paper
for Printed Library Materials, ANSI Z329.48-1984.

Manufactured in the U.S.A.

Contents

Preface

The *Hammer of God* is a most remarkable novel. It has the drama, the suspense, the intensity, and the description of persons, of culture, and of nature that characterize the highest level of literature. The reader gets totally immersed in the unfolding story as well as fully engaged in the many mind-boggling and heart-wrenching dialogues. Holding the reader in a grip like a good detective story, the unfolding events present a spiritual drama of death and life, of despair and hope, of upheaval and peace, of sin and grace—all experienced in everyday life by real people in their relation to the Church and her message.

In this genre, one critic placed *The Hammer of God* as urgent reading, along with *The Man Who Was Thursday* by Chesterton, *Crime and Punishment* by Dostoevsky, and *The Power and the Glory* by Greene.

Another remarkable feature of this novel is that it actually is a trilogy made up of three novellas, each taking the reader to different historic eras while the local setting is the same rural area in southern Sweden.

The author unveils the dramatic confrontation between the Faith of the Church and the many beliefs (and disbeliefs) that battle for the human soul, which basically remains constant even as cultural settings are changed. Faith comes down to a matter of relying either on our own accomplishments to be right with God or on receiving as a free gift by grace the righteousness Christ gained for us. The situation for us today is the same as in generations past, as the three eras covered in the book attest—the first novella (1808–1810), the second novella (1878–1880), and the third novella (1938–1940).

It is commonly understood that the novel's local setting is the Ydre Deanery of the Linköping Diocese of the (evangelical-Lutheran) Church of Sweden. Ydre, no longer a deanery, comprised eight parishes: Asby, Malexander, Norra Vi, Sund, Svinhult, Tidersrum, Torpa, and Vestra Ryd. How the fictitious parish names in the novel (Ödesjö, Näs, Ravelunda, Fröjerum, and Brohult) correspond to the real parish names is anybody's guess.

When Giertz wrote this novel in 1941, he was the pastor in the Torpa parish. It brought immediate fame to the author, as it became the third on the bestseller list in Sweden for that year. Today, more than sixty years later, it continues to be in great demand in many languages. Why is that so? Because its message remains relevant and current to readers in all nations throughout all generations!

This edition of *The Hammer of God* is remarkable for yet another reason: It includes, for the first time in English, the ninth and final chapter ("In the Place of Sinners") of *Stengrunden*, the original Swedish version. Why that chapter was not included in the English version published in 1960 by the Augustana Book Concern in an excellent translation by the Reverend Clifford Ansar Nelson, and again in 1973 by Augsburg Press, is not known. It is now my privilege through the gracious cooperation of the Augsburg Fortress Publishers to provide English-speaking readers with the translation of this chapter. Finally, readers will get the full story of *The Hammer of God,* as the action moves to the eventful stage of the Finnish-Russian Winter War of 1939–1940. On the following pages I am presenting also a brief Giertz biography and Introductory Notes to *The Hammer of God,* which I hope will be helpful to readers not familiar with my native land of Sweden.

On Monday in Holy Week 1997, I had the unforgettable opportunity to interview Bishop Giertz for just over an hour. I asked for his permission to translate some of his works into English. He gave me his permission but added, "Make sure you work with someone whose native language is English." I gratefully acknowledge that my American wife Sylvia and our children Rebecka, Eric, and Christina assisted me in producing that final chapter in a good idiomatic rendering of the American language. I am also grateful to my good friends, the Reverend Larry Beane and his wife Grace, for transferring my manuscript of the translation into a typed version.

—Hans Andrae, Pittsburgh, on Holy Cross Day, September 14, Anno Domini 2004

One of the appointed readings for Holy Cross Day is 1 Corinthians 1:18-24. In his coat of arms as Bishop of Göteborg, Bo Giertz included a few words from verse 18 in the Latin version:

VERBUM CRUCIS DEI VIRTUS
The word of the cross is the power of God—

In the Torpa Churchyard, the Bishop's gravemarker displays his coat of arms:

Bo Giertz:
The Atheist Who
Became a Bishop

As the Twentieth Century was coming to an end, *Kyrkans Tidning*, the official weekly newspaper of the Church of Sweden asked its readers, "Who made the greatest impact on the church in Sweden during the 1900s?" Bo Giertz got more votes than anyone else! Through his inspiring leadership as a pastor and a bishop, and as an author of many bestsellers, Giertz exerted matchless influence in Sweden. And through his literary production, especially *The Hammer of God*, his influence continues unabated amongst Lutherans in many lands. In fact, Giertz (1905–1998) may be compared with his famous contemporaries, C. S. Lewis (1898–1963) and Dietrich Bonhoeffer (1906–1945). All three had somewhat different theological emphases, but each was a brilliant communicator of the Christian faith, not only to his own generation but to following generations as well. Anyone who is guided by these mentors will get an authentic understanding of the Church's faith.

The title of the most popular Giertz biography, *Bo Giertz—The Atheist Who Became a Bishop*, by Algot Mattsson (© 1991, not yet available in English), sums up in a few words the remarkable life of this man. He was born on August 31, 1905. (Note that this volume marks the centennial of his birth, which will be observed with symposia and other events in 2005, not only in Sweden but also here in the USA). Giertz' father was an acclaimed surgeon who already at age thirty-five became head of the new hospital in Umeå, at the time the fourth largest hospital in the nation. Bo, with his sister and his five brothers, usually spent the summers with his maternal grandparents. His lifelong interest in technology was first kindled by his grandfather, Lars Magnus Ericsson, a pioneering inventor in the field of telecommunications and the founder of the global industrial Ericsson enterprise.

Traditional Christian virtues such as honesty and charity were appreciated and encouraged in the Giertz family, though the father was an atheist and the mother an agnostic. All areas of human learning and experience were discussed at the dinner table—all, that is, but religion. As a high school student Bo had often been present when his father performed surgery, sometimes even writing (in Latin) the surgery report in the journal. When Bo Giertz enrolled at the University of Uppsala in 1924, his choice of study was easy—medicine!

However, in the university environment Bo encountered on the one hand a radical atheism displaying an uninhibited egoism. On the other hand, he met students of theology who explained their Christian faith with intelligence and lived their faith with sincerity. Through this experience, Giertz was moved away from his atheism to the faith of the Church. Indeed, he wanted to become a pastor, so he devoted the years 1928–1932 to the required theological studies. Before being ordained in the Linköping Cathedral on December 28, 1934, he served as a traveling consultant for the Church's High School Student Association. He was able to convey to thousands of teenagers his own enthusiasm for the Church and the relevance of its faith even in an age marked by increasing scientific knowledge of the universe and of human nature. A frequent and appreciated (and attacked!) writer, both in church periodicals and in newspapers, Giertz became known to the general public as a bold and gifted expounder of church doctrine as anchored in Scripture, confessed in the Creeds, and explained in the Lutheran Confessions.

Following his ordination, Giertz had three shorter pastoral assignments before he was elected pastor in the small rural Torpa parish in October 1938 (see Preface). Although very busy with his parish duties and with speaking engagements elsewhere (100-200 annually), he managed to be an astonishingly prolific writer during his eleven and a half years in Torpa parish. During this period he produced no less than four major theological works; two novels; a fascinating retelling of the gospel events, *With My Own Eyes* (1947), in a style reminiscent of Walter Wangerin; and also *The Foundation* (1942), a widely-used (225,000 copies sold by 1977) textbook for confirmands, which is even translated into Tamil and Zulu!

With all his literary productions Giertz was aiming at presenting basic Christian beliefs both to believers and to skeptics. That is the purpose of the four theological works: *Christ's Church* and *Church Piety* (both 1939), *The Great Lie and the Great Truth* (1945; number 10 bestseller in Sweden that year), and *The Battle for Man* (1946). It is also the purpose of his novels *The Hammer of God* (1941; see Introductory Notes) and *Faith Alone* (1943).

The setting of *Faith Alone* is Sweden in the 1540s, an era of intensive and decisive confrontation between the Roman

Catholic loyalists and the proponents for the Lutheran reformation, represented respectively by Father Andreas in Fröjerum and Pastor Peder in Ravelunda, in the same geographic setting as in *The Hammer of God*. The heavy hand of state absolutism is everywhere present, as King Gustav Vasa hijacks the reformation movement to extend the state's power over the church, even pronouncing the death verdict on the leading Lutheran reformer, Olavus Petri, although that sentence was never carried out.

In the spring of 1949, Bo Giertz was elected Bishop of the Göteborg Diocese by a large majority of the clergy. This election caused an amazing amount of attention. Never before had a *komminister* (associate pastor) been elected bishop. And to top it all off, Giertz had been pastor of a small rural parish. Torpa was part of a two-parish "pastorat" with the senior pastor residing in the other parish, Asby. At age forty-three, Giertz was also unusually young to become a bishop, especially in one of the most prestigious dioceses. He is, in fact, the youngest bishop elected during the one hundred years since 1905.

During his time as bishop (1949–1970) Giertz did not produce any major works of literature, but he wrote hundreds of articles in church periodicals, theological journals, and newspapers. He traveled abroad extensively on behalf of the Church of Sweden, including visits to India and Tanzania for the consecration of bishops, and to Brazil and the United States as second vice president of the executive committee of the Lutheran World Federation. President of that committee was Franklin Clark Fry, who served first as bishop of the ULCA and later the LCA, following the 1962 church merger. Fry was a church leader to whom Giertz referred with much respect and appreciation.

In 1958 the Churchwide Assembly of the Lutheran Church in Sweden (*Kyrkomötet*) accepted a proposal by the government to open the pastoral office (*prästämbetet*) to women, a proposal the Assembly had turned down a year earlier. Those opposed to this change rallied to form the Church Movement for Bible and Confession, which had no formal membership roster. With Giertz acting as chair, a coordinating committee with representatives from various church groups and organizations planned both nationwide and regional gatherings, some of which attracted thousands of attendees. The movement thus generated considerable support from a very large portion of the pastors and from many active church members. However, the newspapers, political parties, and a great majority of the general public did not accept the biblical and confessional arguments utilized by opponents to women's ordination, and instead accused them of degrading women. This mischaracterization of his stand on that issue was a heavy cross to carry for Giertz through the last forty years of his life.

Following his retirement in 1970, Giertz once again became an extraordinarily productive writer of a great diversity of literature, all with that overriding purpose of telling the good news of Jesus Christ. As Bishop Emeritus he also accepted a great number of invitations as speaker and lecturer in Sweden and abroad, with approximately 300 such engagements annually in the 1970s.

In his later writings, the variety of literary genres is once again evident. *The ABC of Our Christian Faith* (1971) is a thought-provoking compendium for young and old, commissioned by the Church Folk University. *The Knights of Rhodos* (1972) is a dramatic historic novel about the Order of St. John. It describes how a few hundred members trying to stop the expansion of Islam finally had to give up their stronghold on Rhodos in 1522. Giertz devoted meticulous efforts in studying the well-preserved fortifications on that island as well as the well-kept archives of the Order on Malta. This book, a bestseller

in Sweden (30,000 copies in a country not much more popu-
lous than New York City), has been translated into many languages, but not yet into English. Devotions for every day in the
Church Year came out in two volumes, *To Believe in Christ*
(1973) and *To Live with Christ* (1974).

Some argue that Giertz' most remarkable literary accom-
plishment was his translation of the New Testament. He was
planning on writing a commentary to the entire NT. As he
began that gigantic task, he soon realized that he needed a
version of the NT text in contemporary Swedish. The official
Church Bible was dated 1917. There were also more recent
translations available, but they were not entirely to his liking.
So he decided to do one himself. On October 11, 1981, he was
granted an audience to King Carl Gustaf, to whom he presented the first copy of his New Testament translation. During
the years 1977–1982, Giertz published his commentaries to
each of the New Testament Scriptures with the text of the
comments about three times more extensive than the Bible
text itself, a well-balanced ratio appreciated by ordinary Bible
readers, whom the commentator had in mind when he did
this work.

All of Giertz' major works are available in the five
Nordic languages as well as in German. Some are also available in other languages. Not much is available in English.
Only *With My Own Eyes* translated by Maurice Michael
(1960); and a portion of *Herdabrev,* the new Bishop's greeting to his diocese, translated by Clifford Ansgar Nelson,
while he was Pastor of the Gloria Dei Lutheran Church in
St. Paul, Minnesota, and published by the Augustana Book
Concern in 1950 with the title *Liturgy and Spiritual
Awakening.* And then, ten years later, came the great
event—Pastor Nelson's translation of *The Hammer of God,*
which continues to benefit thousands of grateful English-
speaking readers.

Bo Giertz intentionally and successfully integrated elements from the high-church liturgical movement with the best features of low-church piety into a vibrant evangelical Lutheran orthodoxy that is made manifest in the Body of Christ, the One Holy Christian and Apostolic Church.

Introductory Notes

The Swedish title of this book is *Stengrunden,* which literally translated would be "the stone ground." The word occurs frequently in the eighth chapter, *stengrunden och försoningsklippan* (twelve times), where the translator five times opted for "the rock foundation," twice for "the stone foundation," twice for "the stony ground," once for "the rocky base," once for "the stony foundation," and once for "the whole sinful rock of man's natural heart" (page 268). With that latter rendering of *stengrunden,* the translator correctly defines the meaning of that Swedish word when used to describe humanity's sinful condition.

The translator chose "A Heart of Stone and a Rock of Salvation" as heading for the eighth chapter. However, he opted—and I think rightly so—for a more literal translation of *stengrunden* and *försoningsklippan* (*försoning* meaning "atonement"), when he rendered one of the most monumental statements in Giertz' book in this way: "**The stone foundation** of the heart and **the Rock of Atonement** on Golgotha are the two mountains on which a man's destiny is determined" (page 269). I would have preferred those words as the heading for this chapter in the English version. After all, **The Stone**

Foundation is Giertz' title for the whole book, and **the Rock of Atonement** is his chosen expression for the heart and center of the Christian faith, which this author is so eager to show each one of us.

The English title of this book, *The Hammer of God*, is, of course, a reference to the work of God's holy Law. It crushes like a hammer our "good" deeds by which we try to be righteous before God. And as a result, it also exposes the stone foundation, our sinful heart, which we attempt to cover with our "good" deeds. Then we are ready for the gospel. "The whole sinful rock of man's natural heart is lifted and made to rest on the Rock of Atonement" (page 268). In the ninth chapter (now offered in English for the first time) we are reminded about Pastor Savonius, the main character in the first novella, who "more than a hundred years ago . . . was **a hammer of the Lord** . . . who opened the eyes of a twenty-year-old boy." That boy was Eugene Schenstedt, great great grandfather of Gunnar Schenstedt, a major character in the third novella. Giertz wants to convey to the reader that our situation is basically the same from generation to generation even if external conditions may be vastly different. It is through Jesus only (the heading of the second novella), through his atoning sacrifice only and nothing else that we are forgiven and made righteous before God.

———

Henric Schartau (1757–1825) was one of the most influential church leaders of all times in Sweden. He became a chaplain at the cathedral in the university town of Lund in 1785, where for the next forty years he made a deep impact through his preaching, teaching, and correspondence. Town and gown gathered in great numbers to hear

Schartau on Sundays when the cathedral often was filled to capacity and also on Fridays when he offered catechizations in the chancel. Schartau's goal was to give pastoral care and advice as he guided his listeners toward receiving the gift of salvation in Jesus only. As students of theology left Lund and became pastors, the legacy they brought with them developed into a vibrant revival movement within the Evangelical-Lutheran Church of Sweden, especially in the Göteborg Diocese, a movement soon labeled schartaunism.

In his theology Bo Giertz brought together elements from a wide range of Christian movements and thinkers. Except for Luther, no one has had a greater part than Henric Schartau in forming the impressive and harmonious theology that Giertz presents in his literary production. The chaplain in Lund is a major spiritual guide in each of the three novellas that make up *The Hammer of God*. It is a letter from Schartau in 1810 that brings clarity, peace, and joy to fellow pastors Lindér and Savonius. Schartau never published anything, but after his death many of his letters and sermons were printed in many editions, which were and continue to be in great demand. When Pastor Fridfeldt did not know how to preach on Transfiguration Sunday 1880, he grabbed a copy of Schartau's sermons from the senior pastor's book shelves and recited the sermon "Jesus Only" from that collection (pages 170-75). And now Fridfeldt becomes a hammer of God not so much for preaching the Law but for driving home the gospel of Jesus only "like hammer blows" (page 173). In his Lenten sermon in March 1939, pastor Bengtsson is a good "schartauan" when he presents the Order of Grace, how a sinner is brought to his Redeemer.

Part One: The Hammer of God

The story begins in the summer of 1808. Dean Faltin, the pastor in Ödesjö Parish, is giving his annual festive Midsummer party for all the pastors in the deanery as well as for some prominent members of the parish. We know that the year is 1808, because the dean suggests "a toast to the heroes of Sikajoki and Revolaks" in Finland, where the Swedish army had been victorious against the Russian intruders in two battles in April of that year. A heated discussion follows among the dinner guests about the state of affairs in politics and religion both on the domestic scene and on the continent. Since Giertz uses that discussion, covering seven pages in the original Swedish version, to set the stage for the whole book, it is a great loss for the reader that it was omitted in the 1960 American edition. Fortunately, an excellent 50-minute video enactment of the first chapter has been produced with English subtitles, marketed in the USA by Lutheran Visuals (For more information, call 1-800-527-3211).

According to some historians, Finland had been a part of the Kingdom of Sweden for hundreds of years since the reign of King Erik (1156–1160), who after his death was venerated as Saint Erik and patron saint of Sweden. The Swedish army, which was under the command of King Gustavus Adolphus (called "the foremost Lutheran layman of all time") defeated the Catholic forces in the battles of Breitenfeld (1631) and Lützen (1632), both places near Leipzig. The army included a substantial number of Finnish soldiers. Many scholars maintain that the Swedish intervention in the Thirty Years War (1618–1648) was the decisive factor in securing a future for Lutheranism in Germany. A plaque at Concordia Seminary in St. Louis in memory of Gustavus Adolphus says that he gave his life in the battle of Lützen "that the Reformation might live."

The shared destiny of Swedes and Finns in one realm, which lasted for more than 600 years, came to an end through the 1808–1809 war with Russia. In spite of some initial battle success, Sweden was forced to cede Finland to her powerful neighbor. King Gustav IV Adolf was made scapegoat for the shocking loss of Finland and was forced to abdicate. His childless brother Karl (XIII) replaced him on the throne, and the Danish prince Karl August was elected crown prince of Sweden. Following his unexpected death, he was succeeded as crown prince by one of Napoleon's generals, Marshal Jean Baptiste Bernadotte, who became King of Sweden in 1818 as Karl XIV Johan.

In this first part of the book, the reader is introduced to the influence of neology ("new teaching") among the clergy. Neology is a theology that is based on assumptions such as these: man is by nature good; Jesus is not the Son of God; miracles are against human understanding when based on reason and science, and thus cannot happen. In other words: neology is the opposite of orthodoxy ("right doctrine," or literally, "right praise") as expressed in the ancient Creeds of the Church and in our Lutheran confessional documents, which all make up the Book of Concord.

However, even if neology and rationalism had a grip on many pastors, university professors, other intellectuals, and also among people in general, true Christian faith nourished by God's Word and Sacrament was still a strong factor in Sweden at this time, as is so movingly described by Bo Giertz in this book. It is a powerful moment of God's merciful presence, when Katrina leads the dying Johannes to put his trust in Christ alone and receive his Savior in the Sacrament, administered by an "unworthy" pastor. God uses both the Office of the Pastoral Ministry and the Priesthood of the Baptized to bring his amazing grace to save a lost sinner.

The story of this first novella ends in 1810 where it began, the summer banquet in Ödesjö parsonage. In those two years we follow Henrik Savonius, assistant pastor to the dean, in his dramatic development from bringing unrest in the parish with the hammer of the law to affecting peace and joy by proclaiming the good news—and also causing his opponents to attempt to have him removed from the parish. At the 1810 summer party everything came to a dramatic and surprising conclusion.

Part Two: Jesus Only

This part is set in the years 1878–1880, an era when Revivalism was characteristic in Sweden. In the first half of the 1800s, the plague of alcoholism was devastating the land. The Swedes were about to commit genocide against themselves through excessive consumption of alcoholic beverages. The main factor in the dramatic turn-around in the attitude toward drinking and drunkenness was the revival movement that engaged people everywhere in the nation. Many people were converted from the old way of life in debauchery, revelling, and licentiousness (see Romans 13). They were called to a new way of life as children of God marked by the fruit of the Spirit: kindness, faithfulness, self-control (see Galatians 5:22).

However, it became clear that there were two kinds of revivalism. One kind was Lutheran in its experience of sin and grace, law and gospel, and therefore those thus revived (converted, awakened) remained within the Church of Sweden. They knew that it is through faith alone in Christ alone (Jesus only) that we are saved by God's grace alone. In the other kind of revivalism the poisonous element of legalism sneaked in: to be right with God and to be accepted by God you need more than what Jesus has done for you; you first need to live a good, virtuous, and holy life. In other words, you are asked to put the cart before the horse, to yield the fruits of Christian faith, before you put all your faith and trust in Christ alone. And in living such a "holy" life, you cannot have fellowship with "sinners"—and especially not go to the Lord's Supper with "unconverted sinners." Those who experienced their revival in this way left the Lutheran congregations and established "holy" congregations. Only those who confessed that they had accepted Jesus could be baptized and gain membership in these congregations. Baptism within the Lutheran Church was not acknowledged within this kind of revivalism as a real Christian baptism, since the person thus "baptized" had not first accepted Jesus.

Carl Olof Rosenius (1816–1868) has been called "Sweden's most influential lay preacher." He was the most prominent leader for that branch of the evangelical revival that remained within the Church of Sweden. He lifted up Luther's legacy not only from the pulpit in the Bethlehem Church in Stockholm but also through *The Pietist*, a journal he published from 1842, and through his volume of *Daily Meditations*, which thousands of Swedes continue to read. Rosenius' followers formed the Evangelical National Foundation (*Evangeliska Fosterland Stiftelsen, EFS*) in 1856. Many of the EFS people were attracted by the teachings of **Paul Peter Waldenström** (1838–1917) who, although a pastor of the Church of Sweden, became the foremost leader of that wing of the revival that parted from the church. He taught that God, who is love, does not need to be reconciled; there is no need for the atoning sacrifice of Christ as advocated by Luther and Rosenius. The battle on the issue of the atonement engaged the whole nation during the 1870s, causing Waldenström's followers to form the Swedish Mission Federation *(Svenska Mission Förbundet, SMF)* in 1878. EFS and SMF have been about equal in membership numbers through the years. Emigration was another factor that affected Sweden tremendously at this time. Never have so many Swedes emigrated to the USA as during the last three decades of the 1800s. Only two other countries, Ireland and Norway, lost a greater portion of their population through emigration to America than Sweden did. Even today most people in the province of Småland (where I was born) have relatives in the USA, descendants of the more than one and a quarter million Swedes who immigrated here from 1870 to 1920. The main cause of this mass emigration was the shortage of land and work for the fast-growing population in Sweden and elsewhere in Europe. For many emigrants the greater religious freedom on this side of the Atlantic was also a factor.

Part Three: On This Rock

The events in this part occur from 1937 to March 1940. The classical faith of the Church, as anchored in the Holy Bible, the Word of God, and as reclaimed and proclaimed by Martin Luther (1483–1546) and by Lutheran orthodoxy thereafter, was faced with the emergence of a diversity of movements in church and society during the early part of the 1900s. These include the Pentecostal movement, liberal theology, the Moral Re-Armament (M.R.A., also known as the Oxford Group Movement), and ever-increasing secularization (indifference, agnosticism, atheism) in Sweden as well as in most other countries in Europe.

Look in this portion of the book for people who desire to live up to the high ideals of the M.R.A., "the four absolutes:

absolute honesty, purity, unselfishness, and love—in total commitment to God." What did Jesus mean to the followers of the M.R.A.?

Early in the 1900s a strong movement began within the Church of Sweden, under the leadership of young and enthusiastic pastors, seminarians, and laypersons. The so-called "Young Church Movement" wanted to replace the mood of retreat and defeat within the Church with a spirit of advance and victory. They proclaimed that "Sweden is a people of God" and that "the Church is the forgiveness of sin to all people." They organized "crusades" to take this message to new venues, such as to the "People's House" (in Swedish, *Folkets Hus*) to reach blue collar workers, most of whom, though still church members, had drifted away from the Church's faith and fellowship. So many young men desired to become pastors in the 1930s that the Church could not ordain all of them!

Bo Giertz was no doubt influenced by the Young Church Movement, but he deepened the view of the Church and the understanding of the Holy Ministry (the Pastoral Office). He had discovered how both are thoroughly rooted in God's Word as well as acknowledged and explained in our Lutheran Confessions. He conveyed his vision not only to the whole Church of Sweden but also beyond, as his books were translated into many languages. Thus he inspired both clergy and laity to share with people everywhere the good news of Jesus Christ, and to do so with renewed urgency and boldness.

The Hammer of God begins with references to the war in Finland 1808–1809. The conclusion of the book brings us back to another war in Finland, the so-called Winter War 1939–1940. Following the Bolshevik Revolution in Russia in November 1917, Finland declared its independence from that country on December 6, 1917. However, in the beginning of World War II, on November 30, 1939, Finland was attacked by the Soviet Union, the Communist empire that had been established through the Bolshevik Revolution. While 19,756 Finnish soldiers gave the ultimate sacrifice in defense of their country, the heroic resistance of Finland's armed forces, admired by the entire world, caused the death of more than 100,000 invading Soviet soldiers. Still, this could not prevent Stalin from massing more troops against Finland, which was forced to cede some border territory in the peace agreement of March 12, 1940. Yet, Finland retained her place in the family of independent Western democracies, while many of the Soviet Union's European neighbors ended up under Communist oppression behind the Iron Curtain from World War II to the demise of the Soviet Union on December 26, 1991.

Some Giertz scholars believe that Pastor Torvik, the main character in this part of the book, is a portrait of the author himself. I agree with that evaluation. Torvik is the spokesman for Giertz on all issues concerning church and theology, but he also expresses the author's own agony concerning the fate of Finland. When Pastor Torvik's friend, Gunnar Schenstedt, joins thousands of his compatriots to fight for Finland in the Swedish Voluntary Corps, he feels that he too should do that, mirroring Giertz' own thoughts. On Easter Day, March 24, 1940, twelve days after the end of the war, Bo Giertz published a deeply engaging poem with the title "Palm Sunday—Easter" (*Palmsöndag—Påsk*) in *Nya Dagligt Allehanda*, a prominent Stockholm newspaper, giving voice to his compassion—and that of his fellow Swedes—for the brave neighbors who had suffered so unspeakably much in the war. Two years later, Giertz himself had to cope with immense personal pain. In the last chapter of *Stengrunden*, having just learned that a young woman had died at the birth of her baby, Gösta Torvik was "thinking of his own wife who soon would go into the same risk of death" (page 319). This Giertz wrote in 1941. A year later his beloved wife Ingrid died six days after the birth of their fourth child. In his unspeakable mourning, the young father marked this verse in his Bible: "The Lord is just in all his ways, and kind in all his doings" (Psalm 145:17).

Hans Andræ
September 19, 2004

I. The Hammer of God

The Call

A sharp, clinking sound was heard above the hum of voices in the smoke-filled room as the dean touched his glass to that of the captain. He raised it to his lips, but stopped half way and got up from his white arm chair.

"Gentlemen!" He raised his glass in the direction of the card table at the near end of the room, where the gentry from Eksta, Saleby, and Brocksholm were seated. "My friends!" The other hand described a graceful arc which included the clergy of the deanery who were gathered in small groups throughout the room. "I ask you all to join with us in a toast to the heroes of Sikajoki and Revolaks."

Dr. Savonius, the young curate, looked intently at his superior, and then let his eyes move with evident pleasure about the room. It was amazing, he thought, that so much esprit and culture could be assembled in that worm-eaten old parsonage. He remembered how he had packed his books last Advent, choosing only a few authors—mainly the poets of the Gustavian era—to take with him on his exile, as he now left the University and journeyed home for his ordination. He remembered how sadly his fingers had caressed the de luxe edition of Kjellgren and how he had thought, Now you will have to comfort me in my loneliness. As a matter of fact, there had been no loneliness at all in this, his first appointment. The deans' residence at Ödesjö was anything but a place of exile. The elderly dean was a refined and intellectual man, perhaps a bit too conservative and with a touch of the gout of orthodoxy in his make-up, but still a very pleasant man to live with. He was a highly respected spiritual father to his community, where he took the same untiring interest in every matter, whether it be the catechizations in the homes, ancient parish lore, the growing of potatoes, or world politics. He was an admirable figure as he stood there straight and slender as a rod, his forehead high, the mark of authority on his stern chin. He was an honor to his class. Savonius noted with satisfaction that the captain from the manor house, who after all ranked as number one among the parish gentry, looked rather unimpressive by comparison, his jovial but somewhat bloated face sunk deep in his great collar between the epaulets. There could be no question as to who looked more the military man. Nor was there any question as to which of these two the people preferred to listen to at a parish meeting.

Savonius continued to look about him. The last touch of evening sun was finding its way through the leafy crowns of the linden trees. It danced playfully through the wreaths of smoke in the room and cast a warm reflection on the ceiling, which caused the shallow plane marks on the white boards to stand out like ripples on a mirror of water. Farthest away in the room, small spots of light moved over the pearl-gray wallpaper, bringing its stencils into relief, and shining on the dark end boards so that the yellow roses on the handpainted paper edges stood out in all their pretentious elegance.

Across the room, between the two windows of the long wall, stood the pianoforte, with its black and white keys and its straight, fluted legs. A violin was also to be seen. Here the young people were gathered, a bright bouquet of colorful dresses and formal wear. Savonius noted the young people of the dean's own household, the girls from the captain's house, among them the captain's Babette and several others he did not recognize. They had been looking through the pieces of music and whispering among themselves. If only they dared ask the dean to take his guests into the parlor so that they might have the room for dancing, now that Johan-Christofer was home from college and had his violin with him and the latest gavottes in his portfolio.

The pastors were either standing or seated in scattered groups about the room. There stood Hafverman from Näs, large and sturdy, with a tight grip on his long pipe. There were Nylander and Warbeck and the whole contingent of curates from the district. Many of them were strikingly young looking. Several were not yet attached to any parish. In general the cut of their coats was not at all out of style. The only ones who impaired this good impression were Runfeldt and Lindér. Runfeldt was a hopeless rustic; there was snuff on his coatsleeves, his bootleather was cracked, and there was an indescribable atmosphere of stable and sour-cabbage about his thick-set person. He would have fitted better in the back room where the farm foreman and the coachmen were eating their steak. Lindér was a dark Savonarola type, not without fire in his manner, but it was a fire which lost its brightness like a bonfire in the sunlight as soon as the brilliant savants from Upsala began to sparkle with their quotations and witticisms.

The toast was drunk and was followed by the obligatory moment of silence. The only sounds heard were the beating of a bumblebee's wings against the ceiling and the scraping of a chair. One felt a light cloud of sadness stealing through the sunshine and heavy warmth. The shadow of war in the East, which had almost been forgotten in the festive spirit, crept out of its corner once more, bringing with it the winter's tragic memories.

Savonius felt a bit faint. His arms hung limp and the tips of his fingers were numb. He must have imbibed too much again. The next voice he heard seemed to come from a great distance.

The door of the entry hall opened. In the dark doorway stood a peasant. His boots were white with dust, his broad-brimmed hat was held between his coarse hands, whose broken nails pressed nervously into the felt. His knock at the door had been drowned by the voice of the company, but he had finally ventured to make his way inside. Now he stood there, looking about him awkwardly and trying to get his bearings in all this confusion.

"Whom are you looking for?" asked the dean. Soon there was quiet in the room. The searching, reproving glances of all these people caused the stranger to lower his eyes.

"It should perhaps be Pastor Hafverman," he answered slowly, "but otherwise any pastor who is available. A man is sick. He is Johannes in Börsebo. But it is a bit urgent, as he may have only a short time left."

Hafverman crossed his hands behind him as he faced the peasant, who was well known to him. "Why do you seek me here, Peter?" he asked.

Humbly, and without a trace of reproach, the man answered, "I drove the fourteen miles to Näs to find you, Pastor, but learned there that you had left for the home of the reverend dean. So I came here. And now I beg of you for God's sake to come soon. Johannes began to wander in his thoughts even before I left."

Hafverman wrinkled his brow. "But Peter," he said, "Johannes of Börsebo is really from Ravelunda parish."

"Yes, Pastor, but as you know he has lived with us ever since he lost his wife. We are brothers-in-law, he and I."

Hafverman lifted his great head with relief and looked toward the far end of the room.

"Listen, Warbeck, the sick man is one of your sheep. You had better take care of this matter."

It was apparent that Warbeck was not very eager to ride all of fourteen miles through the forest, with nightfall near. He excused himself by saying that the place where Johannes was now living was really in Hafverman's parish and in the opposite direction from Ravelunda. It would not be Christian to expect the poor peasant, who had already traveled twenty-four miles, to make the round trip again. If Hafverman made the call, he could drive directly home afterward. This would be easier for both the pastor and the horse.

"And it would be easier for our dear Brother himself," said Hafverman, with tongue in cheek. "Do you expect the communion set to return to the dean on wings? Or shall I have to return here with it tomorrow? It is not my practice to have church silver delivered by a servant."

The dean lifted his hand to end the wrangle.

"Please calm yourselves, gentlemen. You two remain here. Older people need their sleep. Let the younger men take care of the drudgery. Who among you will volunteer?" He looked at the young assistants.

It became very quiet in the room. Savonius felt that the question was really directed to him, but his eye wandered in the direction of Mademoiselle Babette. The party would last only a few short hours, and after that she would be swallowed up again in the social world of the manor house, where he had no daily entré. He waited with his answer.

The others also waited. The quiet was painful. There was a flash of impatience in the dean's eyes.

"We have had enough of *that* spirit, my dear sirs. If no one will go voluntarily, I shall have to give an order. Dr. Savonius is the youngest among us. He will have to make this pastoral call, and that without delay. Let the driver please go to the kitchen and have a sandwich and something to drink. Hedvig, will you tell Erik to get the horse ready? And now Johan-Christofer will play for us."

As always, there was something firm and definite in the dean's order. The peasant left his place at the doorway. Hedvig slipped out unnoticed, and Savonius bowed a reluctant farewell to the company. Johan-Christofer had already begun to play the violin when, a few moments later, Savonius again peered through the doorway and with dark mien viewed the gay company within.

Savonius was in an unhappy and agitated state of mind when he reached his room. This was hardly a civil way to treat one who had taken his doctorate. He almost regretted now that he had refused to take any shortcuts that might have gotten him a permanent post immediately. He had acted as he did from pure idealism, asking only for an ordinary appointment for the sake of the experience he would get. Now he had to pay for his romantic foolishness. He had absolutely no desire to ride through the dark forest this night. He threw off his blue coat and put on a black one. He put on the clergy collar and bands, threw his handbook into a bag and, after some shuffling of papers on his desk, found the outline of the communion address he had given in church on the Day of John the Baptist. That would have to do. The private communion case, shaped like an hour glass, was in the dean's study. He swung its strap over his shoulder and stepped out into the warm summer evening.

The driver stood waiting beside the carriage. He had hardly swallowed the last bit of his sandwich. The stable boy, who had watered the horse, carried away the empty bucket. Everything was ready. Through the deanery windows stole the sound of gay music.

Now they were beginning to dance, thought Savonius, and I am off for Siberia!

As the carriage swung out under the big lindens, he looked back once more. It was a beautiful summer evening, the branches of the trees kissed his hatbrim playfully, and the dusk was filled with pleasant odors. First was the smell of the soft dust of the roadway and of the new-mown hay, floating on the warm air between the gray log walls of the buildings on either side of the road. Then came the tangy smell of tar and wagon grease and the efflorescence of the barnyard, and the aroma of water plants and ooze from under the stone bridge. In the next moment the fields of the deanery farm came into view, and then the road turned sharply to the north down a long hill. Already there was a fresh stream of air from the lowlands, moist and cool, smelling of birch and sedge. On the right slope edging the valley, stood the church, clean and white. The spire rose broad and stately, the work of some builder in the time of King Fredrik. The south wall now lay in twilight with the dark windows sunk in reverie in the thick stone walls, but on the west and the north the white walls gleamed as if they had been able to absorb all the uncertain light that still glowed pale and melancholy in the northwest.

And now the woods put in their appearance. First was the parsonage pasture, shielded by mothering birches. The grass was well grazed. Between the hillocks stood tall junipers that might well rival the cypresses of the South. They were like funeral guests at a wedding party, thought Savonius. The branches of the weeping birch were the bridal veil, while the graceful young birches were like little girls in white stockings standing in groups and gazing at the glories of the dinner table. But the junipers were like unbidden messengers of death. Really, this could be the theme of a whole long poem, he thought as they rode along.

———

"Pastor, can you tell me how one shall get a deeply distressed soul to believe in the grace of God?"

Savonius found himself suddenly startled out of his reverie. It was the peasant at his side who had broken the silence. He must have sensed that the question came inopportunely, for he continued, a bit uncertainly.

"You'll have to excuse me, Pastor. I was thinking of Johannes, the man who is sick. He is in such vexation of spirit that we fear for his sanity. He has for a long time been under powerful conviction of sin. He has always been a godly man in externals and has not neglected the means of grace. But now these agonizings of soul have come upon him. It seems as though all light has gone from him. He sees only his transgressions. He digs up all that has been forgiven and forgotten in the past thirty years. It is as though the devil had given him a witching glass that causes him to see nothing but hypocrisy and falseness within—and God knows that he sees very keenly, Pastor. It makes one cringe under one's own wickedness just to hear him. But *grace* he cannot see. He has eyes like a cat to see in the dark, but he is blind to the light."

Savonius sat and stared at the edge of the ditch. Unreal, like flowers in a dream, some wild orchids swept by. What should he answer? With what had he gotten himself involved? He must take a little time to think before replying.

"Have you tried to read something of devotional character to him?" he asked. He was trying to feel his way.

"Read?" said the peasant, as if wondering at the suggestion. "Why, we always read at home. And we have certainly read a great deal to him these last days, both from the Scriptures, and from the Hymnal and Scriver's *Soul Treasury*. But when a man has been struck with blindness as Johannes has, he sees only threat and judgment and punishment, no matter what is read. And we are uneducated people, in Hyltamålen. But we thought, Pastor, that you who are a learned man could instruct Johannes thoroughly about the evidences of the state of grace in a converted sinner. For in that case he must understand that he cannot be in such peril of soul as he believes."

Savonius was ill at ease. What was expected of him? Instruct a converted sinner about the signs of being in the state of grace? Never in all his life had he heard about anything like that.

He searched his memory. Large, brown leather-bound volumes with titles in black floated before his vision. He had never taken theology very seriously. The great philosophers had interested him most. But in all of Leibnitz' *Theodicée* he could not recall a single line that even remotely dealt with such things as this. As a matter of fact, he could eliminate everything he had ever read, with the possible exception of *Concordia Pia.* In that volume there had indeed been something definite about the anguish of a frightened conscience. But what was it? He regretted that he had studied *Concordia Pia* so carelessly. He had, of course, always viewed the confessional writings as remnants of medievalism, understandable only against the background of papal darkness. But in Ödesjö the darkness was perhaps just as thick. Such rude means as orthodox theology and true Lutheranism might perhaps be needed to make any headway against it.

But it was too late now to try to find help in such church-historical reflections. He was faced with the necessity of extricating himself from an awkward situation and still keep face. What would he really have to say when he came to the sick man's bedside?

The communion address! He thought about the outline he had taken along, and it frightened him. It was a poetic discussion of the beauty of nature as a revelation of Providence in its wisdom and rule of the universe. Its three parts were presented with feeling. In the first there was a reminder of the lilies of the field as the reflection of the purity of an innocent heart. The second reminded the hearer of the immortal soul's growth in virtue through industrious care of the garden of the soul. Finally, a tender admonition to be moved by the wise kindness of God to discipline and a good life. On Midsummer Day that sermon had sounded so edifying in a church radiant with sunshine and smelling of birch leaves. And Mademoiselle Babette had let it be known afterwards that young Dr. Savonius had both genius and a talent for poetry that she hoped would soon be appreciated as they deserved. But here! The unhappy curate stared ahead helplessly.

The road had once more divided, and had become narrower. A steep hill led to the ridge of the forest. The ground was stony and full of gravel. There were no longer any ditches, and the stone heaps and blueberry bushes reached the ruts in the road. The wilderness on either side seemed to encroach in an attempt to destroy the little road that human hands had built through the primeval forest. Round about firs stood sky high, their branches intertwined, making a black darkness which with evil eyes stared out beneath them.

It was surely midnight by now. A lone bird called, and the individual trees melted together in one forbidding and unfriendly mass. To Savonius they seemed to incarnate this dismal adventure which had been thrust upon him against his will. Somewhere in the deep forest lay this demented man whom he was supposed to try to comfort and calm. If he had been a free student and not tied down with an appointment, he would simply have jumped out of the carriage. But as Dean Faltin's curate he had a reputation—or at the least the possibility of a reputation and a career—to defend. So he clenched his fists under his coat, straightened himself, and resolved to show himself equal to the occasion.

At last the sky began to brighten in the north. The road continued to ascend. Occasionally, when the hills were quite steep, they walked, while the empty carriage blundered along noisily over the stones. No farm gates had been seen for miles. The forest was evidently very dense.

In the bracing night air of the forest, Savonius had become completely sober. He felt a great weariness in his bones, but an almost unreal clarity of mind. Several times he tried by questioning the driver to learn more about the sick man. In between, he tried to prepare a new communion address.

"Now, Pastor, you may ride all the rest of the way. From here on, it is down hill."

Savonius looked up. They had evidently reached the highest point of the Heding hills. He saw ridge upon ridge stretching endlessly before him. In the northeast the sky already glowed a golden red beneath the bank of clouds. A distant lake gleamed amid the forest darkness, and a thin layer of fog arose out of the swamplands.

The curate took his place in the carriage again. For the second time this strange night he felt, thanks to nature's wonders, in harmony with existence. The forest was no longer an enemy. This God-forsaken wilderness had its beauty, too. Now, if he could only set things straight for the sick man! That was the thorn that still remained in his heart.

The road was again a bit wider. A few paths joined it, and the weary horse began to hurry along, knowing that they were nearing home. Clearings appeared in the forest, making it apparent that people must be living nearby. Then a row of small gray buildings loomed up, the road turned, and there against the bare hillside stood a two-story frame house with small square windows.

Savonius had barely put his foot on the wheel hub when the door opened and a woman came out. She looked weary from lack of sleep and her hair was bedraggled.

"And so you did come after all! God be praised!"

"Is he still living?" asked the driver, his voice filled with anxiety.

"Yes, but it has been terribly difficult. To think that you have come at last! Thank you for coming, Pastor. You come in the name of the Lord. Welcome! Please come in."

She was already inside. Savonius had time to note the dirt floor in the entry. The next moment he was in the room to the left. It was the living room, which occupied half the space of the house. The three outside walls each had a little window. Pale daylight crept in from the north, but the room was still only dimly lighted. The air was almost unbearably stuffy. The sick man had evidently been lying there a long time. Fetid exhalations, moldy food, the smell of boot-leather, and medicaments were some of the ingredients of the choking atmosphere. The curate felt a desire to step out, but pulled himself together.

In the corner to the right stood a pull-out bed. It was filled with blankets and pelts in wild disarray. The sick man lay with one knee drawn up. Beyond it only an arm was visible, an unnaturally thin and white arm reaching upward. It was crowned by an abnormally large hand with black pores in the rough skin cracked with calluses. The bony, knotted fingers seemed to be grasping at something. They were thrust apart with wild intensity, only to close again on nothingness; they curled like the claws of a bird of prey and then opened again, ceaselessly repeating the painfully meaningless maneuver.

For the second time, Savonius pulled himself together. He forced himself to turn his eyes from the struggling hand and let them take note of the details of the room. He saw the rough log walls above the bed, the container at its head, which was filled with a few juniper twigs and offensive expectorations, and an old chair on whose wooden seat there were some worn books and a mug of water.

He moved a few steps nearer and heard his voice speak a timid greeting, "God's peace be with you!"

The giant hand was lowered, and from the semi-darkness in the far corner a tortured face appeared, the whites of the eyes glistening. The eyes were wide open with terror, the hair was matted by the sweat of anguish, and the twisted mouth was like a black hole in which two yellow teeth were glimpsed.

This is Horror itself, thought Savonius, the anguish that ascends from the utter darkness of Chaos.

Without really knowing how, he landed on a chair that must have been pushed toward him from behind. Summoning all his power of self-control, he grasped the struggling hand, which strangely enough allowed itself to be moved like a child's. Rough and scabrous, dead as a piece of wood, it lay between the curate's soft hands.

For a while he sat in silence, not knowing what he should say. Then words came to his lips, he hardly knew from whence:

"I wish you *God's* peace, God's eternal peace and blessing."

The sick man shook his head.

"Not for me! Not for me! Eternal damnation, punishment according to the measure of my sin, the judgment of wrath, and the everlasting flames—that is for me. To me he will say, 'Depart from me, ye cursed, into everlasting fire!'"

"But God is *good*," said Savonius quietly.

The sick man looked straight up at the ceiling.

"Yes, God is good, very good. It is just for that reason I am in such a bad way. Pastor, you do not know how good God has been to me. He has sought my soul and bidden me walk the way of life. But I have not done so. He has shown me heaven's purity, but I shall never win it. I sat in Ravelunda church and heard the angels sing. Then I saw my mother in the women's pew, and I thought: Mother has aged, this winter she may die; then I shall inherit the farm. And my heart wept, for I saw that, more than I loved Mother, I loved the filthy dollars. Then the pastor came to the pulpit. Potbelly, I thought. You can play cards and fish for trout, but you cannot feed God's poor little lambs with the Word. But I had not prayed for him. Was that love? I walked along the road and saw the rye in full bloom. Then I thought: Rye as thick as this is never to be seen on the crofter's stony field. But the captain has taken all the good ground for himself. He is rich in this world, but he will burn in hell. Was that love, Pastor?"

Johannes had suddenly turned his fever-reddened eyes toward the pastor and looked penetratingly at him.

"That is how it is with me, Pastor. Day after day, moment upon moment, it is sin added to sin, and nothing but sin."

"But God has no pleasure in the death of the wicked," were the words that came from Savonius' lips.

"But that he should turn from his way and live," said the sick man, completing the passage. "That is why there is no hope for me, Pastor. For thirty years God has given me the opportunity to turn and repent. Thirty years I have been on that way. But I shall never reach the goal. Have I turned from the evil way? No! I have lamented and called upon God. But the heart is just as evil. Falseness and darkness within, pretense and hypocrisy on the surface."

"But confess your sins, and God will forgive you." Savonius tried to give his voice the ring of authority.

"Confess?" said Johannes, and his head fell back with infinite weariness. It was not terror that showed on his face now, but a dying despair that seemed almost more unendurable. He started upwards with lifeless eyes.

"For thirty years, as Thou knowest, Lord, I have confessed my sins. And Thou didst forgive everything—the salt I stole, the grouse I snared, adultery and profanity—all was forgiven. It was like the singing of larks that day in the church, and it was Thy voice, O Lord, that I heard when the pastor read the absolution. That day I knelt in prayer at the gates of Börsebo, and blessedness and peace lay like sunshine on the grass, Lord, all this Thou didst for me. I believed then that I was Thine. But the heart of stone remained. The uncircumcised, adulterous heart continued to be just as evil. I wept and confessed, and Thou didst forgive me afresh. I came with new confessions. Thy grace was great, Lord. Twenty times, fifty times, I came; but I was still no better. Then the door of grace was shut. He who repents and believes will be received into the kingdom. But I did not repent."

Savonius' brain worked desperately. The man was certainly out of his head; his hand was very hot. Still, one could sense a certain logic in his wanderings of mind. The curate knew that sinners could repent and be absolved, but he had scarcely thought that it took place except as the obligatory absolution of adulteresses in the sacristy. But it was evident that this man had long ago experienced sorrow for his sins, which for that matter did not seem to be so great. Why in the world did he, then, doubt the grace of God? Savonius could very well understand that one could doubt such things as the miracles and the sacraments, Adam, the fall into sin, and hell. But grace—nothing could be more obvious than that. Must not all who believe in the Most High God also acknowledge His goodness? Could not even Voltaire be quoted in support of this? But how should he get this strange man to believe it?

Suddenly Savonius called to mind what the driver had said, that if only he were instructed as to the evidences of being in the state of grace, Johannes would surely be able to understand that his soul was in no danger. The good man was evidently right. It was clear that Johannes was unnecessarily troubled. The fragments of a human life that flitted by as he continued his fevered talk showed a piety and godly fear so deep and earnest that Savonius could hardly remember that he had ever witnessed anything like it. This man's soul was completely dominated by the quest for God—that was evident. Why, then, did he not understand that God was good? How could he be made to understand that he had nothing to fear?

Savonius stood up. With an assertion of his priestly authority, he laid his narrow hand as heavily as he could on Johannes' shoulder, and said, "Johannes of Börsebo, I say to you that, if *anyone* in this settlement will die in peace, it is you."

The sick man looked up. A quivering gleam of hope shone in his eyes.

"How can that be, Pastor?"

"You are a better and a more upright soul than anyone I have ever met."

Then the little gleam of light in Johannes' eyes died away. There was a piercing earnestness in his eyes as he looked up at the pastor.

"The Judge will not judge the soul by other souls, Pastor. The books will be opened, and the dead will be judged by what is written in the books. 'Every idle word that men speak, they shall give account thereof in the day of judgment.' And my doom is already sealed."

Savonius' arms hung limply. He was powerless against this chilling logic. The man was really right. Each man would indeed be judged according to his works. He had himself preached on that text at the communion service on Quinquagesima. But he had certainly experienced no anguish of soul.

Not knowing what to say, he sat down. Should he read something? He fingered the books on the other chair. He was glad to find the Church Book among them. He took the worn, brown volume in his hands and paused for a moment. Something about inner conflict and comfort in distress should fit, he thought. But where would he find this?

He did not need to search. The edges of the book were dark with use, and here and there the pages opened readily because their corners had been worn away. He put his thumb in the first notch that showed evidence of frequent use and found the section entitled: "Psalms to be read in soul distress, in cross bearing, and in inner conflict." But then he sat a long time without moving. These pages had been thumbed so much that they had slowly become darkened. Hundreds upon hundreds of times they must have been turned by earth-stained hands. Had not Johannes said that he had been walking that way for thirty years? Was all this the marks of his journey? Quietly, Savonius laid the book aside. He understood that it would do no good to read one of those hymns that the sick man must have read a thousand times without finding cure for his inner despair. He felt unworthy to read anything from this book. He thought of his own beautiful copy of the same church hymnal, its fine white pages clean and unmussed, like the sheets of a bed that is never used.

He felt, suddenly, that someone was looking at him. He turned his head. He had, he realized, almost forgotten the others in the house. The woman, who evidently was the wife of Peter and the sister of the sick man, sat on the sofa at the other end of the room. It was she who looked so intently that he had to turn his head. Her eyes were wide open and lay deep and frightened within dark rings that had come from long night watches. She continued to look at the pastor with eyes that were wise, but sorrowful. Her shoulders drooped and her hands lay in her lap as if benumbed. Her whole being reflected a great disappointment, a last hope that she must have considered crushed. And then, her big, sad, accusing eyes!

Savonius turned his face from her and felt how he blushed. He surmised what the woman was thinking. He had an idea of what she must have gone through during the night in her lonely vigil with the sick man, especially when darkness fell and her husband never seemed to return. Then finally the help had come. But what a sorry help it turned out to be!

A new and painful thought came to the curate. What would these people really think of him? He remembered the gavotte melody that came from the deanery window as a farewell. It must have sounded strange to the driver, who for days and nights had listened to Johannes' feverish soul conflict. He remembered his own unwillingness to go along. What must the peasant think, he who had traveled the roads all day, first to Näs and then to Ödesjö to get a pastor for the sick call? And what was the woman over there thinking? Savonius looked despairingly at his shoes. He had not bothered to change trousers, but was still wearing knee-length stockings, low buckled shoes, and rosettes at the knees. He himself would have been provoked if anyone ministered at the altar in such a costume. Then his hand went to his neck. Yes, he still had the snobbish blue silk scarf wrapped round his collar. Not even that had been replaced by a white one. What must these people be thinking about him?

His eyes sought Peter as he turned them away from the woman, whose glance he no longer wished to meet. He had to turn pretty far before he caught sight of him near the fireplace midway on the inside wall. He was on his knees beside a little wooden chair, his elbows resting on the seat and his face pressed down in his hands.

The curate shyly averted his eyes. How long had Peter knelt there? He was praying, then, while he, Henrik Samuel Savonius, a doctor from the widely reputed philosophical faculty at Upsala and a servant of the Holy Word, had not prayed a single little prayer since coming to this house. For that matter, he had not done so on the journey either, nor even in his room before starting out. When was it really that he last prayed? It must have been at morning devotions yesterday—if indeed he had prayed then.

His first impulse was to bow his head and try to pray. If the woman were not watching him, he might have done so.

But now he was ashamed to show that he had learned from a peasant's example. He remained perfectly rigid in his chair.

The sick man had lifted his big hands and folded them under his chin. The eyes were closed, and he talked feverishly. "Now Johannes stands in prayer in the pasture at Mysebacke. The wind blows, and the angels listen. 'How does Johannes pray today?' they ask." The voice sank to a whisper. "Lord, I pray for the tailor at Hyltet. He beats his wife and milks our cow and spreads poisonous slander about our Anna." The voice was again at its normal pitch. "That is how Johannes prays, and the angels smile and nod approval, for Johannes is praying for his enemy. But when Johannes has said Amen, and sits down to think it over, and he sees how the sheriff comes into the forest and finds the tailor's whiskey still and takes him to court, and the judge puts the tailor behind bars, the thought of it makes Johannes' evil heart feel good. Now the sun is hid by clouds, and cold, cold rain begins to fall. It is the angels who are weeping, 'Johannes has an uncircumcised heart,' they say. 'He is hard though God has been so good to him. He is just as spiteful as God is merciful. Therefore he shall die eternally and will never come to heaven.' 'Who shall ascend into the hill of the Lord? He that hath . . . a pure heart.' But never, never I."

"Be quiet, Johannes! Be quiet!"

It was the woman who cried out thus. She sat with her chin pressed into her hands, staring ceaselessly straight ahead. Her eyes glistened with tears.

"These two are related," thought Savonius. "What if she also goes out of her mind!"

He was so unhappy and despairing that he felt physically ill. The whole scene, the sick man's mad imaginings, which were so irresistibly logical, the woman's worn face red and swollen with weeping, the oppressive air and the stench from the spittoon at his feet—all these got the better of him. He got up and walked unsteadily toward the door. His face must have been white as chalk. He had hardly gotten outside before his repugnance and nausea found release in violent vomitings.

Here then, stood the curate of Ödesjö church in knee breeches and elegant shoes, a blue silken scarf about his neck and a little bit of lace peeping out of the black coat-sleeves, leaning against a projecting log of Peter's house at Hyltamålen. He had too little strength left to be aware of the comical in the situation. All he could see was shame and humiliation. The sun was already shining, the morning song of the birds filled the air, and a well-sweep creaked somewhere in the village beyond the farm.

With a pale grimace Savonius mopped his face with the handkerchief. Now they must be thinking that he imbibed too freely yesterday. Soon the scandal would be known throughout the county. True enough, he had not been real sober when he stepped into the carriage last night. Was this loathsome indisposition after all a link in the chastening Providence provides his children?

If the curate had any further resolution to cope with the situation, it was gone now. He seated himself on the edge of the well, buried his head in his hands, and wept like a child. He was deadly tired both in body and soul, ill to his stomach, and utterly helpless. He felt only a great longing to be back in his study at Upsala.

"Is Johannes already dead, Pastor?"

Savonius looked up, startled. This was an altogether new voice, a woman's deep, warm alto voice. The stranger must have come from down the road. She wore a kerchief over her black hair, which was combed straight back. The face was middle-aged, wise, with soft and gentle lines under the tan.

Savonius' face must have betrayed his bewilderment, since the woman went on to explain who she was.

"I am Katrina Filip from Hersmålen. They have asked me to come because the situation is so critical. We were once neighbors. But now I suppose he has already gone to his rest."

There was a questioning anxiety in her voice and even more in her childlike eyes. Savonius realized that she had innocently construed his strange conduct as the result of his own sadness over Johannes' death. If only she could continue to think that!

"Johannes still lives, but he is in very sad straits indeed," he said hoarsely.

The woman nodded silently and went into the house. The curate sat still a moment longer, undecided as to his course. Finally he rose and followed her. If I am present, they will at least not speak ill of me, he thought. Just inside the door he slumped down on a chair.

The woman was already at the bedside. Peter's wife bent down and shouted in the sick man's ear.

"Johannes, wake up! Katrina is here. It's *Katrina*, do you hear?"

The sick man was in his right mind again.

"Katrina, it was good of you to come. You are kind, Katrina. God will reward you. And me, he will punish. So will He be exalted and declared righteous in all his judgments. But it will go badly for me. Katrina, why is it not as it used to be? Do you remember when we sang the old songs from *The Songs of Moses and the Lamb?* Then my heart was glad in the Lord. But it never became clean. Katrina, I am a sinner, a great sinner."

"Yes, that you are, Johannes. But Jesus is a still greater Savior."

The sick man breathed heavily before answering. He seemed to be going over something in his mind.

"Yes, he is a great Savior for those who let themselves be saved. But my heart is not clean, my mind is evil; I do not have the new spirit."

"They that be whole need not a physician, but they that are sick. He came not to call the righteous, but sinners."

"Yes, Katrina, but it reads 'to repentance.' It is repentance that I lack."

"You do not lack repentance, Johannes, but *faith*. You have walked the way of repentance for thirty years."

"And still not attained to it!"

"Johannes," said the woman, almost sternly, "answer me this question: Do you really want your heart to be clean?"

"Yes, Katrina. God knows that I want that."

"Then your repentance is also as true as it can be in a corrupt child of Adam in this world. Your danger is not that you lack repentance, but that you have been drifting away from *faith*."

"What, then, shall I believe, Katrina?"

"You must believe this living Word of God: 'But to him that worketh not, but believeth on him that justifieth the ungodly, his faith is counted for righteousness.' Up to this day you have believed in works and looked at your own heart. You saw only sin and wretchedness, because God anointed your eyes with the salve of the Spirit to see the truth. Do you have sin in your heart, Johannes?"

"Yes," answered the sick man timidly, "much sin, altogether too much."

"Just that should make clear to you that God has not forsaken you," said the woman firmly. "Only he can see his sin who has the Holy Spirit."

"Do you mean to say, Katrina, that it could be a work of God, that my heart is so unclean?"

"Not *that* your heart is unclean—that is the work of sin—but that you now see it, that is the work of God."

"But why, then, have I not received a clean heart?"

"That you might learn to love Jesus," said the woman as calmly as before.

Back in his corner Savonius had raised his aching head. He followed with fixed attention the conversation at the bedside. Peter now stood at the foot of the bed, and his wife reclined on a chair. Katrina sat on the edge of the bed. The curate was amazed to see that the sick man's hands were at rest. They lay broad and clumsy on the quilt and were perfectly still. His eyes were glued to the woman's lips.

"What do you mean, Katrina?"

"I mean, Johannes, that if you had received a clean heart and for that reason had been able to earn salvation—to what end would you then need the Savior? If the law could save a single one of us, Jesus would surely not have needed to die on the cross. 'Because the law worketh wrath,' and God stops every mouth by his holy commandments, that 'all the world may become guilty before God.'"

The sick man had become perfectly still. His sister fanned the flies from his face. Except for that, no one moved.

"Have you anything more to say, Katrina?"

"Yes, one thing more, Johannes. 'Behold the Lamb of God, which taketh away the sin of the world.'"

He lay quiet a moment.

"Do you mean . . . ? Do you really mean that he takes away also the sin that dwells in my unclean heart?"

"Yes, he atoned for all that sin, when he died in your place."

"But I still have it with me, don't I?"

"Yes, as surely as Paul also still had it with him. Have you never read, 'I know that in me (that is in my flesh) dwelleth no good thing; for to will is present with me; but how to perform that which is good I find not.'"

"Yes, that's how it is," whispered Johannes.

"That is the way it has always been for us, and for all others. 'With his stripes we are healed.' 'He is the propitiation for our sins: and . . . also for the sins of the whole world.'"

The sick man lay breathlessly quiet. Then he whispered, "One word more, Katrina, a sure word, and I will believe it."

The woman got up quietly, took the Bible that lay on the table, and sat down again. Opening the Bible, she read:

"For all have sinned, and come short of the glory of God; being justified freely by his grace through the redemption that is in Christ Jesus."

"Amen. I believe!" said Johannes, in a voice that could barely be heard.

Katrina rose and replaced the Bible on the table.

"Now God's work has taken place. Now you must ask the pastor to give you the holy sacrament."

Johannes nodded slowly. "Master, at thy word I will let down the net." He looked at his sister. "Will you ask the pastor?"

Savonius was already on his feet. His thoughts were in a tumult. If he could only understand these people! One minute he was useless to them; the next they turned to him with reverence, just as if he had not a bit earlier been wholly unsuccessful in the very thing they had brought about before his eyes.

"Pastor!" It was Peter who spoke. "We have fourteen miles to church. Besides, Johannes is my wife's brother, and this may be the last time. Pastor, would you let us partake together with Johannes of the body and blood of the Lord?"

The curate nodded in silence. To think that they wanted this service from him. He took out of his bag the handbook and the clerical coat. Then he opened the communion case, placed the chalice on the table and filled it with wine. The others had quietly smoothed the bed clothes, placed a pillow behind Johannes' back, and tidied the room a bit. Now they were all seated.

Savonius collected his thoughts. As for the communion address, God had already taken care of that, and he could omit one of his own. He folded his hands and offered a silent prayer. He really prayed, an awkward and groping prayer, but full of deep longing. Then he opened the red covers of the handbook, took his place at the bed, and began to read:

"Dear brother, be of good cheer and confess your sins before God your heavenly Father . . ."

Johannes had folded his hands. His eyes looked toward the ceiling. Savonius, troubled about his appearance, turned the pages and found the prayer under the rubric: "When the sick person is very weak." He began to read, slowly and solemnly, "I, poor, miserable sinner, . . ."

The other three got down on their knees on the bare floor. With folded hands and heads bowed low, they joined quietly in the reading. Even Johannes' lips moved. "Against Thee and Thy holy commandments have I sinned by thought, word and deed. . . ."

Savonius could not take his eyes from Johannes. Now it is beginning again, was his troubled thought. It was as though his trespasses had descended like a dark mass on his forehead, and a secret agony once more tightened the wrinkles between his eyes. The curate continued the reading with a fearful heart. At last he came to the words, "who return unto Thee and with living faith take refuge in Thy Fatherly compassion and in the merits of our Savior Jesus Christ." He almost shouted the words. It was like taking hold of a pillar.

Now the confession of sins was finished. In the words of the liturgy, Savonius asked, "Believest thou that God hath given his ordained servants authority in his church through his holy Word to forgive sins, and that my forgiveness is God's forgiveness?"

"*Yes*," answered Johannes, so firmly and so unaffectedly, that Savonius now for the first time understood that this was no formal question read from a book, but a vital question, one that involved the realities of life and death.

"Be it according to your faith! By command of our Lord Jesus Christ I forgive thee thy sins in the name of God, the Father, the Son, and the Holy Spirit. Amen."

Johannes lay perfectly still with eyes closed. The wrinkles about his mouth and between his eyebrows had been smoothed by an unseen hand. Was it a smile that played upon his lips? The smile of a child, a very happy child, thought Savonius.

He read the Admonition and the Words of Institution over the bread and the wine. The holy words restored his confidence. Here, nothing depended on himself. Here he was simply a steward, a nameless link in the long succession of hands which Christ had used throughout the ages to distribute His gifts to men. For the first time he felt it a relief, rather than a compulsion, to be nothing but a servant of the church, without any contribution of his own, and with no other glory to seek than to steward the holy heritage honorably.

He distributed the bread. Dividing one of the wafers made enough for all. Then he gave them the cup. It was then that Johannes suddenly began to speak in a strangely distant voice.

"Listen! Don't you hear the organ tones? I hear the rush of white wings. I hear the sound of many waters. Now Johannes is sitting in Ravelunda church, and never before has the organist played like this. I hear them singing, 'Holy, holy, holy, Lord God of Sabaoth. Heaven and earth are full of his glory.' On the altar the Lord's chalice shines like fire. But the wall is of crystal and the church without a roof, and the angels of heaven ascend and descend. They bow before the chalice, they cover their faces. They say, 'Blessed is he that cometh in the name of the Lord.' Now an archangel takes the cup in his hand. It is like pure fire. Now he comes toward me. Sparks fly from his fingers, he will burn me to death!"

Johannes laid one of his hands over his eyes as if to shield them from too bright a light. The other hand seemed to push something away. But then both hands fell. He became calm again, and his next words were whispered.

"You wanted only to cleanse me, Lord, to cleanse and redeem. You wanted only to save, and now your angel says, 'Lo, this hath touched thy lips; and thine iniquity is taken away. Now you can behold the living God.'"

"He is delirious," whispered the wife. "God keep his mind!"

"He is wiser than any of us," Savonius answered somewhat abruptly. "Let us give thanks and pray!"

He prayed the Thanksgiving and pronounced the Benediction. Then he began to sing the hymn, "Now thank we all our God," and the others, still kneeling, joined him.

For a moment longer they remained in silent prayer. They seemed to be so overpowered by something unseen that they were unable to rise up. Johannes lay quietly on the bed and seemed to be asleep.

When they got up at last, the wife began to talk about breakfast. Savonius declined. He wanted to get home as soon as possible. He was a bit reluctant to force the willing Peter out on the road again, especially since his brother-in-law might die before night. But then he remembered that, if he could get as far as to the big highway in the village, he could get home by hiring a conveyance. It was only a few miles to Hester, and from there he could get a driver to Ödesjö. So it was planned that Peter was to drive him to the inn at Hester. Thereby he would have fulfilled his responsibility.

The wife gave the curate a thankful look. He saw that she was glad that her husband could return so soon. Savonius also was glad. If he had acted badly as a pastor, he could perhaps still be a decent fellow man.

The farewell was brief and with few words. Doctor Savonius looked for at least a hint of irony in the respect which these wonderful people had for their pastor, but he found nothing of that. He was glad that Katrina was to stay. She would do more good than he, if the sick man should be seized with another spell.

———

Now he was off again. The rhythmic slap of the harness and the rasp of the wheels in the sand were the only sounds to break the silence. Savonius noticed that they made way more slowly now, though it was a steady descent. On the way out, the driver's whip had been in use, not mercilessly or impatiently, but with a steady attempt to get the mare to do her best. Now it hung loosely. Savonius understood the difference. It had been a race with death last night; now the matter was settled. There was meaning in everything. And these people thought about others. Even in that respect they differed from him. He remembered with shame that he had forgotten, when they had left a while ago, that Peter might have needed something to eat before starting out again.

He turned to the peasant at his side. His face was emotionless and introspective, his chin jutted out sharply, his dark hair hung thickly behind his ears. The curate suddenly became interested in the kind of life and experience that had produced characters such as these. He wanted to ask—he did not know exactly what.

"Tell me, Peter, how is it that you folks up there at Hyltamålen are so, so . . . I mean that you read God's Word and pray the way you do?"

Inwardly, he thought that, if a physician were so clumsy in asking about the bodies of his patients as he was in inquiring about their souls, he must reckon himself quite inept. He would have reason to ask whether he was really fit to be a pastor.

Peter gave sober and matter-of-fact attention to the question.

"It began with my wife's mother," he said. "In her youth she worked in the vicinity of Kalmar and was awakened through the preaching of Elving. He was a pietist and revivalist. There was something special about my mother-in-law; she could sing and speak in such a way that it was like seeing living pictures on a wall. Johannes has inherited much from her. When I learned to know my Anna, it was my privilege to be present on Sunday evenings when her father read from Scriver's *Soul Treasury,* and when we sang together, and that is how I also was led to walk in the way.

"And Katrina?"

"Her story is somewhat different. She was born up north. They had a pastor who laid much stress on the atonement, and it was from him Katrina learned to understand all this about God's grace. We were neighbors three years. At Katrina's they had Martin Luther's *Postil;* we had the Bible and Scriver's *Soul Treasury.* Every month we traded. But now we have lived far apart for many years."

Savonius was silent again. An altogether new world had opened for him this night. No bridges seemed to lead from this world to his old way of looking at things. In his synthesis of life were found intelligence and grace, the cultured smile at the world's folly, the aroma from warm punch bowls, the music of the spinet. There were the torch-lighted sleighing parties, the fragrance of lilacs, tripping satin slippers along the graceful curves of sandy paths, friendly joviality and raillery—and in the background the expected promotion to higher clerical rank and privilege, carrying with it a round of servants, a private coachman, and a doctor's hat. There was more: there was the effort to advance social welfare and education, schools for children, and an improved agriculture; there was, too, the concern for better politics and parish administration. And, to top the whole system, there was the Supreme Intelligence, the wise and good God, who asked of us a prudent and virtuous life.

The other world Savonius had barely come in touch with hitherto. It lived down among the people, this gray and brown mass which smelled of stable and damp woolens as it sat below him when he stood in the pulpit. He had come close to it when he gave the sacrament to these coarse mouths, which he cared as little about when they smiled in happy innocence as when they smelled of snuff and cheap brandy. He had met it again at the baptismal font, where the godmothers took the wraps off the children and he had to stand in the reek of diapers and frying fat and baptize some red and knotty bundle of humanity. Now, suddenly, he had been forced through the wall of separation and had come to see that world from the inside.

He understood that he had reached a point where the question about God was more alive than elsewhere—though it certainly ought to have been vital in the theological and clerical circles in which he had lived hitherto. And yet he felt that he had learned more about real godliness in these short morning hours than in all his past life. Here the question of the soul's salvation was exceedingly earnest and actual. Indeed, salvation itself was something so real that one could almost see it. As a matter of fact, he had read about all this in Upsala, and he had spoken of it in the ancient words and phrasings of the handbook. But up till now he had always thought about them as a kind of revered symbol of a higher reality, which he knew as Providence and its natural laws and ethical principles. Sitting there in the carriage, it seemed to him that God was just as distant and exalted for him as the cloudless and spacious summer sky above him—infinitely majestic, gentle in his summer warmth, but oh, so far away! For the people he had just learned to know, God was also the earth and the common day. He was as near to them as the Bible on the table or the clothes one wore. He was as real as the ploughed fields and the mountain crags. His wrath was like a tempest and a fever, his mercy like a lovely Sabbath morning. For them, everything was near and palpable. And yet they had the infinity of heaven remaining above them.

And which of these worlds was now the best?

Savonius' mind had become wonderfully clear and keen again. His weary body was pleasantly relaxed on the driver's seat, but his thoughts were transparent as glass. In the early morning sunlight things seemed to unveil their true essence. The road led down into the valley, leafy glades and clearings opened in the forest, at the farmhouses one heard sounds from the dairy, morning smoke rose from the chimneys and there was haying in the meadows. Not a single wisp of cloud showed in the July sky.

Only the sky, that would be quite empty after all, thought Savonius. As empty as it has hitherto been in my faith! Only the heavens! Crystal-clear reason; lofty, transparent ideas; eternal principles: God, virtue, immortality. But here below life follows its own course: French cuisine, soirees, witty lyrics, recent royal pronouncements concerning frugality, the latest news from the war in Finland—and then, on Sunday morning a little address about the precious manifestations of grace from the Most High.

They turned into the village street at Hester. The sunshine danced in the tops of the lindens. He felt, almost physically, how its warm flood spread over the earth and was absorbed by the grass and the flowers, how it flowed into the whole creation as a warming, life-giving, budding, and uplifting power. Heaven must be like that. It must come down to earth, into creation, shine in a broad stream on the kitchen table, through the doors of the cattle shed and the windows of the mill house. It must come thus to bring life into being, that must struggle and be saved. It must not just be above the soil and the dirt, it must be in the midst of it. It must not be far removed from the gray and smelly crowd below the pulpit, but enter deep into its members. It must not have its place within the parsonage fence or the manor house gates; it must be just here where the farm buildings lean their sagging roofs against one another and noisome rills flow from the dunghills in the farmyards.

The carriage had stopped outside the village inn.

Savonius remembered suddenly that he had neglected the most important. He had had in mind to make some plausible excuse for his strange behavior and to try to get Peter to tell him what he really thought about him. Now he stood at the carriage wheel uncertain and ashamed, as he remembered all too clearly the details of his shameful failure.

"Good-bye then, Peter," he said haltingly. "Thank you for the ride. I am sorry I could not do more for Johannes."

"More?" Peter looked at him questioningly. "Pastor, have you not brought him Christ's body and blood? Have you not exercised the blessed authority of the keys, which comes from God? Can a man do more?"

"That I did not do," answered Savonius, and he meant it sincerely. "I could not comfort him."

"Only God can do that, Pastor, and the instrument he chooses. The time has not yet come, but it will come."

"What do you mean, Peter?"

The peasant stood long, looking at the ground.

"It does not behoove me to counsel a servant of the Lord," he said. "But if you will receive it from God, Pastor, it is written in the comforting words in the twenty-second chapter of St. Luke and the thirty-second verse."

Savonius searched his memory.

"What word do you mean, Peter?"

"It must not come from me," said the peasant evasively. "It is too great for me. But if it comes from the Lord, it can be received, and will come as a blessing."

With that, he bowed deeply and got into the carriage and took up the reins. But Savonius felt that he was still not ready to be separated from this strange man. He took a long step toward the carriage, laid his hand on the edge of the seat, looked steadily at the man, and said, "Pray for me, Peter."

The peasant met the pastor's look with calmness. An almost imperceptible brightness spread over his face.

"We have already done that, Pastor. And if you would like it, we will continue to do so—with gladness."

"Thank you," said Savonius as he turned away. He was thoughtful as he walked toward the inn. To himself he mumbled, "Twenty-two and thirty-two; twenty-two and thirty-two."

———

In the Ödesjö parsonage life had awakened as usual. Maja-Lena made her morning rounds. The maids began to put things in shape in the great hall and to move the chairs to where they belonged; there was the clatter of pots and pans in the kitchen, the milk was brought in, and the pleasant aroma of potato pancakes began to filter out into the entrance way. The peace was not broken until Hedvig carried a tray of sandwiches and a glass of fruit drink up to the curate's chamber and found it empty. However unwillingly, she had to hurry to the dean's bedroom, knock at the door, and tell the news.

The dean thought about the steep Heding hills, and feared the worst. All it took was a sleepy driver and an overly tired horse, and there could easily be an accident there. But he did not express his uneasiness.

"I am quite sure they had sense enough to ask the curate to stay over night at Hyltamål," he said. "Don't expect him until noon."

Hedvig had to be satisfied with that.

The dean was uneasy, however, and could not stay in bed any longer. He dressed himself with care, lighted his pipe, and stepped over the high threshold to his study. As he scratched away with his pen and made underscorings and deletions in the statement the county board had asked him to prepare concerning the increasing vanity of the peasantry in respect to dress and manner of life, he again and again looked out through the linden trees toward the place where the parsonage driveway became visible.

The bell rang for breakfast. The dean came to the great hall to conduct morning prayers. It lay at the opposite gable and occupied the whole south end of the residence. The house was said to have been built in the days of King Charles, and the kitchen lay, according to old custom, directly ahead as one came in through the entry hall. The great hall lay to the right, and the dean's bedroom and study to the left.

After morning prayer and breakfast, the dean could not keep from taking a turn down the road toward the Heding hills under the pretext of inspecting the haying. He was never one to show any sentimentality. If a curate was negligent, he would have to answer for it himself. But in his heart he had to concede that he would take it hard if anything happened to his assistant. He had taken a strong liking to the quick-witted Upsala doctor, who was always prepared to make music or put together a bit of verse. Nothing but his fondness for him had made him so brusque last evening. Henrik needed to be forced out into the parish, needed to be thrown head first into the cold water if he should ever learn to swim. As yet, there was nothing of the pastor about the young man. He could preach, indeed, so that the ladies waved their handkerchiefs in applause; but, to put it plainly, the whole thing was nothing but a superficial conglomeration of honeyed phrases. The peasants would choke on such fodder in the long run, and at deathbeds it was just so much froth. The dean had made pastoral calls his own responsibility. But he realized that he must let Henrik begin to eat of the bark bread of earnestness, if he should ever amount to anything as a pastor. If only he has not broken his neck the very first time he left the shelter of the parsonage!

The dean made a wide swing through the fields toward the north, but never farther than that he could see the road. The bell announced the noon meal, but no carriage was yet to be seen. The dean turned his steps homeward, very much disturbed.

——————

When the dean reached the stone bridge and could view the whole of the straight driveway that led to the parsonage yard, a carriage was just moving out through the gates and taking the road in the opposite direction. If he saw correctly, it was the innkeeper's black gelding that trotted down the hill. The carriage must therefore have been from Hester. Wondering what this could mean, he strode along briskly and was soon at the parsonage.

Hedvig dashed out to meet him. She was the dean's oldest child and had managed the household ever since his wife had passed away. Her face, which had taken on an early maturity because of the responsibilities thrust upon her, showed motherly concern.

"Dear Papa, what are we going to do? Doctor Savonius has come back by carriage from Hester. He hasn't slept a wink all night. He looked terribly haggard and wouldn't eat anything. Now he has shut himself up in his room."

The dean drew a secret sigh of relief. It was evident that Henrik still had his arms and legs in good order.

"If he has traveled twenty-eight miles during the night in a hired carriage," he said, to calm her, "it isn't strange that he is tired. Don't bother him. I'll look in on him myself."

The dean was now inside, and climbed the narrow attic stair. Up there the warm air hung thick as a pillow under the rafters of the open room. Dark garments hung in rows beneath the rough roof boards. The flooring rocked under the dean's feet. At the north end of the unceilinged attic where the chimney in its white plaster stood out like a tower, lay the curate's room. A low door, ancient in pattern and almost square, hung on long hinges, and gave entrance to the chamber.

The dean knocked.

Savonius had dozed on the buggy seat during the last part of the journey. It was not until people began to greet him in the village that he sat up, straightened his wig, and brushed the dust from his hat. He would have liked to crawl unnoticed to his room, but Hedvig had seen him coming and was out on the steps before he had had time to pay the driver. He left half of her anxious questions unanswered, and said no in an almost unfriendly way when she tried to get him to eat something. After giving her the communion silver to clean, he proceeded up the stairs with heavy steps.

He had scarcely closed the door behind him before he was at the table and opened his Bible.

"Luke 22:32," he mumbled. So that was it. The Savior's words to Peter on the way to Gethsemane: "But I have prayed for thee, that thy faith fail not: and when thou art converted, strengthen thy brethren."

Two waves of feeling alternated within him. From one direction, came resentment. Did this peasant mean to imply that he was not converted? From the other came a mighty surge drowning every other feeling and filling his consciousness to the brim. This was not the word of a man—it was the Word of God, a sternly clear statement about his condition.

Not converted, supported by the prayer of Another, and yet called to strengthen his brethren! He saw it with almost supernatural clarity, as from outside: he saw himself, slightly intoxicated, red garter rosettes at the knees, stepping into the carriage in the summer night with his head full of gavotte melodies and his heart of selfish concern for his own honor. He had not thought at all about the sick man; he had had no sympathy to spare for him, and much less, any thought for his salvation. He had completely forgotten him who had commissioned him. But far beyond the pale sky of the summer night sat One enthroned who in limitless mercy had prayed for his unworthy servant, prayed that his wretched, bloodless faith might not die completely in the chill night air of raillery and jesting, but that it might be made to burn anew with a warm and living flame. He saw it all as a panorama: the forest road on which Henrik Samuel Savonius, God's unworthy servant, was carried toward the abyss of humiliation, supported by the Savior's intercession, himself forgetful of all that was holy, but remembered by the Holy One he had forgotten. And, in the same melancholy dimness, on another road that stretched before him like a white ribbon, he saw a lone woman, guided by that same great Mercy, rendering the service in which the incompetent servant of the Word had utterly failed. Unprofitable—but still not rejected. Had not God permitted him to administer the Holy Sacrament with his unworthy hands? Had he not been allowed to turn the key that, by the authorization of the Savior, opened the gates of heaven? Had he not been privileged to be the celebrant at the heavenly joy feast at which Johannes on his death bed beheld the angels of God? And had not God now, to cap it all, sent him this message, so overwhelming in its undeserved and overflowing grace: "Strengthen thy brethren." God wanted to use him after all!

He sank to his knees, rested his elbows on the rickety desk, and pressed his forehead against the knuckles of his folded hands.

"Lord, Lord, how canst Thou? Lord, is it thus Thou rewardest my transgressions? Dost Thou clothe me in grace because I have so deeply despised Thee? Lord, I am too insignificant. Lord, I am not fit. Thou knowest my pride. Thou knowest that I have wanted all the glory for myself. Thou knowest that I wanted to be seen and admired, but not to serve and bear Thy cross. Lord, have mercy upon me! If Thou still art not done with me, take me completely!"

He knelt in silence. He seemed to feel that his whole being flowed slowly into the hands of God, that he was lifted out of all the past and gradually poured into a new mould, a new life and a new will which took him in its strong grip. And when God took his soul in his hand, he felt the challenge, "Strengthen thy brethren," as an all-constraining and dominating call.

"Dear Lord," he murmured, "if Thou wilt use me, I will go at Thy bidding."

Now he seemed to see before him the gray, malodorous crowd in homespun, these Swedish commoners, forsaken by their leaders, in danger of drinking themselves to death, and in their desperation being dished out a few miserable sermons, concocted of fine phrase. And yet these men had the strength to bleed and conquer in the war beyond the Baltic. It was to these he was now sent, and he would go forth in the power of God.

He gave a start. Someone was at the door. It was the dean's quick and determined knock. Getting up quickly, he managed an embarrassed, "Come in!" But he had not quite straightened up, nor brushed the dust from his knees, before the dean was in the room.

The dean stood still, apparently surprised. He spoke with an attempt at composure.

"Well, my dear Henrik, it's good to see you again. How did it go?"

"Thank you, sir, it went very well. Johannes found peace; and I, the opposite."

The dean's eyes widened a bit.

"Did it go *that* well?" he said. Yet he seemed to doubt that he had understood his curate correctly. There was a hint of suspicion as he looked him over from the blue scarf to the rosettes at the knees.

Savonius bent over impulsively. Two quick grasps, the sharp sound of ripping cloth, and the two garter decorations landed, torn and tattered, in a corner behind the bureau. He straightened up and said, "Sir, I am through with all this now. I want to be a *pastor,* a real pastor."

Surprise and doubt on the dean's face blended into a bright smile, full of paternal good will.

"Well, my boy, God bless you for that! Though that isn't exactly a matter of the trousers."

Without giving Savonius time to answer, he was out of the room and groping his way down the stairs. The curate followed slowly. The dean stopped for a moment in his study. Savonius stood waiting at the door to the dining room. A moment later the dean came out again with a large brown leather volume under his arm. He pushed the hesitant curate gently into the room, where the noon meal was already steaming on the table.

"Let us eat now, Henrik. For dessert you may take this volume up to your room. It is the sainted Nohrborg's *Postil.*

I have thought for a long time that you should read it a little. It will do you good, and also the congregation. You might very fittingly begin with the sermon for the Third Sunday after Epiphany, which deals with poverty of spirit. And now, let us say grace!"

Savonius bowed his head deeply and devoutly. At the same moment it struck him that he had stood at almost that same spot last evening when the dean had proposed the toast for the heroes of Österbotten. That was not so many hours ago—and yet an eternity. Somewhere in this sleepless night ran a boundary between two worlds. God had led His unworthy servant across that boundary line.

"And I thank Thee, Lord," he murmured.

Awakened by the Law

The house was unusually quiet today. For the first time for a long while the weather was mild, the enormous drifts had begun to melt and become darker, and there was a slow, rhythmic dripping from the eaves. Now and then the snow fell in wet clumps from the trees and landed with a dull splash on the ground, as burdened branches began to raise themselves for the first time in weeks.

The dean found a measure of delight in the stillness. The incessant bustle of the last weeks had almost gone to his nerves. He stood in his study at the window that faced the yard and looked thoughtfully at one of the wings of the house. Today the door was shut and there was no sound of snowy boots being kicked against the flagstone. It was in fact a very lovely day. The events of the last months were almost too much for the dean. He tried to review in his mind all the strange things that had taken place since that night in July when Henrik had received his first jolt.

At first he had remained indoors a great deal, said little, and did considerable reading. Since Johan-Christofer had come home, Henrik had moved to the other wing of the house, to the little room under the gable roof. The dean gazed with some discouragement at its square window, which was flanked by two semicircular wickets. Since Henrik had moved over there, they had somehow drifted apart. The curate was not like his former self. He wore black, and he did not write gay verses as formerly.

The other changes had come little by little. Henrik absorbed the wisdom of the good old postils at every opportunity. First of all, he had given thorough attention to *The Order of Salvation for Fallen Man*. That was certainly good, the dean thought, Nohrborg being one of his favorite authors. Then he borrowed *Concordia Pia*, Luther's *Church Postil*, Pontoppidan's *Collegium Pastorale*, and Fresenius' *Communion Book*. Thus far everything was as it should be.

But when he one day borrowed Murbeck, the dean became alarmed. Murbeck was all right, if read with discrimination. The dean himself would read from that book just before Christmas in order to get the proper amount of salt into his warnings in respect to the wonted heavy holiday drinking. But to read it the week after St. Michael's Day, right in the midst of the Trinity season, that was really going too far. It was not without good reason that Murbeck in his day had been suspended by the honorable cathedral chapter at Lund. If Henrik continued this way, it could go just as badly for him.

No one could deny, however, that the curate's sermons had improved. In that respect the dean felt that his prayers were more than answered.

It was very soon observed that the attendance increased whenever Savonius preached. The dean and his curate served in turn every other Sunday. The church was, to be sure, almost always filled. But now it was almost overcrowded whenever the curate was to conduct the worship. People even stood in the aisles, and people from neighboring parishes were beginning to frequent the services. The dean was disturbed. That was of course nothing but curiosity! He had never been able to tolerate any sensationalism in connection with the Word of God.

Worst of all was the attention of people from other parishes. It had been really depressing of late. From the south came people from Ravelunda. They came in large groups by foot. And from the north, from beyond the Heding hills, came caravans of sleighs that passed the dean's house with tinkling bells. It vexed, first of all, the members of the parish, who were crowded in their pews and had to share their space in the church stables with strangers. Yet their grumbling was easier to endure than the angry remarks of Hafverman in Näs and Warbeck in Ravelunda. They even threatened to report the matter to the Cathedral Chapter. They would charge that the Ödesjö curate was exciting general indignation among honest citizens when, by his affected manner of preaching, he enticed the simple to go outside parish boundaries instead of receiving through the proclamation of their duly appointed pastors the precious principles of religion.

To put an end to this offensive preferential choice of pastor, the dean had resorted to stratagem. At midweek he had changed the preaching schedule altogether, deciding that he himself would preach on the coming Sunday. Henrik was asked to conduct the liturgical service, and the dean had then ascended the pulpit, noting with roguish satisfaction the dismay among the worshipers that filled the church. His text for the *exordium* was Matthew 11:7, "What went ye out into the wilderness to see?" His sermon was a resounding setting forth of the dangers of being drawn by every spiritual wind instead of remaining faithful to the simple Word of God.

His triumph was short-lived. Although he had done away with the announcement of set preaching schedules, and of making known who would conduct the worship on the following Sunday, he still had to let Henrik know a few days in advance when he was supposed to preach. Somehow or other, it always leaked out when it was the curate's turn, and the crowds filled the roads again.

It could not be denied, of course, that there was something remarkable about Henrik's way of preaching. He had always been eloquent. Now a dark glow had come into his voice and a firm control to his thoughts, and it was difficult to escape the implication of his words. If only he were not so intense!

The dean sighed deeply. It was really a shame that so much zeal should be spoiled by such a lack of wisdom! For if dear Henrik was aflame, he was at any rate not careful with the fire. More than once the dean had sat in his pew with eyes closed and his face rigid as though carved in wood, praying in his heart that all these flashes from the pulpit might not be the cause of irreparable harm in the parish.

The dean knew well enough that he was himself by no means a bore in the pulpit. He could preach against both drunkenness and loose living, so that the people bowed their heads in shame. In comparison with Savonius' broadsides, however, his words were like soft western breezes. Worst of all was that Henrik used such pointed and mercilessly concrete examples. If he was preaching about mercy, he would describe the lot of the poor in such a way that the people could picture someone of the captain's many crofters leaving his home at three o'clock in the morning with a sack of grain on his back, how he slaved in the fields, how he must often go without the noon meal in order to get to the mill at last after thirteen hours of labor and after picking up his flour, return home the three miles through the woods, carrying his heavy load. No wonder, then, that the captain fumed at the incendiary speech and the radical and revolutionary ideas expressed.

And then the whisky! When Savonius took up that subject, one got a vivid picture of how the peasant from Bäckafall awoke one autumn morning in the roadside ditch, his feet frozen in the mud. One could hear the rowdy shouts of the peasants from Sörbygd who had stopped at the Svenhester bar on their way home from church and had drunk until they vomited where they sat and were carried out to the woodshed like heavy sacks.

Still, this had to do with actual wrongs which all the people must silently or openly condemn. But what should one say about his constant thunderings against the most innocent little ornaments the women wore? On All Saints Day, the young ladies had wept as usual and used their lace handkerchiefs. At this he had let loose an unpremeditated blast against the slaves of worldliness in their silks and satins, these for whom the blood of Jesus was a sweet perfume barely sufficing to awaken sweet stirrings of the heart, and for whom the Lord's suffering was but a lovely theatrical scene serving to call forth pleasant tears, tears doubly sweet because they gave the coveted occasion once more to show a pair of beautiful hands and a delicately and ostentatiously embroidered handkerchief. When next he preached most of these young women stayed away. Only Babette, the captain's daughter, and a few others were there in plain black woolen dresses.

As for the dean's Hedvig, something was evidently quite amiss. She hung her head, often answered evasively, and refused to dance. She would not even wear her mother's jewels any longer, though they certainly were not gaudy. This had evidently come as a result of the inability of the curate to do anything with moderation.

Today, however, everything was quiet at the deanery. Otherwise, as a rule, people were coming and going constantly. There was always some parishioner—and, for that matter, people from beyond the parish—who wanted to see the curate. Since he now lived in the north wing, he could receive private visitors without directly by-passing his superior. Nowadays most of the errands to the parsonage never got farther than to the north wing. Naturally the dean was a bit jealous. He himself had only a few private consultations during the month. Yet he tried honestly to hide his displeasure. If people must see the curate, he was not going to force them to come to him. But he was a bit suspicious about the nature of all these soul troubles that had developed this winter, this endless chasing for advice from a boy who a year ago did not know the difference between the sleep of sin and the state of grace. Could such goings on be anything more than a foolish spiritual fad?

Today the curate was on a journey. He had left on Friday to visit the chaplain at Fröjerum, that strange man Lindér. He had been invited by Lindér to come and preach. On the way home he was then to conduct a house catechization in Sörbygden. There would therefore be surcease for four days from strange guests who used to steal their way along the snowdrifts as if afraid to meet the dean on the road.

The dean had hardly had time to savor this pleasant thought before a faint sound of sleigh bells was heard from the direction of the village. It might mean a visitor. The dean pondered. Was it someone who wanted to see Savonius? If so, he must be from outside the parish, perhaps from Ravelunda. Then he had come just in time. The dean would see to it that he would not get away without being seen. He would ask him to come into the parsonage, read the law to him, and tell him straight that he could go to Pastor Warbeck if he needed instruction as to the way of salvation.

He could see the sleigh now. The sleighing was fine, and it was approaching swiftly. Before he had pulled himself together it rounded the gate post, and skidded so that the runners struck against the opposite post. It continued swiftly past the wing and all the way to the main steps of the house. It was only when the cutter was right in front of the dean's window that he discovered that the visitors were none other than the captain at the manor house and the youthful Lieutenant von Reiher from Bocksholm.

The dean hurried out to welcome his guests. With carefully chosen words he bade them come in, called Hedvig and ordered wine and cookies.

He directed a questioning look at the captain, who held a roll of documents in his hand.

"What brings me the pleasure of your company today, my good friend?"

The captain, who had seated himself on the sofa, seemed somewhat embarrassed. When he did start to speak, it was in an unusually boisterous and military tone.

"Please understand, Pastor, that in paying you this visit I am actuated by the warmest affection for you personally."

This is no pleasant matter, thought the dean. Putting his hand inside his coat, he nodded quietly, and tried to look both reserved and accommodating. The captain continued.

"Frankly, *cher ami,* I cannot as the king's faithful citizen do otherwise than I am determined to do. I can inform you, Pastor, that we had a very serious consultation at our home yesterday. The baron from Bocksholmen was present, and the young ensign who is with me, who is fortunately home on furlough. We also had the good fortune—entirely by chance—to have Rector Warbeck as guest."

The dean pricked up his ears. What kind of conspiracy was this behind his back? The captain went on with his explanation.

"Well, after a long and very considerate discussion we decided to visit you. The ensign can attest that the opinion I now state is shared without exception by all the gentry of the parish."

The ensign, who sat stiff and reserved in the white armchair, clicked his heels under the chair and bowed curtly.

The dean had already guessed what it was all about and was concerned about giving the conversation a more congenial tone. "Well, Captain," he said, "you really excite my curiosity. It must be remarkable news that has occasioned so solemn an embassy."

"Yes," said the captain, sourly. "It is really nothing to joke about. Ever since last fall a strange willfulness has been evident among the people hereabouts. Honorable old customs are despised, respectable people are being pointed out as ungodly criminals, divisions are created in the homes, and the most hateful invectives are hurled against innocent and useful occupations. And the source of it all, as everyone agrees, is this shameless windbag of a curate."

The dean lifted his hand slightly.

"Calm yourself, Captain. Let us wait with judgment until the examination is concluded. The best procedure would certainly be to call in the curate immediately."

The ensign betrayed himself by a dismayed look at the captain. The dean continued calmly.

"But unfortunately he is away for the time being, and so we shall have to discuss the matter in his absence. And since I understand that it would be beneath your honor as military men to bring charges against a man in his absence, I shall assume the task of speaking in Dr. Savonius' defense. You, my friend, will act as prosecutor, and perhaps the ensign will act as your assistant."

Hedvig came in with the tray. There was a quiet pause. Only the dean chatted pleasantly as he fulfilled his duties as host. He was always in high spirits when the nerves were tensest. When they had had their wine and cookies, he resumed:

"The matter before us, then, concerns certain transgressions by Savonius. Does the prosecutor wish to state the counts of the accusation?"

"Here they are. You can read them yourself. May I ask you to be careful with the document? It is to be sent to the Cathedral Chapter."

The dean's head was in a whirl. Had it gone so far? Without any advance warning! Why had they not consulted him in the matter?

He completed the reading with difficulty. It was a cleverly worded petition on the part of a considerable number of persons in the Ödesjö parish who were most zealous for the welfare of the Church of Christ, asking that the reverend curate Henrik Samuel Savonius be, at the assignment of curates to take place on the first of May, removed from the parish in which his unwise zeal, his fanaticism, and affected manner of preaching had brought about much unrest and confusion. As an example of said confusion, the petitioners simply wished to state that the reputation his fiery sermons enjoyed throughout the district had led to such a flocking of people that the church was overcrowded and the atmosphere contaminated, that the church stables were filled with horses belonging to people of other parishes, that the reverent conduct of the services was interfered with, and finally, that all this entailed the risk of an epidemic.

Furthermore, a sense of honesty demanded that the Cathedral Chapter should not be kept in ignorance concerning the lack of Christian moderation that characterized Savonius' sermons. Thus he had described respected and irreproachable citizens in a way that showed little Christian love, calling them exploiters and slave drivers. He had severely condemned such innocent accessories of women's wear as lace handkerchiefs, plumes, jewels, and necklaces. He had fomented dissension, resulting in the separation of married couples, and strife between neighbors. Finally, he had misused the pulpit by attacks on landowners who insisted on their legal rights to sell travelers whiskey, a refreshing, useful, and widely desired commodity.

The dean could not help thinking that the last sentence was a pretty bit of circumlocution for drunkenness on the church roads.

The communication ended with the suggestion that the tranquility of this former quiet and law-abiding community could be restored in no better way than by the removal of this man, whose Christian zeal could not be denied, but whose revolutionary ideas could lead the unenlightened astray with grievous results.

The dean had finished reading, but kept his eyes on the document. He wanted to gain time. Various ideas chased through his brain. This petition must not go to the Cathedral Chapter. It would have harmful effects on Henrik's whole future. It was sufficiently false to harm his reputation, yet sufficiently true to be confirmed by fairly acceptable evidence. Poor Henrik had really exposed himself to attack. And now he would have to pay for it.

It occurred to the dean that he might say that he could somehow get along without a curate during the coming ecclesiastical year. Then Henrik could be transferred without any hue and cry and without any danger to his career, and the parish gentry would without doubt be satisfied. That would be a painless solution, except for himself. Actually, he was having a hard time to care for his duties of late. Besides, it would, in spite of everything, be difficult to part with Henrik. He looked for another way out.

It was the captain who broke the silence.

"I am sure you realize, Pastor, that we were terribly sorry to have to draw up this painful petition."

"No doubt," was the dean's cool comment. He took note also of the sourly haughty mien of the ensign.

"I am sure we all desire to see that this matter is taken care of without any public scandal," continued the captain. "We have a proposition to make, therefore, which we know must commend itself to your humane mind."

The dean looked at him searchingly.

"We propose that you yourself, having the best interests of the parish in mind, request a new curate. We leave the motivation to you. We have not at all wished to discredit the young man before the churchly authorities; we have only wished to see the danger averted which threatens to stifle all simple and unfeigned Christianity in our community."

The dean felt a wave of indignation rise within him. This was really going too far. To see this old roué and ladies' man making a hypocritical show of honest zeal for pure Christianity, when the only thing he really wanted was to get rid of a free-spoken critic, who had touched upon some of the really sore points of the whole feudal system, and who had thrown a few torches of the Spirit into the cultured darkness of the manor house.

The dean looked sharply at his guest.

"I would advise you, my good friend, not to send this petition to the Cathedral Chapter. In certain respects it is based on obvious misunderstandings. No one will deny that Dr. Savonius has proceeded with unwise zeal, especially with respect to externals and dress. Neither can anyone deny that there are many obvious abuses which are incompatible with sincere Christianity as I myself want to preach it. Drunkenness on the roads that lead from the church is a scandal and a shameful violation of the Sabbath; temperance could be much better in general than is now the case. As regards to the talk about the hard lot of the renters and subordinates, I have myself felt that when this is said in the house of God, one ought not to get angry and protest, but rather go home and search one's own heart and life. When you throw a stick into a pack of dogs, it is the one who is hit that howls, and when God's Word is rightly divided among sinners, it hurts most in the conscience that is most in need of it. I too have renters, Captain, and I must say that on that particular Sunday I found reason to examine myself before our Lord. Nor was I found altogether guiltless."

The captain flushed. The dean's confession had touched him to the quick. He felt that the conversation was in danger of moving in a dangerously personal direction, and so made haste to play his second trump card.

"I have no desire to debate, and I have always been poor at theology. But when it comes to Savonius and his preaching, I have such good theologians as Warbeck and Hafverman on my side. They too have made most serious remonstrances concerning Savonius and his unwise zeal. They have already prepared a communication to the Cathedral Chapter. I have a copy of it with me, for that matter. I thought it might interest you to see it."

The dean accepted the new letter with evident irritation. This looked more and more like a real conspiracy. It was a most unpleasant affair. What would the new bishop think? A petition by a few officers could be offset by a strong statement from a dean; but if the rectors of the two neighboring parishes supported his own parishioners, what in the world would the bishop think? Would he not have to conclude that old Faltin was getting a bit senile, since he had not at all reported any wrong conditions that were causing disorder in the congregation and had even affected other parishes?

Well, what did his worthy colleagues have to say? He glanced through the paper.

It was nothing trifling. The curate at Ödesjö had been the cause of a fanatical schism that threatened all traditional religious practice. He conducted uncalled-for devotionals in the homes outside of the regular church services. This was a plain transgression of the royal order of 1726 forbidding such gatherings. He attracted to these meetings not only his confused partisans in the parish of Ödesjö but also people from neighboring congregations. Although the peasantry in this part of the province were known for their honesty and integrity, said Savonius was in the habit of taking them to task in a scandalous manner, charging that they were spiritually asleep, sinful, and lost. If anyone listened to his deceptive counsels, he was led to separate himself from others by wearing clothes of the plainest and homeliest pattern and refusing to join in the innocent social gatherings and practices which are common in the community. Because of all this, the troubled colleagues urged the Chapter to take action against said disorder by enjoining the people to refuse to follow other religious customs than those that are traditional, and by forbidding said Savonius in the future to say and do things contrary to the demands of his high office.

The dean sighed deeply. This was really much more serious. Hafverman was an energetic man, respected in the Cathedral Chapter for his zeal in promoting public education and for his intellectual gifts. He was a pronounced liberal in theology, which was no doubt the real reason for his interest in the matter. At the recent pastoral meeting, called for the election of a bishop, Savonius had preached the sermon. The dean agreed that he had done well and had spoken in true Lutheran style, but his fellow pastors, and especially Hafverman, had been most critical. Was it proper, they argued, after a whole century of enlightenment, to keep talking about the atonement in this uncivilized fashion? Could any cultured person endure all this preaching of cleansing from sin through the blood of Christ, when everyone surely knew that the only atonement that could avail before God was the cleansing that consisted in following the holy teaching and example of Jesus in a virtuous life?

This had developed into a great conflict, in which the dean sought vainly to intervene. Hafverman looked upon Savonius as a traitor, an obscurant who would attempt to quench the light that was at last beginning to shine, and who would have the church go back to the prejudices of orthodoxy. He thought the time had definitely arrived to make the obscurant harmless.

The captain had his eyes fixed on the dean. He saw that this last salvo had taken effect. Now he brought out his trump card. "It will please you to hear that, having in mind the—shall we say precarious—consequences for you personally, I have persuaded the clergy to refrain, for the time being, from sending this memorial to the Chapter—naturally on the condition that I see to it that Savonius leaves this place. If he remains, I simply cannot help it: things must run their course."

The dean could no longer maintain an amiable tone. This was an attempt to intimidate him. Now he had no desire to compromise. If he dismissed Savonius now, it would be interpreted as compliance in the face of threat. Dean Faltin had never yet retreated because of a threat, and he was not going to do so now. He arose with the papers in his hand.

"Thank you, gentlemen, for being considerate of my welfare, but I cannot exactly agree with your view of this matter. I have the highest confidence in Dr. Savonius in spite of his blunders, which none regrets more than I. If he were now to be driven from the parish, it would benefit neither the diocese nor himself, since he would simply repeat the same follies elsewhere. Nor do I believe that it would do our own parish any good, because I think that then first would there be disorder in earnest among all those who have been influenced by him. The things you gentlemen call disorder are nevertheless for the most part things that have pleased me and that will be of real value for the people some day, if someone understands how to give them wise direction. But I am too old, and a new curate would never be able to put things right. Therefore, I do not believe I should be the cause of Savonius' leaving, as long as he does not himself desire to leave. And now, to show my great appreciation for your recommendation, Captain," he bowed affably toward the sofa, "I beg to be permitted to keep these papers. I shall inform Dr. Savonius tonight of their contents. If he thinks he ought to leave Ödesjö, I will try to make it possible for him to do so without embarrassment. I shall return the papers to you early tomorrow, together with my decision. *Skål!* And thank you for your sincere *humanité* and your unselfish zeal for the good of the parish." The dean drank the toast with an ironical gleam in his eyes. The ensign did not notice it—he played his role with stiff dignity; but the captain cleared his throat. Their glasses touched. The captain regretted the hasty departure, the ensign jingled his spurs, and with a sweeping sound of bells, the sleigh disappeared down toward the village.

Small causes, large consequences, thought the dean, as he looked thoughtfully out of the window. He had not had the slightest intimation of anything like this when he sent Henrik out on that fateful sick call. Was his poor Ödesjö now to figure in the gossip of the diocese as a scandal and Henrik be decried as a gospelmonger? God's ways were certainly strange. If he could only get close to Henrik! But there was an invisible wall between them. He felt almost jealous of the absurd Lindér, who had become a real intimate of Savonius, though ten years older than he.

Hedvig came in for the tray. She had been taught not to ask unnecessary questions. Now too, she was silent, but her whole being was a single, great and anxious appeal. She looked so helpless in her touching concern that the dean had mercy on her.

"They are speaking ill of Henrik," he said. "Just as I surmised. He really could be less self-confident, and not so severe in his judgments from the pulpit. Now they are thinking of reporting him to the Cathedral Chapter for creating factions and playing havoc with the churchly order."

Hedvig had waited. The tray shook in her hands.

"Be calm, my child," the dean hastened to add, "I have just as much faith in Henrik as ever. I will defend him with tooth and nail, if it becomes necessary."

A shy and thankful look was her only answer. She remained standing.

"What do you want, child?"

"Father, they won't remove him, will they?"

"Put your trust in God, Hedvig! You may leave this matter with him."

Suddenly he added, "You must learn to trust him so completely, Hedvig, that you will dare to wear your mother's brooch again, as you always used to wear it with this dress. You must so fully trust in Jesus that you may know that your salvation depends only on him."

"I know that, Father."

"No, my child, you do not know it. If you did, you would not believe that he becomes a less merciful Savior because you wear the brooch that your mother received on the tenth anniversary of her marriage and which she continued to wear for fourteen years with good conscience and sincere faith."

There were tears in Hedvig's eyes. The dean softened.

"You must understand, dear child, that this is a tangled affair, and that we shall need all God's help to clear it up. That means that you cannot give attention to petty things. We must believe, and we must pray in faith. Go to your room, therefore, and put on your mother's brooch, and say to the Savior, 'I treasure Thy grace so highly, Lord, that I dare to carry this ornament, just as my mother did.' Then pray for me and for Henrik that God may guide us aright. We shall surely need such prayer."

Hedvig curtsied and vanished with tears in her eyes. After a little while her steps were heard on the attic stairs. Well, praise God, it was not then any worse with the "disorder" in Ödesjö than that a daughter, despite all whims, could still obey her father.

The sleigh glided over the stones of the narrow forest road with many a sharp scraping and heavy thud. It was thawing, and the runners had begun to cut through the loose snow. This wilderness road had never been worn smooth for traffic this winter.

The Fröjerum chaplain held the reins. It was his errand as host to drive his guest preacher through the forest to Drängsmarken, where the stable-man from the deanery would call for the curate, after attending to another matter there, and then drive him back to Ödesjö. The hired man at Fröjerum could, of course, have done the driving, but the chaplain had his own reasons for taking over the task today. Every hour he could spend with his younger colleague was a feast for him.

The little mission at Fröjerum, which was served by the chaplain, was one of the most desolate parishes in this heavily wooded rural deanery. When Justus Johan Lindér landed there, after many adversities in respect to promotion, it was generally looked upon as a virtual exile. Lindér was not exactly lacking in gifts. He preached with warmth, not to say with passion. Wherever he had served as curate there had been a sensational increase in attendance at services; but, unfortunately, there had also been dissensions, conflicts, and grievances. He had the most unhappy fault of saying more than he intended, and that in the most critical contexts. Twice he had been warned by the Chapter and many times he had been denied a place on the list when nominations to vacancies were made. And once, when he happened to have Dean Jon Dubb as a listener he made a sudden extempore attack on the homiletical eloquence of the times, something in which the dean loved to shine. He had compared that preaching style with dust-covered artificial flowers, empty wine jugs, and withered bouquets, messages that could never produce a living seed.

Every time he preached a trial sermon he was just as unreasonably outspoken. It was said that on such an occasion in Alverum he kept perfectly quiet in the pulpit until there was a deathly silence in the church. Then he had said, "It is no doubt quite painful when it becomes altogether quiet, and you, my dear Alverum folks, must for a long time have caused such a silence in heaven, where for many years none of the angels have been able to sing and rejoice over a single sinner in the congregation who has repented and become converted."

Lindér was odd also in apparel. He never wore a wig as other cultured people did, was always dressed in black, and his housekeeping was as poor as any peasant's. His sermons were as long as they were unpredictable. After the first years of trying dissension, however, his parishioners had begun to be affected by his preaching of repentance, and this stocky and uncouth man with flashing eyes had become a spiritual authority in this forest district. After his conversion Savonius had sought Lindér's counsel, and since then they had met frequently. Gossip at the manor house had it that the dean's curate had been seen running along the road in the dusk of a Saturday evening, and that when some one who had met him asked in surprise where he was bound for in such haste he had answered, "To the chaplain at Fröjerum to get powder and shot, so that I shall be able to fire some telling blasts at you tomorrow morning, you hardened despisers of grace."

———

The sleigh had already crossed the parish border, and the conversation, which had dealt with the marks of a true sorrow over sin, now concerned itself with the future of the spiritual revival. Savonius was optimistic about it. The happenings of the past year were beyond what he had dared to dream. It seemed indeed that the fields had ripened to such an extent that the harvest waited only for the scythe. It had often happened that people had come from a distance only because they had happened to meet one of the awakened ones from Ödesjö. It was plainly evident that concern for salvation burned underneath the hard shell that had seemed so impenetrable.

Lindér was more skeptical. It was surely good that Savonius had been given grace to stir the stagnant spiritual waters of Ödesjö, but there was still much dregs at the bottom that would soon enough show up. And there were ugly fish down there. He counted his own respected superior, Warbeck of Ravelunda, as one of these, who would certainly show up and bite, when the opportunity presented itself. All the gentry would applaud. Since venereal diseases were stealing into the homes and mansions, there was little hope of unfeigned Christianity from that direction. Though they complied outwardly with churchly customs, their hearts were far from the gospel. They had no more interest in salvation than Horace or Rousseau might have had. A little empty rhetoric, a few phrases about virtue, they could still swallow, if only it limited itself to what any somewhat decent individual was considered to be observing already. Sacrifice and simplicity could also be tolerated, if they were presented in quotations from Marcus Aurelius which asked no commitments. But if someone asked them in the name of Jesus to deny themselves and take up the cross, he would be decried without fail as a pietist preacher and an enemy of all human culture.

He spat over the side of the sleigh. The trees stood less thickly now, and the road was uphill. From the hilltop one could see the white fields of Sörbygden lying between strips of forest.

Drängsmarken was the first village on this side of the boundary. Here the house catechization was to take place. As they swung in upon the village street, a group of men who were already waiting outside the Anders place doffed their fur caps. Someone led the horse away, and the two pastors entered the living room, where everything was in readiness for them.

Before the fireplace, whose arched canopy extended to the ceiling, stood a heavy wooden table and an old chair with a high, straight back. This was the pastor's place. A list of those to be catechized lay on the table. The men sat on long benches on the left, while the women occupied those on the right. Young people and children were crowded on the floor, where they sat on blankets because of the cold. Their blond heads shone like a field of ripe grain against the dark homespun of their elders.

Savonius rejoiced at the sight. He recalled the Savior's words, "Lift up your eyes, and look on the fields; for they are white already to the harvest." He led in the singing of the hymn, "Jesus is my joy, my all," after which he offered a warm prayer, for the congregation, its farms and cottages, the poor and the needy, the absent soldiers, for fields and cattle, for deliverance from the ravages of the Russians, and first and last for the eternal salvation of souls, that there might be a true awakening to repentance, and true faith unto regeneration and sanctification in the Spirit. Finally he prayed for all those who had come to be catechized, that as their names were here recorded they might also be written in the book of life in heaven.

He then called the roll and made note of those present. While reading the names, the pastor thought with quiet joy of how, after his experience of conversion, he had been led out among his people, into their homes, and in touch with new and wonderful human destinies and experiences. A year ago, all these men and women were only dead names on a neatly lined paper. Now he saw behind almost every line a face or a destiny. Many of these people were seeking souls; with quite a number of them he had conversed about their soul condition and their troubles, and he had come to know quite well the conflicts and the hidden tragedies also in this part of the parish. As he read, he occasionally put a little question about the health of the person named, or about purchase of land and altered residence, and he sensed that he had become united with these people through a thousand unseen ties of concern and sympathy.

The examination went along beautifully. The dean was a good pedagogue and had taught his parish the catechism as thoroughly as could be expected. The members of each household stepped forward in turn and stood in a group about the table. Savonius kept making explanations and asking thoughtful questions. When the catechization was over, he asked Lindér to take over. The chaplain explained the Third Article of the Creed and commented on certain other matters, such as plumed hats, false prophets, hindrances to communion, and the operation of private whisky stills.

Savonius then preached about true repentance, with Galatians 6:7 as text. This was followed by the singing of a hymn, after which he pronounced the benediction and bade those gathered to depart with the peace of the Lord.

The young people left first and a few of the older folks followed them. But a considerable number lingered. They had gotten up, but remained standing at the doorway or in clusters in the room, hesitant about leaving.

"You know, friends, that coffee will not be served this year," said Savonius. "The dean insists that this be dispensed with at our catechizations, the times being such as they are. We must abide by that."

Jonas, the farmer at Backgården, stroked his beard thoughtfully and said, "'Man shall not live by bread alone, but by every word that proceedeth out of the mouth of God.' And it is that kind of bread we should really like to have in greater abundance. Then too, there are a few things we should like to ask about, now that we have two pastors with us."

"Then we'll sit down again," said Lindér, not at all surprised at the request. "Come and sit around the table." With a few nudgings he got the group to sit in a half circle. Two more benches were moved forward so that the circle was doubled.

It was getting dark already, and the housewife lighted two candles on the table. Their pale flames struggled with the gray twilight of the February evening as it stole into the room from three directions. The light shone on the solemn faces round the table.

"We'll begin at the beginning," said Lindér. "What is the greatest hindrance to salvation in this community?" He leaned forward, his elbows on the table and his hands folded.

The answers were many. Brandy, sinful thoughts, spiritual sloth, worldly cares, lust for money were mentioned. Yes, and the lawsuit over the Bäckafall swampland.

Lindér led the conversation with the skill of a veteran. Litigation and drunkenness were the sins of the self-satisfied. They must be put away before lifegiving grace could be received. The other sins were inherent in man's very nature. They could remain as desires also in the converted, but they must be valiantly resisted. Of acute importance just now was to put an end to this litigation among neighbors. Lindér cleared up the real reasons for the misunderstanding by means of a few brisk questions, and was then ready to give counsel. Jonas must be willing to give up his claim, since he could well get along without that bit of peat bog, but the poor renter, who had the care of many small children to consider, might well bring suit, if only he would keep bitterness out of his heart. If Jonas would voluntarily give up his demand, it might be possible in return to get the stubborn Efraim at Sunnerboslätt, who was the real instigator of the strife, to relinquish of his own account the renter's share of his bog. The crofter lived between the two farms and had his renter's claim on each. Jonas ought therefore talk with Efraim on the morrow and come to an agreement with him. Above all, it was important that everyone beware of being so concerned about their honor or their money that they were in danger of losing Jesus.

A question was directed across the table to Savonius: "Must a true disciple sell all that he has and give it to the poor?"

"I have asked myself that question many times," said the curate a bit uncertainly. He had really felt compunction because of his fine books, and did not know just how to answer. But Lindér, who did not condone any evasiveness in respect to the Word of God, quickly interrupted.

"Zacchaeus didn't do that when he became a true disciple. The Lord shall be the owner of everything, but he must have someone to steward his property. Woe to him who uses God's money for luxury and vanity, to satisfy the lust of the eyes and the joys of the belly. But God's money must not, on the other hand, be given away carelessly. Let God rule the heart; he will then rule also the farm and the money."

"How shall ill-gotten goods be restored if the owner is dead?" was the next question. Savonius showed a touch of admiration as he looked at the man. Had he not as much admitted that he was a thief?

"He who is able to do so should pay the amount in full. But if the owner is dead, the money may be given to the poor or to someone who has suffered loss innocently."

The man nodded thoughtfully.

"What, then, about the man who can't pay?" The question came from the far end of the circle.

"He will nevertheless receive God's forgiveness and must ask forgiveness of the man from whom he has stolen. It would be wise to speak to your pastor about it."

The next question came from the housewife in the home where they were guests. "How great shall our sorrow over sin be, if it is to be sincere?"

"So great that one is willing to give up the sin," answered Lindér promptly. "Crocodile tears mean nothing in heaven. But he who wants to be freed from the sin has the true sorrow, even though the heart feels as hard as a stick."

The questions began to come more and more freely. A daughter from a neighboring farm family dared to ask about what was troubling her.

"How shall one know for sure that one is called by the Spirit of God?"

Savonius thought a moment. After leafing through the register of names, to identify the questioner, he answered.

"Christina Jonsdotter. Your name is listed among the baptized. You are called by God himself. You need never doubt that."

"But if one does not feel anything?"

"Then God feels so much more deeply."

She blushed, but said nothing further. Then a new voice was heard.

"How often should one go to the Lord's Supper?"

It was again Lindér who answered.

"That depends a little on how you ask the question. If you ask how often you *must* go, it may indicate a stubborn heart that wants to buy God's grace as cheaply as possible and that does not really want to be with Jesus. If that is the case, you must pray God to convert you. If, on the other hand, you ask how often you *ought* to go, our Lord's answer is, 'As oft as ye do this,' and that means that you must do it oftener than the great majority, who commune four times a year just for the sake of propriety. And if you ask how often you *may* go, you are showing the right hunger for grace, and my answer then is: Go in the joy of the Lord as often as you can. But do not be careless about the preparation!"

Gradually the conversation came to touch on more general questions, and chiefly the ill will toward seeking souls in the parish. It was felt that the winds of opposition blew strongest from the gentry, coldest from the manor house, and mildest from Saleby. Only the other day old Schenstedt had even gone so far as to bestow faint praise on his gardener, the elderly Aron.

"You are not like the other pietists," he had said. "You are merry and can sing a gay ballad at times. If you will promise to keep from excesses and to show moderation also in Christianity, I'll give you half a barrel of rye right now. There should be moderation in everything."

Aron had answered him, "You can keep that rye, Baron, because the condition you require is too difficult for me. *Moderate* means, does it not, that the amount shall be the proper amount? And the right measure of Christianity is to love God with all one's heart and one's neighbor as oneself. I still have far to go to measure up."

The baron laughed and sent for half a barrel of rye, nevertheless. No one could say that Baron Schenstedt lacked in generosity.

The conversation continued. The windows became dark as dusk fell thick outside. It was time to close. A hymn was sung. Savonius conducted evening prayer. Then he said farewell to the people and to Lindér.

When he was already at the door in his fur coat, waiting for the driver from the deanery to hitch the horse to the sleigh, one of the remaining peasants asked to have a word with him alone. Savonius stepped into the room again.

"I just wanted to say," said the peasant, "that I have discovered just today that they have evil designs against you at the manor house. Yesterday von Reihers, Baron Schenstedt, and Warbeck were there, and the captain said this morning that you will be reported to the Cathedral Chapter, if you do not leave the parish of your own free will. They prepared a document late last night and they all signed their names to it except Baron Schenstedt, whom they took to task for not going along with them."

The news left Savonius speechless for a moment. Then he called out through the door, "Lindér! Lindér!"

The housewife, who looked out from the kitchen, announced that the chaplain had already left. Savonius did not know what to do.

Two or three others had joined them. They were evidently aware of the situation, and their attitude was one of bitter determination. "God helps his witnesses," said one of them. "But you must promise us one thing, Pastor."

"What then?"

"That you will not forsake us."

"That decision is not mine; it belongs to the Chapter."

"But if you *can* stay?"

"Then I will stay."

"Is that your promise, Pastor?"

Savonius was affected by their concern. Was he really needed as much as that? Then he would surely stay at his post.

"That is my promise," he said. "I will not of my own accord ask for a new assignment, if I am allowed to stay on in Ödesjö."

"Then God will surely keep the right shepherd for his little flock," said the peasant with solemn joy.

The sleigh stopped at the door. Savonius was anxious to get home without delay, and so bade his friends a hasty farewell. "Remember that you are always welcome at the deanery," he said, with a special glance at the man who had asked how one should be able to receive forgiveness even though one could not restore that which had been stolen.

The darkness had now fallen. The murky sky was starless and seemed to merge with the dark forest. Only when they reached the open fields could a faint margin of light be seen. Once they were on the highway, they made good progress, and the driver, who was eager to get home, gave the horse free rein.

Savonius slumped in the seat, his thoughts unhappy. He had indeed preached with sharpness, but with no other end in view than to awaken the indifferent and startle them to awareness of their condition. And now there were those who, having listened, had sat down to conspire against him. What had they been able to discover that might be considered offensive by the Chapter?

The horse slowed pace. They had reached Vänneberga, and sleighing was poor on the village street. Savonius remembered that terrible Monday in November when the crazy farmers from this place, while returning from church after drunken carousing all night at Sinkan and Svenhester, got the wild idea of racing with their sleighs, though most of the early fall snow had thawed during the night. He had been out on a sick call that morning and met them on the hill on the other side of the village. The horses were foaming and bleeding at the bit and whip lashes had left streaks on their sweaty backs. He had jumped out of his rig and run toward them, wild with rage. The first sleigh had stopped; a slavering, snuff-specked face had raised itself above him, and the cursing drunkard had in the next moment let him feel the sharp lash of a whip like a coiling snake on his back and shoulders. He had been carrying the communion case by the strap, and the lash of the whip had loosened the catch so that the two halves fell apart, revealing the red lining which shone like a bloody wound. In the nick of time he had prevented the silver from falling into the dirt of the road. The next moment he had lifted up the chalice with both hands and, taking position in front of the sleigh, shouted, "Keep striking! It is the cup of the Lord you blaspheme and the holy blood of Jesus you would mingle with the dirt!" The peasant had become stiff as a statue. He had gazed with bloodshot eyes and finally realized what he had done. Then his whole body had begun to shake, he had fallen on his face in the sleigh and wept like a child. He had to be carried inside. Three days later he had come to the deanery. That was the beginning of the revival in Sörbygden.

To think that the Cathedral Chapter should now be asked to intervene, so that everything could return to the good old peace with drunkenness, cursing, and cruelty to animals! Surely no Chapter in all the world could be so blind that it would decide *against* God's work of renewal! Surely Christian people, aware of the real condition that prevailed, would not knowingly defend this cursing and gambling, this adulterous and besotted misery?

———

At the parsonage, lights shone in the dean's study and in the parlor. Savonius was met in the hallway by the dean coming from one direction and by Hedvig coming from the other. The dean greeted him with unusual heartiness, and Hedvig invited him to supper.

The dean's first question at the table was about news from the south. How was Lindér getting along?

Savonius could report that the chaplain at Fröjerum had been in a sparkling mood. He had gotten the assessor and the innkeeper reconciled; the odious old man at Svinnsjö had been warned by the church council, the farmer at Liden was happily married to his housekeeper, and the two drunken farm hands who had tried to stop his sleigh one dark night at the Eneberga mill he had thrown over the fence. Among the crofters more and more were beginning to think in earnest about the one thing needful. But among the freeholders there continued to be small pickings for the kingdom of God.

Savonius' lightheartedness was strained. He wanted to get to another subject.

"And how are things at Drängsmarken?"

"Well, the attendance was good, and there had been no treat. It was a very quiet meeting; the answers showed intelligence and a quite remarkable spiritual maturity and experience. The widow Kristin was feeling better; the farm hand at Backgården had been called for military service; the frost was deep, but the fall rye was in no danger."

The dean wondered about his curate. He had not been so talkative for a long time.

"You didn't by any chance call at the manor house?"

"I would have liked to, sir. I understand they had an assembly there yesterday to promote the high interests of the church of God."

"So, you have already heard about it?"

"Only hints. Have they been here?"

The dean nodded. "But we'll eat first," he said.

———

In the dean's study, the fire still glowed in the gaily decorated stove. The dean motioned Savonius to be seated on the sofa. He took up the captain's document first.

"Here is what they have cooked up," he said.

The curate read. A shadow flitted over his face and made two wrinkles between his eyebrows.

"This is the most foolish thing I have read in a long time," he said.

"Well, perhaps not foolish exactly, but rather cunningly malicious," said the dean. "Lies and halftruths all the way through."

"Do you think, sir, that the Cathedral Chapter would bother at all with such a document as this?"

"Yes, I am afraid so. The fate of a memorial of this kind depends not only on what it says, but rather on the signatures underneath it. If both the captain, Crefedlt, and von Reiher have signed it, the Cathedral Chapter is not likely to throw it into the wastebasket. Its fate will hang also on the kind of witnesses they can get. And here you have the crowning witness."

He handed the curate the letter from his brother clergy.

The two wrinkles on the curate's brow deepened and became a dark knot of anger.

"This is infamous," he said. "Should not a pastor have the right to gather the people of his own congregation for prayer and the preaching of the Word? Does Warbeck expect Anders at Drängsmarken to let his brother-in-law from Ravelunda stand out in the snow when I come to his house so that he won't get to hear me? Is the church to be a congregational meeting where sinners must be called 'yeomen of good character' just because they pay their taxes and attend church? Shall the church of Christ begin to judge souls in accordance with royal statutes instead of by the laws of God?"

The dean looked intently at his curate.

"You still have something to learn about humility, my son," he said. "They won't get you on *those* points. If I surmise correctly, things will be hotter in respect to dress and laces, and jewelry. Evangelical confession views such things as adiaphora, but you have sometimes made them commandments and have bound people more strictly than does the Word of God."

"But do I not have the Word of God on my side?" shouted Savonius.

"That is something the learned disagree about, as you well know. And you have both Luther and Melanchton and evangelical Christianity in general against you."

"That is not true. Surely both Francke and Murbeck belong to the evangelicals."

"There are legalists, and there is work-righteousness also among them, you see. But it is directly contrary to the very heart of the freedom of the Christian man. Such things lead only to distress of conscience—or to self-righteousness."

At that moment Hedvig came in with two cups of coffee on a tray. Savonius stood stiffly where he was. He had just now discovered that she was once more wearing the gold brooch in its accustomed place. The blood seemed to turn to ice in his veins. So—even she! Even here opposition was being shown. Now he must not budge an inch.

"With respect to ornaments," he remarked curtly, "Scripture says distinctly that the outward adorning of women should not be a braiding of hair, the wearing of gold or costly apparel, but should be something of the heart, free from vanity, the adorning of a meek and quiet spirit."

The dean smiled archly.

"And so you would forbid my little Eva-Lotta to braid her hair after this! Or do you intend to ask the women of Sörbygden to refrain from doing up their hair properly?"

Savonius was taken aback by the dean's words. He had never thought about braided hair in that light. If the women could not braid their hair, how should they wear it?

"Look up the context of the passage from First Peter more carefully," the dean continued, "and you will find that it refers to how women should seek to win their men who are unbelievers. They are simply told not to resort to affectation and coquetry, for that would convert no one. Rather, they should display a quiet and sincere godliness which wins souls without words. You must remember, Henrik, that he who depends on works of the law is under condemnation. Remember, too, that nothing is to be refused that one receives with thanksgiving to God. It is good, the apostle says."

"In that way you can defend almost any kind of worldliness," said Savonius. "Thank God for the steak, thank God for the drinks; eat, drink, and be merry! And then we cure their drunkenness and ulcers with a drop of the blood of redemption! I can't swallow such a doctrine."

"You will understand it better, when you have tried to cure your flesh by means of self-mortification and self-sacrifice," said the dean dryly. "Good night, Hedvig. Sleep well, my child, and don't forget to thank God for a good mother, when you take off her brooch."

"And now, Henrik, we must face this thing in earnest. The captain and his friends have given us an ultimatum. Either you leave Ödesjö by the first of May, or these documents will be sent to the Cathedral Chapter. That is the way things stand. I have promised them an answer by tomorrow morning. What have you to say?"

"What do you say, sir?"

"My answer has already been given. Though I regret some of the blunders of which my curate has been guilty, it is not my wish to send him away unless he himself wants to leave. Therefore, the answer will depend on you. You can sleep on the matter until tomorrow. It is not without significance for your future. If you choose to leave, I shall simply write the Chapter that, until further notice, I intend to get along without an assistant, in which case you will be transferred without any ado."

Savonius looked absently straight ahead. The wrinkles had left his forehead, and a grateful calm had taken their place; there was even a hint of a smile on his lips. He saw in his mind's eye the rude peasants of Drängsmarken and the smell of their damp homespun seemed again to be in his nostrils; he heard again their voices say with childlike confidence, "Pastor, will you promise not to leave us?" Yes, he had promised to remain. It was by God's providence that he had been urged to make this promise a few hours before he was confronted by this decision. Now he had no choice.

"Thank you, sir," he said. "I think I can give my answer right now. I will stay on here, if you will let me."

"Of course you may," said the dean, "even though I sometimes think that you have been sent to try me. But I ask you to remember this, Henrik, if you choose to battle, that you are not immune to attack and there are bad gaps in your armor."

"I am not afraid," answered Savonius. Since the dean had nothing further to say, he said a hasty goodnight, went out through the entrance hall and was about to make his way across the yard to the other wing. Then, with his foot on the threshold, he looked back.

"But I want to say this, sir, that if the Cathedral Chapter sides with freethinkers, drunkards, the profane, and the exploiters of the poor renters, and against those who seek to win the lost for the life in God, then the Chapter is a Babel of the devil, and I will then leave the ministry. Good night!"

The dean sat down dejected at his desk. He fingered a bronze paper knife and thoughtfully scratched his head beneath the edge of his wig. Then he tossed the knife away, folded his hands and bowed his aged head low against the table.

Poverty of Spirit and the Light of the Gospel

The summer wind shook the tops of the birches, the leaves glittered, and the soughing was borne through the open windows into the church. Outside the walls people stood on the sand walks, trying to catch what was being said within. Some had brought long benches from the parish house and stood on them outside the open windows. Inside, people sat on the window sills. In the nave people were packed tightly in the pews, and the aisles were filled by those who had to stand.

The services were always well attended, but the crowd today was a bit larger than usual. This was due partly to the fact that the spring work on the farms was done and the warm summer had come in earnest. The comfortable warmth also contributed to the spirit of devotion. It was no longer necessary to strike the heels together to keep warm, and the constant coughing that was so common was no longer heard. The silence was broken only when someone of those who were standing changed position and a coarse wooden-soled boot scraped against the stone memorials on the floor, or when a child tried to say something and was vigorously silenced.

Savonius was speaking from the pulpit. The sermon was finished and the announcements made. Now he was speaking to the confirmands, who stood in the chancel. He could see only the white headcloths of the girls, since they faced away from the pulpit. He saw more plainly the gray rows of boys, their awkwardly folded hands, their new, stiff woolen stockings, and their shy glances beneath flaxen forelocks.

He spoke sternly.

"'You cannot drink the cup of the Lord and the cup of devils,' says the apostle. You cannot with the same lips take the name of the Lord in vain, swear by the name of Christ and the enemy of souls, or speak words of evil jesting, and with those lips receive the blood of Jesus shed for the atonement of your sins. Or would you make trial of the Lord?

"There may be those among you, who while yet being prepared for this holy moment cursed with their lips, used the cross of Christ as a flippant expletive, useful to express alarm over a broken dish or surprise at an unexpected visit. How can you today with the same lips receive the holy God himself, he who is a burning fire against all unrighteousness? Must you not with fear and trembling cry out, 'Woe is me! for I am undone; because I am a man of unclean lips?'"

As he spoke, Savonius searched his own life. I too, perish, he thought. I myself have unclean lips. How have my words been this past week? Vain talk with the driver, whose favor I sought but about whose soul I little cared. Hard words to the captain, when I ought to have excused him. Pride in the garb of humility when I told about my vexations of spirit to the peasant from Sörby.

"And you, confirmands, you who have never earnestly sought your salvation through a faithful reading of God's Word, you who have unwillingly learned what you were forced to learn about the way of salvation, but who were never earnestly intent on using the Word in your homes, how can you now come to this table, prepared for the disciples of the Lord, and where he, the allseeing One, awaits those, and those only, who hear his Word and receive it in upright hearts?"

All the time another voice was speaking within him. "Lord, Lord, why do you place me here to condemn, I who am just as great a sinner myself? How many times I have used God's Word only as much as I was obliged to in order to be able to preach without endangering my reputation, but not a paragraph more. Have mercy on me, O Lord! I am a sinner."

"And you confirmands," continued the audible voice with the same strength, "you who live in uncleanness and secret lusts, you who delight in sinful company and silly love songs, you who are greedy for everything that stirs the passions, just so you do not lose your reputation for modesty and good morals, how can you today meet the Lord who sees in secret and searches the heart and the mind!"

Again that voice cried within him. "Lord, why must I stand here, I who would rather stand with the boys and blush and feel ashamed as they do? Why must I speak like this when my heart is full of stains and would cry out for mercy? Why must I swing the terrible whip of Thy Word, when I should like to go down to my poor children and say, 'Come, children, and let us behold the Lamb of God that taketh away the sin of the world?' Perhaps he has a ray of hope also for us."

"Repent, therefore." It was again the prophet of the law speaking. "Seek forgiveness for your sins today in honest contrition. Do not dare to come to the altar without first promising your Lord an earnest amendment of your life and a holy striving and effort to put away your sins."

But again his own heart cried, "Lord, I do not myself dare to make such a promise. How many times I have promised to abide in the Word and live by it, to humble myself, to seek nothing but Thy glory! But how have I kept my resolutions? Lord, have mercy upon me!"

The conclusion of his address was like a mighty and majestic rumble of distant thunder. The children knelt once more. Savonius and the dean proceeded to the altar. As usual, the curate did the chanting.

"Lift up your hearts unto the Lord."

There was the noise of creaking benches and stomping feet as the congregation arose, but it was all drowned in a wave of song:

"We lift them up unto the Lord, our God."

"Let us thank God, our Lord," sang Savonius.

Again came the response like the sound of many waters echoing under the temple arches. It came like a flood of joy:

"It is meet and right so to do."

Then again the lone voice of Savonius, as he chanted the thanksgiving.

"It is truly meet, right and salutary that we should at all times and in all places give thanks unto Thee, O Lord, Holy Father, Almighty, Everlasting God, through Jesus Christ, our Lord . . ."

When we sing we have time to think. Whether it was the lifting power of the melody itself or the immediately gripping effect of the congregation's responses that was the cause, Savonius experienced a wild longing to be able to thank and praise, to be able at least for a brief moment to be free from all accusations of conscience and to rejoice in childlike spirit as before. The ancient words of the liturgy brought comfort to his wounded heart. They spoke neither about repentance nor the putting away of our sins, but only about God's power and glory. He thought of all God's ordained servants, those poor sinners, commissioned like himself, who had stood at this altar, clad in the same worn, old chasuble, looking up at the same carved figure of Christ, from whose side the redeeming blood flowed down into the chalice. Had they perhaps after all, at the last, by some miracle of grace, found release from the smiting swords of the law? Did they now share in that life, whose unspeakable joy he could only dimly imagine, each time he sang that it was truly meet, right and salutary always to thank and praise the holy God for his wonderful goodnesses. His goodnesses—dared he sing about them, when he had so often misused them?

He *must* in any case sing about them now. And so he continued chanting:

"And especially for this mercy which Thou hast shown us, who because of our sins were in such misery that nothing remained for us but condemnation and eternal death . . ."

Yes, such misery is mine, he thought. And not only mine, but that of my confirmands also, and of all men. Strange that the words here are so certain and inescapable! He continued reading.

"And no other creature in heaven or earth could save us."

The curate thought, as he read, that this was certainly as true as the words said it. "Strange, how like us the people of old were!"

"Thou didst give Thy only-begotten Son Jesus Christ, who is of the same divine nature as Thyself to be made man for our sake, didst lay our sins upon him and let him suffer death . . ."

The words he read were so simple and true. Yet he wondered what had become of conversion. Where in the Preface was it really to be found?

"As he hath conquered death, is risen again, and liveth for evermore, even so all they who trust in him shall through him be victorious over sin and death and inherit eternal life."

Trust in him? Was that the only requirement? Was that really sufficient? But should not those who put their trust in him *be victorious* over sin and death? Savonius knew that he had not been victorious over sin. He had never before been conscious of so much sin in his heart as in these last months.

Now he had come to the Words of Institution and had other things to think about. The dean handed him the elements, first the wafers and then the chalice, so that the Words of Institution should be properly read over them. Then followed the singing of the jubilant Sanctus. Savonius chanted the Lord's Prayer, after which the dean read the Exhortation. Savonius' thoughts were far away, but he suddenly realized this and accused himself for his lack of devotion. The members of the confirmation class came forward to commune at the first two tables. Then the older communicants made their way to the altar through the crowded aisles, moving carefully through the ranks of the confirmands up to the altar rail. The dean watched them and made mental comments as his eyes picked out one or another among them.

There comes Johan from Vännerberga, he thought. You are tall and ugly, Johan, and ill humored too, but if I am able to judge correctly, the Lord is hammering away at your heart, and it is my belief that you will not die without a true faith. And there is Gustaf. It is a long time since you were here last. God bless your communion today, so that you will soon be back again. And all these peasants from Sörby—that is different from what it used to be. God make you humble, so that the fever of holiness does not get into your bones and make you Pharisees!

The curate, who stood at the left of the dean, also took note of those who came forward. He noted with joy the many faces from Sörbygden. We can at least count on you, he thought. The communion table will not be defiled by you. He saw Johan from Mellgården, and was troubled. Ought he not be denied communion? Did not everyone say that he was the father of Lina's oldest boy? And Gustaf from Hästveden? So he was taking the required annual communion today. Didn't he look like a reluctant Judas, as he stood there with his clumsy figure and his twisted mouth?

At that moment his breast seemed to be pierced through as by a flame of fire. Who was he to stand here and judge? What did he know about Gustaf? Was it perhaps nothing but natural aversion and lack of love, coming from his own depraved nature, that pronounced judgment? Was he not himself a sinner who needed all the atoning power of the chalice in his hands? Could he receive it rightly himself when he was so unmerciful in his judgments while administering it at the altar? Would not judgment without mercy fall upon him who showed no mercy?

Another table was now to be served, and Savonius had to leave his thoughts behind. As he passed from one to another with the cup, he hoped that he might see Katrina from Hersmålen among the guests. He really needed her help just now. He had a feeling that he himself was on the way to the kind of darkness in which he found Johannes that night at Börsebo. He had tried many times to remember what it was that Katrina had said to the dying man that night. But when he tried to recall the words, they became lifeless phrases, as powerless for his heart as all the hymns and Bible verses in which he had sought help. For every word of comfort he found, some new demand which he had not fulfilled immediately intruded and silenced the promise of grace so that he was certain that it could in any case not be valid for him.

The dean, who had distributed the bread, had now mounted to the altar, and stood looking out over the people. A tear was beginning to shine in the corner of his eye. The congregation had just begun to sing the communion hymn, "Jesu, Priceless Treasure." One could feel the surge of joy and the feeling of reverence as they sang. For thirty years he had had occasion to see how much feuding and drunkenness, how much hardness of heart and bitter defiance of both God and man, prevailed in the parish. Still he felt overwhelmed at this moment by the divine power of redemption which, despite all, was at work year after year, so that in spite of everything there were many who lived the hidden life with Christ in God, and so many, too, in which the work of the Spirit was gradually progressing. Just as the sun streamed in with its warmth and gave color and brightness to the dark garments on the men's side of the nave, so the sunshine of grace fell upon hard hearts, so that there was hardly a soul who was not aware of something of its glory, and very few who would not sooner or later be led to seek forgiveness. He thanked the Lord who did not weary in his labors with this stiff and stubborn people. He thanked God for every worship service that again brought the stamp of heavy boots and the creaking of the pews and that gave still another opportunity for the struggle between the Word of God and the sinful nature of man. He thanked God for every confessional service, opening anew the portals of repentance and forgiveness for the people of his parish and reaching some stained soul with the words of absolution. He thanked God for the church itself, standing like a fortress in the village, a mighty storehouse of heavenly treasure, where Sunday after Sunday he could stand and pour out the heavenly seed, even as the sexton with his scoop dispensed grain at the parish storehouse and filled the bags of the poor. In quiet joy he returned to the altar rail to serve the next table of communicants.

Now it was the curate's turn to pause a moment at the altar. He poured wine from the large silver flagon to fill the chalice. It revolted him to see the coat of arms of the von Reiher family inscribed on it. Even here the sanctity of God's house and people must be stained by the spirit of worldliness and vanity. Even to this holy place the enemies of God must intrude and forever place their stamp on the sacred vessels. Was there anything at all that was not marked with vanity, sin, and hypocrisy? He saw this obdurate throng who today sang the hymns so vigorously that they echoed through the church, but who tomorrow would be cursing, quarreling, and carrying on as wickedly as before. Had he not this day dispensed the sacramental treasures to these confirmands, of whom probably only a third were true Christians? Again and again at the altar rail he had to ask himself with a start, "Is this the face of a disciple?"

He fell to his knees. Was there perhaps greater reason to despair of his own soul? Sin and hypocrisy! Did not these terms describe his own heart? Would not a priest of God receive a severer judgment?

He got up from his knees and returned with heavy steps to the altar rail.

When the last round of guests finally had left the rail, bowed toward the altar, and returned to their pews, the pastors gave the communion to each other, after which the Thanksgiving and the Benedicamus were read, and the service was over. Through the three exits the large congregation streamed out of the church. The young men walked quickly to the stables. The rest stood in groups in the church yard and engaged in conversation.

The dean and his assistant proceeded down the slope toward the brook. The rye was green and swayed with the wind. The wild chervil crowded on to the path from either side, streaking the white blooms against their trouser legs. The dean led the way with weary feet, a quiet peace mellowing his stern features. Savonius followed with bowed head, and Eva-Lotta brought up the rear, carrying her father's books under her arm and dangling a bunch of keys from her finger.

When they were half way up the rise of the parsonage hill, the dean paused and drew a deep breath. He turned to the curate.

"Do you think we'll get mail today, Henrik?"

"Since it hasn't come earlier, it can just as well wait until Tuesday's delivery."

"True. But I have a presentiment. There was a Chapter meeting last Tuesday, and the matter could well be settled by now."

The dean continued his walk. No one spoke. The matter had been discussed enough during the painfully long period of waiting.

After Savonius' refusal to capitulate voluntarily, the course of events had moved slowly but surely in the channel that had been determined beforehand. The dean had immediately taken measures to defend his curate and had sent a personal letter to the dean of the cathedral, in which he had asked to be allowed to keep his present curate, whom he valued highly both because of the fearlessness with which he denounced sin without respect of persons, and because of the zeal he had displayed in conducting house catechizations and in this and other pastoral activities had sought to better the moral standards of the people in general. As a special reason for his request, the dean cautiously added that his present curate might sometimes, because of his fiery temperament and his burning zeal, have gone further than a more mature wisdom would have prescribed, for which reason he considered that it would be wise and helpful to permit him to remain under his tutelage for a few years and thus be prepared to serve this diocese in the way his unusual gifts give reason to anticipate.

The letter had evidently proved effective, since when the complaints of the captain and the clerical brethren had been dealt with by the Cathedral Chapter it was decided that the matter should rest until further investigation could be made. Until further notice, Savonius was therefore to remain at Ödesjö. The summer passed without any further development. Savonius preached as usual and conducted house catechizations, though always with an awareness that he was being watched. Something sharp and chilling had come into the atmosphere.

Then came the autumn, that terrible autumn in which Finland was lost to the enemy. The dean paced the living room sleeplessly at night. No one seemed to take further note of the fuss raised over a poor little curate. But in November the affair suddenly entered a new stage. Rector Hafverman had discovered that many married couples in his congregation had of late begun to go to the Lord's Table separately. He immediately suspected that improper influence lay back of this new departure. One Sunday after morning service he summoned a wife for interrogation and with grim satisfaction discovered that it was Savonius who had introduced this new order of communing separately. He wrote a new and sharper memorial to the Cathedral Chapter, which now felt that it must have an investigation made. This investigation was left with Dean Faltin, who was in no hurry to take action. When his investigation was at last concluded, Hafverman considered it so one-sided that he and Warbeck challenged the findings of the dean and by the presentation of new claims forced the Chapter to return the papers once more to Ödesjö. The dean was angered and refused to have anything more to do with the affair. The Chapter then weighed the matter for three weeks, after which it turned the matter over to the dean of the neighboring district to the west of Ödesjö. However, this man was old and in poor health and did not dare to venture forth in the cold of winter.

It was not until the first days of May, 1810, therefore, that the impartial investigation that had been asked for could be undertaken. The aging Dean Sommarling was not a very able leader, and Dean Faltin shook his head many a time as he read the final record of the proceedings. In spite of many changes, he was still not satisfied when at last he signed his name to the document.

It was now a full month since the papers had been sent in for final action. For more than two weeks both the dean and his curate had eagerly awaited each mail delivery. To the very last they had hoped that the decision would arrive at least before the day of the great reception which was given each year at the deanery at midsummer time for all the gentry and the clergymen of the district. The dean had almost hoped that this traditional festive day might become a day of reconciliation. When the matter had been concluded from the juridical point of view, he intended to make a speech in which he would generously acknowledge all the good that might reasonably be found in the contending parties, and then, he had hoped, all things would be well again. These had certainly not been happy days for the worthy dean. Hafverman and Warbeck had nothing to do with him except in the line of duty. He had been able to keep the captain and others of the gentry from fomenting public conflict in the parish only by the exercise of all the authority he possessed and by his ability somehow to attribute the highest motives on the part of all concerned. It was fortunate for him, that their further utterances bearing on the case were received in writing. He had even lauded their insinuating petitions, admired their spirit and acumen, and had said that they provided him with refreshing reading matter. Thus he preserved at least the appearance of amiability and comity.

Now the day of the gala summer party was at hand. The guests from a distance were awaited as early as Monday morning. Hafverman had sent his regrets, saying that an important pastoral duty would unfortunately keep him from coming. Warbeck, however, would be present, as also the usual members of the upper class.

———

The dean and Savonius had entered the garden through a back gate and had walked in the shade of the ash trees up to the house. There were as yet no signs of carriage wheels on the driveway. The dean looked into the study, but he saw no mail on his desk. The regular day for the mail was really Monday. But since the mail arrived at the nearest town by Saturday evening, it sometimes happened that it was sent along with some carriage on its way to the inns at Näs and Ödesjö. For that reason mail could be expected at almost any hour on Sunday.

Savonius went quietly to his room, stretched out on his bed, and clasped his hands behind his neck. The humidity was like a warm blanket. He closed his eyes, and could not keep the thoughts from coming. He hoped he might be spared any visitor before dinner. A fly flew against the window, began buzzing again and, having found the open half, vanished into the sunshine outside.

———

Savonius was roused from his dozing. Someone had stepped over the threshold below, and was slowly ascending the stairs.

The curate had immediately gotten up. He smoothed the covers quickly, put on his coat, and sat down at the table. He snatched at a book, but let it lie. Playing a part, you poor wretch! he thought to himself.

The steps had reached his door. It was a coarse hand that knocked.

"Come in! God's peace be with you!"

"Thank you!"

The man remained standing hesitantly after lifting his boots over the unusually high threshold. At the pastor's invitation he seated himself on the farthest chair. Savonius knew him well. It was the shoemaker at Långaryd, near the border of Fröjerum parish. He had experienced a spiritual awakening the fall before and had visited the parsonage once before after a morning service. He had given the impression of being a frank and resolute character, not given to compromise. He had not had any coarse sins to be sorry for, but he had wanted to make a clean breast of his worldliness, and had received good counsel and admonition.

"How are things with you, Anders?"

Savonius noticed that he was trying to make his voice sound patriarchal and weighty, and again felt ashamed of himself.

"With me, it is well, Pastor," answered the shoemaker with a certain vehemence. "But it is the sins of the worldly that are such a burden for the Christian."

"I know that, Anders. What in particular is bothering you now?"

The shoemaker bit his lips, lowered his eyes, and began to speak.

"It is all the sin in my own home. Let me tell you, Pastor, it isn't easy to be a child of God when one has to be surrounded by so much abomination. In the first place, it's my brother. He is altogether unconverted. As you know, we work together and he had been taking his meals at our house. But since I became spiritually concerned, I will allow no whisky in my house. Now he has a bottle of his own and drinks right before my eyes. I have asked him to stop, but he refuses. What shall I do with him, Pastor?"

"Patience, Anders, patience. Is he difficult and uncontrollable when he is drunk?"

"Drunk?" The shoemaker fidgeted. "He doesn't exactly get drunk. But he drinks in my presence. It is with me as it was with the just Lot who was vexed with the filthy conversation of the wicked, and with seeing their unlawful and adulterous deeds."

"Well, what does Karin say?" Savonius knew that the shoemaker had a fine wife, who was known to be a godly woman.
"That is the worst of all, Pastor. She has begun to side with him. She says we should let the matter rest so long as he is sober. Besides, she is always crying and fussing. And she can't discipline the children. She lets them dance in a ring, sing foolish songs, and play worldly games. She permits them to wear ribbons in their hair, and to sail their birch-bark boats on the Sabbath. They are allowed to dress their dolls like society ladies. But now I have thrown the boats and the doll dresses and the ribbons in the fire. There must be an end to the lust of the eye and the desecration of the Sabbath. And my brother will have to leave the house. If he wants to drink, he can do it in his own room at the cabin."

"But my dear Anders, think what you are doing. It is certainly better that the brandy bottle stands in Karin's cupboard and that you both see when he drinks. If he takes the bottle with him to his room in the cabin and drinks by himself, it will only get worse."

"But, Pastor," interjected the shoemaker, "surely a believing man must not be forced to endure ungodliness before his very eyes."

Savonius said nothing. He did not himself know just what he should think about this situation. Anders was too severe—and too sure of himself.

"Listen to me, Anders," he said. "After all, you have been awakened, you know your Savior. *Your* soul is certainly not endangered because there is a bottle on the table."

"No, but I don't choose to tolerate such wickedness. I see red every time the bottle appears."

"Wait a bit, Anders. If your brother is unconverted, it is surely *his* soul that is in danger. Then the most Christian thing is to do what will best serve his soul."

"And that is to deprive him of his brandy."

"If that could be done, yes. But to send him off to his lonesome room in the cabin with his brandy, that is not Christian. Rather be patient, Anders, and be agreeable toward him, until his day comes and God seeks him."

The shoemaker looked dubious. Savonius continued.

"The godlessness round about us, that which *others* do and say, is never the worst thing. The worst dwells within ourselves, Anders."

The shoemaker looked up, wonderingly.

"What do you mean, Pastor?"

"I mean pride and our own righteousness."

"But, Pastor, I have always been known as an unpretentious man. That I can say without bragging. I certainly am not proud. And I do not want to be self-righteous but *righteous*. Then I certainly must see to it that what is sinful is put out of my house."

"Out of the heart, too, Anders."

"But I surely have got rid of it in my heart, Pastor. It is true that temptations come once in a while, but then I say with Joseph, 'How can I do this great wickedness, and sin against God?' How can I use strong drink or go to the dance hall? How could I put a ribbon in my hat, or wear embroidery? How can I use profanity?"

Savonius looked long at the man, not knowing what to think. There was something hard and bitter about him that impressed him painfully. Could the shoemaker really be as free from sin as he tried to make out?

"There are some things I must ask you about, Anders. Has there been strife and unpleasantness at home because of all this?"

"Can you have any doubt as to that, Pastor?"

"What have you tried to say to your brother?"

"I have rebuked him roundly and told him that he is a wicked and accursed slave of sin. I have told him that I cannot bear to see him so long as he continues to drink, and that it is no more than right and proper that he should land in hell, when he is unwilling to repent."

Savonius was silent a moment. Then he said, "Do you love your brother, Anders?"

"Yes, of course, I love him."

"Of course? And still you think that it is only right that he should be damned forever?"

"But if he will not repent?"

"Then he will not be among the blessed, that is true. But certainly that cannot bring any one of us the least satisfaction."

"But otherwise we are *mistaken* altogether, Pastor."

"Would you not wish to be mistaken, if that could save your brother from hell?"

"But, Pastor, what meaning is there then in all we have given up?"

"Is it not reason enough that it was granted you to begin to live with God ten years earlier than your brother?"

"But then I could just as well live in sin and have glad days."

"*Glad* days? Do you really believe that they would be happy days? Happier than you are now? If that is true, then your heart is indeed poorly converted, Anders."

The shoemaker stared wide-eyed at the curate.

"Why should my conversion be doubted, Pastor? Have I not done everything you have said?"

"'Though I bestow all my goods to feed the poor, and though I give my body to be burned, and have not love, it profiteth me nothing.' Thus it is written, Anders."

The shoemaker sat silent for a moment. Then he said, "You are speaking profound things, Pastor. They might do for learned people, but I am a simple man and will stay by these simple words of God: 'The soul that sinneth, it shall die.' 'Save yourselves from this untoward generation.' 'Be not unequally yoked together with unbelievers.' It was my intention to ask you to come to my house and talk sense with Karin, but I can see that it is better that I do it myself."

There was sharpness in his voice. Savonius answered sternly.

"Don't forget love, Anders. And let the children play; it is natural and proper at their time of life."

"'What concord hath Christ with Belial?'" answered the shoemaker. And with that he bowed, and took his departure.

The curate was in turmoil. The awakening could, then, develop in that direction! Or was this really a fruit of the spiritual movement in the community? What was it, then, that had gone wrong? In a broad sense the man was right in maintaining that he had been following the counsel given by his pastor. Nor could one doubt his honest intention to separate himself from sin. But it did seem that everything had become a matter of personal honor for his self-satisfied heart, which was set on adding his conversion as another laurel among his trophies. And what had he really meant by those final words? Was it only that the children's play belonged to the works of the devil, or could he even have implied that the pastor was the Belial with whom he no longer wished to speak? What hypocrisy! First, spitefully assigning his brother to hell and then, considering himself Christ's true servant above his own pastor!

"Henrik! Dinner is ready."

It was Hedvig who called from the stairway. He had a feeling that she had only been waiting for the visitor to leave. Had they really been waiting for him? He rushed down the stairs. While walking through the dim, cool corridor, the thoughts came to him: Do *you* love the shoemaker now? Do you have love in your heart? You who judge your parishioners are under the same condemnation as they.

Monday morning came, and there was still no mail. The dean surmised the worst. The regular delivery would be at noon, just when the guests would have arrived. They would naturally want to hear the latest news. The clerical brethren would want to see if there was any circular from the Cathedral Chapter, or some new pronouncement. Everything would be examined and opened. And *if* the decision in respect to the curate came today, anything might happen. If Henrik had been exonerated, it would surely be difficult to preserve the neighborly amity with the gentry and Warbeck. If Henrik had fared badly, the dean feared that he might carry out his threat to have him unfrocked. The dean had not failed to notice how critical Henrik was of many things in the church, how the lazy worldliness of his fellow clergy irked him, how impatient he was with their complacent heterodoxy, and how he reacted to the nominal and formal religiosity of the social upper crust. Should the Cathedral Chapter side with the heretical and ungodly coalition, there could well be a terrible explosion and a scandal unsurpassed in these parts. And all this at his summer party, which he loved and looked forward to with keen anticipation!

It had rained a little during the night. The morning was cool, and wooly, low clouds still rolled over the Heding hills when the sun at last broke through in earnest above the church meadows. In the parsonage, last minute preparations were being hurried through in the kitchen; one heard the clatter of dishes, the scraping of chairs as they were being put in place, and the cook's shrill voice calling out orders. Meanwhile, the first carriage rolled into the yard.

It was the chaplain from Fröjerum. He jumped down like a boy, bowed to the dean, kissed Hedvig's hand, and put his arm around Savonius like a wrestler and spun him around. All the wrinkles of his swarthy face registered delight.

"I scarcely need to ask how my good brother is feeling today," said the dean. "Have you by any chance been notified of a royal promotion to some great church?"

"No. Reverend Dean, it's better than that. I have gotten three of my most notorious despisers of God's grace to creep to the foot of the cross, as pious as confirmands. And Löske-Maja at Kvarnfallen, that hussy, has died a Christian. That is as great a miracle as that which took place in the valley of Ajalon. My own Lisa presented me with a wonderful baby boy last Wednesday. And here in my pocket I have the invitation to the big party at Ödesjö, to which I have looked forward for months. Could anyone be more fortunate?"

He threw out his arms again and drew Hedvig and Savonius toward the dean and included the three in a mighty bear hug. Laughter, rejoicing, and congratulations echoed over the place. The chaplain broke away quietly and took Savonius aside. As soon as they had come a little way into the orchard, he asked if there had been any news from the Cathedral Chapter. Savonius answered that the verdict could be expected today. Lindér whistled.

"How are you getting along otherwise?"

"Well, thank you," was the answer Savonius intended to give, but he changed his mind and said instead, "miserably, Brother. Never before has it been so desperate with me."

"So! What seems to be the matter?"

"Oh, it's nothing—and everything," said Savonius, as he clenched his hands. "I wish there were some special sin, one that I could take hold of. But it is just a doughy mass of wretchedness that is boiling over. Pride and uncleanness, greed for money, laziness, and lack of delight in all that is holy—there is neither beginning nor end to it. I cannot even confess it. If I try to tell God about it, it is like dipping from the sea with a spoon—you get a bit of a wave, but the great deep is still there."

Lindér had suddenly become very serious. Yet he whistled softly.

"You, too, Henrik!"

"Too? What do you mean? Are there others, then? That must not be. It is bad enough that there is one who has failed so completely in that which he has wanted most of all: to become a true Christian."

"Here you see another," said Lindér, and beat his own breast.

"You don't mean it, Lindér! You must not joke about such a serious matter. Don't you understand? I *want* to be humble, but I seek only my own honor. I keep wondering what the peasants think of me. I am jealously concerned about my reputation as a revival preacher. I *want* to serve God only; but if I get a few of my spiritual poems published in some calendar, I wonder right away if there will be an honorarium. When someone praises my sermons, or some troubled soul from another parish thanks me, I begin immediately to think how through all this my reputation may spread and I might receive a call that would be more advantageous. And if I am called to conduct a funeral, I wonder in my greedy heart whether I shall get a fee for it. And this is only a small part of my misery. Such is my condition!"

"Well, you have your counterpart right here," said his friend, as calm as ever. Suddenly he began to speak in another vein.

"My little boy was baptized yesterday, and was given the name Henrik. He wasn't named for you, you old sourpuss, but for that new man of God in Lund."

"In Lund?" Savonius looked confused. "Faxe's name is Vilhelm, isn't it?"

"Of course his name is Vilhelm, and he is really no particular man of God. Let me tell you, they have a little man down there who is a chaplain like myself, but a prophet of God in his ability to teach. His name is Schartau. Last Christmas I knew as little about him as you do. But then I received a letter from my cousin Malcolm. He sent me a copy of Schartau's study on the catechism. It was like a powder blast for my stony heart, and like salve for the wounds of a fatally wounded man. In late winter I was in the same blessed anguish of soul as you are now experiencing. I was badly bruised. My whole body and soul were sick. Where pride ended, lust began; when lust choked, self-righteousness put in its appearance. Then, in my misery, I wrote to Schartau. Two weeks ago I received his answer. There was healing power from God in that letter. The scales fell from my eyes.

"Henrik!" There was suddenly a powerful eagerness in his voice, as he stood still on the walk and reached forth his hands. "We have never understood this matter of salvation before, even though we have stood amid the storms of a spiritual springtime. We have divided people into converted and unconverted, we have applied every sermon to the self-secure and to the believing ones, we have imagined that when a man was brought under conviction, it was only necessary that he should see his sins, contritely confess them, and come to Jesus in faith and he would be born again. And all that we accomplished in three days, or three weeks, or months at the best. No, my boy, it could take three years, or thirty sometimes. One sees the Lord's happiest disciples going about and singing about salvation only because they have stopped living in drunkenness and adultery and contempt for God's Word, having felt some blessed movement of grace in their hearts. In Lund, they call that the state of being awakened. And the hardest bit of the road remains. If the Spirit of God has been allowed to crush the outward sin, so that one begins to live without intentional transgression, that is only the first, small beginning."

They had been walking along the path past the raspberry bushes and had not come to the lilac hedge that fronted the turnip field. Here, farthest down in the garden, a grove of birches extended into the meadows like a bastion with its boulders and blackthorns. Here the dean had cleared a fenced and sanded area and placed some benches where one could sit and enjoy a pleasant view of the sloping terrain. A few hundred yards from this spot the main highway ran between the fields. In the north the dark church spire rose high above the trees, and toward the south lay the village with its gray farm buildings, its straw stacks, and its red dwellings.

Savonius opened the little gate.

"Let's sit down here," he said. "Do you mean to say that the corruption of sin is alike in all people?"

"Yes, just as surely as every man has heart and liver and lungs in his body, every man has the corruption of sin within him. 'For out of the heart proceed evil thoughts, murders, adulteries, fornications, thefts, false witness, blasphemies.' Have you not read that verse of Scripture?"

"And that you say with the calm of a contented cow! Don't you realize how dreadful it is? If I alone had utterly failed in my Christianity, it might do to speak so, but think of all these others! Here we meet together, sing and pray and talk for one another's edification, believing that we are thereby engaged in driving sin and Satan out of the parish, and yet we are told that he still has his cloven hoof within the doors of our hearts. What will become of all our cherished work of revival? And what will become of us? Don't you realize how dreadful it is?"

Lindér sat relaxed, his legs crossed, and one arm hanging over the back of the bench. He gazed up through the birch leaves and seemed to be absorbed by the vision of something lovely and captivating.

"Of course it is dreadful, and still I am so full of joy that I should like to take the whole world in my arms. This is the great secret of redemption, you understand, that God has drawn a cross over all the sinfulness of the world both without and within us. Do you believe that Christ died only for the sins you committed before you became spiritually concerned? He would hardly have needed to die for them—you could put them away by your own strength. That you begin your day with the Bible instead of with Molière, that you deny yourself a nip of brandy on Saturday nights, that you no longer write coquettish verses with double meanings—that is only picking burrs from your coat, something you can get rid of yourself. But the corruption of sin is something that you cannot put away yourself. For this you need a Redeemer, one who suffers in your place; for otherwise you might as well give up every thought of heaven right now."

Savonius sat in silence.

"Now perhaps you will understand why I am so happy, even though I have seen the hopelessness of my condition and that of all others. Some 1800 years ago our situation became different; through the righteousness of One, righteousness unto life comes to all men."

Savonius continued to be silent.

"What actually opened my eyes," continued the chaplain, "was Schartau's statement in his letter showing that all my despair up to this point was a work of God, but that, if I remained in it, it would be a temptation of the devil. It was the work of God's Spirit that in connection with my awakening I came to see that there was much more sin in my heart than there had ever been in my actions during the years when I was a confident sinner. It was a work of God also that I came to see that I was so corrupt that I could not do the least little thing to bring about my conversion. But it was a temptation of the devil that I now nevertheless wanted to establish my own righteousness and secretly hoped that I could help myself and would not need to accept grace as the penitent thief had to do. And the very worst temptation lay in this, that I tried to become a works saint in respect to those things in which it seemed as if I could win victory and accomplish something by myself. It was for that reason I constantly became more strict in the matter of dress, and so careful about every word that I went about without opening my lips for fearing of losing my lovely halo in the dust, while all the time I was unwilling to recognize my pride and my antipathy toward Warbeck."

"But," Savonius said, "you are still talking only about sin. How did you find help?"

"Man, don't you understand that all this is in itself a gospel? For it is a blessed gospel that one is brought into despair, not by sin, nor by the superior force of Satan, but by the Holy Spirit of God, who would save one's poor soul from becoming a legalist and a hypocrite, and whose purpose in it all has only been to let the overpowering glory of Christ shine forth. In other words, Henrik, the Spirit would show us that one may receive forgiveness without making atonement by one's own sorrow over sin and without any personal merit or self-betterment; that one may be a child of God, one's sinful nature notwithstanding."

He let his hand rest heavily on his friend's knee. Savonius bowed his head slowly and hid his face in his hands. Above him the birches sighed in the wind, and the sun as it shone through the branches made dancing spots of light at his feet. He took no note of this, for his thoughts were far away, at Peter's home in Hyltamålen a warm July night two years ago. He had wished to meet Katrina from Hersmålen again to seek help for his heart. Now God had sent him another helper. But the help was the same. He felt as if he had stumbled against something eternal and unmovable, something at the innermost core of existence, something that was at the same time hard as rock and as soft to the touch as the gentle hand of a mother.

When he looked up again, he saw as in a dream a carriage approaching on the road from the north. The driver wore a high bluish-black hat with a yellow plume. It is the gentlefolk from Eksta, he thought. Good God, let me be alone yet a while with this bringer of good tidings!

"To think that one could be so blind," he said slowly.

"I have thought the same. Yet I have come to see that this blindness is a clearer seeing than I had before when I believed that God's forgiveness was the most natural thing in the world. This despair over sin is after all a part of the Spirit's enlightenment. Actually one sees more clearly all the while, though one is looking down at the dark pools of evil in the slough of sinful corruption. But it is important to look deeply into it, for one will otherwise imagine that it is possible to get across it by oneself. So one makes a few hops from hummock to hummock, but is soon mired. At the very worst, one does not even dare to admit that one is stuck fast, but claims that one is already across, only because one is no longer in the company of the self-secure sinners on the farther shore. This leads to a selfish satisfaction with one's own penitence and a merciless judgment of the children of the world. There have been evidences of something of that kind in my congregation among people who have begun to be concerned about their souls."

"Among us too," said Savonius, and thought of yesterday's visitor.

"But now we must look upward and forward. Light, reconciliation, peace! He is our peace!"

"And then? What is now to happen?" asked Savonius.

The carriage from Eksta had turned the corner at the village, and the well-groomed horses trotted in lively tempo up the hill toward the dean's house. Another carriage soon followed. It came from the south.

Lindér had already started speaking again. "As you say, what is now to happen? Justus Johan Lindér is now condemned to death and lives as a lost and condemned sinner day by day by the grace of his Lord. He sits like a bird and eats from his Redeemer's hand. And in between he sings happily in the sunshine. Henrik, we must start again from the beginning. We have thundered like the storm, we have bombarded with the heaviest mortars of God's law in an attempt to break down the walls of sin. And that was surely right. I still load my gun with the best powder when I aim at unrepentance. But we had almost forgotten to let the sunshine of the gospel shine through the clouds. Our method has been to destroy all carnal security by our volleys, but we have left it to the souls to build something new with their own resolutions and their own honest attempts at amending their lives. In that way, Henrik, it is never finished. We have not become finished ourselves. Now I have instead begun to preach about that which is finished, about that which was built on Calvary and which is a safe fortress to come to when the thunder rolls over our sinful heads. And now I always apportion the Word of God in three directions, not only to the self-satisfied and the believers as I did formerly, but also to the awakened, the anxious, the heavy-laden, and to the poor in spirit. And I find strength each day for my own poor heart at the fount of redemption."

Savonius thought again of his experience with Anders the day before; he thought about his confirmands, about Johan at Mellgården, and about Gustaf's mouth with its Judas twist.

"And the result, Brother? Do you note any difference?"

"In the first place, I myself see light where formerly I saw only darkness. There is light in my heart, and light over the congregation. Before, I was in despair over my people at Fröjerum and at their impenitence. I see now that this was because I kept thinking that everything depended on what *we* should do, for when I saw so little of true repentance and victory over sin, helplessness crept into my heart. I counted and summed up all that they did, and not the smallest percentage of the debt was paid. But now I see that which *is* done, and I see that the *whole* debt *is* paid. Now, therefore, I go about my duties as might a prison warden who carries in his pocket a letter of pardon for all his criminals. Do you wonder that I am happy? Now I see everything in the sun's light. If God has done so much already, surely there is hope for what remains."

Again a carriage rolled into the parsonage yard. Savonius did not want to look in that direction.

"But what about the sinners, then? Will they not become still more hardened?"

"There is that danger, to be sure. One must seek to divide the Word of God rightly. But I'll take that risk. There are so many prisoners who have sat in the same cage as I and who have already been set free since the gospel has come to its own in Fröjerum's pulpit. That alone makes the risk worthwhile. Besides, the self-secure sinners surely also have need to catch a glimpse of the gospel. Three of the worst despisers of grace among my people have had a blessed soul experience this spring. It was not the law that did it. So long as the thunder rolled, they simply crawled deeper down in their holes. But when the sun began to shine, they lifted up their heads, and our Lord laid hold on them."

Again there was the sound of carriage wheels, this time down on the road. This time Savonius could not help looking in that direction. It gave him quite a start when he saw that it was the mail delivery.

The chaplain saw it too, no doubt. He said nothing about it, but changed the subject of their conversation.

"Henrik, my boy, what a privilege it is to be allowed to preach the Word of God in our generation! When I took up preaching fifteen years ago, there were no brightening signs such as we now see. Then one was to preach about true virtue, which consisted in raising potatoes, paying taxes, and in not forgetting to buy the king's brandy. As late as last year I sighed bitterly over this darkness, which fools called the enlightenment. But I believe now that this century, which began in deepest shame, will nevertheless make some good contribution. Things are beginning to show signs of life everywhere. Mark my words, springtime is near, and the fig trees are in bud. Now it is up to us to work faithfully, each one of us in his appointed place as long as we are granted the privilege."

He had gotten up from the bench. "It must have been the mail cart that arrived," he said. "Let us see whether the Cathedral Chapter had been able to reach a decision yet."

The carriages had been arriving at the deanery one after another. Those that had brought the gentry of the parish turned at once and drove empty away amid the cracking of whips. The buggies of the clergy creaked slowly toward the church stables.

The dean stood on the steps with Hedvig at his side. The sun shone on flounces and dress-coats; the talk and laughter, gay and pleasant, was like the murmuring of the wind through the tops of the elms, which caused the last drops of the night's rain to fall upon the tiles.

The captain was amiable and gay. He noted with quiet satisfaction that the curate was not present, and loudly praised the dean's beautiful flowers. Warbeck and von Reihers talked about the unexpected death of the crown prince at Kvidinge and about the alarming rumors of unrest in the capital. The young people gathered around Hedvig, and wanted to know why Johan-Christofer had not been able to get home from college.

It was then the mail-carrier's cart was seen coming up the parsonage hill.

The dean had instructed Eva-Lotta to keep him from driving up to the house. She was to receive the bag of mail at the gate and carry it the back way into the kitchen. She was already at her place beside the white gate-post. The cart stopped as expected, and a moment later Eva-Lotta was crossing the lawn toward the wing with the heavy bag hanging by its strap from her shoulder. Unfortunately, the pastor from Brohult happened to be standing on the grass conversing with two of his colleagues. Partly out of helpfulness, partly out of curiosity about the news from the great world, he lifted the bag from the girl's shoulder and brought it to the dean.

Now everybody's attention had been called to what was going on. The bag with the tensely awaited news from Stockholm was the center of interest for the entire company. Eva-Lotta, who had so ingloriously failed in the errand entrusted to her, had already found a certain compensation through running to fetch the key, which with a curtsy she handed her father, barely a second after the pastor from Brohult had reached the dean with his booty.

There was, then, nothing else the dean could do than to open the lock, lift out the contents, and examine them. The two newspapers were immediately turned over to the captain and Baron Schenstedt. The bundle of letters was untied. A letter for Karin was handed to Eva-Lotta who skipped away with it across the walk. Several certificates were returned to the bag without further notice. The dean would have liked to dispose in the same manner with the two large envelopes in his hand. But once again bad luck pursued him. Warbeck, who stood on the steps at his side, had caught sight of the seal of the Cathedral Chapter and called the dean's attention to it. Immediately all the brethren were on the alert and pressed forward. Could this have something to do with tithes? Or with the new regulations to govern clergy and parishes? Would the dean please open them?

Somewhat unwillingly, the dean broke the seal on the first letter and unfolded the crisp, stiff paper. When he had read a few lines, a touch of red came to his cheeks. His eyes skimmed over the page and finally stared glassily at the concluding sentences. His cheeks had turned grayish pale.

Warbeck had understood what it was all about when his eye happened to fall on that final resolution. He whispered theatrically, "It's the decision about Savonius."

There was complete silence in the group of clergymen. No one moved. The dean continued to stand motionless with the Chapter's statement in his hand. The silence caused the gentlemen who were reading their newspapers to look up. In a moment the tension had spread. All eyes were on the dean, and a few furtive whisperings brought the news to everyone: the verdict had arrived.

It was not the dean, however, who broke the silence. Instead, voices from the outside were heard, and then Lindér's dark and sun-tanned face appeared through the hedge. Close at his heels followed the curate. They came forward to greet the others, but when they suddenly felt that all eyes were focused on them, they stopped and looked about them in amazement. In the next moment they understood the situation. Lindér shyly stepped a few paces aside. Savonius straightened up and looked directly at the dean.

At last the dean spoke.

"May I ask you to come to my study for a moment, Henrik? A communication has arrived which concerns you, and there is a letter for you personally from the Cathedral Chapter." He took up the second letter with its red seals.

"Thank you, sir," said Savonius. "I gather that this is the decision of the Chapter. You may as well read it here, so that all may hear it. The contents will perhaps be of interest to everyone."

The poor fellow! thought the dean. Is there no end to his arrogance? Now he really thinks he has won the battle. Well then, he will have to take his punishment from God.

With a strong and clear voice, in which there was nevertheless a slight tremor, the dean began to read, while everyone listened with rapt attention. A few fixed points finally began to emerge out of the welter of ponderous official sentences, following an awkward introduction which sought to recapitulate all that had entered into this complicated affair. It was declared as evident that the accused curate, said H. S. Savonius, had on several occasions given counsel in religious matters to persons who were not members of his own parish; that he had not in these cases properly emphasized their Christian duty to seek in the first place and with confidence the counsel of their own spiritual advisers; that he had on some occasions, as evidence showed, counseled married people to go separately to Holy Communion, thus encouraging them to depart from accepted Christian practice in the community; that in his sermons he had failed to show the moderation and spirit of love which one expects of a servant of Christ and which is enjoined in the Church Law; and that he had, in his unwise zeal, pictured as sinners honorable citizens who, as is well known, have observed all their prescribed religious duties; for which reasons the Cathedral Chapter has found cause to enjoin that from the day on which this decision reaches him, said H. S. Savonius is to refrain from exercising any pastoral activity in said parish of Ödesjö; that he be commanded to appear before the Chapter to receive kind and earnest remonstrances and warnings; and that with respect to further service in the diocese its decision will be governed by the circumstances that might arise at the time of said warning. All of which the honorable Dean and Knight, etc., etc., shall immediately make known to the parties concerned and by public announcement on the following Sunday in Ödesjö church.

The dean was deathly pale as he finished reading. Lindér had folded his hands and kept looking steadily at Savonius. The captain seemed, in spite of his triumph, to be affected unpleasantly, his face turned red and the ridge of his collar chafed nervously against his neck. Old Baron Schenstedt shook his head thoughtfully. Only young von Reiher looked haughtily at his conquered enemy with half closed eyes.

Savonius himself was as pale as the dean. He stood all the while erect and with arms hanging motionless. His eyes were directed upward, and his lips moved slightly.

Then he pulled himself together and looked at the dean.

"I thank you, sir. It is a good thing for all of us that this matter has finally been concluded. And the verdict is kinder than if I should have had to pronounce it myself. It will be hard for me to leave Ödesjö. Not until today have I really understood the depth of the message I ought to have preached. Now I beg you all to forgive everything I have said and done that has been lacking in love. When it comes to zeal, I regret that I have been too lukewarm in seeking the good of your souls, and that I have made distinction among people, so that I have loved the little more than the big. With regard to love, I regret that I have wounded and chastised more than I have bound up and healed. But most of all I am sorry that I have so seldom preached the full gospel of unmerited grace, which I long for and need more than any of you. My only prayer now is that God in his grace may wipe away the memories of all that was faulty and wrong and let that grow and increase which has truly been the work of his incorruptible Word. And I pray also that there may now be peace and that our hearts may be free from all hard feelings, just as I now would thank God that he still, perhaps, may have some use for me, a sinner, in his church."

While Savonius was speaking, something unusual had happened. The dean had raised his hand and wiped two tears from his cheek. Now he stepped down, went to his suspended curate and threw his arms around him.

Then he turned to the assembled guests, and said, "My dear friends, none of you will misunderstand me, if I say that from this moment I love my curate as though he were my own flesh and blood. And may there now be peace in the congregation, the peace of God which we sinners need so desperately."

Once more there was perfect quiet. Then old Baron Schenstedt came forward silently and shook hands with Savonius. His two sons followed, then two of the pastors, then Warbeck and the captain and all the others. It was almost as though they were congratulating him for something.

When the greetings were over, the dean clapped his hands and said, "Ladies and gentlemen, dinner is served. May I ask you to step in to the dining room?"

After much bowing and crowding, the motley company moved slowly, slowly in between the white deanery pillars. No one noticed that the chaplain from Fröjerum waited until the last and paused a moment below the steps. There he bowed his head in his hat, as though he were saying a thanksgiving in the sacristy after a morning service. Then he too went in to the banquet table.

II. Jesus Only

Three Days
before Christmas

"So! Stand there and be ashamed!"

The rector put back a bound volume in his meager bookshelf. He had just finished the reading of Professor Myrberg's severe criticism of Rosenius' *Commentary on the Letter to the Romans.* Though its theme was the divine love, it was full of salt and pepper and was rough-shod in its treatment of the orthodox man of God. Also on the table lay a sharp reply to Myrberg's critique by one of the rector's colleagues. With a gleam in his eye he squeezed in the two antagonists side by side in the bookcase.

"In my house, at least," he mumbled, "you will have to try to live together in peace, just as you will have to do in heaven, if you expect to get there."

He got up and stamped his feet. The floor was uncommonly cold. Not in many years had it been so bitterly cold in Advent and since the snow was hardly an inch deep the cold penetrated the house with even greater intensity. In the tile stove, which was decorated in mottled green, a fire crackled and the dampers rattled noisily in the draft. This was the third fire today—but what good did it do!

The rector went to the window. Through the peep holes at the top of each pane which the frost still left clear, a tangle of frost-covered branches could be seen in the bluish winter dusk against the faded green silk of the evening sky. The smoke from the renters' cottages rose perpendicularly to the sky. No sleigh could be seen.

There was a knocking at the door and the housekeeper, Mrs. Holleman, popped in her frostbitten nose.

"Dear Pastor, won't you have something to eat? My good waffles will be tough as leather, if we wait any longer."

"Calm yourself, Lydia," the old man answered and made a friendly gesture with his pipe. "You can enjoy the waffles yourself. For my old palate they will be just as tasty after two hours. And when the new curate arrives he will at least not have to eat his first meal all alone."

The firmness with which the door closed again showed that Mrs. Holleman strongly objected to the decision. A stream of ice-cold air had had time to come in from the hallway and was now creeping forward along the floor. No attempt was made to heat the halls during the winter.

The rector moved to the hotly burning stove and stood with his back to it. Standing with his feet apart, he made sure that his robe should not be singed by touching the hot dampers. His favorite dressing gown barely covered his black suit and all the layers of vests and other garments that he wore to seal in the warmth. His arms were short, and the tasseled cord was wrapped twice about his stomach as though it were a package that threatened to come undone. His boots were just visible beneath the hem of the threadbare robe.

One could not easily determine the rector's age. His sideburns and the little that was left of his hair were silver gray, but the round face had a look of youthful freshness. His eyes, which peered forth from behind his narrow glasses, were large and full of wonderment like those of a child. His cheeks were soft, and a gentle smile played unfailingly about his large mouth.

Actually, the old man was somewhat provoked at the moment. It was of course just three days before Christmas, and one could expect the train to be quite a bit late. Then too, sleighing was difficult with so little snow on the roads, and it was some fifteen miles to the station at Näs. Yet it was anything but pleasant to have to keep stamping one's feet on the floor in the cold and to be unable to do anything sensible while awaiting the new curate, who was coming from Linköping.

Well, who would it be this time? The rector had had a number of assistants. To tell the truth, he could not say he had had a happy time of it since this miserable rheumatism had forced him to ask for a curate. How should a rheumatic old man be expected to continue year after year to break in young colts for the Cathedral Chapter? His problem was exactly like that of the poor crofters with their beasts. When the steer measured ten span at the waist they had to begin to use him, and when he had barely reached twelve span and learned to walk straight in the furrow, they had to get rid of him and would have to rely again on nothing but wild calves.

The old man fumed at the recollection. They had sent him a drove of good-for-nothing young oxen to fool around in his fields these four years. They were the plagues of Egypt in a new form! Rinell, the little, fat one—that was the turtles. All he did was to sit on the sofa, glutted and bloated, blinking his eyes, and waiting for food to be served. Emptander, with his whining voice and his skinny legs, might be the grasshoppers. And Svenson, he was like the swarm of flies, always buzzing around in the kitchen—if the maid had not moved to Saleby, who knows what might have happened? But Skagerbom, misfortune itself—he was the darkness, indeed, the great Darkness!

The old fellow walked the floor again. It was getting darker. The light in the room was a melancholy blue. His fur coat and his leather cap hung on a hook near the door; they could not be left in the hallway in this bitter cold. Piles of papers and envelopes lay on nearly all the chairs. A few maps, a glassful of pencils, and a few samples of minerals on the untidy desk betrayed the interests of the man outside his vocation.

The rector continued his meditations at the window.

What nice Christmas present would the Cathedral Chapter give him this year? This time he had at least let them know that he wanted a devout boy, a fellow he could ask to make a sick call without having him look as if he had been asked to eat nails, or at least a decent fellow who could be offered a drink without immediately asking for four. The bishop had promised to do his best. It would be interesting to see what the best which the Cathedral Chapter could send would look like. The rector did not let his expectations rise too high.

From the window he walked slowly back to the desk, drew his robe closer about his legs, and sat down. It was already beginning to grow dark, and everything was strangely still, as it can only be on a winter night in an isolated country parsonage in which the household has stopped its usual functioning in the process of waiting involuntarily for something. Only the fire crackled and threw flickering streaks of light across the floor.

The rector pricked up his ears. Could it be bells that he heard? There was no doubt about it, and from the right direction, too. Now one could hear them clearly from the hill that led down from the village. The old man pushed back the desk chair and got up. Mrs. Holleman must have heard the bells too, for someone was going through the opposite hall door that led to the kitchen.

A sharp, screeching noise was heard in the yard as the sleigh runners cut through the thin snow. Heavy boots kicked against the stone steps. Through the door a steaming horse could be seen, its mane white with hoarfrost. The driver, whose muffler was wrapped about his mouth to the tip of his nose, pushed in a black trunk, and the curate followed in its wake. He, too, looked more like a big piece of luggage than anything else. His slight figure was evidently stiff with cold and he moved awkwardly in his short mackinaw, under which at least two other coats could be seen. The coarse shoes were encased in galoshes that seemed a bit too large and therefore made a shuffling noise as he walked. A narrow face showed itself under the fur cap, which was pulled down far over the head. His nose was red and pointed, and at its very tip hung a large shining drop.

The rector stood in the open door of his study and made no attempt to pass over the threshold to the icy floor of the hall.

"Welcome, Pastor. Step in! No, don't hang your things out there; bring them into the study. Anders! Will you please carry his trunk up to the east bedroom? And now let me present my housekeeper, Mrs. Lydia Holleman."

It took some time to get the various outer garments off from the young man, who was frozen stiff. In the process the rector had time to acquaint him with the parish: 1,487 souls at the beginning of the year; a fine traditional churchliness, though—God help us!—there had been considerable separatism this last year. The saddest situation concerned the Lord's Supper. In some quarters, going to communion in church was likened to eating with the swine. The separatists had their own communion societies, or rather, two of them, as the Baptists had kept to themselves since last fall. No doubt it all had its explanation in his own decrepitude. He was physically unable to travel about in the forest sections to look after his people. For that matter, what would our Lord himself do with such an ill-starred place as this Ödesjö? When the Church permitted a worn-out old man and his miserable curates to mismanage the vineyard, then God perhaps had to send the freelance preachers to care for men's souls. It did seem to him sometimes that our Lord could have found wiser and better servants than those colporteurs who of late had been carrying on and laying waste at Svedjefallet and Hyltamon.

Pastor Fridfeldt, whose aching limbs were slowly coming to life again, spoke only a few words in answer to the rector's chatter, but he listened with considerable interest. This was his second assignment and he wondered much what it would be like. Himself a child of the revival movement, he had ever since he was sixteen been carried along by its mighty sweep and had had the good fortune of serving the first time under a "believing" minister at Vikbolandet. About his new senior pastor he had heard many strange rumors, however. Fridfeldt had an indefinite feeling that he belonged to those who were against the awakening, that he might be one of the scribes, who were the sworn enemies of the pietists, or "readers." But he had never learned the actual facts about the situation here.

He was first given a few minutes to get settled in his room on the second floor. Then he went directly to the table for the evening meal. The rector read the table prayer, and Mrs. Holleman sighed a hearty Amen. Fridfeldt thought he might have found an ally in her.

The conversation at the table dealt, at the cautious suggestion of the curate, with the free religious movements. He wondered if it would not be wise, in order to save Christianity in Sweden from schisms and eventual chaos, to ignore all doctrinal controversies and concentrate on the most essential, inviting all who believed in the Lord Jesus Christ in truth to unite in the work for the kingdom of God.

The rector maintained the point of view that the revival movement could well, and with more permanent gain, have stayed in the Church, and defended the place of baptism and confirmation in their relation to such awakenings among the people.

"Awakened people also have children, and when they are once brought into the world there remains the duty of nurturing them. We have had revivals before in these parts, and always it has gone badly for the children. Either the revival burns out with the older generation, or it becomes necessary to begin to reckon the children as Christians and nurture them with catechism and confirmation and all the churchly ministrations, as the Church always has done."

Fridfeldt did not feel too happy about the situation. Though their conversation had been carried on earnestly and in all friendliness, he felt somehow that the rector did not grasp what was most essential in the whole question, and that he was in some ways a stranger to the spirit of revival. Did he know through personal experience what it means to be born again?

His superior must have noticed the shadow of displeasure that was beginning to show on his assistant's face, and made a genial effort to smooth things over.

"Now, now," he said, "let us not argue further, but give ourselves to the enjoyment of the meal. Lydia, my frozen feet need something to warm them today. Will you please get the cognac?"

"This solves the problem," thought Fridfeldt. "At any rate he is not a true believer."

As for Mrs. Holleman, she was very evidently different. She seemed genuinely unhappy when she went to the cupboard and took out the liquor. Fridfeldt was strengthened in his regard for her.

"You must not think ill of us, Pastor," she said with embarrassment. "The rector has his own ways, which I am unable to affect. If I had my way, this bottle would not have a place in this house. I know nothing worse than drunkenness."

The rector nodded in kindly agreement.

"Then we are almost of one mind, Lydia. Drunkenness is next to the worst thing I know. The worst is self-righteousness. If I had to choose, I would rather be a drunk hired man at Österby fair than to sit self-righteous and self-satisfied at a pious coffee party."

"But now, Pastor, you are really horrid."

Mrs. Holleman looked with a mixture of indulgence and holy indignation at the always imperturbably genial old man. He gestured calmingly with his rough hand.

"Come, come! I only mean to say that a drunkard may repent and fill heaven with joy, whereas the ninety-nine righteous ones, who need no repentance, bring nothing but sorrow and vexation to God and his angels."

"But the drunkard must really repent," said Mrs. Holleman with conviction.

"Of course, of course, Lydia. The publicans also repented, and sinners eagerly sought our Savior. But the righteous and the Pharisees stood far apart and sneered at them. But let us not judge. It is not so sure what you and I might have done *then*."

I know what I would have done, thought Fridfeldt, without looking up from his plate. If one has given one's heart to him *now*, one surely knows that one would have done so *then*.

The atmosphere had become a bit tense. It was only the rector who did not seem to notice it. Or did he, nevertheless? At any rate, he brought up another subject for conversation, and described in broad terms the natural phenomena and physical geography of this strange and variegated region.

The waffles, the special company treat at the parsonage, were soon on the table, and were accompanied by Mrs. Holleman's excuses. When two big helpings were eaten, the coffee was brought in. The old rector seldom drank coffee. His stomach thrived on a noggin of liquor, but coffee was not good for him, he said.

After the table prayer, they passed again through the dark and unheated hallway and entered the study.

The rector lighted the table lamp. In its pleasant glow the details of the room stood out in soft relief.

The desk was large and heavy. It had carved oak garlands between the ornate heads of the pillars, and protuberant brass ornaments. The bookshelf contained for the most part leather-bound volumes in brown and black. Countless miniatures almost covered the striped wallpaper of the room. Largest among these was a painting in brownish green hue of some castle on the Rhine. Beside it hung an etching of the wounded head of Christ. There was also a black console with a Swiss boy in mottled porcelain, an inscription in pearl: "By grace are ye saved," and an oil print of a child with a guardian angel. Elsewhere, nearly every inch of wall space was filled with small pictures in black frames with figures in water color. Fridfeldt looked at them with interest, but was not able to make out what they represented. His eyes searched the room, and found them everywhere—between the cabinet and the door, above the tasseled sofa, and all the way to the heavy draperies. He looked carefully at the nearest one, trying to make out what it could be. The rector noticed it and began to describe the picture.

"That is a Savolax infantryman, my boy, the 1803 model if I remember correctly. And there above it, you have all the others from the Finnish war." He had taken the lamp in one hand and let its light fall on the pictures. In the other hand he held his long pipe and pointed with its stem. "Those," he said, "represent the various Finnish regiments that have fought in European wars." He identified the various pictures, and talked warmly about patriotism and courage.

"Where in the world have you been able to find all these pictures, sir?" asked Fridfeldt, who had not honored all this military glory with a glance, but had with increasing wonder taken stock of the ugly little man who gesticulated with his pipe and energetically kept pulling his head deeper into the turned-up collar of his dressing-gown.

"Just a hobby, my boy, just a hobby. Even as a boy I began dabbling with colors, and little by little it has added up to this. The big difficulty is to choose the right colors. The models may be found in illustrations everywhere."

Fridfeldt seated himself on the sofa. He felt that he must not put off confessing where he stood. This strange old man with his brandy and his soldiers should at least learn what kind of assistant he had gotten.

"I just want you to know from the beginning, sir, that I am a believer," he said. His voice was a bit harsh.

He saw a gleam in the old man's eyes which he could not quite interpret. Was approval indicated, or did he have something up his sleeve?

The rector put the lamp back on the table, puffed at his pipe, and looked at the young man a moment before he spoke.

"So you are a believer, I'm glad to hear that. What do you believe in?"

Fridfeldt stared dumbfounded at his superior. Was he jesting with him?

"But, sir, I am simply saying that I am a believer."

"Yes, I hear that, my boy. But what is it that you believe in?"

Fridfeldt was almost speechless.

"But don't you know, sir, what it means to be a believer?"

"That is a word which can stand for things that differ greatly, my boy. I ask only what it is that *you* believe in."

"In Jesus, of course," answered Fridfeldt, raising his voice. "I mean—I mean that I have given him my heart."

The older man's face became suddenly as solemn as the grave.

"Do you consider *that* something to give him?"

By this time, Fridfeldt was almost in tears.

"But sir, if you do not give your heart to Jesus, you cannot be saved."

"You are right, my boy. And it is just as true that, if you think you are saved because you give Jesus your heart, you will not be saved. You see, my boy," he continued reassuringly, as he continued to look at the young pastor's face, in which uncertainty and resentment were shown in a struggle for the upper hand, "it is *one thing* to choose Jesus as one's Lord and Savior, to give him one's heart and commit oneself to him, and that he now accepts one into his little flock; it is a very different thing to believe on him as a Redeemer of sinners, of whom one is chief. One does not choose a Redeemer for oneself, you understand, nor give one's heart to him. The heart is a rusty old can on a junk heap. A fine birthday gift, indeed! But a wonderful Lord passes by, and has mercy on the wretched tin can, sticks his walking cane through it, and rescues it from the junk pile and takes it home with him. That is how it is."

Fridfeldt said nothing. Though it seemed sacrilegious to speak about the Savior in connection with such an ungodly thing as a walking stick, he saw that the old man's intention was certainly not sacrilegious. He felt this by the very tone of his voice. When the old man continued, his voice was gentler still.

"And now you must understand that these two ways of believing are like two different religions, they have nothing whatever to do with each other."

"And yet," he added thoughtfully, "one might say that there is a path that leads from the lesser to the greater. First one believes in repentance, and then in grace. And I believe you are on that path. But now we must argue no longer," he said briskly. "It probably does not pay, nor can I ever convince you with words. But out there"—he pointed with his pipe toward the dark winter night outside—"out there you will find a strict and demanding teacher."

Fridfeldt looked puzzled.

"The congregation, my boy. The congregation is the best teacher a pastor can have. Remember what I tell you now: In this congregation you must keep your tongue in discipline if you would be able to lead souls. But since we have gotten in on this subject, we might as well begin right away. Have you your almanac with you?"

The rector had seated himself at his desk, and motioned the curate to sit down beside him.

"You had better jot it all down," he said. "Well then, you take the Christmas matin service, it is the most exacting. I'll have to try to take the forenoon service. By that time they'll all be sleeping in the warm church, and eloquence is not so important. I'll preach on the Sunday after Christmas, and you on New Year's Day. Look up the texts tonight and tomorrow we'll make up a preaching schedule. The next item is the calls on members. We usually visit the very poor before Christmas. You had better start tomorrow with the Christmas baskets."

"Christmas baskets?" Fridfeldt looked puzzled.

"Yes, Mrs. Holleman will make them ready, you need not trouble yourself about that. Tomorrow at one o'clock Anders will be here with the sleigh, and then you two will make the rounds according to the list and leave a basket at each place. Mrs. Holleman has sometimes helped me with this, but I have noticed that the result is too much sighing and too little of the true doctrine. You had better take care of it. Just follow my directions. Better write them down.

"1. Lotta at Sågen. Anders knows where it is. She is to have a basket, and you are to read a daily meditation to her. Take both Roos and Rosenius with you. Do you sing?"

"Somewhat," answered Fridfeldt modestly. Actually, he thanked God for a fine tenor voice.

"Good. Sing for her, 'I know in whom I trust.' Put special emphasis on the singing of verses two and six. Read from Roos' book the evening meditation for the second of June. The old woman is strong in confession, but weak in deeds. Don't give her syrup, but salt.

"2. Frans at Sjöstugan. There is a fine old man. Put down: a basket and a meditation from Rosenius. Take something comforting. The reading for October seventh about the shield of faith will do.

"3. The widow Clara at Sjundefall. Let her have the large basket. She has six little ones. You'll hardly be able to do any reading amid all the noise and confusion, but sing for her. I suggest either 247 or 250, and some other hymns of comfort. Remind her of her promise to come and see me once in a while.

"Then there is number 4. That is Mother Tilda at Finnarödja. She is not to have a basket, since she is fairly well off. She should really be called on some time between the holidays, but since you will be over in that direction, you might as well look in. Tell her that you will come with the Lord's Supper on Tuesday after Epiphany. We'll have more to say about that in a moment. She likes to tell about how wonderful it is to be a child of God, but cut her off sharply and say, 'Unto whomsoever much is given, of him shall be much required.' There could be more of the spirit of neighborliness up at Finnarödja," he added by way of explanation.

Fridfeldt sat quietly in his chair. Now and then his pen scratched away. This was a long memorandum just for tomorrow. Then followed a round of visits to be made the third day after Christmas, and still another on the fourth. After Epiphany a number of calls would have to be made on shut-ins and disabled who had not been given the Lord's Supper for as long a period as the rector had been without a curate.

Fridfeldt did not know what to think. Even though nine tenths of this might be considered routine duty, there was nevertheless a good deal of real concern for souls in the old pastor. How this could be so in view of his drink at dinner and his great enthusiasm for the military remained a puzzle to the curate. Perhaps a struggle was going on inside the old man himself. He was beginning to have a real liking for him.

Time had passed while the rector talked. He looked at his watch and said, "Forgive us if we seek the night's rest rather early here. I am old, as you are aware, and I need to go to bed with the chickens. Will you ask Mrs. Holleman to come in and we'll have our prayers."

The curate groped his way through the dark hallway and found the kitchen door. Inside sat Mrs. Holleman beside the large stove, whose canopy extended out toward the middle of the room. She had placed the lamp on the mantle and had moved her chair close to the stove. Her feet rested on a wooden footstool. Embarrassed, she closed the illustrated magazine she had been reading.

They returned to the study. The rector remained at his desk, Mrs. Holleman took her usual place on the sofa, and the curate sat down on a chair near the stove.

The rector first read the meditation for the day by Rosenius. Then they sang all the verses of hymn 440, after which the old man offered a prayer in his own words. It was a prayer unlike any that Fridfeldt had ever heard. There was thanksgiving for God's mighty works in creation, for the stern glory of winter, for the Christmas that was soon to bring its special joy, for a roof over one's head, and for the salutary discipline of pain and sickness. His intercessions, too, were unique. He prayed not only for his congregation, for the aged and the sick, for the scalded child at Bältefall, and the sick mother at Svenhester, but also for the crops under the snow, for freedom from the disease that threatened the farm animals, and for milder weather for the crofters and their beasts. Finally, he prayed for poverty of spirit, for a right trust in God's grace, and for the final favor of dying one day as sinners won by the Savior's merits.

In the midst of all his wondering about his new superior, the curate experienced a warm human fellow feeling for him. Where he sat with folded hands, he prayed quietly in his heart for the old pastor's salvation.

Springtime
in March

"Praise, laud, thanks, and glory,
Praise, laud, thanks, and glory,
Praise, laud, thanks, and glory,
Our God and our Lamb!"

Confident and strong, the song rose up toward the stars. The informal meeting following the service was concluded, and the crowds were homeward bound through the woods, singing on their way. Springtime was in the air. There was the scent of wet snow and supple birch boughs. In the ditches, water from the melting drifts still flowed and rippled beneath its thin crust of ice. On the road, too, the night frost had left a crust on the water in the wagon tracks that sounded like tinkling glass beneath the feet.

Among the last ones in the crowd was Olsson, a member of the church council. His broad shoulders were hardly visible in the dark as he strode on heavily through the icy mud. That did not bother him, for he felt as though he were walking on clouds, and was inspired by a heavenly enthusiasm and an unearthly joy. This was the day he had longed for and prayed for. Now the promises were being fulfilled, now showers of blessing were falling on the dry fields of Ödesjö. Since God had heard his prayers and had sent the rector a believing assistant everything had become transformed. He had sensed a note of revival already in the young pastor's sermon at Christmas matins. When the slender and unprepossessing youth got into the pulpit he seemed to grow in stature under his vestments and spoke with an intensity and joy that warmed the heart. His presentation was plain and popular, too, and filled with illustrations and examples. It was easy to follow along and easy to remember what he said.

The news that the new curate was a true believer spread like a prairie fire through the parish. As early as Epiphany they had dared ask him to come and preach in the mission house at Hyltamon. He had without hesitation promised to do so, and it had been glorious. Fridfeldt was one in heart and soul with the so-called "readers," knew all the beloved gospel songs, and was not afraid to go right to the point and ask people about their soul condition.

And then it had come!

It began slowly at the revival meetings in the chapel after Quinquagesima. The crowds were large. The Spirit was at work. One evening Anders the blacksmith surrendered himself to God. Gunnar from Rusthållet and his wife followed, and after that the ice was broken. It was now the middle of March, and meetings followed in quick succession. Homes were opened for gatherings as never before, and everywhere there was good attendance. There was an atmosphere of tense expectation, in which great things were hoped for from God and anything could happen.

Olsson had been as happy as a child and had thanked God on his knees. He was himself nurtured by *Pietisten* and Rosenius' *Daily Meditations*, and it had disturbed him deeply to see the rector growing old and to mark how he was letting the reins of leadership slip from his hands. He had been grieved also at the spirit of division that had come into the parish.

But now! The revival had scarcely begun before the hatchets were buried. There was a new unity and amity among the people. They prayed and labored together for the salvation of the unconverted, and one and all seemed to turn to the young pastor as their leader, without ill will or reservations of any kind.

The deacon had by this time gotten down to earth again after his enraptured feelings. He looked at the slender figure of the curate who walked at his right. To the world he must have appeared most unimpressive. His head bowed forward a bit and his knees bent slightly as he walked. His galoshes trampled heavily in the half-frozen mud. He walked in silence, as if he were thinking about something.

Pastor Fridfeldt was actually far away in his thoughts. The events of the past weeks had quite overwhelmed him. To think that he, poor sinner, should be permitted already in this, his second assignment to be in the midst of a revival and, humanly speaking, be the Lord's instrument in its promotion! Everything in this congregation had seemed so unreal, everything had gone so well that he could see nothing but the hand of the Lord in that which had taken place. The very fact that he had so early in his ministry here been recognized as a true believer and acknowledged as spiritual leader, gave evidence of a degree of spiritual life in the community which he had not dared to expect. That they so unitedly received and supported his message gave him a joy that words could not express.

The meeting this night had been another demonstration that the age of miracles was not past. In the large hall at Nysäter the people had occupied every inch of space on the long, rough planks. They had crowded also the hallway and the kitchen, while some listened through the open doors. He had talked about the prodigal son and pictured the love of the Father with a joy and a power that were not his own. Once again he had felt the overpowering greatness of this new message that God was love, pure and unchangeable love. He had urged all the straying and lost to remember that they had a Father who yearned for them. He had used an illustration they could all understand: the father who sat alone in the old home and wrote to a dear son or daughter in America who, though absent from the home nest for many a long year, was still the object of that father's unquenchable longing and deep concern. He had then begged them not to bring sorrow to the heart of the heavenly Father. A wave of emotion had flowed through the gathering, and the call and appeal of the Spirit and the touch of God's presence were felt almost like a physical impingement. And then it had broken loose! Almost all had remained for the after-meeting. Men and women had fallen on their knees; no one knew how many they were who asked to be prayed for. One after another had stood up and thanked God with a jubilant or tear-choked voice, because he had at last found the way home and had fallen into the heavenly Father's arms.

―――――――

They had now reached the main highway. Here the crowd broke into groups, each going its own way. The singing had stopped. The cool night air had caused the church warden's thoughts to revert to everyday concerns and he remembered his promise to his cousin Erik Svensson at Bältefall. The cousin belonged to those who had separated themselves from the church and formed their own communion circle, but they were nevertheless on good terms and were often together.

Today Erik had sought out the church warden before the meeting and had told him the story of certain sorry events that had taken place. They had agreed to talk it over with the pastor, tonight if possible. There was no other way than to ask the pastor to come along to the church warden's house. The pastor was a bit surprised at the request, but when he understood that it concerned a matter of importance, he made no objection. Mrs. Holleman was disappointed, to be sure, but it was really not far to the parsonage and she could well continue on alone.

The church warden's wife was evidently aware of the matter, since the coffee tray stood ready on the table before the sofa. The three men sat down. The pastor sought to get an edifying conversation started, but the other two had very little to say. When they had had their coffee, however, the church warden presented the matter in a straightforward manner.

"We wanted to tell you, Pastor, that something very distressing has happened among the believers, something that will create offense if it becomes known."

Fridfeldt looked up with concern. "What could that be? Among the believers?"

"It is Daniel and Karl-August in Vänneberga who are at outs."

The curate knew them both. Daniel was the richest man in the village. He owned a farm of about 160 acres, as he seemed to remember from the records. He was a pillar among the believers and had been present also this evening. Fridfeldt remembered the man's broad shoulders as he had taken note of him at the prayer meeting. Karl-August, on the other hand, was a poor man and lean of body; he was the owner of barely fifteen acres. Tonight, contrary to his usual custom, he had been absent.

The church warden continued.

"Karl-August came to Daniel's place last Monday and asked to buy some hay. He can only feed two cows, and because of the poor crops last summer has scarcely enough for them. Daniel answered that he did not have a wisp of hay more than he needed himself. Karl August pleaded, 'If I can't buy hay, I'll have to slaughter the cow. She is a good milker,' he said, 'and I'll get nothing for the meat if I have to butcher now at the end of the winter.' But Daniel refused to help him. Then Karl-August said, 'If you won't sell me any hay, you must at least buy the cow. I simply can't slaughter such a fine cow.' So they bargained, and Daniel got the cow real cheap. He paid in cash, and fetched her on Monday evening. On Tuesday the cow took sick, and this morning they had to slaughter her. The cow must certainly have drunk something poisonous, seeing she had been burned black inside. Now Daniel is abusive and tells everyone that Karl-August knew all about this and had cheated him with intention."

"How can he believe that?" asked the pastor. "Karl-August had first tried to buy feed for the cow. That ought to be evidence enough."

The church warden's eyes fell. Erik Svensson had twisted his watch chain tightly around his left forefinger and was unwinding it again.

"That is not altogether certain, Pastor," he said, without looking up. "Daniel has his own way in business. Karl-August is no beginner either, for that matter. It could be that Karl-August cooked up the whole story about the hay just to make Daniel unsuspecting and so be able to free himself from blame afterward."

"But that is surely preposterous," cried the pastor. "That would be falsehood and deception beyond end. And how foolish would it be, besides! If Daniel would only have been willing to sell him the hay!"

The church warden shook his head sadly.

"Karl-August certainly knew that Daniel would never sell any hay for a cow he had good prospects to buy at a bargain. There was no risk in this transaction."

Leaning over, the pastor gripped the edge of the table so firmly that the tips of his fingers were white.

"But this is too terrible. It *can't* be as you think. Karl-August is certainly man enough to know that the matter would be found out."

"Yes," said Erik Svensson, "I am sure he understood. That's why it was so fortunate for him that Daniel got possession of the cow as he did. It is not exactly honorable for a rich farmer not to have a bit of hay left over for a poor renter's beast and then force him to sell, and in the next place buy the cow himself at a bargain and have enough hay to keep the animal himself. Most anyone would have borne the vexation and have forgotten it, rather than make an affair of it. But Daniel has his own way in business matters, and now he is irritated and does not care about anything, but says he will sue Karl-August unless he gives him his money back voluntarily."

The curate had sunk back on the sofa and sat with his head bowed in his hand. What was this? Could such things really happen? And among God's children? He saw the two men with his mind's eye: Daniel, heavy-set and coarse, with plump features and sharp eyes. He had often testified at the meetings and spoken of the necessity of being separated from the world. And Karl-August, had he not constantly urged young and old to give themselves to God? Had he not prayed for the other farmers at Vänneberga—there were at least two up there who were known to be unconverted. What would they say now? And what would become of the whole revival, if the opponents of the "readers" should again triumph?

He looked up, and asked, "Where was Karl-August tonight?"

"They say he is at the mill," said Erik Svensson. "That could very well be, because the miller is working night and day since the water started flowing down there again. But I think there were special reasons why Karl-August made his visit to the mill just tonight. It's likely he didn't want to meet Daniel at the prayer meeting."

The pastor had gotten up. He walked stormily back and forth, breathing heavily.

"Do such things happen often?" he asked suddenly.

Both the others lowered their eyes.

"Not often," said the deacon hesitantly, "and yet *too* often. There's need for revival also among the believers, it seems," he added.

The pastor stopped, made an awkward turn, and stood with his hands deep in his pockets.

"We cannot now determine just where the deepest lying fault is to be found," said the pastor. "We must first try to heal the worst wounds. If the situation is really such as you say, then it will work great harm to the revival and will bring dishonor to the name of God. Cannot the differences between the two parties be settled peaceably?"

"That is just what we wanted to ask you, Pastor," said the church warden. "The simplest way would be if we could persuade Karl-August to return the money and take the meat. Someone should speak to him about it as soon as possible."

The pastor seemed to hesitate.

"Will one of you go with me tomorrow?"

"I believe Karl-August is still waiting at the mill for his flour," said Erik Svensson. "It's not far to go." He looked at the pastor hopefully.

"If you'll go with me, we'll go immediately," was Fridfeldt's prompt decision. Yet he felt terribly uncertain. What should he really say to Karl-August?

It was about eleven o'clock. The stars were shining. The wind blew softly and carried the scent of decaying leaves and melting snow from the fields.

The mill was at the brook above the church village. The noise of the big wheel could be heard from afar. Evidently it was still working.

The nearer the three came to the mill, the more uncertain the pastor felt. It would not be easy to charge a religious man with dishonesty without clear evidence.

Under the mill bridge the water churned in brown eddies. Chunks of ice crashed against the stone abutment with a roar that drowned out the sound of their steps. Inside the mill room a pale light glowed. There sat Karl-August, his coat collar turned up, his legs stretched out, and his hands deep in his pockets. Two other farmers slouched sleepily over the rough table.

Erik Svensson stepped in alone and greeted. "So, there you sit. Yes, I have just come from the meeting. There is something I want to talk with you about. Will you come outside a while?"

Karl-August got up and followed. When he caught sight of Fridfeldt he shrank back.

"Is it you, Pastor? Are you out so late?"

"Yes, Karl-August," said Fridfeldt, with an attempt at calmness and authority, "and on an important errand."

"One would think so, at this time of night," Karl-August answered nonchalantly.

"Yes, Karl-August, it is a matter that concerns God's church. It affects the good name and reputation of the faithful. You know, of course, that the cow you sold Daniel yesterday died this morning?"

"Yes, I have heard that they had to slaughter her."

"And you know, Karl-August, that she had drunk some poison."

Karl-August looked toward the side. It was impossible in the dim light to make out the expression on his face.

"What are you saying, Pastor? Are they so careless with such things at Daniel's place that the cattle can get at them?"

"Karl-August," said the pastor, helplessly, "you must not become angry, but this affair looks very bad. All the worldly scoffers will surely link the sale of the cow on Monday and her sudden death this morning and will draw the conclusion that one brother in the congregation has deceived the other. Such offense must not be allowed."

"That is surely nothing to take offense at, Pastor. If in God's providence it was Daniel rather than I who had to slaughter, then it only upholds the poor man's right. Besides, he got the cow so cheap that he'll lose no more money on the slaughtering than he can well afford."

Fridfeldt hardly knew that to say or do.

"But my dear Karl-August, Daniel is going to sue you. The matter will come to court. There will be gossip and trouble without end."

A hint of sarcasm played on Karl-August's lips.

"And that you believe, Pastor! I must see it first."

Fridfeldt became more and more convinced that the man was guilty. But he did not know what to do. He looked toward the bridge. There was the sound of hoofbeats on the oak planks.

The white spot on a horse's nose showed in the dark and in a moment a wagon stopped. The men had stepped into the darkness under the overhanging roof. The driver noticed the men at the wall and came closer for a look at them, as he greeted, "Good evening!" It was Daniel. It gave the pastor quite a turn when he recognized the voice.

"So here you stand? And the pastor too, and Karl-August. Well, I have really been waiting for you. Strange how long it sometimes takes to grind two sacks! Or maybe you didn't want to come home until Daniel was asleep. But now I have found you after all, and now the matter will have to be settled. Will you give me back my money, or won't you?"

"But listen, good friends!" It was the pastor who answered. "As believing brethren, we must settle this matter peaceably. I have just offered Karl-August an honorable solution. Certainly no one will say that it was his intention to deceive."

"Yes, I claim that it was," shouted Daniel. "He has always been a sneak and a fox, and this thing has been premeditated fraud from beginning to end. To come and make it appear that he needed help and to beg for mercy, and all the time wanting only to cheat his neighbor! That is a thing so base that he ought to go to the penitentiary for it."

"Jonsson, Jonsson!" shouted the pastor. "Do not throw stones! Neither of you is without guilt in this affair."

"What are you saying, Pastor? Have I any blame in the matter? Have I not paid honestly for the cow? Didn't we settle on a price?"

Now the pastor was ready to despair.

"But Jonsson, you know it is a sin to refuse to sell a little hay to your neighbor, saying that you couldn't do without it yourself, and then nevertheless buy the cow and put it in your barn. You know what is written, 'Give to him that asketh thee, and from him that would borrow of thee turn not thou away.'"

"Sin? Is that sin? One can see that our pastor is pretty young and doesn't understand business matters," said Daniel, quite undisturbed.

That was too much for the pastor. He took hold of the lapels of Daniel's overcoat and shook him.

"But man," he said, "don't you understand that this will end in hell? Can't you see, Jonsson, that your heart is just as unconverted as any drunkard's or adulterer's can be? Don't you realize that you are the equal of harlots and thieves when you shut up your heart against a brother in need?"

This was the end of Daniel's patience, too. He tore himself loose from the pastor's grip.

"Did you say unconverted, Pastor? That a minister should say that to me! I'll tell you one thing, Pastor, before you had outgrown your baby shoes, I was saved and born again, and I'll not let a state church preacher call me a whoremonger, drunkard, and thief. I could sue you for that, too. But now let's settle this business. Karl-August, do I or don't I get my money back?"

Karl-August backed a bit to a position between the pastor and the deacon.

"You ought to be glad the cow died on you, since you didn't have a wisp of hay to feed her. The meat is yours and the money is mine. You can have that settled by the court."

"Then there will be a lawsuit!" shouted Daniel. The next moment he turned away and got into his cart. The whip flashed, the ice crunched under the wheels, and he was swallowed up by the darkness.

The three men stared at one another. Karl-August had slowly slipped into the mill house. It was evident that he felt that the matter had been discussed with finality. There was nothing else to do than to go home.

Erik Svensson was the first to break the silence.

"You must not be angry with Daniel, Pastor. That is just his way. He can't help it and doesn't mean anything bad with it. It will soon blow over."

Fridfeldt said nothing. It was not the abuse heaped upon him that disturbed him most, he had deserved that. He had gotten excited, and he had been a poor curer of souls. What really crushed him was the insight he had just received into the weaknesses of believers. Was it really like this behind the pious words, the warm prayers, and the hearty singing? In what could one then put his trust? Where really was the borderline between believers and the children of the world?

"Friends," he said, when he finally turned to his companions, "I want to look upon this as God's call to holy warfare against the flesh for all of us. And I propose to begin with myself tonight. There must be no sin remaining in us. We have responsibility also for others. And for the revival, too. Those who wait for the Lord must not be put to shame because of us."

The others nodded. They had certainly had similar thoughts.

Now they had reached the village, where their roads separated.

"What shall we do now with the people at Vänneberga?"

"Pastor, might it not be well for you to talk it over with the old rector and ask him to go there tomorrow?" said the deacon.

"Would you come with us?"

"If the rector wants me. If so, let me know. I'll stay home tomorrow."

They shook hands and separated. When the others had gone a few steps, Fridfeldt looked back and said, "And then let us pray earnestly for sanctification and victory over the flesh."

———

The March morning dawned with a bright sun. The robins sang and chattered in the lilac hedge, where buds were beginning to break forth. There was a steady drip from the melting ice in the eave troughs.

The shades in the corner room on the southeast were the first to be raised. It was the old rector's bedroom. He was reading his Bible before the clock had struck six. Life next awakened in the west gable room on the second floor, where Mrs. Holleman had her quarters. She was reading from a book of meditations by Spurgeon. Last of all, light sounds were heard from the east gable. There the curate had his rooms, and there he began his day by pulling on his trousers and falling on his knees in prayer at his bedside. This morning the prayer was brief but fervent. His resolve of the day before rested upon him like a powerful hand. He dedicated himself wholeheartedly to the Lord. Then too, the memory of the miserable affair at Vänneberga sent him hurrying down to the study, where he found the rector already at work.

He had imagined that it would be humiliating to tell about the sorry state of affairs among the believers, but the rector viewed it all matter-of-factly and was not greatly disturbed. The carriage was ordered and a message was sent to the deacon.

At nine o'clock the parsonage buggy carried them south on the highway toward Ravelunda. Fridfeldt felt more at home north of the church hamlet. There the revival had been more evident. Down here at Vänneberga it had one of its last outposts. Beyond it lay Sörbygden where the spiritual life was of another type. There one could both smoke and confess the Savior; there the doctrine of total sinful depravity was preached, and it was said that whisky might be found also among the awakened. The rector liked the people of Sörbygden, but the curate expected little good to come from that direction. He had always considered Vänneberga the last bright spot southward on the map. It was therefore all the more humiliating that this wretched affair had occurred in Vänneberga.

It did seem today as if all evil had conspired to bring Vänneberga into disrepute. When the rector's carriage entered the village the most terrible oaths and curses could be heard from the direction of Daniel's farmyard. When they came nearer they saw that most of the Vänneberga farmers with the womenfolk and dogs were gathered outside of Daniel's cattle barn, where a one-horse cart stood waiting.

The excitement was extreme, and blows could be exchanged at any moment. Indeed, a fight had already become something more than a threat, since some of the men were trying to hold in check Johan from Mellgården, who swore and cursed, while Daniel stood before him white as a sheet and with a streak of blood on his cheek. His wife hid her face in her apron and wept bitterly.

The rector swung his carriage into the yard. The effect of his arrival was enormous. Everyone was dumbfounded and stood there in complete silence. Slowly and clumsily the rheumatic old man stepped from his carriage and stood in the mud, his head sunk deep in the collar of his fur coat.

"God's peace, dear Christians," he said quietly. "You ought to be ashamed. What would you have me think of you?"

He motioned to one of the men who had been holding Johan to come nearer. "I am sure you are impartial, Edvin," he said. "Tell me what this all means. Does it have something to do with the cow that was slaughtered here yesterday?"

Yes, that was it. After a few brief questions the rector had learned the salient facts. Daniel was just now set to take half of the cow to market. The others had watched him load the cart. The atmosphere had been irritating. Then Johan had come along and said something provocative. Daniel had given as good again, and Johan had become furious and taking the shoulder of the disjointed beast had hit Daniel on the head with it. In the last moment the others had rushed in and stopped the fight.

The rector nodded quietly.

"I am going to see Daniel now," he said. "And I'll not leave Vänneberga until this whole matter is settled. But first I want to talk with Johan. Olsson," he said, turning to the deacon, "will you go out and get Karl-August? But don't let him in until I give the word. Give me a hand, Fridfeldt, I'm afraid I'm stuck in the mud."

Slowly he crossed over to the house, and stepped uninvited into Daniel's parlor. He seated himself on the sofa without taking off his heavy coat. There was no heat in the room. Fridfeldt stood guard at the door.

Johan actually came in. Fridfeldt looked at him critically. He knew something about the man's life. Johan was a godless old pagan, a real roughneck.

Johan stepped to the middle of the room and stood there with cap in hand. The old pastor sat half reclining on the sofa.

"Listen, Johan," he said. "Should a Christian man act as you did a while ago?"

Johan was silent.

"I would never have said that," thought Fridfeldt. "Johan ought to be told that he is not a Christian at all."

"Do you think you used language that one baptized in the name of Christ should use?" continued the rector.

Johan kept silent.

"Tell me, Johan, do you think it was pleasant that I happened to come here and heard the kind of language you used?"

"No," said the farmer glumly.

"Of course it doesn't mean a thing that your old confirmation pastor had to listen to it. But what do you think God thought when he heard it?"

Johan made no answer.

"I believe God must have thought something like this, 'I have baptized that boy, he belongs to me; but he has not done very much to honor me.' That is what God must have thought."

Johan turned and twisted unhappily.

The old pastor reached out his right hand. "Do you see this old hand? Shall it have to testify against you on the day of resurrection?"

Johan had a questioning look.

"You see, Johan," the rector continued, as he touched the thumb and index finger of his trembling hand together, "these two fingers can also bear testimony. They have held the holy Body of Christ and offered it to you, and you have received it with your lips. Today, with those same lips, you have called upon the powers of darkness and cursed your neighbor. Do you think a Christian man ought to do that? Yes or no?"

"No, Pastor."

"I knew it, Johan. You think just as I do, then." His hand was still stretched forth. "I do not intend to withdraw this hand until it is able to bear witness *for* you, and not against you."

Again Johan wondered what his old pastor meant.

"Will you promise me two things, Johan?"

"What would they be, Pastor?"

"First, I want you to promise me that you will not go to sleep a single night without a prayer for forgiveness and for strength to become a better Christian."

Johan scratched behind his ear.

"But if I should forget it some night, Pastor?"

"Then pray the next morning instead. Do you promise?"

"I do, Pastor."

Johan reached forth his hand.

"Wait! One thing more must be seen to before my old hand can witness for you again. Will you promise to shake hands with Daniel after I have talked with him, as an admission that you have acted foolishly and want everything to be forgiven and forgotten?"

"I promise, Pastor."

They shook hands. As the rector drew his hand away he lifted it a moment. "With this poor hand as instrument, God has both baptized you and given you the holy sacrament. Now God has used this same withered hand to seal a covenant with you for your own happiness and salvation. See that you keep the covenant. God bless you! Now you may go. Let Karl-August come in now! And bring in a Bible."

Karl-August came in, together with Daniel's old Bible in its brown leather binding. As Fridfeldt closed the door, he thought if he treats the ungodly as Christians, how will he then proceed with believers?

"Fridfeldt, will you open the Bible to the next to the last chapter of The Revelation of St. John, the eighth verse I think it is. Let me see it. Now place the Bible on the table. Karl-August, put your finger on the eighth verse. Can you make it out?"

"Yes, Pastor," said Karl-August, wondering what it was all about. "It is here at the bottom of the page."

"Good! Answer me one question, Karl-August. Did you know that the cow was sick when you sold her to Daniel? No, do not answer yet. Read first what is written where you are holding your finger."

Karl-August bent forward and stumbled through the verse: "But the fearful and unbelieving, and the abominable, and murderers, and whoremongers, and sorcerers, and idolators, and all liars, shall have their lot in the lake which burneth with fire and brimstone: which is the second death."

"Good, Now you see yourself in what company a liar lands—among the unbelieving, the idolators, and the whoremongers in the lake that burns with fire and brimstone. Think now before you answer. Did you know that the cow was sick?"

Karl-August had shrunk together and looked even smaller than he was. Against dark stubble, his skin looked pale and yellow.

"Yes," he whispered.

"Praise God for that," said the rector. "Now there is hope for your soul. Now we'll both lend a hand in settling this matter. What is the first thing for you to do?"

"Ask God for forgiveness," whispered Karl-August, without looking up.

"Good, and then?" It was as though the rector were conducting a catechization.

"Give back the money."

"Splendid! And what more?"

The last requirement was more exacting. The man writhed in agony. He could not get it over his lips.

"I suppose I'll have to help you, then, though you ought to be able to say it yourself. You must ask Daniel for forgiveness. Are you willing?"

"Ye-e-es." Karl-August was all a-tremble. Fridfeldt felt an infinite sympathy with him. This was indeed penitence that hurt.

"God bless you, Karl-August. Now the angels of God rejoice, for now a lost little brother has found his way home. Go home now and get the money. Let me next talk with Daniel."

The door opened, and was closed again.

Daniel stood pale and tight-lipped before the rector. He had washed away the blood from his face.

"You have been shamefully cheated, Daniel," said the old pastor. Then followed a pause. "Now things are going to be set right again."

Daniel looked up in surprise.

"Karl-August is going to return the money. He has already gone to get it."

Daniel's face brightened perceptibly.

"And he is going to offer you his hand as a sign that he is asking you to forgive him. Will you take his hand and the money and let everything be forgotten?"

"Gladly," said Daniel. He could not have dreamt of anything like this.

"Well, then, that matter is cleared up, and you have been vindicated. And that is good and well. But now there is another person by whom you have been shamelessly cheated, and this has to do with greater sums. This has to be cleared up so that the wrong is righted."

Daniel had a perplexed look.

"You see, Daniel, last Monday there was a great council in heaven, much like the one mentioned in the book of Job. The good Lord said, 'The Adversary has had much to say of late against one of my servants down in Ödesjö, and I shall have to put him to test in order to discover if there is any truth in all this talk about his love of money and his greed for a thick wallet and many fat cows.' And then God sent along a poor little crofter who begged to buy a bundle of hay. And God said to His angels, 'Now you will see that my servant is honest and faithful and will let the man get his bit of hay cheaply.' But the Adversary also stole away and reached Vänneberga and sat down by the window and whispered, 'Don't be a fool now, Daniel. If there is no fodder to buy, the cow must be sold, and you can't buy a cow as good as this one every day and at such a price.' Then there was a tenseness in heaven, and all the angels wondered if Daniel at Vänneberga would allow himself to be deceived by his worst enemy. Well, Daniel, how did it go? Did you allow yourself to be deceived?"

Daniel was silent.

"Daniel, Daniel," said the rector, "now the heavenly Father is looking at you again. Last Monday he was pretty much discouraged about you. Will he be so again? It's hard to speak sometimes, Daniel, but it can be much worse if one keeps silent. Answer me now: Did you let the devil deceive you last Monday?"

"Yes, Pastor, I did."

Fridfeldt heard himself draw a sigh of relief. The innermost knot, the most difficult one, had been cut.

"God be praised for that word, Daniel," continued the old pastor. "That is the most significant testimony to the power of God that you have given for a long time. Well, Daniel how shall we now be able to right this matter that you let yourself be deceived when God put you to the test and asked you to help a poor neighbor? Don't you think it would be best if we helped him today instead?"

"What have you in mind, Pastor?"

"This is what I have in mind. Karl-August is not a rich man. He has suffered a great loss in being forced to slaughter his best cow. How much do you think the meat is worth? What would you have gotten for the half of beef you planned to sell today?"

"Perhaps fifteen riks-dollars."

"And what is the price of a new cow?"

"Between fifty-five and sixty-five."

"I suggest that you keep half of the meat which I understand your wife is already salting down. Pay Karl-August fifteen riks-dollars for that when he returns the purchase money. If we reckon the cost of the other half at fifteen, he will still be short twenty or thirty dollars before he can buy another cow as good as this one. Now, then, let us take up a collection."

He took out his billfold.

"I will give five dollars. How much will you contribute, Daniel?"

"Ten," said the farmer, who had already put his hand inside his coat for his pocketbook.

"What remains we can surely pick up in the village. Johan will be the first to give." With a nod toward Fridfeldt, he added, "Now you may call them in."

Fridfeldt called in, not only Johan and Karl-August, but also the deacon and the other men who were outside. It took only a brief moment to conclude the matter. The penitents did not have to say anything. The rector spoke for them. Handshakes were exchanged, the purchase money was returned, and in a few minutes the collection was completed.

Karl-August burst into tears when he received the money. The rector spoke briefly on the words, "Ye are the body of Christ, and members one of another." Then he asked Fridfeldt to lead in the singing of "Christians, while on earth we wander," which was followed by the benediction. There was an atmosphere of quiet and solemnity, in sheer contrast to the yells and curses that had greeted them as they entered the village.

Fridfeldt felt at one and the same time impressed and perplexed. He could not quite approve treating everyone without distinction as a Christian. But he was happy about the results. When they came outside, the sun shone with a warmth like that of summer. The sand was springy beneath their feet, as the frost was beginning to loosen. Farther on, at the gate, it was already firm and dry. The rector leaned against his young curate and was helped into the buggy with some difficulty. He waved to the men who stood silently in the gateway with uncovered heads.

As the carriage sped homeward through the countryside, where the black furrows of the fields began to show through the blanket of snow and the hazel bushes that edged the ditch were beginning to bud, they began to talk about old parish happenings. Olsson and the rector sat in the back seat, and the curate sat on the cloth-covered board facing them. The deacon always had something of interest to recall as they passed each farm. Here, for example, was the place where they had dug out of the snowdrift the team of oxen and the hired man who had perished in the storm on that evil Tuesday. Here was Brännan where they kept bar for the churchgoers and where peasants from the Jämshögs district would sometimes be lying drunk as swine until Tuesday morning.

"The drinking was surely terrible in the old days," continued the warden. "Liquor was supplied stealthily behind the church barns. The bell ringers seldom went into the tower without taking a bottle with them. Most everywhere along the way—at Anderstorp and Svenhester and Sinkan, for example—one could stop and have a drink."

Fridfeldt looked intently at his superior. This would be good for *him* to hear, he thought.

"It is really a miracle of God that you, our dear rector, were able to put an end to this miserable business," said the deacon. "I was of course just a child at that time, but I remember the storm of anger that swept through the parish when you did away with the whisky sales at the church and closed the still at Södra Hult. That was the time they hurled the whisky glass at you. Father told us about it when he came home. I was home that day taking care of the cows."

The old pastor just smiled.

"That glass was worth a great deal," he said. "The dash of whisky I got in my face seemed to change the whole atmosphere. These forest people are genuine. From that day on, they wanted to make amends, as it were, and the opposition vanished."

Fridfeldt could hardly believe his ears. Surely it had never entered his mind that the rector was, in his way, a champion of temperance.

"And all this you have done, sir," he declared. "Why do you never say anything about this? The separatists ought to hear about it."

"One ought not talk about oneself, it may hide Jesus from view."

Fridfeldt wondered if there could lie a little sting in the soft-spoken words. He liked to talk about himself and his spiritual experiences from the pulpit.

The water splashed about the wheels and the horses' hoofs would sometimes strike a still remaining crust of ice and sometimes sink softly in the muddy ruts. The sun shone with pleasant warmth. The old pastor dozed a bit. This had almost been too much for him. The deacon tightened the blanket around his legs and also the carriage apron, and purposely kept silent. The old man's face sank down in the fur collar and his eyes peered half-closed into the sunlight.

Many conflicting thoughts were at work in the curate's brain. He thanked God that there was peace once more in Vänneberga. At the same time, he could not get away from a feeling of shame because such a thing could happen among the confessed disciples of Jesus. And both the deacon and Erik Svensson had intimated that such things were not exactly unusual there. Perhaps there were many still unsettled and unforgiven sins among those who participated week after week in the meetings and labored with him for the gospel. He felt that the very thought of such a possibility lay as something slimy and ugly upon his heart.

His thoughts continued to churn within him.

There must then be something wrong in connection with the revival, something that did not function properly. Fridfeldt agreed with Erik Svensson that a stronger preaching of sanctification was something that was sorely needed. He was taking this to heart personally. Again, as yesterday, he felt that a mighty hand was pointing to his own breast. He must accept the judgment. He realized that he had allowed himself to be lulled to security by his successes. The crest of the revival had lifted him higher than was wholesome for such an inexperienced Christian. He had without suspicion accepted all who accepted him, and had taken for granted that they were true children of God for the very reason that they had accepted him as their leader. He had thought himself a powerful evangelist and shepherd of souls last night at the prayer meeting. God had therefore found it necessary to humble him so deeply and to show him that very night that he was unable to restore a faulty brother. He had fallen short in respect to love, he had become sinfully angry. And today God had moved him from the place of leadership to that of a doorkeeper. He understood that this was a sign that he must make a new beginning.

While the rector's carriage moved along slowly toward the church village he was engaged in a severe and searching self-examination and struggled earnestly in prayer.

It was not until late that same evening, when he finally rose from the place of prayer at his bedside, that the struggle was over. But then he lay, spirit and soul and body, a whole and total sacrifice delivered into God's hands.

Transfiguration Day

W hat a morning!
If the young pastor had not been so absorbed in his thoughts, he would have been as filled with enthusiasm at the glory of creation in all its summer splendor, as were the birds who sang everywhere in the ancient maples. The air was perfectly still and clear. There was no haze in the early morning, nothing but pure sunshine. In the north, the Heding hills showed a solid wall of trees sharply etched, and the prairies round about the church village were revealed in clear detail in their rich summer colors.

It was Sunday and the festival of the Transfiguration of Christ. He had really gone outdoors at this early hour to get some inspiration for his sermon, to which he had not been able to give much preparation. But he was still too disturbed to be able to think clearly. He had to read that letter once more.

When he came home late on Saturday from a preaching tour, the letter lay on the table awaiting him. He saw immediately that it was from Conrad and he opened it with eager hands. Conrad was his schoolmate and his spiritual twin brother. They had knelt together at Bethlehem Church at

Hötorget and surrendered themselves to the Lord; they had sat side by side at the mission house in Upsala; they had been fellow guests at the Lord's Supper one of the first times it was served privately to the little company of believers. Conrad had not become a theological student, but a language teacher. During the last few years he had taught at Örebro. Fridfeldt took out the letter and read it again:

———

"Dear Brother in the Lord:

"God's Peace!

"You are the first to whom I write about the greatest day in my life. How gloriously happy I am at this moment! For the first time I am truly conscious of having become a Christian.

"I am baptized. I am baptized with the true baptism according to the will of Jesus and the testimony of the Scripture. What a release! I cannot describe it with words. The struggle was difficult, but now it has been fought through to victory. To God alone be the glory!

"First let me tell you something about what preceded my conversion. Ever since my arrival here I had been unhappy, and things became worse rather than better. I found that I was *not* a Christian, as I had long imagined that I was. I experienced no victory over my evil thoughts, my pride and vanity continued to plague me, and storms of carnal desire threatened my ruin. Oh, what misery! I cannot describe it.

"I tried all sorts of cures. I prayed much. It helped for the moment, but soon the old thoughts were back again. I read the Word of God more diligently than before; but even as I read I was assailed by desires whose dreadfulness I dare not describe.

"Then by God's guidance I met in the Mission Society at this place true Christians, to whom I opened my heart. They opened my eyes and showed me that I had no power in myself and could find no victory over sin until I had fellowship with the Holy Spirit through a true baptism. Together we searched the Scripture. And, Brother, though you are an ordained pastor, you must admit that the Scriptures nowhere state that children shall be baptized.

"Thus I was led to see that *faith* and *confession* must come before baptism. It meant a difficult struggle with my pride. Should I, a Doctor of Philosophy, become like a child again and be buried with Christ by baptism unto death? If God had not so completely crushed me with the terrible knowledge of my sin, that I was left totally without peace and joy, I suppose I should never have taken the step.

"But now it has happened. Praise God! The days since then have been the happiest of my life. Now I have entered the new life and am conscious of its powers. The storms of temptation are stilled, a sweet peace reigns in my heart, and I walk in a light such as I had never known before. Oh, that all who lack joy and peace might know and understand how wonderful it is to surrender wholly to the Lord and walk in the way of obedience to the very end!

"I am writing this to you, Brother, because none other in all the world is nearer and dearer to me. Let me hear from you soon. Tell me what you think.

"Good-bye, then. May the Spirit of God guide you to the full truth!

"Your humble Brother,
Conrad Y."

———————

Fridfeldt sat down and put his hand to his head.

The way of obedience to the end. Was this God's Word to him in this most crucial hour of his life? Truly, this letter must have come from God!

How strange that two lines could run so parallel in their development! What Conrad described in his letter was an exact description of his own conflict. Was not that which God had let his dear friend in Örebro experience in every phase the same as he had passed through since coming to Ödesjö? That spiritual decision in March when he had committed his soul to God as never before had not been so final a breakthrough as he had himself thought it to be at the time. Actually, things had assumed the old tenor. The revival had stagnated. When the spring farm work began again with the return of sunshine and warmer weather, the crowds at the meetings dwindled. The spirit of those who did come was not the same. Pale faces with big, hungry eyes had given way to a tanned and vigorous everydayness. There was never now the old lift and spiritual glow which had formerly humbled the proud and attracted even the most sluggish. It filled him with doubts and agonizings of spirit. Was the whole revival movement allied in some way with undernourishment and bodily weakness? He dared not admit such sacrilegious thoughts to anyone, but he was trying anxiously to assess the fruits of the revival, and became still more depressed.

Nothing had gone as he had hoped. Many had definitely lost their fervor, and stayed away from the meetings when they noted the general decrease in interest and attendance, in other words, when the movement lost its sensational character. Others remained faithful, indeed wonderfully so, but their testimonies were rather powerless. However much they declared the joy of salvation, their eyes betrayed a secret uneasiness. He surmised that they also struggled with secret doubt as to the genuineness of their experience. The only one in whom he thought he could detect a true work of God was, strangely enough, Johan from Vänneberga. He had begun to come to the meetings regularly and his life too was changed, but he had never committed himself to God in the usual manner.

Fridfeldt was greatly tortured by the thought that the lag in the revival might perhaps be due to his own fault or failure. He had to admit to himself that he had not been the tool of the Lord that he ought to have been. He had been fully sincere in dedicating himself to God, and had wanted to crucify his sinful self even unto death. It had indeed become a death struggle, but without resurrection to new life. The first three weeks after his commitment he had actually lived in a new light, but then it had again deserted him. One April morning, when heavy, slushy rain beat against the windows of his room, he had become terribly conscious of it. He had just come home from a long after-meeting at Hyltamon. He had stayed in bed longer than usual that morning and as he lay half awake improper thoughts came to plague him. He got up dull and out of sorts when Mrs. Holleman called him to breakfast. He had gone down to breakfast unshaven and unkempt, his usual bedside prayer neglected. He was mute and unresponsive while the rector talked about boyhood memories from high school days in Jönköping. There was something charming about the old man's memories as, with an admixture of Latin terms, he told of the wild adventures, the singing about the bonfires on Walpurgis night, and revealed a trace of the country boy's furtive longing for the homes of the wealthy in the city, their celebrations and dances. All these memories from a past and wicked world had somehow captivated him. Back in his room again, he felt a strange longing for books, laughter, and companionship and, indeed, for the pomp and vanity of this world which he had long since renounced. He tried to read Rosenius, but to no avail. Instead, he had gone down to the office to write extracts of the parish records. It was not until the evening of that day, a half hour before he and Mrs. Holleman were to start for the prayer meeting at the shoemaker's, that he was able to collect himself and overcome his spiritual torpor. But he remembered what his thoughts had been on the way to the meeting: that all he had prayed and done was only that he might be able to witness with power, only that he might preserve his reputation among these people as a believing and Spirit-filled minister.

Ever since that day he was pursued by an appalling compulsion to test his innermost motives. The results were shattering. He noted that he was especially careful and correct in respect to everything that Mrs. Holleman saw or heard. He knew that she worshiped him almost to the point of idolatry. He knew, too, that she was the channel through which life in the parsonage was brought to the circle of believers in the parish. What Mrs. Holleman thought and said determined to a large extent the direction of pious opinion. He was careful, therefore, to remain in high regard with her, and showed a sympathy and amiability such as he had never shown the senior pastor. He tried resolutely to overcome this temptation, even affecting a certain curtness and abruptness toward her. If he had been sitting in his room in the morning reading the Bible, and she came in to dust, he would carefully close the Bible and hide it under some worldly books. He would not parade his piety before her. His sermon outlines, on the other hand were allowed to lie in full view, since the particular group of believers she belonged to did not look with favor upon a preacher who wrote his sermons. And yet—when he was done with one sin, another put in its appearance. When with all these attempts he finally succeeded in dampening the romantic adoration of the housekeeper and had instead to hear some reproach or other, he got disgusted with her and suddenly began to see her as sanctimonious and narrow-minded.

Fridfeldt halted abruptly. Absentmindedly, he had crossed the lawn and was on the orchard path. He faced a mock-orange bush whose white blossoms swayed delicately before him.

"That is how my faith ought to be," he mumbled to himself, "but instead it is like a crushed and dusty thistle at the edge of the road."

Where did the fault lie?

Had he not labored in the garden of his heart until his hands were bloody? Why had there been such paltry fruit for God? Had he not denied himself everything? He had burned the last colored neckties when he found that he kept choosing among them. He had only black ones left. He had left unread the three novels he had received at Christmas. He had even given up coffee when he noticed how he longed for it after dinner and that it had become a desire for him. This had of course caused no little embarrassment, since Mrs. Holleman kept urging him to accept the fragrant poison, and for fear of losing his halo in her sight he had not dared to give her the real reason. At last he told her the reason, that he was developing a craving for it, and so wanted to give it up entirely, as he had done with tobacco and liquor, in order that the temptation might not have power over him. Mrs. Holleman had become very much offended. She drank coffee herself. Why then should the pastor call it a sin? As for the senior pastor, he had only done what he seldom did: he had sighed.

However, all these attempts had brought him no peace. What was wrong?

Had he received God's answer this very morning? "The way of obedience to the end." Had not God led him along the same paths as Conrad? During the revival in March he had had some fellowship with the Baptists. He had found them to be strict and earnest Christians. The place and significance of baptism had therefore become a burning question for him also. He had felt for some time that the baptism of infants had no real significance for the Christian life. Making too much of baptism served only to make nominal Christians more entrenched in their false security. After all, everything hinged on conversion. But it had never occurred to him that a true conversion should also include a new baptism. In searching the Scriptures, he could not now help noting the role which baptism played in the first Christian church. Could he then be satisfied any longer with a baptism which in his own eyes had never meant anything?

"The way of obedience to the end." That way was hard; yet it had a singular attraction for him. He would have to give up the ministry. But was not that a fetter that must be broken? Ought he not as a free evangelical preacher serve the revival movement which God had let come to his country? Had not Ekman recently taken this bold step? It must be wonderfully great to sacrifice all and go out, free, poor, and burning with the zeal of an apostle! But he lacked peace. If only he could gain the peace of God, he would gladly walk the way of obedience to the end.

For a moment doubt rose again. What if the peace that Conrad wrote about should be only a passing thing? He had felt much the same way during those short weeks at the end of March after his own coming to terms with God. What if Conrad's wonderful peace should take wings after only a few weeks!

He resisted his doubts. It *must* not be so! For that would mean that there was no way left to peace. And it was surely a dispensation of God that this letter should come just at this time. Tonight a decision must be reached. The question had become acute. For a few months now, he and a little group of mission friends had been studying the Bible together with the Baptists. There were several who leaned toward rebaptism, among them Erik Svensson, the cousin of the church warden. They must have noticed that he was moving in the same direction. They were waiting to hear their pastor's decision. Tonight there was to be a special meeting at the home of Jonas Ahlberg, the local leader of the Baptists, and Fridfeldt had half promised to give a resumé of what they had thus far deduced from the Bible. It meant he would have to take a stand.

By now he had reached the currant bushes farthest down in the orchard, where a narrow border of grass followed the fence. He fell to his knees, overwhelmed by emotion and inner tension.

"Lord, Lord," he prayed, "I have no right to ask anything of Thee, but if Thou wouldst guide me aright, show me a clear sign. Lord, Thou seest that I wish to walk the way of obedience. But give me, I pray, a sign to assure me."

"Pastor! Pastor Fridfeldt!"

It was Mrs. Holleman who called. She was on the gravel path at the upper end of the orchard between the apple trees. Embarrassed, Fridfeldt crept out from behind the currant bushes.

"Pastor! There's a sick call to be made. You must go to Sjöstugan."

Fridfeldt hurried with long steps up the path. Before he had time to ask, Mrs. Holleman gave further information.

"It is Frans, a heart attack, they think. You'll have to hurry, Pastor."

He ran to the study and came out with the bag containing the communion service hanging from his shoulder. He had not taken time to put on his hat, but hurried bareheaded into the yard. The peasant lad from Skräddarluckan, who had brought the message, ran before him in his bare feet to show the way.

Directly across the pastures, it would take about a quarter hour, if one walked fast. The pastor wiped the sweat from his brow and tried to recall what he knew about Frans at Sjöstugan. He had been there twice before, once just before Christmas, and then again at Easter. Frans had once been a grenadier in the army. He was known to be a godly man, who always spoke quietly but with mature understanding about spiritual things, as one who had a personal experience of the new birth. His errand was therefore not especially difficult. The old man would undoubtedly be worthily and well prepared.

The path led over a fence, and already the little house could be seen through the trees standing on the shore of a little lake that glittered in the sunshine. The boy slowed down. Fridfeldt caught up with him, wiped the perspiration from his forehead for the last time, stepped into the low vestibule and, after a gentle knock, slowly opened the door that led into the room. A woman was crouched in a chair at the bedside, dabbing her eyes with her apron. She jumped up and turned her eyes, red with weeping, toward the pastor.

Fridfeldt saw at once that there was little he could do here. The old man was obviously already paralyzed and entirely unconscious. Now and then he spoke a few incoherent words. One hand fumbled with the blanket, while the other lay powerless. By asking a few questions the pastor learned what had happened. The tailor next door had looked in earlier that morning and had found Frans so ill that he immediately sent for his own wife Hedda and sent word to Frans' youngest daughter, who was married and lived quite a distance down the lake. She had rushed away from the breakfast dishes, taking her youngest in her arms but leaving the older children at home. When she arrived, Frans was still able to speak, but immediately afterwards his condition became worse. Now she stood there, alone and in tears. The tailor had gone to her house to look after what was most necessary, but he would soon be back.

Fridfeldt sat down on the edge of the bed. He tried to talk with the sick man, but there was no sign of recognition. He bent over and shouted in the man's ear, but received no recognizable answer. Occasionally they could make out what the old man said, but he spoke of far-away, distant things, about rock blasting and oxen.

"Father was always such a good man," said the weeping daughter. "I know, of course, that he will have it better now, but it is so hard to part with him."

"When I got here," she continued after a moment, "I said, 'You are thinking about Jesus, are you not, Father?' And he answered me, 'I am not able to, Lena. I can't think any longer. But I know that Jesus is thinking of me.'"

Again she wept.

The pastor sat in silence. The truth that Jesus is thinking of the sick one seemed to him a comforting pillow on which to rest one's head when death is near.

Just then something startled him. The woman had heard it, too. Had they heard aright?

Yes, they had both heard it. The old man had uttered an oath; they had heard it plainly. It was as unlike him as it could possibly be. Fearfully, the pastor bent close and looked at the man's lips.

"Right turn!" he shouted with an oath. "Can't you lift your heels? Right turn!—No, Lieutenant, we're to advance by companies.—Skål, fellows. It's ten cents a drink."

The woman shook with sobs and covered her face, as if she felt ashamed before the pastor. Fridfeldt did not know what to do. Frans had been a soldier, and it must have been dim memories from the days at the Malmen camp grounds that haunted his brain. The pastor knew that he had not been a Christian at that time of his life, but was not all that forgiven and forgotten now? Why should all this sinful mixture well forth now in his last moments?

Frans continued his vague imaginings. Now he was at the marketplace. As far as they could make out, he was remembering a transaction involving a calf. "He cheated me. I got a dollar and a half too little. I'll get even with you yet."

Again sin, thought Fridfeldt. He did not dare look at the daughter.

For a while now, Frans chattered about inoffensive and inconsequential matters. Once he touched on religious matters. The subject was grace, but what he said was not clear. Suddenly he said very plainly, "She does not pray as much as I."

Fridfeldt could not help thinking how alike we all are within, after all. The same jealousy, the same pride, the same unloving heart. Frans was having the same trouble that he was having.

But he also thought about how it would now go for Frans. As long as he was conscious he had faith. That seemed quite evident. But beneath the thin shell of his conscious faith this evil still dwelt within the heart.

"Just as it is with me," mumbled Fridfeldt almost audibly. In the next moment he was gripped by an anguished thought. What if he were to have a stroke and were lying in his bed delirious! He saw it before his mind's eye in grotesque reality: his bedroom at the parsonage, the poor wooden bed, his face thin and pale, his unruly hair more than usually disordered, and his eyes closed. He imagined the old rector sitting at his bedside, kindly and troubled, and Mrs. Holleman wringing her hands in horror at his blasphemous imaginings. For what might come over his lips? Improper rhymes he had learned as a boy, coarse and sacrilegious words he had used as a high school youth before his conversion, sensual pictures that still today plagued his imagination. Not to mention his conceitedness and his eagerness to keep up appearances and make a good name for himself, all of which filled his soul. What if all this should well forth in his dying moments, and Mrs. Holleman should get up at the meeting-house and tell how the pastor she had thought so wonderful had died like a profane man and a libertine?

"And even now you are thinking about your own honor!" This accusation, spoken inwardly to himself, fell upon his soul like the lash of a whip. He was, then, so wholly concerned about his honor and success in life, that a death in sin frightened him only because of the evil consequences to his reputation. But if he were dead, what would it matter what people said about him? But how would it go with his soul? And with the souls of those to whom he preached? Must they not think of Christianity as nothing but humbug and hypocrisy?

Well, was it really anything other than hypocrisy? Here he was supposed to bring comfort, and was himself as chockfull of sin as this dying old man. The only difference was that he was still in possession of his full senses, and in the interest of his good reputation must cover up tightly all the uncleanness within. As for the poor old man, his lid had fallen off, and everything lay bare. But for God, to be sure, everything was always naked to his eyes.

The old man had begun to breathe heavily. His chin had fallen and his mouth was wide open. The baby, which had been sleeping on the sofa, now awakened and began to cry. The woman looked helplessly at the dying man and went over to quiet the child. But the boy, who was perhaps six or eight months old, was determined to be picked up, and would not respond. The mother took him up in her arms and tried to hush him as best she could, and then laid him down again. She wanted to be free to give attention to her old father, who could not be expected to live much longer. But the baby went into a tantrum. He tried to roll off the sofa, and yelled despotically at the top of his lungs. It was as though some evil power was grimly bent on disturbing the peace of an old man's dying moments.

The pastor could endure it no longer. He decided to carry the boy out and in this way try to put an end to the noise. The woman must be spared, and there must at any price be quiet in the room. It was hard enough on the nerves to listen to the rattle in the old man's throat. "Lena, you must stay with your father," he said as he picked up the boy.

And so it came about that the revival preacher suddenly found himself standing outside the little cottage in the blueberry bushes with a wildly screaming boy in his awkward arms. The little fellow tried in every way to show his temper. He stiffened himself and shouted down every inept attempt on the part of Fridfeldt to talk to him. He was thoroughly provoked at this stubborn and selfish little creature, who though not yet a year old still showed much the same self-will and stubborn desire to command attention as its elders. Surely, human nature from the cradle to the grave was bent on having its own way, trying to dominate others and make its own will supreme.

Fortunately, the tailor and his wife came along. Fridfeldt turned the child over to them and asked that they remain outside. He remembered the wandering imaginations of the old man. He himself went inside again.

The woman was now on her knees. She held her father's paralyzed hands in her own and rested her forehead against them. Fridfeldt also knelt at the bedside. He prayed quietly to Him who does not break the bruised reed nor quench the dimly burning wick.

A succession of death rattles were heard. Then everything was still.

The pastor called to those outside to come in. He laid his hand on the old man's forehead and spoke the benediction. The child continued to howl at the top of his voice. The woman, still on her knees, turned to Fridfeldt with a long and anguished look.

"Tell me, Pastor, do you believe he died a blessed death?"

The question pierced his heart like a spear. What should he say? He had wanted to ask the same thing himself.

"God is very good," was his evasive reply. He tried mercifully to make his voice as reassuring as possible.

Then he looked at the clock. It was almost half past nine. At ten o'clock the morning service at the church would begin. It was time he was on his way.

He took farewell shyly and was soon hurrying over the fields. The communion case, which had not been opened, dangled in its strap from his shoulder.

The morning worship! He would be preaching in half an hour. As yet he had not the slightest idea what he should say. It was Transfiguration Day. He was himself as far away from the Mount of Transfiguration as anyone could be. He ought to be thinking of his sermon, but he could not get his mind off the dead man. Death could, then, be that strange even for a believer! So much of the old sinful nature could be left in a man! *If* such a man could be saved, on what grounds would it be? His faith? But that, as they had seen, was gone at the same moment that his consciousness clouded; and behind it all the sin lay in ferment to the very end. His conversion? No, much less could it be that. It seemed to be swept away like a loosely applied sticker when the man's will was paralyzed by his illness.

And what about the baby? Such a screaming, self-willed bundle, filled to the brim with selfish obstinacy, could it be saved? Why, it could not believe at all. But the evil nature was there, the same evil nature that was active in the old man to the very last.

And finally, what about himself? Did he not have precisely the same corrupted nature as the child and the old man? Was not this the only difference, that at this moment his will and his thought had stretched across the dark abyss a thin coating of conscious faith and personal commitment? As long as this thin, trembling layer of faith remained intact, he was therefore a believing soul. But what if his will should no longer be able to make that commitment? What if his thought should be shattered and faith's thin shell broken? What if a hardening of the arteries should set in, and he should be unable to will and to direct himself?

He looked at the watch again. Twenty-two minutes remained. He was just turning in upon the footpath behind the swine shed. It would take ten minutes to get to the church. He had less than fifteen minutes in which to get ready.

Mrs. Holleman waited eagerly and nervously on the parsonage steps. Despite her urgings and remonstrances, he refused to go to the table. Instead, he sent her with a message to the senior pastor, who had already gone to the church. She was to go to the sacristy and ask him kindly to choose the hymns, assuring him that when the bells rang for the service the curate would be there.

Up in his room the curate went limp. In the manner of revival folks, he knelt beside his chair with his elbow on the seat. He was surely in need of that support now. Darkness, doubt, unanswered questions—and a sermon to preach without any preparation. What a Transfiguration Day!

When after the prayer, he snatched the service book from his desk, his eyes happened to fall on a little volume that lay open there. It was Schartau's *Fifteen Sermons,* a little book the rector had let him take long ago. He had not read it, to be sure—what good did it do to stir among the dead bones?—but yesterday, when he was searching for a theme for his sermon, he had opened it and had discovered that there really was a sermon in it for Transfiguration Sunday. His eyes fell on the verse of Scripture on which the *exordium* was based, "And when they had lifted up their eyes, they saw no man, save Jesus only."

Here indeed was the very kernel of the Gospel text on which he was to preach. He leafed through the first few pages. This was not at all bad! In any case, there was a string of Bible verses in bold type. If he had these before him in the pulpit, he would surely be able to get some thoughts and points of departure.

He rushed down the stairs and almost ran along the parsonage drive. He felt tired. That was not strange, as he had had nothing to eat all morning. At the stone bridge he slackened his pace. Below to the right lay the church, shining white against the green foliage of the trees. He turned off the road and followed the footpath along the brook and across the fields, which had just begun to turn yellow. He walked slowly up the hill to the church.

In the churchyard the people, who stood about in black groups, greeted him reverently. A few belated carriages rattled toward the church stalls. In the bell tower the ringers, who had evidently been waiting for the pastor to arrive, turned to their task. The bells began to peal.

In the sacristy the rector, the organist, and the church wardens waited in quiet and ceremonious expectation. Only a few whisperings were required to take care of essentials, and before he was fully aware of it, Fridfeldt was kneeling on the plush-covered hassock at the altar.

He had never really cared for the liturgical altar service. It bothered him to be bound by a fixed ritual. It had therefore always been his practice to make little changes and additions, and to put as much feeling and personal touch into it as possible. Today he did not feel able to do this. Strangely enough, it was a relief to be allowed to read them as they were, ancient and hallowed words that fell as heavy, life-giving drops on his heart.

Then came the difficult moment. He stood in the pulpit. The opening prayer had been offered. Before him lay Schartau's little book. He had had time in the sacristy to glance through the *exordium* and had been struck by its power and manly austerity. He decided he would simply read that introductory part without any additions or deviations.

Thus it came about that the city curate of Lund preached in Ödesjö church on this Sunday fifty-five years after his death. First, he pictured the Transfiguration, which had ended with the three disciples daring again to lift up their dazzled eyes to behold no one but Jesus only. Then he went on to describe how this lifting up of the eyes or lowering of them was a picture of the soul's condition at different stages on the way of salvation. "When a sinner first has the eyes of his understanding opened, they are directed downward upon his own unblessed and lost state. The law constrains a man to look chiefly at himself, and drives him to compare his corrupted nature with the holiness of God and his guilt with the righteousness of God."

Why, this describes my own condition, thought Fridfeldt. He read on:

"But afterward the Holy Spirit lifts the eyes of our understanding to Jesus only. It is a blessed thing when a believing soul looks in the Word for Jesus only."

That I have not done, thought Fridfeldt. I have looked for penitence, for amendment of life. I have taken stock of my deeds, but I have lost sight of Jesus in all this mess.

He noticed that he was reading without knowing what he was reading about. With much resolution he began to concentrate on the words before him.

"It is a blessed thing when the faithful soul in prayer fixes his uplifted eyes of faith on Jesus only; when he does not look about him to lay hold on his own scattered thoughts, nor behind him at Satan who threatens him with the thought that his prayer is in vain, nor within him at his sloth and lack of devotion; but looks up to Jesus, who sits at the right hand of God and makes intercession for us."

Fridfeldt saw that this applied to him. To think that he had not understood this before! Now he continued to read with the true joy of preaching, as a discoverer who presses forward, charmed and drawn by ever new visions.

Now came the first main division of the sermon proper. In it Schartau developed the aim of the awakening, namely, to lead the soul to Jesus only. The law is the pedagogue, the schoolmaster, to lead to Christ. For Christ is the end of the law for righteousness for everyone who believes. He could see it almost as on a canvas spread before him. There ran the endless way of the law, bordered by naked trees whose supple branches hung down like whips. Steeper and steeper grew the pathway that pushed toward heaven. Stains from wounded, bleeding feet made the stones of the way red. He saw himself walking there, a hair-shirted penitent. But suddenly Christ stood there in the middle of the road. Now his old thoughts gave way to something new and wonderful: Jesus only, righteousness for each and every one who believed. The pathway had an end!

The way of obedience to the very end! He had suddenly left off reading, and was speaking freely:

"The conscience, our own anxiety, and all slaves of the law bid us go the way of obedience to the very end in order to find peace with God. But the way of obedience *has no end.* It lies endlessly before you, bringing continually severer demands and constantly growing indebtedness. If you seek peace on that road, you will not find peace, but the debt of ten thousand talents instead. But now Christ is the end of the law; the road ends at his feet, and here his righteousness is offered to everyone who believes. It is to that place, to Jesus only, that God has wanted to drive you with all your unrest and anguish of soul."

The second part followed. Like hammer blows aimed with unerring precision against the head of a nail, the words "Jesus only," recurred again and again and sank ever deeper into the consciousness. *Jesus only,* the foundation of faith, and man sees nothing else, believes in nothing else, builds his hope on nothing else, when through the awakening he has had his eyes opened to see his state of corruption and condemnation.

It is only through the gospel that a man can come to faith, for the gospel deals with Jesus, and with Jesus only. If therefore there be any doctrine that does not deal with Jesus, let it deal with whatever experience or glory it may, it is not the gospel.

Fridfeldt thought of the doctrine of baptism about which they had cudgeled their brains. What had they really been discussing? They had talked about faith, confession, personal commitment, works—but not about Jesus.

Jesus only as the ground of our justification—that was the next hammer blow. Just as a man, when faith awakens, ceases to look at himself and sees nothing but Jesus only, so God also looks not upon the man who believes nor does he see his indwelling corruption and his sins, for they are atoned for by Jesus.

Neither does God in his grace reckon with the good deeds of men, for God looks only upon the dear Son and will not look upon man and his good deeds, and this in order that he may not have to look upon man's sins and count against him the very sins with which all human good deeds are tainted, and so be forced to punish them in his righteousness.

Again a transfiguring light shone before the rapt eyes of the preacher. This, then, was the solution: Sin always remains, yet is always atoned for! Perhaps there was salvation after all for Frans at Sjöstugan. Again he saw a picture: A large cross rising heavenward, overshadowing the whole community from the bluffs of Heding to the plains of Sunnerbo. An eternally valid atonement, effective to cancel the judgment; a merciful love, stretching out its arms to all these evil hearts, in which sin is still in motion like reptiles in a snake pit. Jesus only!

His joy was almost ecstatic as he began to read the third part, which had to do with Jesus only in sanctification, as the strength thereof; with the warfare against the corruption in the heart, with evil thoughts, desires and sinful habits, for which there is no cure in heaven or earth except in Jesus only. Once again he saw clear sunlight illuminating his condition, when he read the words, "That which once and for all and immediately is reckoned as yours in justification will be worked in you little by little in sanctification." Little by little! He had wanted to see it *all* realized and accomplished at the beginning of the road if he was to dare believe. Now he was privileged to *believe all,* appropriate the whole infinite inheritance at the beginning of the road, that afterward through the long years he might draw upon it and invest it amidst the realities of the everyday life.

He concluded by saying, "Do not ask to be like this or that one, but pray that you may be like Jesus. Do not attempt to imitate the gifts of others or simulate their measure of grace" (nor Conrad's either, he thought), "but walk in your Savior's footsteps."

This was without doubt the shortest sermon he had ever preached. But he felt that it contained more of God's Word than anything he had hitherto spoken in Ödesjö. Quietly, tired but with a sense of security, he read the announcements, the general prayer and the Lord's Prayer. Then he went directly to the altar and concluded the service.

So it was all over. The postlude was played, the pews creaked as the people got up and the pew doors squeaked. With halting steps, the rector approached the sacristy.

"Thank you, Fridfeldt, thank you! Today you were a powerful preacher."

The curate reddened.

"Not I, sir."

"No, of course not, my boy. I know that. Schartau stood behind you, and behind him stood Jesus only. A good preacher must always have someone behind him. And everything must come from that One. If it can then take its way through the preacher's heart, so much the better. And this sermon went through the heart."

"And to the heart," said Pehrsson, the church warden, quietly. Fridfeldt looked at him with surprise. The rough, prosaic man met his glance with open, thankful eyes, but said nothing further.

Just as Fridfeldt took his hat and was about to bow his head in a word of silent prayer, Olsson, the church warden, touched his arm and handed him two old numbers of *Pietisten.*

"You should read these, Pastor. Here Rosenius himself writes about baptism," he said. "I heard there was to be a meeting again tonight to discuss that subject," he added by way of explanation.

Fridfeldt understood him. Olsson was a clear-sighted man. He must have surmised that the young pastor was wavering with respect to baptism.

"Wouldn't you like to come along tonight?" he asked.

"You must not take it ill, Pastor," he said with a somewhat hesitant expression, "but I would consider it a wrong against God if I should put my baptism in question. I accept God's Word and sacraments with reverence, but I pass no judgment upon them."

Fridfeldt said nothing. The reprimand struck home, but perhaps he needed it. He bowed again for the final prayer, and left with the rector.

The sun was already lower in the sky, but it was still warm. The young pastor came walking down toward the church village. The fine white clay dust settled on his shoes and powdered his black trousers. His clerical coat was unbuttoned. It was really his custom to change into his civilian clothes for the afternoon meeting, but today he had not done so; he simply had not given any thought to the matter.

After dinner he had rested a while. Then he had read the two articles by Rosenius about baptism. He was still not quite clear about the subject. This day had brought him too many deep impressions. On top of it all, Mrs. Holleman had criticized his sermon. It had not appealed to her as much as was usually the case. The pastor had not cited as many examples nor told of experiences by way of illustration, and she had not been greatly moved by the sermon. Fridfeldt confessed all about his use of Schartau, thereby sinking a bit lower in her esteem. She had never dreamed that a Spirit-filled pastor could be guilty of that.

As for himself, he was discovering the painful truth that this pious woman did not after all have any particular appreciation for the pure Word of God, but wanted touching stories instead. He felt that he was very much to blame, since he understood that his own manner of preaching could easily lead people to think of the sermon as a bit of spiritual entertainment.

The meeting tonight was to be held at the Ahlberg home in Ödesjö. Ahlberg himself was a Baptist by conviction and the only "reader" in the vicinity of the church. He was esteemed as a man of honor, showed hospitality both to the people of God and the worldly, and had helped many to find spiritual clarity. Here a group of those especially interested were to meet and discuss and pray together about baptism.

When the pastor entered the room most of the participants had already arrived and were seated along the walls. Fridfeldt was aware as soon as he came in that they had been talking about him. It was Anders-Johan from Västergården who dared to voice the matter.

"You wrote your sermon today, Pastor?" he asked.

"No, I had nothing written. I read a sermon from a book. I came from Frans at Sjöstugan directly to the service and, as I did not wish to preach without sufficient preparation, I made use of a published sermon instead."

He looked about him, questioningly. Some had their eyes lowered, others looked at one another. It was evident that opinion had not solidified with respect to this matter.

"We simply mean that it would have been just as well if you had spoken by inspiration of the Spirit," said the village storekeeper.

"No, Isaksson, I could never have preached such a sermon." Now the farmer's wife from Bäckafall felt that she must say something.

"Our pastor is too humble," she said. "Have we not heard you preach the dear Word of God so that our hearts came near to melting within us! You must dare to believe more in the freedom of the children of grace and beware of the churchly leaven."

Fridfeldt lowered his eyes. It was easy to become disconcerted in the presence of such purposeful and strong-willed people. He sat before all these unruffled and authoritative persons like a pale and spindly school boy. Fortunately, one of the sturdiest among them came to his rescue.

"We think a good and Spirit-filled sermon was heard today, Pastor. If you have more of that kind, we should be happy to have you come and read a bit for us at the meetings in Sörbygden. It is more important *what* is preached than *who* preaches. What we heard today did us good. It was the true gospel."

"But the Spirit must be present," spoke up the storekeeper. "And the Spirit flees when we stick to the letter. The Spirit is liberty, but written sermons and ceremonies are the letter that kills."

"The letter that kills is the law," said Fridfeldt. "That is the clear teaching of Scripture. The law kills by condemning us to death. But printed letters do not kill. The Bible is full of printed letters; it is, nevertheless, full of spirit and life. If someone sits down and prepares a sermon based on Scripture, and writes down the sacred words on paper, it would be strange indeed if the Spirit should leave for that reason. And if one selects good words of Scripture and reads them before the altar as prayers or texts, it is certain that the Spirit can be there too."

He was suddenly aware of the fact that he was defending the liturgy of the church. That had never happened before. But he sensed the danger of a new enslavement to forms developing which would force the spiritual life into an arbitrarily tailored straightjacket, which was both poorer and more rigid than the one that had come down from their forebears.

"And since you believe so firmly in the witness of the Spirit in the heart," he continued, addressing Isaksson, "I can myself testify before my friends here that, as I was reading the sermon in church today, God's Spirit filled my heart with such light and clarity that I saw truths in the Word that had long been altogether hidden from me."

The other farmer from Sörbygden fingered his heavy gold watch chain and spoke.

"It was much like that for me too. I have never before seen the truth about grace and sinful corruption so clearly presented. One toils with the flesh but never gets it put to death. One wonders, then, if perhaps the conversion was not genuine, or if no more grace is to be found. But today I have come to understand that the saving foundation does not lie here" (he beat upon his chest), "but in Jesus only. If He has redeemed my corrupt human nature, I can continue on the narrow way with confidence."

"But a true Christian must nevertheless have a pure heart," said the housewife from Västergården.

The farmer looked at her long and searchingly.

"Do you, then, my dear woman, have a pure heart?" he asked. The woman flushed.

"If one *truly* prays God for a clean heart, it is certain that one will receive it."

"Have you asked God to give you a pure heart?"

The woman avoided his glance and twisted a bit.

"God is almighty," she said, "and he will answer our prayers. *If* one prays aright for a clean heart, then one *must* receive it."

"When were you saved, my friend?" asked the farmer.

"Fifteen years ago," the woman answered, somewhat irritated by all the questioning. Did someone question that she was a child of God?

"Then I believe that you have kept praying for a clean heart for fifteen years. But you still have not got it," said the farmer calmly. "It has been the same way with me. But today I have come to understand that also my unclean heart can stand under grace for Jesus's sake. So I shall be saved as a sinner, and Jesus only will have the glory."

"Sinners will not be saved," said the woman, sharply, "but only he who repents and believes."

"True," said the farmer, "but to be converted means to take refuge in grace. It is to believe in Jesus, in Jesus only. It is a salvation for sinners. There is no other salvation."

"Do you deny, then, that God can make an evil heart clean?"

It was a storekeeper who asked the question. He looked sharply and with distrust at the ones from Sörbygden.

"It would be wicked to deny that," Fridfeldt hastened to answer. "God can do whatever He wills. But it is neither true that God *must* give a man a clean heart, nor that he *must* have a clean heart, before he can become a child of God. God saves us by grace, even with our unclean hearts. Our state of grace rests not on our heart, whether clean or unclean, but on the righteousness and merits of Jesus."

After some further discussion, during which other believing friends from the villages out Jämshög way had arrived, the hour for the announced discussion about baptism had come, and Ahlberg himself took the chair as leader.

He read a portion of Scripture, after which all knelt, and he led in prayer.

"Yes, we thank Thee, dear Lord Jesus, that Thou hast permitted us to be gathered here in Thy name. We thank Thee for Thy promise to be with us every day. We thank Thee that Thou wilt perfect us in a new covenant, which is Spirit and not letter. We thank Thee for Thy purpose to put Thy law in our minds and save us with a perfect salvation to serve Thee without spot ..."

Ahlberg prayed at great length. Fridfeldt found it difficult to maintain a spirit of devotion. He felt that there was a veiled disunity in the air, which brought something artificial into the prayer fellowship. He noticed how this dissension showed up in Ahlberg's prayer, which became a sort of compendium of his own doctrine of sanctification. In passing, even his views on baptism got into the prayer.

Fridfeldt suddenly remembered that, following the usual order, it was his turn to pray next. It bothered him. It would be hard for him to pray from the heart, when he felt that his every word would be critically weighed. He knew the belligerent wills and the curious expectations that filled the atmosphere. When Ahlberg had at last said Amen, and the others had added their Amens, he therefore limited himself to praying a quiet "Our Father," adding a few words at "Thy will be done," and praying the Fifth Petition twice. When he had finished he still had a feeling that what he had done was not conventional here. During the remainder of the prayer period he prayed silently for peace of heart and clarity of thought.

Ahlberg got up from his knees and sat down at the table as a sign that the prayer session was over. He looked at the pastor with his dark and intelligent eyes.

"May God now grant us a spirit of peace and unity as we continue! First, we would ask our dear pastor whether he has any statement to make concerning the subject that we are met to discuss."

Without getting up from his chair, Fridfeldt made reply. "I am surely betraying no secret when I tell you, my friends, that the conversations we have had hitherto have only brought me closer to the baptism of adults. I have learned to understand those who permit themselves to be re-baptized. This morning I prayed to God in great anguish for direction in this matter. I am convinced that God has answered my prayer."

No one dared breathe. Ahlberg bowed his head in his hand as though he scarcely dared look at the pastor for fear that the tension might be too much for him.

"The answer which I believe I have received from God," continued the pastor, "really lies in a question which God forced me to face this morning through a special providential experience. This question I now want to bring to the attention of all of you here."

Everyone, Ahlberg included, looked intently at him.

"Can a little child be saved? And, if so, on what grounds?"

The answer came from many directions. "Yes, 'for of such is the kingdom of God.'" "Yes, for Jesus said, 'Suffer the little children to come unto me.'"

"On that, then, we are agreed," said the pastor with a nod. "But on what ground?"

They looked at him questioningly.

"I mean, are children prepared to enter the kingdom of God just as they are, or must they, too, be made partakers of the salvation in Christ?"

"They must be saved by Jesus," said one of the farmers from Sörbygden. "Is it not written, 'That which is born of the flesh is flesh,' and 'Except a man be born of water and of the Spirit, he cannot enter into the kingdom of God'?"

"That is, without doubt, what is written," said Fridfeldt, "and without doubt the Scripture means that all mankind from Adam on is under the rule of sin and death. There is none righteous, and all are included under the judgment. But all can be redeemed in Christ. It had not until today occurred to me that this included the children. The sinful corruption about which we were talking a while ago is the natural state also of the children. That was what I was led to see this morning. And I think all of you must have seen the same thing."

"Yes, everyone must surely know that," said a peasant woman from the big woods country. "I have raised nine children. Some were gentler and some more stubborn in disposition, but long before they were able to talk plain, they could show envy, fight, and try to grab another's syrup sandwich. That is inborn."

A smile stole through the congregation. Mother Ahlberg opened a window toward the yard. It was very warm.

"Yes, that is inborn," said Fridfeldt. "We carry our corrupt sinful nature with us from the cradle. From life's first day we belong to the race that is under judgment and in need of salvation."

Ahlberg began to detect in what direction the discussion was leading. Thoughtfully, he remarked, "But is it not written that the little children belong to the kingdom of God?"

"No, the passage states that of such is the kingdom of God. The kingdom of God belongs to the children and to the childlike. That is the very opposite. The children needed to come to Jesus to become partakers in the kingdom of God, just as much as publicans and all other sinners. That is why they must not be turned away. Jesus did not say, 'Let them play in peace. They are already blessed.' Instead, he said, 'Suffer the little children to come unto me, and forbid them not.' Then he laid his hands upon them and blessed them, and received them into his kingdom."

"But he did not baptize them!"

"Neither did he baptize anyone else. He took people directly into the kingdom. But to his church he has given baptism, that through this gateway we might be brought into the kingdom of God. He has given us no other way of entrance. 'Except a man be born of water and of the Spirit, he cannot enter into the kingdom of God.'"

"But children cannot believe," said Ahlberg, whose eagerness was increasing. The others listened in complete silence.

"'He that believeth and is baptized shall be saved.' Thus faith is necessary for baptism."

"No, not for baptism, but for salvation. Jesus does not in that passage say what is necessary in order to be baptized, but what is necessary in order to be saved. Faith and baptism are two that belong together. Don't you see, Ahlberg, how dreadful it would be if children could not believe? In that case they could not be saved, either."

Fridfeldt was himself startled by this thought, which just now came to him. Was this just juggling with words? But then he remembered Frans, the dying old man, and his grandchild, and he felt that there was a deep and edifying connection.

"It may very well be that we have drawn wrong conclusions regarding faith," he continued. "Faith does not dwell in our brain or in our thoughts. Faith is not a work which we accomplish; it is not a gift that we give to God. Being made righteous by faith does not imply that faith is some kind of payment that will serve as well as our almsgiving and good works. Is it not written that the kingdom of God belongs to those who are poor in spirit? Faith is, then, a poverty of spirit, a hunger and thirst, a poor, empty heart opening toward God so that He can put His grace into it. When God bestows His grace upon us, we are born anew and become partakers of the new life."

The farmers from Sörbygden nodded assent. Those who followed the leadership of Ahlberg had a questioning look.

Ahlberg himself looked intently at Fridfeldt. It was evident that this was new to him, but also that he was honestly trying to understand it.

"But must not a man nevertheless *himself* open his heart?" he asked.

"Of course—if he has himself closed it. But I am wondering if it is not so with the little children, that their hearts are not really closed to God. Why do little children more easily enter the kingdom of God than we grown-ups? Why do we read that unless we receive the kingdom as little children we shall not at all enter it? Why do we as adults have to become like little children in order to enter the kingdom? Is it not because a child's heart is open so that God can fill it with his grace, shed his Spirit upon it, and regenerate it? When we grow older, it becomes more difficult, for then resistance begins; we are stubborn and evasive and shut up our heart by intentional sins. Not until the heart is opened in conversion have we become as little children—and then we can enter again into the kingdom."

He became silent, utterly surprised at his flow of words. But he had caught a vision, had glimpsed a solution to his search. In order not to lose it, he began to speak again.

"How is it now, friends? If faith means to receive God's grace in our hearts, and if the child's heart is always open toward God, it surely follows that the child is able to believe. It can, then, certainly receive grace. If, however, faith resided in our heads, in our thinking and understanding, it would not be possible. When we therefore bring a little child, with its corrupted nature, to God in baptism, what can hinder God from being gracious to it, taking it up into the kingdom of God, and giving it forgiveness of sins? Look," he said, as he held out his hands in the shape of a bowl. "This is your heart, a vessel full of corruption, being born of sinful nature and having evil desires at its bottom. When you were born into the world, the vessel was open toward God. You were not for that reason a child of God, for the vessel of your heart was not that of an angel, but a bit of corrupted human flesh. Then you were brought to baptism. God poured his Spirit as a stream of grace into this vessel. It was still sinful, and evil tendencies lay within it, but it was all covered by forgiveness; over it lay a white cloth, the righteousness of Christ, the redemption of Christ. You were then a child of God, for Jesus' sake. Then you grew up. Perhaps you were guilty of intentional sins and lived in unbelief. It was as if your heart were covered over again." Here he lifted one hand and held it over the other as a lid. "Then things were really bad. But you know that God took hold of you again, and there was penitence and confession and faith." The covering hand was removed, and the hands together again formed an open bowl. "This is your spiritual state today. The sinful nature still remains, and the struggle against sin and for sanctification of life continues. Some hearts become almost clean in this life, while others retain so much of the bitter dregs that it takes extreme watchfulness and care to keep it from flowing over into intentional sin. Yet, over us all shines the atonement, and all of us have exactly as great a portion in that which is the foundation and content of our salvation: Jesus only.

"And when you shall die some day," he continued, with hands still extended, "and your consciousness is clouded, you may lay your broken vessel down, with all the darkness that is still within it, before the throne of grace and say, 'I know whom I have believed.' In the heart, evil may still bubble forth and wrong desires rise up and, though your mind is no longer active, your lips may perhaps form wicked words. What does it matter? It is only the old nature that is falling to pieces and letting the black contents run out. The new nature already rests securely on the Rock of our salvation, Jesus only."

He let his hands drop. He saw old Frans all the while before his mind's eye. So now he had an answer also to the question raised by the circumstances of his death.

There was a long silence in the room. Finally, Erik Svensson spoke up, with a voice that seemed a bit unclear.

"Our pastor has really given us a sermon of his own that we shall not soon forget. As for me, I am putting all my trust in my first baptism and do not need anything else. I think we ought to sing a song and leave for our homes."

When the others nodded approval to what had been said, Ahlberg made haste to ask for the word. He was not content to have the discussion end at this stage.

"To me, this is such a new way of thinking about faith," he said, "that I hardly know just what to say about it. You asked a question, Pastor. May I now ask one of you?"

Fridfeldt nodded assent.

"Can you mention a single passage of Scripture that states that a little child can actually be born again?"

"Not one, but two," said the pastor, after a moment's thought. "We have already heard them. One is, 'Except a man be born of water and of the Spirit, he cannot enter into the kingdom of God,' and the other, 'Whosoever shall not receive the kingdom of God as a little child, he shall not enter therein.' Do you see what I mean, Ahlberg? The first passage, then, says that God's kingdom is received through regeneration in baptism. The other states that children can receive the kingdom and that it is just they that receive it in the right way. If, then, it is the children who enter the kingdom in the right way, and if that way is to be born again, it also becomes clear that children really can be born again. And it becomes equally clear that we all received the kingdom of God when we were baptized as children."

Ahlberg looked straight ahead as he gave thought to Fridfeldt's words. He was uneasy, but was not ready to dismiss the matter yet. He felt, however, that perhaps it was best that the group should disperse now. He therefore asked the pastor to close with prayer. Fridfeldt felt grateful for the way in which the conversation had given him an opportunity to look at himself and see anew the meaning of grace. He respected Ahlberg. He sensed that they both lived by the same grace. Might it not be that all honest Christians must after their separate strayings return at length to the Rock of Redemption?

Fridfeldt prayed a brief prayer for three things: the oneness of all believers in Christ, for fellowship on the right foundation, and for willingness to acknowledge one's own faults, forgive others, and by daily grace to live always in that poverty of spirit which made Jesus only great and indispensable. He closed his prayer with the words of a hymn:

> *Rejoice, my soul, and bless his name*
> *Who to the lost and fallen came*
> *To open heaven's portals.*
> *Rejoice that God will mercy show,*
> *The broken covenant renew*
> *With us poor sinful mortals.*
> *Now be*
> *Glory*
> *Ever given*
> *God in heaven;*
> *Peace unending*
> *Be to earth from heaven descending.*

It was the first time he had prayed in the words of a hymn at a prayer meeting. Then he got up from his knees quickly, not wishing to risk another prayer duel. Instead, he suggested they close the meeting by singing, "Rock of Ages, cleft for me."

As the group broke up, a bit tumultuously, some gave the pastor a warm handshake without saying anything, while others looked aside in embarrassment and pulled their hands away abruptly when they said farewell. It was only when they were outside and on their way that they began to converse.

Fridfeldt himself remained standing a few moments and talked with the two men from Sörbygden. He would have liked very much to learn more about their inner thoughts. But they had little to say, and soon took their farewell and went to Ahlberg's stable for their horse.

Fridfeldt stopped on the hill as he was nearing the parsonage. The sun had now sunk very low on the horizon, and the tree-crested hill cast a broad shadow over the fields below. Beyond them rose the church, its tower tinted with sunset gold. The summer clouds had gathered themselves into snowy and cottony mountains in the east. The sky was infinitely clear, broken only by the quick darting of the swallows.

For a moment Fridfeldt thought of turning to the left and visiting Sjöstugan, where the old father had died. Then he remembered that it would soon be supper time at the parsonage, and he would hardly have time for the visit.

Walking up the hill, he felt an altogether new love for the church in the valley below. Was it, perhaps, because he had seen so much wrong and thoughtless despising of it this day? One ought not despise one's old parents, he thought. The church is really the mother of us all, and it was she who administered the baptism by which we one and all became Christians.

Christians? Yes, that is the term that must be used. He could understand now that the rector was right when he treated his parishioners as Christians and that it was only natural to place Christian demands on them. This he now acknowledged, for the truth of the sinful corruption of human nature and the truth about the atonement and grace and baptism had become clear to him this day. The rector had been right, as right as it is that God has called us in holy baptism.

At the parsonage gate stood a pair of ancient lindens, which tonight were filled with the hum of bumblebees. The pastor stopped and listened. As he stopped to enjoy the clean smells and sounds of nature, his eyes strayed through the trees and flowering bushes to the yard within. Spots of light illuminated the red tile roof, a few bands of light streaked across the gravel all the way to the lilac bushes, while right across from the main veranda the old wing of the parsonage lay in clear sunshine. Beside the steps were climbing rose bushes, old and almost lifeless, yet there were still some red flowers among the dry and thorny coils. The old rector was sitting on the steps, warming himself in the sunshine, leaning peacefully against the railing, his hands folded in his lap.

The curate suddenly felt himself warmly attached to this man through a wave of sympathy and respect. He quietly seated himself below the older pastor on the steps. Neither spoke for quite a while.

Then the old man began to speak quietly.

"It is strange to think that sixty years ago old Dean Faltin stepped on the same gray planks, on which we are sitting. And if I am not mistaken Savonius, of blessed memory, also set his foot upon them. I heard much about Savonius when I first came here as a minister. The old folks said there was fire on his lips, fire from above. He died later of smallpox. Though he labored here only about two years, his work was in evidence still when I came, and especially in the southern part of our parish. Later, when the newer evangelism came, it was of deeper character there than anywhere else. One can see marks of it among the Sörbygd people still today. We are all, to be sure, inheritors, and much has happened here before we came."

"You are right, sir, much has happened here before us. It is a great thing to be an inheritor."

It was plain to Fridfeldt that the old pastor had noted a personal emphasis in his words, but he did not let on that he had noticed it.

"It is a great thing to receive a heritage," he said quietly. "I begin to understand now that not everything began with the revival. Behind Waldenström stood Rosenius—and Rosenius no doubt had the deeper vision. And behind Rosenius were Schartau and Sellergren, and surely many others. Yes, much happened before our day. It is wonderful to stand in the same pulpit, to learn of them, and to carry forward the work they began. Sir," he said suddenly, without turning, "can anything be greater than to be a pastor in God's church?"

The old man reached out his thin hand and laid it feelingly on the younger man's shoulder.

"Fridfeldt, Fridfeldt," he said, "today you have really brought me joy."

Mrs. Holleman appeared on the steps across the way and called them to supper. Silently the two men arose, the older with difficulty, as he stretched his rheumatic legs, and the younger with boyish clumsiness. The trousers of both were equally wrinkled, and on both the clergy tabs stood ludicrously awry.

———

After the meal, Mrs. Holleman offered a cup of coffee, as was the custom on Sunday evenings. The old pastor declined with thanks as usual, and lit his pipe instead. A faint smile played on the curate's lips, which was quite unusual.

"Tonight, Mrs. Holleman, you may pour a cup of coffee for me, if there is plenty of it," he said.

Mrs. Holleman clapped her hands.

"Praise God, Pastor, you have finally given up your foolish notions!"

"I am not sure that foolish notions describes it," said Fridfeldt. "Say, rather, a curse."

"A curse?"

"Yes, the curse of the law. That is what God has freed me from."

Mrs. Holleman remained standing dumfounded at the china closet, holding the cup she had taken out.

"The law? Surely, Pastor, you don't mean that God's law forbids us to drink coffee, in the way it forbids sinful pleasures?"

"God's law forbids all selfishness in thought, word, and deed, Mrs. Holleman. And that law applies to everything human, if you get right down to it. I would neither dare drink this cup nor continue this conversation, if I were trying to live a life free from sin. But there is another way. 'The life which I now live in the flesh, I live by the faith of the Son of God, who loved me, and gave himself for me.' On that foundation I shall drink coffee from now on. And perhaps, following the footsteps of my Master, the day will come when I shall dare to go out and sit with sinners and drink a glass of wine with them."

"Shame on you," said Mrs. Holleman. "Now you are talking just like the rector."

There was a grave silence. The curate drank the cup of coffee set before him, thanked Mrs. Holleman, and asked to be excused. He wanted to visit Sjöstugan before it would be too dark.

Once more he walked between the lindens. There was still a streak of the day's warm light at play in the treetops. He carried within him a great new light and a joyous message which would cause a pair of anguished eyes in that humble cottage to shine with happiness before this Transfiguration Day was over.

III. On This Rock

New Life

Through the tender mercy of our God;
Whereby the dayspring from on high hath visited us,
To give light to them that sit in darkness
*   and in the shadow of death,*
To guide our feet in the way of peace.
Glory be to the Father, and to the Son,
And to the Holy Ghost:
As it was in the beginning, is now, and ever shall be,
World without end. Amen
They shall be abundantly satisfied with the fatness of Thy house;
And Thou shalt make them drink of the river of Thy pleasures.

The deep bass voice filled the empty room, which resounded with the monotone of the reader as though it were a sound from a distant seashore. At the Gloria Patri the tone rose a trifle as though lifting itself into a hymn of praise, and with the antiphon dropped again to its former level.

The April sun flowed through the two windows and painted large golden panes on the worn wooden floor. The curtains and even the curtain hooks had been removed. The room was completely empty. The dark brown wallpaper with its large designs in gold and black was pale in spots and showed plainly where pictures had hung and where the china closet had stood in times past. In the center of the ceiling a severed wire hung from a greasy plaster ornamentation.

On the exterior wall, halfway between the windows, stood the only piece of furniture in the room, a miniature altar with two brass candlesticks and a small crucifix hanging above it on the wallpaper. In front of the altar stood a low prie-dieu with a white rail and red plush upholstering, evidently intended to be used at weddings in the parsonage. Behind the prie-dieu stood Pastor Torvik with a blue prayer book in his hand, from which he was reading. He was a big, heavily built man. His chest was enormous. His arms were long, and his wrists unnaturally slender. His hair was extremely blonde, and his eyebrows seemed almost white against the sunburned face. His features were plain and angular, his cheeks protruded too far, and his nose had a slight depression at the middle as if it had figured in some childhood accident. His forehead was high, and his large head came to a point in the back, where a few strands of hair stuck upwards from an otherwise smoothly groomed head of hair.

Pastor Torvik finished with the *Laudes,* knelt in a brief moment of silent prayer, made the sign of the cross, and then walked pensively through the room. His clergy coat was unbuttoned and hung clumsily on his heavy body. He had his hands deep in his pockets.

He stopped at one of the windows and whistled softly. The sun shown warmly, and the gravel outside the window was dark and moist in the thawing weather. On the lawn last summer's grass, which had never been cut, lay yellow, snarled and uneven. A cat snatched at the big blue flies which had awakened to life, and scared away the gray sparrows from the unclipped lilac hedge. Farther away he glimpsed the old and decaying apple trees. A big branch which had been nearly severed last year hung dead and dry between the other branches that were beginning to bud.

The pastor took note of the neglect and ruin and thought to himself that it was a picture of his parish. The devout among his people were all old and moss-covered; their days were numbered and they could no longer withstand the storms of this new age. The young were like rank weeds, unkempt and undisciplined, eaten up by the moss. The very foundation was itself like loam when the frost leaves it—all moral standards were in dissolution, wherever one put one's foot it gave way, and one's shoes were muddied.

He turned away and slowly left the room and went out into the yard, his shoulders slumping and his hands in his pockets. His first year in the ministry had been altogether different from what he had expected. Coming from a poor laborer's home, he had never dreamed of becoming a minister until he was won for Christianity at one of the student camps during his last year at high school. At Upsala he had quite naturally been drawn into the new theological thinking and had accepted the historical view of the Bible, an undogmatic and independent attitude toward the Confessions, and a warm enthusiasm for the church of his fathers. Through the influence of some of his friends he had become interested in liturgical matters and in his last year at Upsala had begun to go more often to the Lord's Supper.

And then he had been assigned this position as vicar at Ödesjö. Already at his ordination he had heard that things were not as they should be in this parish. The rector who had died all of a sudden had been a tragic figure, alone, divorced, and with his financial affairs in sad confusion.

When he stepped off the bus in the church village and walked up the hill toward the parsonage for the first time, he wondered greatly how he would find things. No one had met him at the bus stop, and when he reached the stately lodging house which stood across the road he learned the reason. Through some misunderstanding, he had not been expected until four days later. The keeper's wife, who was much embarrassed and disturbed by it all, had gone with him to the parsonage.

What a sight it was! Pastor Torvik halted in the middle of the large living room. He could still picture the scene that met his eye when he stepped into the room for the first time. Though it was nearly a year ago now, every detail was etched in his memory. The floor had been tramped on with muddy shoes so that the sand grated under his feet wherever he walked. Crunched wrapping paper, torn old ledgers, and some ragged novels lay in a corner. A broken garden table leaned against the wall, and some small pictures still hung about the room. Among the pictures was one of the group of children in costumes from the beginning of the century, a photograph of a sad-looking old woman with straight hair combed tightly back, and one of a weak-chinned and mustached student. On the floor stood some old pots containing flowers long since withered.

The other rooms showed the same neglect. Here and there were chairs with broken legs or seat; in a corner, a cracked pitcher and a coat with torn lining. Scattered about were old newspapers, letters, curtain remnants, and some dirty saucers used as ash trays. The woman who took him around kept apologizing. The old pastor had no close relatives, and some very distant kinsfolk had come and auctioned off everything a few weeks after the funeral. Everything should have been cleaned up before the vicar came, of course, but they had not gotten started yet.

Most repulsive were the tobacco stains. Mrs. Karlsson had excused them with the explanation that the old pastor chewed tobacco and could not rid himself of the bad habit of spitting on the floor.

The loathing returned and Torvik had a sense of nausea as he stood in the sunshine. He opened a window. Then he walked through the rooms, entering first the old dining room toward the west, which stood entirely empty. The wallpaper was torn, and there were cracks in the tile stove. Then he came to the kitchen. Here, perpetual twilight reigned and the sooty hood of the large fireplace jutted out in the room like a castle wall, and everything was dark brown with age and soot. From the kitchen he crossed the hallway to the study and opened a window there also. Would it be possible ever to air out his predecessor from this old crow's castle? Were the old memories pasted firmly to the walls?

He remembered the coming of autumn with its long and lonely evenings in the empty house. The owls hooted from the ancient maples outside, and he sometimes thought he heard eerie footfalls in the living room. He saw in imagination the figure of the old parson as it had been formed by the furtive remarks of the people, as marked by the unfortunate events of twenty years ago. These events had cost him a divorce and a year's suspension from service and had left him bitter and brokenhearted, and he sat alone stained with tobacco and his eyes suspiciously roaming around the walls. When darkness and autumn chill crept into the rooms as the young vicar sat at his desk in the study, a feeling of forsakenness and anguish stole into the house. No outsider could imagine what fortitude it took on such evenings to grope his way with a flashlight out into the living room to light the candles on the altar and read the service for the last canonical hour in the pale light while his breath froze in the raw, cold air.

The worst thing about this house, worse than the loneliness itself, was these dark memories, a cursed fate woven of broken marriage vows, hoarse and fretful voices, and an old man's restless steps. These created the very atmosphere of the house, they seeped into the chronic smell of the damp and moldy flooring, of rat dung, and of decades of dust piled up behind tile stoves that were beginning to crumble.

Pastor Torvik sat down at the old study desk, a cumbersome thing of oak with sculptured heads and bombastic fittings. He rested his head in his hands.

This, then, was the church of the fathers as it appeared in its reality! For twenty years no record of communions had been kept and there had been no celebration of the Lord's Supper except in connection with confirmation. There had been no visitation of the sick for a decade, as far as he could discover. Many a time the old rector did not conduct a Sunday service. It was even said that, rather than hold a service for four or five persons, he would sometimes ask those who had come to return to their homes voluntarily. The collections had seldom amounted to ten crowns in a quarter year, and baptisms were hardly known in the community, since they had begun to baptize all children at the maternity hospital.

How had he really lived through this first year?

First, he had the parsonage cleaned and scrubbed. Next, he bought some furniture for the room just beyond the study, so that he might at least be able to receive visiting parishioners properly. Up in his east gable chamber he had his bed, a wash stand, an unpainted table, a stained pine bureau, and three small, unmatched chairs. Mrs. Karlsson came three days a week and cleaned. He ate his meals alone at the Karlsson home.

By the end of his first year he had at least gotten his finances to balance. He had found, a few weeks after moving in, that he had gone pretty much in debt through the purchase of the furniture and other things that he absolutely needed in order to get established in this deserted house. At the same time he had to take care of the installment payments. Having no one at hand to turn to for temporary financial help, he had borrowed a bicycle and had made a humiliating trip to the rector at Ravelunda. Fortunately, this man was a man of honor, a rustic gentleman with orthodox ideas who was always ready to help and had considerable experience in the affairs of this world. Torvik had gone to him more than once when he was at the point of losing the last spark of courage because of his loneliness.

And then he really got going in the parish work. If he had hoped that it would be a thankful task to take hold with fresh initiative in working a neglected field, he was soon disappointed. After the large crowds that had come the first three Sundays, the average attendance dropped to thirty or forty each Lord's Day. And it stayed at this point. It seemed as if all living religion in this area was centered in the mission house at Svedjefallet. There was, to be sure, also a little group in Sörbygden connected with the Foundation. With the last mentioned he had gotten at odds from the beginning. At a funeral in those parts he had presented the modern exegetical view of "the legend" concerning the virgin birth, and since then it was obvious that he was not regarded with confidence in those circles. The "northeasterners" did come to church now and then—rather often in fact, considering that they had so far to go—but they were wont to sit with heads aslant and with watchful eyes, and on the lookout for false teaching.

Communion at the Lord's Table was, however, his greatest disappointment. He had preached and admonished, he had invited and importuned, but to no avail. If he announced a communion service, even regular churchgoers who were known to be churchly minded in other respects stayed at home. The only people who came to the Lord's Supper with any regularity were the northeasterners. He honored them for that, even though he realized that this was not in any way the fruit of his efforts.

What would the future be like? In three more weeks the year of his assignment as vicar here would be at an end. Then the rectorship would ordinarily be assigned to a regular incumbent. But since it was still an open question whether or not the pastorate should be united with that of Näs, and it was thought that because of the shrinking population it could be cared for by a curate, there had been no election, and its care for a year or two would be assigned to a temporary rector. This would mean that such a person would receive the full salary. Torvik could hardly hope for such a fine promotion after a single year's ministerial experience. He would therefore have to be resigned to further roving as assistant within the consistory. For that reason he scanned the newspapers anxiously each Thursday for any news about the diocese. It would certainly cause him no sorrow to leave Ödesjö. But he wondered with a certain anxiety what adventures and disappointments his next assignment would bring him.

There was no use denying that he longed to be back at Upsala. He had done some work already toward the licentiate examination, and had done pretty well in the history of religion. Also during this last year of solitude he had found time to do considerable reading. And since he was more and more convinced that he was not fit to be a parish pastor, it would be better now than later to prepare himself for a post as a teacher.

His parish work had really not been encouraging. He was too shy to talk with people, would rather sit undisturbed at home and read, and literally had to force himself to make sick calls and visit the shut-ins. He did not, for that matter, feel competent to talk with these people. One day during his first weeks, a Pentecostalist lady evangelist had come to ask for a letter of transfer, and they had begun to converse about baptism. He had had a hard time of it. Afterward he combed through his library for something substantial about baptism, but had neither found any facts as to the antiquity of infant baptism, nor concerning its Biblical grounds. The only thing he found, which no doubt might be correct in itself, was that the legitimacy of infant baptism could not be based on individual proof texts, but must rest on its whole inner association with the central content of Christianity. But certainly you could not effectively make such a statement to a Pentecostalist preacher or, for that matter, to anyone else in these parts.

And then there was the case of the girl whom the district court had sent him for instruction as to the seriousness and importance of an oath. It was a paternity case. He had talked briefly of one thing and another, and since she wanted her papers immediately, he had salved his conscience by noting that she had a good confirmation record. So he had filled out the certificate. Three months later she was found drowned— had drowned herself, people said. Since that day, an additional black shadow crouched behind the doors of the desolate parsonage.

He could continue in this manner the recital of an endless succession of failures. There was the first draft evader, who came one stormy day in January. Once again it was a battle without honor, ending in sorry retreat. Then there were all those old fashioned believers with their plaguing questions. It was evident that they wanted to feel his pulse, and to discover what thoughts he had about the Atonement and about the believer's freedom from the law. What did he know about such things? They were not satisfied with a few pious phrases; they wanted factual answers. And they knew their Bibles. After a few embarrassing defeats, he had stopped arguing with them. He had memorized very few Bible verses himself. He had always been taught that this constant use of proof texts was a mistaken theological method. It was important, rather, to analyze every matter in accordance with the gospel. What irritated him was that he was never able to show why the spirit of the gospel insisted on just that answer to a question which he was accustomed to give. The others could always point to the letter of the Scripture, and that always made an impression.

Pastor Torvik shook his broad shoulders in disgust. He took up a book that happened to lie opened under some county notices. It was Cumont's *Die Mysterien des Mithra*. At that moment the telephone rang.

A timid and faltering woman's voice asked to speak with the pastor. She informed him that the old woman at Kvarnlyckan was ill and had asked that the pastor come and give her the Lord's Supper.

Torvik felt a strange mixture of surprise, of irritation at being disturbed just as he was ready to engage in the studies planned for the day, and of joy at finally being asked to give pastoral service. Of course he would come, and immediately. He hung up the receiver.

He already had on his clergy coat. It was a matter of principle with him to wear it weekdays, as well as Sundays. He opened the safe and took out the old and worn leather communion case. He made sure that there was wine in the silver flask which fitted into the hollow foot of the chalice, and that there were wafers in the host box. He sat down a moment and turned the pages of his handbook. This was the second time he was summoned for this kind of service since ordination. He was not very familiar with the ritual. He had no concern about the preparatory address, since he could always speak about the significance of the sacrament. That was one of his favorite subjects.

It was fortunate that he knew the way to Kvarnlyckan. Before leaving he had, however, refreshed his memory concerning the old woman by referring to the church records. Johanna Kristina Johansson, born Gustafsdotter, a tailor's widow, born March 8, 1852, widowed August 19, 1927—that was her life story in a single line. She was known as "Mother."

But he was not sure about which given name, Hanna or Stina, she went by.

After a warm walk across pastures and fields, the pastor arrived at Anneberg. It was a house with a steep, divided roof and wide gables, and was quite recently built. Yet the sight of it gave him an uncomfortable feeling, as he remembered that his opponent in the conflict about the church heating system, carpenter Joelsson, lived here.

So he was now again thinking about that episode! Why could he not forget that insult? It had started over a trifling matter. The one ministerial gown that the church possessed was of the ancient, absurdly narrow "rat-tail" type. Since it was moth-eaten and ragged, he had sent for a new one. When he presented the bill to the treasurer, the man showed surprise and asked that, in the interest of proper procedure, he get authorization from the church council before paying it. Torvik had therefore presented the matter at the next meeting of the council casually as a mere formality. Young Schenstedt, owner of the Saleby estate, had then spoken with unexpected sharpness and declared that it was an old custom at Ödesjö never to spend beyond the budgetary amounts, and that since the apportionment for unexpected items was already used up, he could not authorize the expenditure without the consent of the parish. Torvik felt insulted and indignant and said something rather bitter about letting the sacred service of the Lord be administered in old rags green with age, such as even the smallest manor house would be ashamed to nail to the wall of an attic closet to keep out the draught. Since that day Schenstedt had been his adversary.

He had learned this when the heating system in the church was under discussion. There were two old stoves whose smoke painted black mourning bands on the ceiling. When the winter cold finally seeped through the massive walls of the church the burned-out stoves were wholly ineffective. The air right under the ceiling and near the stoves was warm, but the pews were as cold as if they had been standing out in the churchyard. He had then brought up the subject in the church council and asked that he might secure bids for a new heating plant. Schenstedt had at once made things difficult, insisting that a parish meeting should be called to guarantee the necessary funds. Later, when various plans had been proposed and he himself expressed the conviction that a low-pressure steam heating system would be most advantageous, Schenstedt had naturally urged the adoption of the cheaper project proposed, namely, a hot air system. When a day in March had finally been set for the meeting, Schenstedt had conducted a purposeful agitation for his plan. The meeting was well attended, sharp words were exchanged from the very beginning, and the arguments on both sides were heated. When Schenstedt finally alluded to the business about the cape as an example of the vicar's arbitrary way of dealing with public funds, he had used his gavel in protest and asked him to stick to the subject under discussion. Schenstedt had answered that it was useless to discuss a question when the chairman was party in the case and used his position to silence all criticism of himself. He had even suggested that the chairman should relinquish the gavel. Naturally he had refused to do so and had appealed to the meeting, which gave him a vote of confidence, even though it was not unanimous. With respect to the heating system, however, the majority had voted with Schenstedt. On top of all this, there had been a pretty bitter account of the meeting in one of the newspapers. It was generally believed that Schenstedt was in back of this, too. Torvik had the feeling that he was being laughed at behind his back. It made him furious.

What was more lamentable was that Schenstedt was in reality an intelligent and alert individual. He belonged to an old family that had owned Saleby for more than a hundred years. Long ago the head of the clan had borne the title of baron, but there were some doubts as to the actual rank of the family, which was thought to be of Danish origin. The present owner, Gunnar Schenstedt, was at this time about thirty-five years of age. He had qualified as a student at Lund and had studied there a few terms, but had changed his course of study and had finished at the forestry school to prepare himself for the care of the large forests at Saleby. His handsome face with the brown eyes and the dark skin gave the impression of gentleness and restlessness in combination. He was broad-shouldered, a bit shorter than the average, and always well-dressed. He was sensitive and unpredictable. Torvik had the impression that he belonged to the problem people who like to talk about themselves and to be at the center in anything in which they take part. At the same time there was something boyishly impulsive and unaffectedly loveable about him when he showed this side of his nature. He lived alone at Saleby. Occasionally, his sister visited him, and of late had been making longer and longer stays. She was of the same restless nature, and it was said that her marriage—her husband was a captain in Stockholm—was not too happy, and that she was wont to come to Saleby when she wanted to get away from her husband for a while. But she did not exactly feel at home in Ödesjö either, since she did not fit into that rural milieu. Certainly she was the only woman in the parish who smoked cigarettes and could mix a cocktail. These things did not make her any more popular.

It was in any case too bad that the cultured and broad-minded Schenstedt, the only person in the parish with an academic education, who should have been the pastor's best friend, had instead become his most dangerous adversary.

Torvik was thinking about these unpleasant things as he continued on his way through the pasture on the other side of Anneberg. After a few more minutes of walking he caught sight of Kvarnlyckan. It was an old crofter's cottage.

The pastor stepped into the entrance way and knocked. No one answered from the living room. Then he tried the kitchen door, and heard a growling answer. Bending his head low, he entered the room. It was often the case in these old houses that one could not stand erect but had to bow the head and sometimes bend the knees a bit. To his surprise he found the sick woman sitting up and fully dressed on the bench behind the kitchen table. She had small eyes and a pale, plain face. There was a fire in the kitchen stove, and the coffee pot stood on it. No other person was visible.

When he began to ask about her health, he was given a detailed recital of all her sufferings: the arthritis in her hands, the dizziness, the pains in her chest, and the swollen legs. Torvik listened patiently. He had learned that old people should be allowed to tell their story in full. But it did seem to him that this almost pleasurable dissection of the afflictions of a lifetime was a little strange in one who was about to receive the Lord's Supper. He realized that it might possibly be because she had not had opportunity to recite her ills to anyone for quite some time. He therefore listened patiently to all she had to say, nodded occasionally, and put in a word here and there. The impression grew that this talkative woman was not as ill in body as he had imagined on his way to her home. When she finally reached the present moment in her account and began to tell how she now felt, she did seem to become weaker, her eyelids closed, and she looked ill. The pastor was not really convinced, however. He felt it was time for him to say something.

"And now you want to receive the Lord's Supper?"

The old woman sighed. She said she wanted to be prepared to die. She felt that her strength was departing from her, and she did not want to be found dead in her home some morning without even having had the opportunity to be shriven. Two tears rolled down her cheeks.

"Well then, you know, Mother Hanna, that it is necessary to examine oneself before communion."

"Yes, Pastor, and I know that I am worthy."

The words startled the pastor. He had encountered those who believed the opposite, but he had never before heard anyone make *this* claim.

"You know that when you have examined yourself, you must confess your sins."

"Yes, Pastor, we are all sinners."

"If therefore there is anything special, you can confidently tell me about it here. You know that I am not allowed to tell it to anyone, but will be as silent as the walls."

He was glad that for once he could serve as a shepherd of souls. The feeling that he was a father confessor was increased as he saw a gleam in the woman's eyes that seemed to suggest that she really had something to confide to him.

"Since you promise not to tell anyone, Pastor, there is one thing I want to tell you." She leaned forward over the table and lowered her voice. "The assessor in Eksta is a thief."

Torvik could scarcely conceal a smile. The man of whom she spoke was chairman of the pension board, and was as honest a man as ever walked.

"The assessor in Eksta? What, then, has he stolen?"

"He takes my poor money, Pastor. He has been oppressing me ever since my husband died. Then he cheated me out of eighteen crowns, which part of my inheritance I never received. And when later I was to get a pension, he saw to it that I got less than Evert in Hästhagen. Where do you think that money goes?"

"But you must understand, Mother Hanna, that it is because Evert does not own a penny that his pension is larger. If you had not received a little inheritance from Johansson, you would have received as large a pension as he."

The woman winked knowingly.

"Pastor, you don't know the assessor. But I know him, that bloodsucker. He has always dealt unjustly with the poor."

"But, Mother Hanna," said the pastor, who had a sudden inspiration, "*if* it is as you say, and the assessor has acted wrongly, then you must forgive him with all your heart."

"Forgive him? Never, Pastor. I'll never forgive him until he lays that money on this table."

In his consternation, Torvik struck both hands on the table.

"But, my dear woman, he who will not forgive will not be forgiven."

"If the assessor will come and place the money on the table and *ask* for forgiveness, I'll give it to him."

"But that is not the way we are to forgive. To forgive is to remit everything another owes and not to mind that he has done wrong. Remember the parable of the unmerciful fellow servant! He had been forgiven ten thousand talents. He ought for that reason also have forgiven what his fellow servant owed him. If you are to receive forgiveness for your sins, you will have to forgive everyone who owes you anything."

"But there must be justice in everything, Pastor. I have never treated anyone so wrongly as the assessor has treated me. Then it surely is not just that I should forgive him unless I get my money back."

Torvik saw that it was hopeless to continue the discussion.

"You cannot come to the Lord's Supper in that spirit," he said with sternness.

The woman looked up at him, surprised and indignant.

"Am I, then, not worthy?"

"He who is unwilling to forgive cannot receive forgiveness. If you will not forgive the assessor, you cannot receive the sacrament."

"Well then, I'll go without it," she said.

Torvik stared at her in shocked surprise. There she sat with her taut wrinkled features. She looked straight ahead unyieldingly, not allowing her eyes to meet those of the pastor, her hands pressed hard on the table top. What was really her inner state? Why had she asked him to come?

"But, Mother Hanna," he said in a conciliatory tone, "I can see very well that you nevertheless sincerely long to receive the Lord's Supper."

"Oh, you don't need to urge your wares on me. If you think I am so big a sinner that I am unworthy to receive the sacrament, I'll not beg it of you."

"But, my dear woman," said Torvik, sadly and uncertainly, "do not get angry. I have never said that you are a greater sinner than others. We are all sinners, of course. But a sinner must forgive other sinners, if he is to receive forgiveness himself."

"You say that, Pastor, only because I am a poor woman. Were you speaking to the assessor in Eksta, it would sound differently."

Now Torvik had had enough.

"If you do not wish to receive communion, then I must thank you and take my leave," he said.

"Oh, there's nothing to thank for," said the woman, looking straight ahead. Torvik took his bag, which contained the black cape and the communion case, stooped at the doorway, and was again outside in the fresh air.

He straightened up and breathed deeply. Such, then, was the second call he had made as pastor and soul shepherd during the year since coming to Ödesjö. This self-righteous old woman, who wanted the sacrament only to bring attention to herself on account of her sickness and to enjoy the sentimental effects of the pastor's visit, thus represented exactly half of the spiritual need that could be found in his congregation. He returned home embittered.

It was only to be expected that the old woman would not keep silent about what had occurred. She would of course concoct an unpleasant story to embarrass the pastor. And of course there would be people who would believe her. Soon he would have nothing but traducers in Ödesjö. The sun shone with the warmth of summer. Yellow pollen filled the air and water ran in rills between the hummocks. When at last he came to the road he was perspiring heavily. With hat in hand and coat under his arm, he continued his walk through the pasture until he came to the parsonage fence, turned in at the white gate posts and entered the yard slowly between the old linden trees.

At that moment he thought about the eagerness and anticipation he had felt two hours before when he had hurried away on a pastoral errand, hoping to find some dying person to whom he, as the consecrated servant of the church, could administer the holy sacrament. That was the dream, and this the stark reality. Did not the knotty tree trunks laugh at him?

When he came to his room he took off the coat and changed shirts. Just as he was about to put on the starched collar, he paused a moment and stood holding it in his hand. Then he threw it on the bureau, opened the drawer and looked through its untidy contents for a soft collar and a red tie. Then, from the clothes closet under the roof boards, where a cluster of flies buzzed about the open window, he took his summer suit of gray tweed.

Mrs. Karlsson's eyes were big with surprise when at two o'clock she saw the pastor coming to dinner in this civilian elegance, which besides the suit and red tie, included colored socks and tan shoes. He offered no word of explanation. As usual, he carried under his arm a book with some unintelligible title, and from this he read during the entire meal. Mrs. Karlsson would have liked to ask, but since she surmised that the transformation had something to do with a forthcoming engagement, she considerately kept silent.

Pastor Torvik, who was absent-mindedly helping himself to still another dessert pancake while at the same time reading Cumont, had as a matter of fact not the least thought of marriage on his mind. His whole inner being seethed in desperate revolt against this existence, into which destiny had forced him. One moment he told himself that God must have adjudged all evangelical Christianity unfit to live, and that the Reformation was really an unfortunate falling away from the Church of God, and that this apostasy was now being punished. The next moment he felt that the fault was that Christianity had completely lost its hold on the Swedish people. The nation could never again become a people of God. One or another ecstatic sect might still be able to make some headway among simple souls open to suggestion, but for a university man it would be better to withdraw and have one's faith in private, and let the whole sorry mess proceed on its way to catastrophe. Between times, he tried to impress on his mind the fundamental plan of the Mithra temple at Heddernheim.

All that afternoon he read the history of religion. In the evening he said a brief prayer. He would skip the Compline. Sitting at the table, he prayed for light and guidance. In his heart he was already sure of the way he would take. He would go back to the university at Upsala. Shivering with the evening chill and inwardly ill at ease, he went to bed, and tried half unconsciously to formulate in his thoughts the most suitable form of request to the Cathedral Chapter for a leave of absence.

An endless road stretched toward the horizon. It was bordered by tall poplars which swayed and rustled in the storm. A strange, warm wind, heavy with humidity and noxious fumes, swept across the fields and robbed those outdoors in the night of their breath. It must have been early dawn now, and the low clouds that tumbled their twisted shapes in the sky showed in their rifts a pale light which was like a streak of blood trembling in the gray sky.

Torvik walked as in a dream. He scarcely felt the ground on which he trod. With every step, he was lifted from the road by the terrific onset of the storm. In the semi-darkness he caught a glimpse of other figures, all walking in the same direction, bent forward in the wind, with outstretched necks and half closed eyes and faces that appeared a ghostly white in the pale light.

Suddenly it brightened. A fiery light beamed high above the clouds. It fell from the vaulted heavens earthward in waves of light that spread into the night in ever widening circles. Wave followed upon wave, till the light reached the horizon of the plain in glittering surf. The clouds seemed to roll onward in ragged carmine shapes, while in the azure zenith a whiteness of unbearable brilliance was revealed.

A sound with the ring of steel cut through the storm, a trembling, brittle, metallic tone, as if the very dome of heaven had been set in vibration by a mighty blow. The sound became more intense, a whining roar, a wild and anguished crashing, hiding within it infinite depths of darkest terror.

Existence itself was shattered.

Far beyond the possibilities of all earthly laws of sound, a primeval thunder rolled and crashed, laden with annihilating power and overwhelming terror. High above all earthly light, shone an unfathomable and indescribable brightness. The dome of heaven was riven, and the Power revealed itself and descended, over-mastering and annihilating in its might.

Torvik saw how the poplar leaves shriveled and the last living branches drooped toward the ground, as if the life in them had been commanded to withdraw. He saw people throw themselves headlong to the ground, hiding their faces in their hands. He was enveloped by light and gripped by the Power. He felt that it filled his innermost being. He sensed how it possessed him and always had possessed him. Freedom and self-sufficiency faded like empty illusions. Everything was infinitely dependent and unconditionally bound to the Unspeakable. Life was not his own, but flowed into him every second from above, and he felt with fear and trembling that that flow could be broken at any time and that his body could at any moment succumb to death and dissolution like the withering trees. He realized that everything was a gift and a loan, that every cell in his tissues acknowledged the Power as its source and owner, that the Infinite was one with the life in his members and pulsed warmly to his very fingertips, pumping the blood through the arteries, holding his psyche together, so that the chain of his thoughts did not break.

A quivering sound shot through the sea of light and everything was enveloped by the penetrating peal of trumpets. Earth trembled and gave way, and the void was filled with glittering and reverberating chords.

Christ is coming, he thought, and the kingdom of heaven is like a king who takes account of his servants.

———

He stood in the presence of the Power and the Glory. Beneath him and behind him was an endless and engulfing darkness, a chaotic night of cold and terror. He felt the darkness clutching at him, he heard its cry from the depths, heard how it heaved and tumbled. He felt its approach from behind. Chilled to the bone with fear, he reached out for something to support him, but everything was empty nothingness. Before him he had the Power and the Majesty, to which he dared not lift his eyes. He had only the perception of a glowing, molten mass, of a consuming heat that could destroy him at any moment, should it come but a hairbreadth closer. He heard royal lips speak with other-worldly clearness, brandishing words like shining blades of steel. He was conscious of horsemen rushing by, the whirr of white wings. Somewhere above his trembling shoulders the *Book* must be lying!

Now that Book was to be opened. He was being lifted up. With startled wonder, he looked down as from above upon his own life.

He saw a wide, white church with bare walls. The sun shone in from the northwest. It was an evening in late summer. The chancel was bright in the rays of the sun. The chalice mirrored the warm light in unnatural splendor. At the wide altar rail young lads knelt shoulder to shoulder. Kneeling with them was himself, a tall overgrown high school student who had been overwhelmed by God. He stammered awkward prayers, his heart overflowed. Now he knew why. From above, from a bridge of light, came a flowing down from the Infinite One and poured itself upon him, suffusing his being like a corposant, touched him so that he trembled in blessed ecstasy. In the chalice the blood glowed a dark ruby red. A drop of the Infinite fell from the rim of the lifted chalice upon his heart and marked it with a living fire-red seal. And a voice was heard, saying, "Called of God."

The page was turned. He saw himself with a schoolmate in a rowboat. A breeze rippled the water gently, leaving a triangle of waves in the wake of the boat. Heard his comrade's voice: "Tell me, what were you really doing at that meeting you attended?" And he heard his own voice telling some stories that were vulgar and suggestive. As the laughter resounded over the water, a voice was heard clear as the ring of steel: "Thou art weighed in the balance and found wanting."

Again a page was turned.

The sun illuminated the edge of the ditch where the weeds waved in the wind. There he lay with his marching shoes propped against the clay bank, his uniform unbuttoned, and his hands clasped behind his head. Above him on the field edge sat the horseman, a giant of a man, puffing his pipe. He spat and remarked with disdain, "And when you have dug through all your books at Upsala, what will you do then?" And he heard his own voice answer with feigned indifference, "Well, I'll think about it. Maybe I'll be a teacher." But a red longing glowed in the heavens and sought for a way to the horseman's heart and for a witness to be borne. And a stern voice sounded from the thin summer clouds: "Whosoever shall be ashamed of me and my words, of him shall the Son of man be ashamed when he cometh in the glory of his Father."

The page was turned again. The street lights shone through the November fog, which rose raw and cold from the stream which flowed through the old university city. He saw himself with turned-up collar hurrying across the bridge with a book under his arm. He ran down the street with swift steps as though he were fleeing Someone. He felt his cheeks growing hot. He remembered exactly what book it was. He had borrowed it from one of his student friends at the fraternity house, saying something about the necessity for keeping up with modern literature. His comrade had agreed, bolstering his stand with some literary clichés. But they had not looked each other in the eye, knowing only too well that they delved into this trash, though neither ever had time to read the classics. And the Voice spoke, sadly: "But fornication and uncleanness . . . let it not once be named among you."

Again a page was turned, with quiet, relentless consistency.

It was Sunday morning. The cathedral bells rang heavily. A gray, cold morning light filled his student lodging, whose small dormer window looked out upon the ugly yard. He turned toward the wall, tired and heavy-hearted, to get some more sleep. A shame which he would not admit ached within him. After a night like this he ought not go to church. But a note of doom mingled with the heavy cathedral bells: "They have made them crooked paths; whosoever goeth therein shall not know peace."

Now the pages were being turned more swiftly.

There was the fraternity banquet at the beginning of the last seminary term. Loud peals of laughter echoed through the room. There were clever jokes with the professors and instructors as targets. There was festive gaiety in the smoke-filled room. Viewed now from above it had a grotesque aspect. He saw himself sitting there, the red seal of God on his heart, created to be God's own, called to serve him. There sat this possession of God and imagined that he was a free spirit, with self-complacency's unlimited right to heckle others, for whom he ought rather to have prayed, rejoicing over the sins of others which ought instead to have saddened him.

Similar scenes presented themselves. There was the dinner in the old coffee shop, where the latest public disputation scandal was delightfully dissected. There was the hazing of new members at the fraternity house. There was the midnight hike with the boys to the end of the promenade and the big argument about the election of a housemaster. What had become of responsibility and service? And of brotherly love?

The scenes kept changing. He saw himself on a warm June day walking outside the Chapter house in Linköping wearing a tall silk hat, waiting for his ordination examination to begin. At his side walked a comrade from Lund whom he did not know. They made a fumbling attempt at contact with each other, but since neither knew anything about the convictions of the other, they talked only about the assignments they might possibly be given. This led to conjectures about the older pastors under whom they might serve. They joked about them without shame, and tried to appear witty and clever. Then he was in Ödesjö. The pictures flickered before him as though they were produced by a jerky old motion picture projector. Black spots kept creeping across the picture and, oddly enough, always seemed to thicken about himself. Seen in this macabre light, everything appeared shabby and tattered. There lay the old prostitute at Ölstorpet on her dirty sickbed. As for himself, he was at home reading Frazer's *The Golden Bough*. The day passed; the old woman swore in her pain, and now and then looked with helpless hunger through the window toward heaven. The night went by. Again he started the day with reading Frazer. Toward evening Lotta from Skräddarlyckan came with the news that the old woman was dead. Above the howling of the wolves, he heard a prolonged and tragic cry: "If thou speakest not to warn the wicked from his wicked way . . . his blood will I require from thy hand."

Sermon preparation, distracted musings, then reading the newspapers, or filling out some certificates—these made a welcome break in the routine. Saturday came, bringing the mail and a new issue of the church quarterly. That day passed. Late at night one might hear the scratching of his pen. His sermon never got finished, never was written in full, nor thought through. It was not based on prayer or the Word of God. Much of the same sort of thing he was now clearly aware of.

Then there were the meetings of the church council and that unpleasant parish meeting in March. In this strange light from above it was all laid frighteningly bare. He tried in vain to give his attention to Schenstedt in order to discover how his intrigue and malevolence would appear in this light. He saw only a little, immature child, behind whose broad shoulders and dark skin hid a hungry soul that knew no peace. He saw how the heavenly light reached down again and again in flickering bands to lay hold of the child in the man's soul, but was constantly repulsed. Then he heard his own voice, hard, irritated, and malicious. It cut through the air like a sharp dagger and wherever it struck the bands of heavenly light were cut off, the severed ends fell like chrysanthemum petals to the floor, and Schenstedt stepped upon them with his feet, a haughty and mocking smile upon his face. But somewhere in the distance a cry of disillusionment was heard. The ground shook with the tramp of many feet, there was the clang of armor and lances, and from heaven great drops of blood fell, the hotly burning spray from the agitated chalice, which overflowed with the wine of the stern wrath of God.

He fell to the ground.

Only one thought possessed him—how to get away, to hide himself in the earth, to feel the rocks and cliffs crashing over his head. But there was no place to hide. He sank into empty nothingness. He felt an enveloping darkness underneath, a concentrated evil will possessed with the satanic joy of destruction. It widened into a gaping abyss, a black pit of eternal terror, to the bottom of which he fell with dizzying swiftness.

His chest was being constricted as if by bands of steel. A shout of horrible anguish came like a dry, hot stream over his lips.

The next instant he again rested on something solid. He heard the familiar squeak of the steel springs of his tourist bed and saw some pale reflections dancing on the ceiling between the big brown moisture spots.

He jumped out of bed and stood on the cold floor, clearly aware of his trembling knees and of the flapping of his pajama top, icily damp against the beads of perspiration on his chest. The next moment he staggered to the door and locked it securely. Then, still only half awake, he went to the window and raised the shade.

A pale daylight shone through the naked crowns of the maples. There had been a frost during the night and a grayish-brown pastel shade tinted the branches of the trees. There was an infinite quiet.

Shaking with cold, he went back to bed and pulled up the blankets. He was finally able to think straight, but still felt the terror in his bones. Never had he had such a nightmare. He had had dreams often in the past, long dreams that hung together with some sort of logic. But this was something else. This feeling of anguish had a primitive power beyond anything he had thought possible. From the point of view of religious psychology this dream was of great value to him. He had experienced a visible manifestation of what was known as *tremendum* in the idea of God. He had read about such things, but had always thought about them in a purely theoretical way. Now it would be possible to understand better certain primitive rites—just as, for that matter, did Luther and Bunyan and the others for whom anguish of conscience played a religious role.

He began to tremble again. Would this terror never leave him? Was it his old heart trouble that was coming back? Or was it simply that he had eaten something yesterday that did not agree with him?

He turned over again in the creaking bed. The day had dawned, and details could now be clearly distinguished. It was four-thirty in the morning.

Suppose there was after all a bit of truth behind the mythological symbolism of his frightful dream! Could a human soul really be lost? Then surely that must be as terrifying as what he had experienced in his dream.

And he, himself? He could not get away from it. The judgments he had heard were not just sickly fantasies. There was bitter truth in many of the bizarre pictures presented.

He lay prone on the bed, his hands folded and his face buried in the pillow. Was there after all something of the voice of God in this nightmare? If so, it could not be misunderstood. As a Christian, he was weighed in the balance and found wanting.

He sat up. There was no purpose in lying there and torturing himself. He might as well get up at once. As he dressed, he came to the conclusion that he would not let this experience pass without thinking it through. He could at least subject himself to an honest self-examination. Perhaps there was some meaning in all this.

He lit a fire in the tile stove, which had not been touched since yesterday. Then he went downstairs for his Bible. His eyes happened to fall on the book shelf. After a moment's hesitation, he picked out two small volumes and returned with them to his room, which was already becoming comfortably warm from the crackling fire in the stove.

He sat down beside the unpainted table at the window and bowed his head in his folded hands. When he had sat thus for quite a while, he picked up a card on which were printed in blue and red the words, "Quietness before God."

Be quiet. This was the first admonition.

Remember that you are now in the presence of the Living God.

Once again he was seized by a crushing sense of insignificance in the presence of an overwhelming Power. As he sat here, he realized that he was completely borne and supported by God's power. He could feel the pulse beat in his wrists. Without a constant fresh supply of God's creative will, it would beat no more. Life, which made it possible for him to raise his eyes and look out through the window or move his foot under the chair, was then a gift which he must accept second by second from God's hand. At any moment his Lord and Owner could take back the gift at will and bid him give an account of his stewardship of it. He would be held responsible for every minute of the day which he was now entering upon, and in which he was supported by the Almighty. He must live in the presence of this Lord. He dropped to his knees and rested his elbows on the edge of the table.

Self-examination. This was the next item on the card. *Ask yourself: Am I willing to commit myself wholly to God?* The very thought made him dizzy. He felt at the moment as if he were stepping on an ice floe that, with a roar, had broken loose from the shore. Where would a surrender to the whims of the river take him? Would the road ever lead back to Upsala? Would he ever again be able to devote himself for a single day to his books? Would he be able as before to lock the door and reserve certain hours for himself and for his own interests as *liber studiosus?*

But in the same moment the thought struck him that it would after all do no good to try to break away. God possessed him already. He was responsible for every moment as it was. And the stream would carry him relentlessly toward the place where it would be apparent that all this talk about taking care of oneself or living as a free individual was a miserable illusion. It would be folly to hesitate in the choice. It would be cowardly and disloyal. Now he would commit himself entirely. He would be a good soldier and take orders.

Am I willing to break with every sin of which I am conscious and give up everything that weakens the sensitivity of my conscience and my love of God?

That he must do, he agreed. The Lord helping him, there must be an end to laziness, fear, antipathy toward people, desire for applause, and sensitiveness to the slightest criticism. He had been trying to excuse himself with the claim that he was not qualified to be a parish pastor, when as a matter of fact it was his own comfort-loving, cowardly, and self-centered ego that was unfitted for life among others and for serving them.

He continued to read point by point. He came to the four absolutes: absolute honesty, purity, unselfishness, and love. They were four mortal blows aimed at his way of fulfilling his ministry, from the episode of the vestment to the neglect of the old and the sick.

Next on the card were these words:

Am I willing to live in a right relationship to all men?

Also with Schenstedt?

Am I willing as quickly as possible, guided by God's Spirit, to make amends for the wrongs I have done my neighbor?

Here the demand grew more exacting. There was no way of escaping it. He squirmed under God's grip. Nothing less would do: He must go to Saleby.

He still delayed the decision. But he had already given a half promise. He wanted only to wait for the right moment and the best approach.

He continued with the prayer card, prayed in great earnestness for the forgiveness of his sins and for grace to make a new start.

He sat down again and opened the Bible. He read the twelfth chapter of Romans with earnest consideration, and became more and more convinced that he had never been a Christian. He began to read with ever greater eagerness. He read Philippians, the third chapter, and the First Letter of John, making frequent pauses and underscoring certain passages. It struck him as he read that he had certainly never before read the Bible in this manner; simply to discover how he himself might become a Christian.

The sun had risen outside, and the golden yellow morning light filled the room and shone on the papered door with its ugly grease smudge around the keyhole. The birds were singing and rejoicing and the hoarfrost was already being transformed into shining moisture on the resinous buds of the trees.

"Now the sun is rising also upon my life," thought Torvik. "God shall have the power and the glory. And for me, now, service and obedience begin."

It struck him that, up to this day, everything had been just the opposite. It was he himself who had the power, also the power to choose a suitable life philosophy for himself. His problem had been whether or not Christianity really sufficed. He had tried to be modern in his thinking about God. He had defended Jesus and declared that he must be considered as the unequaled example also for our day, even though one must of course pass by that in his teaching which was determined by the historical situation and had significance only for his own era. He had championed Christian morals and tried to show their superiority to both affirmation of life, psychoanalysis, and the modern nationalism. But all the while it was he that passed judgment and assumed the right to accept or reject. His standard of measurement was that of science and modern man. The validity of the Christian faith depended entirely on whether he found it worthy of acceptance.

But now it had become perfectly clear to him that the real problem was not whether Christianity was sufficient, but rather whether his own Christianity measured up. His right to judge was shattered altogether. It was no longer he who passed judgment on the religions; it was God who was passing judgment upon him. He was a sinner who must start again from the beginning.

He continued his reading. He looked through a number of pamphlets which friends at Upsala had given him. In those days he had entrenched himself behind a wall of reservations. But now he was eager to read all this about Christian renewal and about the all-inclusive revolution that begins with the individual's total self-commitment.

Toward breakfast time Mrs. Karlsson again caught sight of the pastor in his civilian summer suit. For the first time in a long while he was not carrying a book under his arm. He looked pale, but his greeting was more cordial than usual and he even spoke a few words as she brought in the food. Between times, his thoughts seemed to be far afield. She was surer than ever that her theory as to his engagement was correct.

All day long Torvik battled with himself. He read, he prayed, he walked to and fro in the garden. When the sun began to top the pine trees in the west, where the last outcroppings of the Heding hills toward the south loomed beyond the Saleby woods, he was finally ready. He took his bicycle and started off.

In front of Saleby manor house were two large stretches of lawn with apple trees and lovely pines. A thick hedge separated the orchard from the highway. Wrought-iron gates swung from two huge pillars of roughly hewn stone.

Torvik left his bicycle at the edge of the ditch outside the gate. Protected from view by the hedge, he walked back and forth a few times and looked down the road toward the church, much as a prisoner through a barbed wire enclosure. Then he turned resolutely and made his way slowly through the gateway.

Before lifting the heavy knocker, he mumbled a prayer. He was greatly excited and aware of the rapid beating of his heart.

He was admitted to the hall which through an arched entrance led to the living room. Here Schenstedt's sister made her appearance. She was dressed in brown-striped sport clothes. She met him with a radiant smile.

"Well, well! Is our pastor honoring us with a visit?"

There was just a hint of reproach in her friendliness, and Torvik felt that he blushed. It was really true that he had neglected to visit Saleby. Could that perhaps be the first reason for Schenstedt's animosity?

"Marianne, will you call the Master? He is showing the new gardener where to plant some trees." The added remark was for Torvik's information.

He was invited to the main hall, which was furnished in the best manor house style, and landed somewhere in the middle of the enormous divan.

The two were soon engaged in conversation, but it was mainly the captain's wife, who was a charming hostess, who kept it going. She asked about how everything was at the parsonage, about the food at the boarding house, as to the pastor's plans for the future and what he thought about the war in Spain.

Torvik heard the opening of the outer door, and stiffened visibly.

The next moment Schenstedt stood at the entrance to the room. His finely chiseled features expressed an embarrassed friendliness, mingled with half unconscious suspicions.

"What a surprise!" he said. "Welcome to Saleby, Pastor. You are in mufti today?"

"Yes. It seemed more pleasant to come as an ordinary human being," said Torvik. He was himself surprised at the calmness with which he spoke.

Schenstedt looked at him a bit uncertainly. He began to talk about the muddy roads. There was good reason for that, since Torvik's clothes were bespattered above the ankles. Embarrassed, he curled his big feet under the sofa.

"May we serve you some refreshment?" asked the sister.

"No, thank you. Please don't go to any trouble for my sake," said Torvik. "I shall have to leave very soon. It is only a very personal matter I would like to talk over with the squire."

It had taken an effort to say it. A retreat was no longer possible. Schenstedt's sister joked a little about what secret parish matters the gentlemen had to discuss, matters in which no woman in Ödesjö had ever had a say, in spite of their right to vote. Then she left the room.

Schenstedt looked questioningly at the pastor. He did not appear unfriendly, but it was apparent that he was prepared to draw sword if necessary.

"I have come to beg your pardon, sir, for having acted wrongly toward you both at the church council and at the parish meeting," said Torvik.

Schenstedt opened his mouth slightly, and his eyes widened. Then he lowered his eyes and turned very red. Torvik continued to speak.

"I realize now that I did not act as I ought. I was wrong already in the matter of the vestment. I ought to have acknowledged from the beginning that my behavior was nonchalant and high-handed. And at the parish meeting, sir, you were absolutely right in considering that I was making use of my position as chairman to maintain an indefensible position. For what I have mentioned, and for everything else I have said and thought about you, I sincerely ask your forgiveness."

Schenstedt now looked quite unhappy.

"But, dear Pastor, there is no occasion for it. I really have nothing to forgive you."

"Yes, sir, you have," said Torvik, and extended his hand.

"That we will not discuss. *If* there were anything, you know, Pastor, that as far as I am concerned no grudge is borne." He took Torvik's hand. Then he looked down again and blushed like a school boy.

"Then, Pastor, you'll have to pardon me in return," he said, "because I am not at all sure that I acted like a true gentleman in the matter."

Torvik could hardly believe his ears. He stammered a few words, and since they could no longer stand there holding hands, he said something about being glad that the matter was cleared up and promised that in the future he would not take sides in the question of the heating system, but would be content whatever the solution. He asked to be remembered to the hostess, and said farewell.

When he was almost at the gate, he heard running steps behind him, and when he looked back, he saw that it was Schenstedt.

"If I may, Pastor," he said, "I'll walk with you to the village. I have urgent business to see to at the municipal office."

They walked together down the muddy road. Torvik pushed the bicycle before him. It made splashing sounds as the water dropped from the dirty tire.

Schenstedt began to talk about Saleby and its past history. This naturally led to the mention of his own family. He talked about his mother, whom he had never seen, and about his father, the lieutenant who had met his death thirty years ago as the result of a riding accident. He had his grandmother to thank for whatever real upbringing he had had. She was still living, but very seldom visited Saleby. She was a godly woman. As a child she had experienced the great revival which visited Ödesjö at that time. Though Schenstedt had often laughed at her, he acknowledged that he had never met a better person.

"And deep down, sir, you would want to be like her yourself," Torvik remarked. Though it was a bold suggestion, he somehow felt that Schenstedt had led the conversation toward this subject on purpose.

"Maybe, maybe not. It's not so easy, let me tell you, Pastor."

He hesitated a little. Then he said, "Pastor, I have learned tonight to trust in you as an honest man. I had honestly thought that your religion was humbug, but I see that I was mistaken. Will you tell me straight out how you came to be a minister? I mean, how did you come to believe in God?"

Torvik began to tell about his childhood days, about his irreligious years at high school and college, and about his first encounter with God. He told about how he began to pray in an exploratory way, how he made contact, how his academic doubts were resolved when he learned to look upon Christianity from the historical point of view. Finally he admitted the humiliating truth that it was really not Christianity in earnest until he came to realize on this very day that he must place himself radically at God's disposal and make a thorough housecleaning and rid himself of everything that separated him from God and from other human beings.

It was evident that Schenstedt listened with interest. Very soon he began to speak quite unreservedly about himself, about the childhood faith that his grandmother had implanted in him, but which had vanished as early as the first term at Eksjö. During his years at the Forestry School he had become a confirmed materialist, both in theory and practice. But now, at home in the forests and in the rooms at Saleby, where his elders had left their well-worn hymnbooks, he had again gotten another fundamental view of life.

"I do not know whether I believe in God," he said, "but I am at all events religious."

They had arrived at the village crossroads. It was nearly dark. Torvik had the feeling of having come from church. This was the result, then, of his daring to go God's way! Now he decided to venture a further step.

"In the final analysis, doubts always come as a result of sin," he said.

"What, then, is sin?"

"It is everything that separates us from God and from other people."

Schenstedt seemed to be considering the answer.

"That might be almost anything. Am I right?"

"Whatever it is, it must be confessed and righted."

When Schenstedt did not reply, the pastor made haste to pursue the matter.

"Since we are already at the parsonage," he said, "perhaps I could let you have a couple of pamphlets that have been of great help to me?"

Schenstedt laughed pleasantly.

"So, you are a colporteur, too, Pastor? Well, I have no objection."

They entered through the parsonage gate. When Schenstedt, a few minutes later, reappeared, not only the prayer card, but also a few brochures were in his pocket. He whistled thoughtfully as he realized that he had talked in easy familiarity and friendship with his former foe.

It was not until the vicar had said good-bye from the stairs that he began to think how strange it was that Schenstedt had not used his automobile this evening, but had walked the four kilometers on foot. The only explanation was that they might have time to talk. Had this man really walked all this distance on muddy roads tonight only that he might talk about God? Perhaps there were others in the parish, for that matter, who were longing and waiting for an opportunity to talk about faith and the difficulties of faith.

Ashamed, yet happy, he crossed the yard to his supper. He did not care to read the Compline this night either, but he prayed a long time in his room. He prayed for all those to whom he had shown little true love, and he prayed that at least during the days that remained for him at Ödesjö, he might serve God in spirit and in truth. Finally he prayed for light to guide him on the way he was now to walk in a new obedience.

Why should it be so difficult to receive guidance?

He bowed his head in his hands and waited quietly. "Speak, Lord, for Thy servant heareth," he mumbled. Before him on the table lay a notebook and a pen.

Since Wednesday he had spent a long quiet period at the table in his room. He read his Bible with sincere hunger, and he planned his day in God's presence. There was no difficulty in respect to the immediate duties. He had the sick to visit, letters to write to old friends and enemies, one or another wrong within the parish to clear up. During these days he had succeeded in setting right almost everything by which he had given offense in Ödesjö. It had not been as easy in many places as it was at Saleby. Sometimes they just looked at him in mute embarrassment, but everyone, with the exception of the old widow at Kvarnlyckan, had shown him respect.

Only one thing was now lacking: definiteness with respect to his immediate future. Should he continue his studies? He had already written his application for leave of absence. But would he dare to mail it? He was not sure.

He finished dressing and went down to the desk in the office study. It was Saturday. Preparation of his sermon was almost completed. For the first time in many months he longed to enter the pulpit. He felt that he had a message that pressed powerfully for utterance and sought to be spoken as the Spirit dictated. Just as the Word had condemned his half-heartedness, even as it had shown him the deceptive falseness in a religiosity which made faith a mere lovely feeling for a few enjoyable hours, he was now eager to preach that Word about the Christ who must rule over our work, our possessions, our rest, and our very being with the power of a dictator.

After adding a bit more to his sermon, he went to breakfast. A cold, torrential rain lashed the pools in the yard. He hardly noticed it.

In the room where he ate at the boarding house, the week's mail was awaiting him. The milk driver from the village delivered it at this time of day. He opened the bag eagerly and looked at the large brown envelopes. No, there still wasn't anything from the Cathedral Chapter. He took the newspaper and sat down at the table.

―――――――――

Back in the parsonage he again assumed the listening attitude, his head bowed in his hands. Still no answer! Why did God keep silent?

At twelve o'clock the bus would be leaving with the morning mail. It was the last opportunity for the day to post the letter. He really ought not wait any longer with his application. But did he really dare take this step before he was sure of God's will? He prayed afresh.

At twenty minutes after twelve he got up, resolutely sealed the large brown envelope, put on his raincoat, and walked down toward the village. He dug his hands into his pockets and took longer steps.

At the post office he first shook off the water that had gathered in the crown of his hat, and then with his fingertips carefully drew forth the envelope from his briefcase so that it might not be soiled, and gave it to the postmistress. Just as he was about to leave, she remembered something, bent down behind the counter, picked up an envelope, and handed it to him.

"Pastor, here is a letter that was forgotten when the mail went out today."

Torvik thanked her and was on his way. When he came out on the veranda he took one look at the envelope and stopped short. It was from the Cathedral Chapter.

He was just beginning to open it when a car swung around the corner, its front wheels splashing cascades of water. The brakes were applied just as it neared the post office entrance. The door opened, and Schenstedt jumped out.

"Hello, old boy!" he called out as he hurried up under the cover of the veranda roof. "I've been looking for you. You must promise to come and see us. My sister is bound to talk with you about—uh—serious things, you understand, such as we talked about on the road yesterday. I can't tell her all about these matters. Thanks for the books. We have both read them."

Torvik stared at him. Had the spiritual development in Ödesjö, which had been dormant for so long, suddenly begun to move at a gallop?

"Thank you. I'll surely come," he said. "When should I come?"

"Could it be tonight? But perhaps it would not be right to invite the pastor out on a Saturday evening."

Torvik did not answer. He had opened the letter from the Cathedral Chapter. It contained an official folio, with "An Appointment" as superscription. In a single sweep of his eyes he had caught the gist of the statement: "The vicar Gösta Torvik is asked to remain as temporary rector in the pastorate of Ödesjö parish."

His head was in a whirl. Was this God's answer? This letter—and then this Schenstedt, who stood here and invited him to his home as a friend and a Christian brother? And this on the very day on which he had planned to retire from parish work and go back to his studies!

Schenstedt roused him from his musings.

"What's wrong, lad? You look as though the heavens had tumbled down on you."

"Not far from that. Wait a moment."

He was already inside the post office again. At the last moment the postmistress opened the outgoing bag of mail and pulled out the large envelope. He tore it to bits and threw them into the wastepaper basket, laughing at her surprise.

The mail bus was already signaling out in the street. The postmistress hurried out the back way, and Torvik went out again to finish the conversation about his visit to Saleby. It would be the first visit he was privileged to make in Ödesjö for the purpose of talking with ordinary healthy and sound people about God.

A Heart of Stone
and a Rock
of Salvation

"I think you can blame yourself, Pastor. If one whips the flock of God with the scourge of the law instead of guiding it to the springs of living water, everything will eventually go wrong. No one can endure unlimited lashings."

Torvik stared at the woman who was seated on the office sofa and who spoke so freely. She spoke without bitterness, and with a certain motherly concern and warmth, which made it impossible for one to be angry with her.

The woman was from Sörbygden. She had come with the milk truck that morning to attend to her errand. It was of delicate nature. It was to let the pastor know that Margit, who had been a servant at his home for an entire year, had now, scarcely two months later, allowed herself to be re-baptized. The woman was Margit's aunt and her only near relative in the community.

She had presented her view of the case. Margit had experienced an awakening at the parsonage, there was no doubt about that. But she had never found rest and assurance in God's grace. She had only examined and tried her deeds, had confessed her sins and fought her temptations, but had never found peace in the wounds and shed blood of Christ. She had never heard anything about the grace of baptism, nor about the robe of Christ's righteousness. And now she had become convinced that she could never be saved unless she were baptized again. Those who counseled this had also spoken to her about the precious atonement. Was it strange, then, that she had joined their ranks? Mother Lotta wept over the fact that she had not been allowed to keep the girl at her house, for in that case she would have attempted, poor as she felt herself to be in such matters, to point her the way through the veil.

Torvik listened quietly. He had heard such complaints before. Since his marriage more than a year ago he had found many things to reflect on. His Britta was from an old family of "readers" which remained closely allied to the church. Much of that, which he in his soul struggles had only found with great difficulty and in part, seemed to belong to her very being since childhood. Her gentle criticism of his preaching was that it only proclaimed Christ as a source of strength and an example and an illustration of the four absolute demands.

"Let me tell you, Pastor," the woman continued, "it won't do to offer Moses a forty percent agreement and expect him to be satisfied with our becoming absolutely pure and loving and honest, as you are always talking about. One will certainly not be saved on that foundation. It will be nothing but patchwork. It will not result in a whole and acceptable righteousness, as the heart will surely attest, and it will certainly not do as a basis for salvation. Those outward sins, which one can pluck away as one rids the padding of a sofa of vermin, one by one, are by no means the worst. And that is true also of those sins of thought that you can take hold of as you would a bug and show the Lord, and say, 'Here it is.' But the corruption of our nature, Pastor, the sinful depravity, that remains where it is, and I should like to see, Pastor, how you would turn that over to God."

Torvik listened, amused. This remarkable woman really meant well, and he knew she was a sincere friend of the church.

"But Mother Lotta," he said, "you surely do not mean that one may give up trying to be pure, truthful, and loving."

"My dear Pastor, how can you believe anything so wicked about me? Of course, you must preach that we should be pure and perfect in love, but you should not say that we should be this in order thereby to be saved, but must say instead that we should live thus because we *are* saved by grace."

"But there isn't really any difference, is there?"

"Yes, Pastor, it makes this big difference, that a poor, tortured soul, seeing the whole ugly tangle of his sins, dares to look at Jesus instead of at himself. If Margit had understood this, she would never have strayed from the church."

Torvik remained silent. There was something in what she had said. The more wholeheartedly he sought to break with sin, the more painfully aware he was of something lacking. The more energetically he pursued the evil in order to discover its inner source, the more apparent it became that there were not only single dark wellsprings of evil within him that with a little determination and will power might be stanched, but that the whole inner soil was a morass and deep down a frightening dark flood appeared that he feared he could never master. The woman had spoken truly. It was indeed impossible to commit this to God. With a trace of irritation in his voice, he asked:

"But can you tell me, Mother Lotta, what might possibly be able to help overcome the corruption that I have in my heart?"

The woman looked up at him as if shocked at the question.

"The blood of the atonement, Pastor; nothing but the atoning blood."

"Dear Pastor," she continued, "since I am reproving you in this way, there is one thing more that I must say."

It was as if she were speaking to a boy. Torvik could not help smiling.

"Since you have gone to so much trouble for my sake, you must at least have some refreshment."

"Britta, dear," he called to the kitchen, "will you bring in some coffee? Mother Lotta from Drängsmarken is here and teaching me the cure of souls."

"Well, Mother Lotta," he said as he sat down again, "how was it again? Out with it now! I need what you may give me."

"Yes, Pastor, there was something else that I believe caused Margit to leave us. It is that you deny baptism."

Now Torvik became almost angry with her.

"Deny baptism? That is not true, Mother Lotta."

"Examine yourself, Pastor. When Margit went to communion the first time after her awakening—on Judgment Sunday, it was—Marianne at Saleby also communed, as you will remember."

"Yes. What then?"

"But she is not baptized, Pastor."

The pastor felt a wave of resentment. Now she is really pharisaical, he thought. He was about to answer, "Shall you cast out the one whom the Lord receives?" But he kept his tongue in control. Marianne's story was not a pleasant one. She had become converted through Schenstedt and his sister and had been coming to church faithfully, and had then asked to go to communion. Schenstedt had talked with him about the matter, and they had agreed together that it was pure formality to insist on her being baptized when she was already Christian. She had therefore gone with her employers to the Lord's Table with his acquiescence. He was at the time absolutely sure that he had acted rightly. But now he kept silent. When the miserable situation developed at Saleby, Marianne had become lost. She was employed at the café in Svenhester, and was considered not to be leading a proper life.

The woman remained quiet a moment before continuing.

"That Sunday you preached that one must obey God every hour of the day. But by your actions, Pastor, you preached that one does not need to obey God in the matter of baptism."

Torvik swallowed and lifted his hands from the table as if about to say something, but the woman gave him no opportunity.

"Pastor, if one should obey God in such matters as tax returns and making change, one ought surely also obey Him in respect to baptism. All transgression of God's commandments will be punished. Now Margit got the idea that baptism has no real significance in the church. No wonder she turned to another sect, to whom it at least means something."

Torvik kept silent.

"As for Marianne, it would surely have been better, Pastor, if you had instructed her and baptized her. Perhaps then she would not have fallen away. Now she says that Christianity is a fraud. A Christian should be absolutely pure and good, she says, but not a single one is that. That's the way it goes, Pastor, when one only teaches the law instead of emphasizing the atonement."

Torvik had leaned his forehead against his clenched hand. He had no desire to say anything. When the woman again spoke, it was with lowered voice, as if she feared her own words.

"And now that I have come here to contend in all friendliness with you, Pastor, I must say that I could never understand that you, who make so much of obedience, can permit women to speak God's Word at meetings. That is clearly forbidden in the Bible."

"But Mother Lotta, you are now talking like a real minister yourself."

"Yes, the Lord be merciful to my sinful soul! I know full well that I shall have to give an account on the last day for

every idle word I talk as I sit here. And if there were no atoning blood, I should not have dared to come. But, Pastor, no
woman has ever been permitted to speak among us at our
meetings. Then the old preachers read God's Word. God help
me! Rather than let them see Mother Lotta standing in the
pulpit, I would lay my old head on the railroad track. It has
been more than enough that God has given me five children
whom I have tried to nurture by the Word of God. And if a
troubled soul has come, I have of course tried to comfort and
help with the truths of Scripture. But to be a teacher in God's
church and a shepherd for the flock, that is another matter.
Only an ungodly self-security would make one believe oneself
capable of that, when one was not called and ordained."

The pastor did not lift his forehead from his hand. A year
ago he would have contradicted at every point. The revival
was then at its peak. Since he had won Schenstedt and his sister as friends and allies, and the sister had been reunited with
her husband, they had all been animated by an active and
contagious Christianity. And when some friends from
Stockholm had come to help, and when Mrs. Jonsson at
Glanstrop and the Arvidssons at the freehold had been won,
it almost looked as if an avalanche of revival had come over
the congregation. He remembered the great crowds on the
church hill the Sunday Schenstedt preached, and he could
still see the throngs at the schoolhouse during the week of the
parish mission when all those who had been won stood up
and bore witness.

The woman must have been thinking of the same events,
for she touched upon them as she continued to speak.

"You ought not let so many of the newly awakened
preach the Word to us, Pastor. It is certainly good to hear that
they have come part of the way, but beyond that they have little to tell. No one is ever saved by his conversion, but only by
the death and resurrection of Christ. But of that they never

speak. Do not the Scriptures say that he who would lead a congregation ought not to be a novice, a beginner in the faith, 'lest being lifted up with pride he fall into the condemnation of the devil'?"

Now the pastor's wife knocked at the door and invited them to have coffee. Mother Lotta had evidently finished her errand. She did not need much urging, but followed into the room where the little home altar stood against one inside wall and the sofa used for devotions against the other. Mother Lotta settled down in a corner of the sofa like a little black bird.

Torvik kept very quiet. His old melancholy had begun to return of late and the visitor's words had not made it any easier today. During the revival he had lived in an ecstasy that was almost too wrought-up in character, but he was aware that he had forced this gladness by the power of his will. It would never have flown so freely of itself. Now when difficulties had begun in earnest, he was often deeply distressed.

Difficulties, indeed! It was not only that he had been unable to enlist any new helpers for a long half-year. The older ones had, in addition, caused him one concern after the other. Schenstedt's sister was once more separated from her husband after a series of terrible scenes. This was so much more serious in its effects, since their reconciliation had been generally referred to as proof of the genuine quality of the revival as a whole, not to say of Christianity as such. Still more serious, he felt, was the fact that he himself had such great difficulties. He carried on an almost hopeless struggle to keep his prayer life healthy and vigorous. The old pattern of self-examination and commitment had lost its edge also for him. It was an altogether hopeless task to search out all sin and make amends for it. It was no doubt a sin that he thought good old Magnusson looked slouchy and repulsive; that he noticed how he changed his tone in speaking with Britta because he heard some parishioner entering the hallway; that during the morning hymn at prayers, he would think about how to meet the cost of fuel for the stoves; that he told the deacon thoughtlessly that he had to leave the party at his house early in order to prepare his sermon, when as a matter of fact he really wanted to write letters that Sunday night. Yes, all of this was no doubt sin, but what good would it do to confess all this before men? And what did it mean to make a break with such sins? He would have to tear his evil heart from his breast!

And his prayers! Every day he fought despairingly to keep his prayer life from going stale. Every day the quiet hour seemed to grow longer, and it became more impossible to keep his scattered thoughts from intruding on his devotion. Now he thanked God for family prayers. There was at least some order to them. But it was thanks to Britta that this was so. When they were first married, he had at first preferred that each of them should have a private devotional period and then share their experiences. But one day Britta had let him know that they were now sufficiently acquainted with each other's sinful corruption. Now she wanted to hear something about Jesus instead. Then she had proposed that they use the old and worn book of prayers by Roos, which had been used in her childhood home. Since then their maidservant had joined them; they had sung a hymn and prayed the Lord's Prayer, after which he had read one of the terse doctrinal meditations. He was, in spite of all, glad for that. In the midst of all these other things that were shaking now, this old-fashioned Bible faith seemed like a firm stone bridge.

He had much more to thank Britta for. She had even been able to get somewhere with the widow at Kvarnlyckan. He had himself called on her again and tried to win her by confessing his own sins. She had only smiled with malicious joy and said, "You see, now, things aren't as good with others, either." Later she had spread the most fantastic tales about his confessions to those who came to see her. Britta had gone there and had not spoken a single word, either about the soul or about God. She had bound up the woman's bad leg, brought her some conserves and helped her write a letter to her daughter in America. On her birthday she had given her a copy of the new hymnal. However Britta had gone about it, it was certain that the woman was nearer the kingdom of God now than she had ever been before.

———————

While the pastor at Ödesjö sat in thought and helped himself mechanically to sugar and cream, Britta Torvik began to talk with the woman in the corner of the sofa. The two were soon on the best of terms; there was a spiritual kinship of some kind. Mother Lotta had a never-failing interest in individuals and their salvation. In this respect she was like the pastor's wife. They began to talk quietly and earnestly about the homes in Sörbygden, without the least hint of gossip, but rather with the loving concern that weighed each soul on the scales of eternity as earnestly as if it were a matter of their own salvation. The old woman's final verdict concerning everything that looked gloomy and hopeless was always the same, "We'll have to leave that." She meant, "in the hands of God," but that was so self-evident to her that she never needed to say it.

The pastor said nothing. He just remembered that it was the people down there in Sörbygden who were thought mainly to have voted against him in the election. A few months after he had been made temporary rector, the parish boundaries had been changed. Ödesjö, which since medieval times had had its own rectors, was placed under Näs, and the curacy was declared vacant. He had of course sought it, and had been elected by a slim majority. He did not feel very much concerned about the strong opposition, since he had never expected the work of God's Spirit to meet with nothing but applause; but it really irked him that it should be just these old-time believers at Sörbygden who did not want him. If they had made as much propaganda for their candidate as his own friends had made for him, who knows what the outcome might have been? When it was all over, however, these people had shown themselves loyal, and had continued to go to church and to the Lord's Supper. As for himself, he had determined not to show any trace of disappointment, and whatever division there was had been healed.

Tonight he was to conduct a Lenten service at Sörbygden. He was not altogether happy about it. It would not be easy to preach about the sufferings of Christ in a way that would satisfy them down there. He had planned in a special way to win their confidence if possible and at the same time help them spiritually. He had asked Rector Bengtsson from Ravelunda to come and preach the main sermon, after which he and Schenstedt would speak briefly. In that way they would first hear the kind of sermon they were accustomed to and would swallow without blinking, and at the same time he would have opportunity to give them some salty and wholesome truths to carry home with them.

Mother Lotta got up and thanked them for their hospitality. When she had put on her coat and was ready to go, she curtsied.

"I have talked too much again," she said. "May God forgive me. Now I want simply to leave a word of God before I go, so that I shall not finish with something foolish. I say in the words of the apostle, 'Our mouth is opened to you . . .; our heart is wide.'"

She curtsied again and took her leave.

Torvik returned to his office without saying a word. He stood with his hands in his pocket, looking out upon the gray winter sky. Light snowflakes fell on the crust of ice and the thin ridges of snow still remaining after the recent thaw. As he stood there, everything seemed to melt together. The branches of the trees became a blurred, dark pattern against the gray of the sky. Tears came to his eyes. Had this little woman been able to turn him upside down like this? Was it the criticism? Was it not, rather, the love that characterized her bearing? He longed to be able to understand and to be one in heart with the people in Sörbygden. Why were not such Christians produced up here? Why could not the whole-hearted commitment which he preached and practiced bring forth one such fruit as this woman?

―――――

At twelve o'clock the bus came, and Torvik stood at the post office to meet it. Pastor Bengtsson alighted. He was a short, stocky man, with alert black eyes and rather thick rustic lips. It had been decided that he should spend the afternoon at the parsonage. Schenstedt would later take them in his car to Sörbygden, where the service was to be held at the Lutheran mission house. Kind as always, Schenstedt had promised to drive the rector back to his home in Ravelunda after the meeting.

The two men walked slowly in the falling snow up to the parsonage. They had to walk slowly, lest they slip on the ice. The visitor made kindly inquiry about conditions at Ödesjö. Was the baby well? How had church attendance been since Christmas? Had the new heating system proved satisfactory? When would the next communion take place? And how did it go with the revival? There was a little good-humored banter in the last question. Torvik rather took for granted that his more conservative colleague did not have a very high opinion of revivals in general and of this one in particular. But he was determined not to give an answer in kind, but to be absolutely honest about the revival, and admitted therefore that it had not been anything to shout about. No new recruits were being won, and of those on whom he thought he could rely one after the other came and lamented how little he had been able to do of that which he had promised himself and his God.

"So?" said the rector with noticeable surprise. "In other words, it turned out very well for you."

"Don't joke about the failure, Olle."

"I am not joking at all. These are, on the contrary, very serious matters, so serious indeed that the life and death of souls may depend upon them. You must know that when God's work gets started in a man, he will sooner or later experience desperate need, the need that is created by God's Word. Then the situation is the very one you now see: one would, but cannot."

"But what, then, shall a man do?"

"And you ask that, you who are a pastor? What follows illumination by the law?"

"I haven't the slightest idea."

Bengtsson made a complete halt and pushed his hat back in a gesture of astonishment.

"I thought so. When will they learn at Upsala not to send out people to shepherd souls until they have learned the ABC's of Christianity? Have you never read the catechism?"

"If I have read it, I have in any case forgotten it." Bengtsson stood with legs apart, his hands clasped behind his back.

"Listen Gösta. I am telling you that you are an immoral man. By a Church decree you are obligated to teach your catechumens the catechism of 1878, and the law of the Church enjoins you to conform the content of your sermons with the main parts of the catechism so that people may learn to know how they are related and thus be established in the doctrine of the church."

He saw that his friend wanted to say something, and silenced him with a quick movement of his hand.

"Yes, I know what you want to say, that no one follows the catechism strictly, and that may be so. You are nevertheless obligated to teach your people the Christian teaching found in the catechism, the full evangelical foundation of faith and way of salvation." Taking his friend by the arm as they continued their walk, he said, "Let me teach you what you ought to have known long before you stepped into the pulpit. When an individual has been called through the power of the Word—in other words, the very thing that has been happening in this congregation of yours—that person is first enlightened by the law. He understands that there is something called sin that he must be careful to avoid. He becomes *obedient*, you see. That is the first awakening. Thus far it has perhaps come here and there in Ödesjö by now. But then comes the second awakening by the law, when one sees the miserable condition of one's heart. I am going to preach about that tonight. Then one understands that, with all one's best deeds, one is and remains black as a chimney sweep. Then the danger is really serious. A person will then say, either, 'If my condition is so terrible, I may as well wallow in the dirt,' and go away and sin again. Or he will say, 'I am after all not as black as Karlsson or Lundstrom and their card-playing cronies, since I do not sin intentionally, and surely the Lord must make some distinctions on the last day,' and he goes away and becomes a self-righteous Pharisee, and all is lost. Or his eyes are turned from his own miserable condition and he catches sight of the Lord Jesus Christ, who died for just such black rascals as himself. And he hears that it is *faith* that makes righteous, and not works. That is the enlightenment through the gospel. Therefore *everything* here in Ödesjö depends on whether you can rightly preach the gospel and guide souls to the Redeemer. Answer me honestly: Are you not aware of this yourself? Yes or no?"

"Yes," answered Torvik clearly and definitely. The rector did not let go his arm.

"Well, lad, are you able to give them the true bread of life, so that they will not faint?"

"No," answered Torvik, just as plainly.

"You are an honest man, Brother," said the older pastor, "and I believe God has chosen you to be an instrument of blessing. But you can do nothing of yourself. First we must make sure that everything is clear with regard to your own conversion."

Torvik stiffened at these words. He felt that he was helpless and exceedingly vulnerable in the face of such rude soul cure. He looked anxiously at the stocky comrade at his side, but saw only the black spread of his slouch hat.

"Be converted?" he said with a show of irritation. "Let me tell you, Olle, I have been converted twice, and that should be enough. The first time was at college, the second as pastor here in Ödesjö. How many times does a person have to be converted?"

"As many days as one lives," was the immediate reply. "But first the conversion must be properly completed through repentance and faith. And that is something God must do, and not you. It is evident that He has gotten you a considerable distance on the way. But you lack faith. You lack the right faith in Jesus only. And that is why you are unable to show others the way to faith."

Torvik would certainly have made objection if Britta had not said something like that just the other day. Instead, he simply asked, "What, then, shall I do about it?"

"Read the Bible, of course."

"I read the Bible every day."

"I believe that. But how do you read?"

"You mustn't be so critical, Olle, of everything a poor fellow does. I try to read devotionally and for edification, so that I take to heart that which I feel is meant for me."

"Feel, feel! That is just what is wrong. Don't you believe the Bible is God's Word just as truly, no matter how you may feel? Don't you see, Brother, that this won't do? Here you are with your sore conscience and your awakening by the law, and you are as sensitive to every single threat of that law as a sore tooth to ice water. But since the conscience is dead as clay toward all the gospel promises, you feel nothing when God's Word speaks about Jesus, who died for us sinners, and about the righteousness that comes from God and which one may believe in spite of every accusation of one's conscience. Because you make your feelings your barometer, you pass by the gospel and are held fast in the law. Look in your Bible and see if the passages you have especially marked are not just those that speak of what *you* shall do. But you have not given half the attention to that which tells what Christ has done through his atonement."

Torvik gave inward assent to that. It was true, completely true. But he said nothing.

"We are in the midst of Lent, Brother," said the rector. "Read God's Word now as God's Word, without skipping anything. Underline heavily everything about what our Savior has done for us. And if you like, write 'For me' in the margin. You need this yourself, and it is your duty to preach it to your congregation, as well."

They were now at the parsonage. The old wing with the curb roof, which strangely enough was located directly in front of the main building, looked dejected where it stood in the snow and seemed to sleep. The intention had been to tear it down at the last renovation of the property, but Britta Torvik had asked that it be left standing. Perhaps it might some day be used for youth work of some kind, or as a guest house.

In the parsonage itself the same sunny joy prevailed as was common when brethren visited one another on preaching missions. The baby, now five months old, had to be shown to the visitor. Pastor Bengtsson gave his competent opinion of the way the renovation had been done. He found fault with the furnace, and approved the new cabinet in the office. Then Mrs. Torvik invited them to the coffee table. For the second time that day the curate sat at the long table facing the sofa in that room where family devotions were held. He noted that the pastor from Ravelunda sat in exactly the same corner of the sofa where Mother Lotta had sat in the morning, and could not help making comparisons. Did God mean to send him one critic after the other today?

Perhaps he needed it. The woman from Drängsmarken and this bluff older brother in the ministry were both talking sense. While Britta and the rector reviewed most of what had happened in the two parsonages since Advent, Torvik sat lost in thoughts. He began to feel at last that he had gotten under the shell of the question that faced him and to the kernel of it. After all, it had to do with the Word. Could he accept the Word as Christianity's self-evident foundation?

In the conversation that followed, in which Britta also put in an occasional word, his objections to certain doctrines were honestly presented but he was at a loss to defend them against the Scriptural convictions and insights of the rector. Only one objection remained.

"But must we not, nevertheless, hold to a historical view of the Bible?" he asked.

"What is that?"

Torvik was amazed at the question. The old pastor answered it himself.

"There is room for anything and everything in that phrase. It can be pure rationalism, which considers everything in the Bible to be relative, uncertain, and extensible, so that the final result is that you need not agree at any point unless you wish to do so. The authority of the Bible is in that case rejected, and man himself, his reason, his conscience, his modern scientific spirit, and everything else that is blind and straying, has become the guiding star of religion. It can of course include some other things that are much finer and better, this historical view of the Bible. But as far as salvation is concerned, I do not think it matters whether one has a historical or an unhistorical view of the Bible. Everything depends on whether we have a *religious* view of the Bible."

Now it was Torvik's turn to ask, "And what is that?"

"That is faith in the Bible as the voice of God, so that if you read it to hear what God would say to you, you actually hear God speak. For my part, I have the simple belief that the Bible is exactly as God wanted it to be. That does not mean, perhaps, that every detail is set forth systematically for science, as in an academic treatise. But it means that every little detail has been given such a form that a human being who seeks salvation will be helped to find the truth."

Torvik appreciated the considerateness of his guest, who was satisfied with making this statement and did not use his opportunity to attack specific errors, which his young colleague had been influenced by. The curate sensed that he had been directed toward something that he would do well to think about in quiet meditation.

A lovely afternoon had passed. The soft winter twilight had enveloped the low-ceilinged rooms with a blue veil of quiet and contentment. They had sat long in conversation after the dinner. Soon the car from Saleby would come to take them to Sörbygden. The men went to the office to choose hymns and plan the evening service. The pastor's wife also had duties to see about. She would not be attending the meeting, as she had the baby to care for.

When they came to the office, the rector looked his young friend over.

"You ought really put on your clerical coat when you go out to preach," he said.

Torvik blushed. Was there to be more criticism?

"It's not laziness or indifference. It's a matter of principle."

"That doesn't make it any better. Would you respect an officer who as a matter of principle appeared at maneuvers in mufti? Or a Salvation Army soldier who doffed his uniform when his corps was assembled in the market square?"

Torvik was becoming irritated. "You must certainly understand that I want to come as an ordinary human being."

But the rector continued his argument.

"Then you are sailing under false colors. You are no ordinary person. You have been ordained by the Church as a servant of the Word. You have been elected and called by the Christian congregation at Ödesjö to be its pastor. You get support from the fields which godly forbears donated for the pastor's upkeep. It is pure dishonesty to take the money, if you want to be just an ordinary person."

"You are bound to misinterpret everything, Olle. You know very well that I don't want to make myself great through my office. I only want to remind myself and others that what a pastor is comes, not because of his office, but because of what he is in himself."

Bengtsson straightened up and laughed.

"You are the proudest man I ever met, Gösta. What are you in yourself? A sinner. Do you really enter the pulpit because you think it is because of *your* piety, *your* faith, and *your* prayers you are called to be the leader for the Christians in Ödesjö? Then you might as well stay home. If you expect to continue to preach, you had better do it because you have been appointed by God to do so and have his Word to hold fast to. And that Word remains just as holy a Word, though a poor servant with many shortcomings proclaims it."

Torvik smiled.

"If I did not know you so well, Olle, I would conclude that you are just looking for an excuse for laziness and comfort for a pastor's unrepentant heart."

Pastor Bengtsson suddenly became very stern, stern as a father who is rebuking a stubborn son.

"Tell me one thing, Gösta. Are you a poor and weak servant, or are you not?"

Now Torvik, too, became serious.

"I am a poor and unworthy servant," he said.

"Then you had better put on your clerical coat, Brother. Do not come any longer as the remarkable Gösta Torvik, but come instead as the humble servant of God's Word at Ödesjö."

Torvik still wanted to contradict. But the clerical coat did command respect. People respected it, though it was perhaps in a way a respect for the Word. He kept silent.

Just then the window shade was illuminated from outside by the lights of an automobile. The conversation was cut short. Torvik threw some books into the bag and hurried out into the hallway where Schenstedt had already showed up, his smiling countenance framed by his fur collar. A moment later they were on their way.

―――――――

The headlights illuminated the broad, straight highway through the communal forest. Schenstedt drove carefully. He was familiar with the road, and knew exactly where the ice was treacherous under the blanket of snow.

They had only had time for a hurried greeting at the parsonage. Torvik took up the conversation again where he sat in the rear seat with Pastor Bengtsson.

"I forgot to ask how your sister is, Gunnar."

"Thank you," answered Schenstedt in the pleasant tone of voice which was characteristic of him this last year. "She left for Stockholm yesterday. She is to marry Rothmann as soon as she has obtained her divorce."

Torvik was stunned. He had known for some time that something was wrong at Saleby. Everyone in the village knew it. This Rothmann had often visited Saleby. He was an energetic and pleasant American who was in Sweden to look after some matters pertaining to the metal industry. Then there had been scenes again, violent disagreements between Inger and her husband, sufficiently public to make a painful impression on the many who were accustomed to look upon Gunnar Schenstedt and his sister as champions of an uncompromising Christianity. Sometimes when Torvik called at Saleby and saw this Rothmann with Inger he felt an inner revulsion. But he rid himself bravely of this feeling and told himself that this was not the way to think about a fellow man, much less about a fellow worker in the battle for the kingdom of God.

And now it had happened! And he had been kept completely in the dark about it. This hurt him deeply—there had been such mutual frankness before, and they had shared everything together. His first thought was for his friend. How would this affect his faith? It must surely be a terrible problem for his happy and undeviating faith in the gospel of absolute obedience. How could he speak so calmly? Was this just a mask to hide his despair?

Schenstedt must have surmised something of the consternation his announcement had brought the two pastors, but his voice was as pleasant as before as he pursued the matter further.

"I am well aware that this may seem strange to you, who are pastors. But I am sure Inger is following God's will. She and Sten have never been compatible, and since she now loves

William, it would have been cruel to stand in the way of her happiness. I feel this very strongly."

Feel, always feel! That's just what's the matter! Torvik heard an inner echo of the rector's voice at the parsonage gate. Now his colleague sat quietly at his side. What was he thinking? He perhaps thought it best, since he was within the boundaries of Ödesjö parish, not to cause any trouble nor to interfere in the pastoral care that was another's concern.

"I know very well," Schenstedt continued in the same affable tone, "that it might seem as if this divorce were contrary to Bible teaching, but I think you will both agree that the Spirit is more than the letter, and that we must follow that which we have felt to be God's way. In the last analysis, the Bible is merely the contemporary clothing of an eternal content, and one can both actualize it oneself and bear witness concerning it to others, even when one is formally at variance with the letter."

Torvik's blood froze. He had in fact said practically the same a few hours ago, but he was not prepared to arrive at *these* conclusions.

When at last he found his tongue, his words came slowly and with care.

"I can't say how deeply this pains me, for both Inger's and Sten's sake. And for the congregation's sake, too, I must add. The effect will not be good, either among those who have come to a decision or among the opponents."

"In that I know you are mistaken," said Schenstedt calmly. "Inger has simply pursued the course she considered right and proper. And I have myself counseled it. Truth may seem dangerous, but it always frees and cleanses. When one follows the light within one's heart and has inner assurance of God's intention, it can never be dangerous, except for one who does not dare to walk in God's ways also when they run against our human opinions."

The visiting pastor could no longer keep silent. He was very pale, and his voice was like a bow held taut over a trembling depth of passion and zeal. It was in direct contrast to Schenstedt's calm and sonorous voice.

"You must remember, sir, that here the individual soul and its eternal salvation is at stake. We must reckon with that, whether we would or not. And it becomes most serious when we are responsible also for the souls of others, as for example when one gives counsel in marriage matters or goes forth to preach to others. The Savior has given us those terrible and solemnizing words, 'Whosoever causes one of these little ones who believe on me to sin, it would be better that a great millstone be fastened round his neck and to be drowned in the depths of the sea.' In their light we dare not live or teach in conscious conflict with the Word of God."

"I understand, Pastor, that you must view the matter in this light," said Schenstedt, with a toss of his head that reminded of his old ways. "That is your conviction, and you do right in following it. I, too, have a personal conviction and have the right to follow it. Each of us will therefore have to speak tonight according to his own experience and his own way of seeing things. One can do no more than follow one's conviction."

"Yes, my dear sir, one can follow God's Word. A man should not follow his convictions but determine his course by God's Word."

"Yes, but what then is God's Word? That will always remain a matter of interpretation. And then you are after all referred to your own conviction."

"But there is *something* that stands firm. There are difficulties of interpretation also in secular laws and regulations, and yet the result is not chaos. If it is stated that divorce is forbidden, then it is forbidden, and one may not interpret it as if it were the opposite."

Schenstedt shrugged his shoulders.

"Our views of the Bible are altogether different," he said. "To you, it is a book of laws; to me, it is the spirit of Jesus that matters."

"Then, sir, you'll have to explain to me how the spirit of Jesus can speak anything other than God's Word."

"That is due to the law of evolution, Pastor. The Spirit will lead us into the whole truth. What was valid in Jesus's day is not necessarily valid today. Not even his own words are so unalterable that his Spirit cannot change them."

And this man Torvik had asked to come and speak tonight! At the thought, he wiped beads of perspiration from his brow.

"How can you know what the Spirit says today?" asked the pastor from Ravelunda. His voice was like cold steel.

"It becomes a matter of conscience."

"It means, then, that the conscience is the highest authority. No, thank you! Then both of you and I are lost. The conscience does indeed know quite a bit about the law, but it knows absolutely nothing about the promises of the gospel. Can the conscience tell you whether Jesus was crucified? Can it say whether he died for our sakes? Can it determine whether he rose again? Can it know that he is to return again to judge the world? These are the chief truths of the gospel, and no man would have the faintest idea of this, if we could not read it in the Word. Christianity must therefore cling to the Word to the end of the ages, or it must cease to be Christianity, since it would no longer have the gospel of Christ to proclaim."

Silence reigned in the car. The atmosphere was explosive. Torvik sat in his corner, infinitely unhappy. He took a side glance at the rector, and saw his face as if chiseled in stone. What could he be thinking? He had, indeed, gotten support for his earlier suspicions.

The back of Schenstedt's head was a mute puzzle. He drove with elegance and ease on the narrow forest road, which they had now turned in upon.

Torvik tried to collect his thoughts. He was aware of the tension as two strong wills opposed each other like a pair of buffaloes in head-on conflict. If the worst came to the worst, there might be a battle royal between the two at the mission house. He spent some moments in thought; then folded his hands and sat in silence. At last he turned to his companions.

"We'll have to drop theology now," he said, "and give a little thought to the arrangement of the meeting. Suppose we follow the usual order. After the first hymn, I'll read the whole of the section from the Passion history. Will you kindly speak first tonight, Gunnar?"

"Well, if that is your wish," said Schenstedt with just a touch of stiffness in his usually pleasant voice, betraying that it was not altogether without effort.

"Good! Then we'll sing another hymn. Perhaps you'll select it, yourself. Then you speak, Olle, since you are the principal speaker, and I shall make some closing remarks. Will that be all right?"

He felt better when he noted their silent agreement. The first skirmish was won and the deployment luckily assured. If Schenstedt should say anything foolish, Bengtsson would surely know how to set the light in its place again; and if Bengtsson offended in any way, he, Torvik would have to try to smooth things over.

Torvik busied himself with the selection of hymns and was barely through when the car slowed down to a stop in front of the yellow frame wall of the mission house.

Inside, kerosene lamps shed a soft light. The house was well filled, and silent nods greeted them as they walked to the front pew on the men's side. They sat down and bowed their heads in prayer.

After the first hymn, Torvik read the text. It was Part Three of the Passion history, which included four dramatic incidents: the betrayal by Judas, Peter's denial, the trial before Caiaphas, and the suicide of Judas. It was very quiet in the room; old men sat with half-closed eyes, as though they saw the scenes enacted before them. The long but tragically freighted story came to an end, and once again feet were heard scraping against the benches.

Then Schenstedt stepped to the platform. His bearing was casual as he leaned against the lectern and spoke with his familiar ease. He based his remarks on the words of Jesus to Judas, "Would you betray the Son of man with a kiss?" and said that he wanted to remind his listeners and himself of how easy it is to betray the Master most shamefully when one pays him the most reverent homage. He explained that he, too, before his conversion, was all for the church, had been a member of the church council, and had supported every measure taken to put an end to anti-religious activities in the nation, although he had with heart and soul, and day after day, betrayed Jesus by his disobedience. But after he had come to understand Jesus's demand for a radical and uncompromising obedience, he had been forced to sacrifice all external interest and place himself instead under the inward guidance of God.

So far, Torvik thought, all was well, though he did feel that his friend exaggerated both his superficial churchliness before his conversion and his inward obedience now.

Schenstedt continued to develop his thought. There were of course many other ways of betraying Jesus than with a kiss. All of them had this in common, giving God something other than a full and unrestricted obedience. There were those who stressed redemption in order to get away from thorough-going repentance. Others made the Bible a protecting shield against God's demand of absolute surrender. Or the pure doctrine would be made an excuse for a lazy unwillingness to walk in brave, new paths. All this was self-deception. The important thing was not what one believes but what one does. It is not necessary to be hesitant about God's will. The living Word of God, which is something other than the letter, penetrates directly to the heart. It fills the soul with the clear light of the Spirit, as soon as one is ready to obey. For those who are guided by God, all human inventions collapse, all ceremonies are hollow, the doctrine is an empty shell. Only one thing remains: the clear demand to dare at every moment to do just what God commands, without consideration for the opinions of men, without regard for religious custom, ancient dogmas, or traditional beliefs about what the Bible teaches.

Torvik sat way over by the wall in the front pew. By his side sat the visiting pastor, absolutely still, with terrific power concentrated in his frozen features, and with his eyes riveted on a plaster replica of Thorvaldsen's *Kristus* on the front wall. Somehow, Torvik, as he looked at the rector, thought of a time bomb the moment before the explosion. He peeked over his shoulder at the men behind him. They too sat motionless. Some looked directly at the speaker, and the lines between the eyebrows seemed to deepen. Others sat with eyes half closed, as if they had attained an otherworldly peace far removed from all human error and could no longer be swayed by any winds of doctrine.

Schenstedt spoke with increased eagerness. There was something in his voice like the crack of a whip, something sharp and at the same time authoritative. He pictured man's situation, alone with God, placed under the immediate command of God, forced either to obey every second, radically and without hesitation, whatever God's demand might be, or otherwise to cease being a Christian. He pictured man's attempt to find something to support him. He was unwilling to stand naked and alone beneath God's unrelenting rule. He would like to be loosed from the position of absolute servitude, in which one can never know what God may demand in the next moment. For that reason he has created the doctrine of the church: It is so comforting to have something that is always and at all times the same. For that reason, too, he has raised the Bible to the place of God: Here at least, one knows what is written and does not need to fear that God will the next minute demand the opposite. That is the reason why he is so delighted with pious old customs and churchly ordinances: He does not then have to walk the dangerous way of God, which is narrow as a steel rail, and on which there is absolutely nothing to cling to but the command of God, which every second reaches those who each day afresh decide to walk the way of complete obedience.

He finished with an admonition to all his listeners to break in pieces the false crutches, to reject their old, shielding prejudices, and to dare to make the leap into the void where nothing exists and nothing matters but God, the soul, and obedience. He who refuses to make that leap ought for honesty's sake cease calling himself a Christian.

In closing, he announced the hymn, "Life, death, alike, are here at stake," and left the platform.

Torvik was filled with thankfulness that he did not have to preach next. He felt ashamed in the presence of the farm folks who had built this mission house that the Word of God might be preached among them in its truth and purity, and who in spite of all misgivings had willingly opened its doors and asked their pastor to come and "read" the Word, as they expressed it. He had to admit that he did not himself understand many of the nice dogmatic distinctions, but this at least was certain, that if Luther, whose picture hung on one wall, and Rosenius, who looked down from the opposite wall, could have heard what was said there tonight, they would have turned over in their graves. And there must, then, have been a stirring of revulsion also in the breasts of these oldsters, for they really understood Luther and Rosenius, and clung with moving loyalty to the old evangelical heritage. To tell the truth, Torvik would not spread accusations of conscience. He had himself told Schenstedt, when they were planning this meeting, to give them some "bitter pills." A few months ago he would surely not have reacted so strongly against this kind of message as he did now—if it came from the right person. But because his eyes had this night been opened, and he had seen the consequences of this "undogmatic" faith, he was violently agitated by the attacks that had been made on the doctrine of the church and the written Word. Or could his aversion simply be due to his feeling that some of Schenstedt's bitter pills were intended for him personally?

Pastor Bengtsson now stood at the lectern. After the prayer, he began to speak slowly and quietly as if he feared that the dam might give way entirely if he should let loose too much of the emotion with which he was loaded.

He began by asking how it was possible that Peter should deny his Lord. On the way to Gethsemane he had surely been the picture of loyalty, a man of complete obedience and genuine devotion to his Master. He was prepared to forsake everything, to go both to prison and to death for his Master's sake. But then Jesus had said something very strange. "When you have turned again, strengthen your brethren." Just as if the enthusiastic disciple had never been converted!

That night Peter and all the other disciples had learned by experience what all their good intentions were worth. Had it depended on their obedience and their ability to fulfill God's commandments, they would have been eternally lost. But fortunately, there was something more than God, the soul, and obedience. There was a Redeemer who died in the place of his unprofitable disciples, and His atonement was the only thing that counted when a sinner was to be made righteous before God.

He began to describe salvation in vivid and drastic terms. He showed how God throws out the lifeline and takes hold of the soul that is drifting like a helpless craft down the stream toward the great waterfall; how he first lifts the soul to the solid ground of the Word by teaching him to attend church, to read and hear the gospel; how he then by the same Word chastises his evil propensities, and teaches him to flee sin and to seek to live without reproach.

He continued with increasing vigor.

"To begin with, this struggle against sin is pure joy to the awakened soul. It is as when a home owner begins to clear the land around his new house. The stones fly and the spade digs happily. But when a person is at work on the field of his heart, he gradually makes the dismaying discovery that there are more stones the deeper he gets. He keeps discovering new sins right along, and they become more difficult to move the more deeply they are intrenched in his inner life. One might possibly break with drinking and profanity and desecration of the Sabbath in a single evening. But pride, that desire to talk about oneself, or to find fault with others are likely to remain still after many months of penitential struggle.

"Then one day, when a man is battling sin and is trying to clear the stones from the heart's field, sweating at the task yet hoping finally to get rid of the last ones so that he may really see the garden grow, his spade strikes solid rock. He digs and scrapes on every side; he tries again and again to budge the rock. Then the terrible realization dawns: It is stony ground through and through. When he has hauled away load after load of stone and dumped them outside the fence, he still has not succeeded in making a garden that can begin to bear fruit for God. He has laid bare a ledge of granite, which never can support a living, fruit-bearing tree.

"This is the rock foundation we know as the sinful corruption of our human nature, the sinful depravity that remains even after a man has separated himself from all his conscious sins. It is this stony ground that explains why a man is just as great a sinner before God after he has offered God the best he is able to give of obedience and commitment.

"Standing on this rock foundation of sinful corruption, a man has three possible choices. He may depart from God in unbelief as Judas did. That road leads to death. He can make a show of clearing away the stones, as the Pharisees did. The stones that are visible to men may then be put away. One becomes temperate, honest, industrious. One may take a bit of this soil of self-righteousness and plant therein such flowers as will be a sweet fragrance to one's own nostrils, such as kindness, helpfulness, support of missions, zealous activity for kingdom causes, witnessing, and preaching, or perhaps an extreme abstinence in respect to food and drink. And then one walks among these flowers and considers that the work is completed. But in the sight of God, the rock foundation remains, and on Judgment Day the flowers have long since withered.

"The most dangerous of all temptations is to tamper with the yardstick. God has sent his Holy Spirit to convince the world of sin. The Spirit dwells in the Word. Did not Jesus say of the words he spoke that they are spirit? He who strays from the Word will never be convicted of sin; in any case, he will never know the terrifying depths of sin. He never gets down to the rock foundation. It is with him as with the farmer in the legend, who was to build a bridge. He took a tapeline into the woods to measure with. But when he measured his longest poles they were nevertheless too short. Then he cut off a part of the measuring line, and declared that the poles would be tall enough. Even the holiest and strictest adherents of the cult of absolute obedience are careless in the same way when they believe that they can stand the test before God even for a moment by virtue of their works of the law. They have shortened the measure. They use a tapeline that is like a rubber hand. It is called one's feelings, one's conscience, or one's own perception of God's will. These can all be stretched or pressed together, consciously or unconsciously, so that they fit most anything. There are two signs of falsifying the measure that are inescapably sure. One is that a person considers himself, his deeds and his life good enough to find acceptance with God; the other is that he calls that right which the Word of God calls wrong.

"Only he who acknowledges God's Word without objecting to it or seeking to reduce it, and who accepts it wholly as God's Word, gets down to the rock foundation of the heart and discovers the law of sin that dwells in his members. Only such a one understands that he needs not only repentance, but salvation. But when he understands that, if he is to be saved at all, he must be saved by grace, that is a work of God. It was to that place he wanted to lead the soul, when he laid bare the rock foundation."

At this point the speaker made a sudden shift in his line of thought and began to speak about something altogether different.

"Outside Jerusalem, there is a hill of yellow, naked stone, ugly and hard as a dead man's skull. Long ago men bored a socket in this rocky hill and planted a cross there, and on that cross they hanged the only one of our race who was righteous and had perfectly fulfilled the law. God permitted this to happen because, although he had tolerated sin in former ages, he wanted once and for all to show that he was righteous and that sin is followed by condemnation and punishment, and that he will not countenance any tampering with his standards of holiness. But so wonderful is God that he let all the curse and penalty of sin fall upon the Innocent One, who freely gave himself in death for us. He was made a curse for our sakes. Thus he redeemed us from the condemnation of the law. He was made sin for us that we might become the righteousness of God. He bore our sins in his own body on the tree, and by his stripes we are healed.

"That is why the rocky hill of Golgotha is the most holy place in the world. The way of obedience leads to the foot of that cross. There one stands, a poor wretch, like Peter on that first Good Friday, full of shame and despair, looking upon his crucified Savior, whom he had been unable to follow. There it becomes apparent that the Lord's best disciples are unworthy of him. They are all betrayers and deniers, sharing in the guilt of his death. But there, at the cross, it also becomes clear that the Lord himself makes atonement for their sins. Where the way of obedience ends at Golgotha with judgment upon us, everyone who believes may nevertheless stand on this Rock of Atonement. There the way of grace begins, the new and holy way through the veil, the way that is sanctified by his blood.

"The stony soil of our heart, the rock foundation of our corrupt human nature, need not, therefore, be the basis for judgment upon us. It can be sprinkled with the blood of Jesus, just as the hill of Golgotha was when drops of blood fell upon it and it was transformed from a place of execution to the Rock of Atonement. God marks the evil heart with the sign of the cross and makes a man righteous in Christ. The whole sinful rock of man's natural heart is lifted and made to rest on the Rock of Atonement. It still remains flinty rock. Man, as he is in himself, remains a sinner. But the guilt is atoned for, the curse is lifted, and he can come confidently as a child into the presence of God and, thankful for the wonder of redemption, begin to live to the Savior's glory. Then the fruits of faith begin to appear. A fertile soil now covers the rocky base. It is the good soil of faith, which is watered by grace. Gradually something begins to grow that would never grow there before. Thus the backsliding Peter, when he had experienced the *great* grace, the grace that the penitent thief received on

Calvary, could become both an apostolic leader and a martyr witness to the faith. Yes, he then witnessed no longer concerning *his* faith, but concerning the Savior, and could finally make the supreme sacrifice of his own life with confidence, the sacrifice he was unable to make as long as he lived by his own resolutions and his own righteousness."

The rector made a momentary pause. Then he began a new line of thought. It was apparent that he was improvising.

"The stone foundation of the heart and the Rock of Atonement on Golgotha are the two mountains on which a man's destiny is determined. If he remains on the stone foundation of his natural fallen state, he is lost. Only *one* way leads from that stony foundation to the Rock of Atonement, a firm stone bridge built once and for all. It is the Word. Just as only the divine Word can convict man of sin and lay bare the soul to its rocky base, so nothing but the Word can reveal the truth about the Redeemer. The external Word is as inescapably necessary for the gospel as it is for the law. No one who is awakened in earnest would ever be able to believe in the forgiveness of his sins, if God had not built a bridge leading to the Rock of Atonement. The supports on which it rests are baptism, the Lord's Supper, and absolution; the arches are wrought by the holy Word with its message of redemption. On that bridge a sinner can pass from the stony ground that condemns to the Rock of Salvation. But should a single one of the arches be allowed to fall, then is man condemned to remain eternally under the law's condemnation, either as a despairing sinner or as a self-righteous Pharisee.

For a very long time, Torvik had not as much as stirred. He drank in every word. Though he had the feeling that Bengtsson was all the time wrestling with Schenstedt and with unyielding strength demolishing his false teachings, he was at the same time aware of the rich measure of soul cure that was intended for the people of Ödesjö and their pastor. He felt grateful. This rough and ready fighter did, after all, have a goodly portion of tender concern for wounded souls. And since Torvik himself belonged to that number today, he accepted the gifts as coming from God.

Not until Pastor Bengtsson had closed with a prayer for the grace of a true faith that works through love, did Torvik remember that it was now his turn to speak. He felt like a college student who dreams that he is standing before a great audience and has not the least idea what he shall say.

Suddenly he got an idea. While the hymn was being sung, he mounted the platform, took the Bible on the lectern, and opened it. His hands trembled as he sat down and began to turn the pages. Fortunately, he found the passage he was looking for, and again took his place at the reading desk.

Facing all these alert and expectant eyes, he was again definitely aware of a critical attitude. But tonight he was not hurt by it. His eyes sought the picture of Luther and then that of Rosenius. He felt that he was an inheritor of all the spiritual life that had been homed within these walls. He felt like the disciple who was privileged to enter upon the labor of others.

Tonight his prayer was the simple, "Lord, sanctify us in Thy truth. Thy Word is truth." Then he began to speak, slowly at first.

"I had really planned to speak tonight about courageous confession and give a little testimony from my own experience of how difficult it can be to confess Christ. But just now another admonition of the Word has suggested itself to me so forcibly, that I must say something about it. The exhortation is found in the third verse of the Letter of Jude, and reads as follows: 'It was needful for me to write unto you and exhort you that ye should earnestly contend for the faith which was once delivered unto the saints.'

"Today it has become clear to me that the Christian faith is a sacred heritage, which must be faithfully preserved, if it is not to be dissipated. There is only *one* Savior. He has lived *once* here on earth; he has spoken certain definite words that can never be changed or recalled, and he has accomplished saving works, whose validity endures to the end of time.

"As long as the world lasts, all Christianity is bound to this Jesus Christ. Just as no one could be a disciple of Jesus during his lifetime only by agreeing with this or that word which he spoke, or by acknowledging the principle of love or something else which one selected from his teaching, so it is no more possible for anyone to be a Christian today by holding to an abbreviated, reinterpreted, or modernized gospel. In those days a man was a disciple by following just this Jesus of Nazareth, hearing him, obeying, believing, and accepting him. Today one becomes a disciple by being united with this same Jesus of Nazareth, being baptized to him, nurtured by him in his church, and receiving his gifts. These gifts are the same today as then. The same words reach us through the Bible, the same feast is celebrated in the Lord's Supper, the same forgiveness is pronounced in the absolution. The conditions of discipleship are the same, salvation is the same. Once and for all, he suffered and died and rose again. Once and for all, the faith that embraces all this has been delivered to the church. And this is the holy and unchangeable faith for which the Word here bids us contend.

"I choose this day to turn away from all that is my own and to consecrate myself to contend for the apostolic faith. I would no longer censure it or make myself its master, as you know that I have done. I would no longer add to it or subtract from it, because I dare not claim to be wiser than the Lord and his apostles. I will not point to my own experiences, but will rather with Paul glory in my weakness. God has shown me that I am a sinner. Perhaps he will now in his mercy also let me be saved in the old way, by grace alone."

He paused a moment. His voice had become uncertain. Hastily, he concluded his remarks.

"My dear friends, it may seem to you that I have, after all, done what I said I had realized one ought not do—I have talked about myself. When next we meet I shall try to come to you with a sermon about Jesus, our Savior. I cannot do it tonight, but would instead admonish each one of us here, and most of all myself, to contend faithfully for the faith that was once delivered to the saints. Amen. And now let us sing the last stanza of Hymn 78, 'Dear cross, the glory of our faith, the depth of God's eternal plan.'"

Torvik had never before spoken so briefly. Nor had he ever, he thought, spoken so poorly. But the effect was such as it had never been before. A warm wave of humility and gratitude billowed through the room. It did not go so much to the pastor as to some point beyond him. It made him both glad and ashamed.

When he left immediately at the close of the service, little Mother Lotta from Drängsmarken greeted him. The eyes closed in her wrinkled face as she whispered so that no one else should hear, "Now the Lord can let his poor servant depart in peace, for now he has heard the prayers of his people, and has let a new day dawn for those who dwelt in darkness. God bless the witness!"

With that she curtsied and vanished, as if she feared she had said too much.

———

At first, silence reigned in the car. When Schenstedt began to speak, he made no reference to what had been said at the meeting. He began to talk about recent world events, and mentioned especially the fate of the Czechs. Torvik admired the sure tact by which he led the conversation to a field where all could meet on common ground after the evening's conflict.

Pastor Bengtsson got off at the Ravelunda parsonage. He thanked Schenstedt for the ride and recommended that serious consideration be given to the first chapter of Galatians. Then he said "Good night!" without any further remarks.

The auto took off in a northerly direction toward Ödesjö. Torvik sat in silence. The day had been so full of experiences and decisions that he found it difficult to get a total impression of it. He felt, however, that he stood face to face with something that was reminiscent of those critical days in his life two years before, when his future path began to be clear to him.

It was not until they reached the old gate lodge at Saleby estate, that he began to speak.

"Gunnar, I hope we shall survive this day without any bad blood. And I trust there will always be a hearty and sincere honesty between us. You understand that I agree in the main with Pastor Bengtsson. We cannot depart from God's Word."

"Certainly no one has wanted to do that! I dare affirm that my position is at least as Christian as yours. For that matter, I have approval for it also from within the Church. Look here!"

He produced a folded newspaper clipping. It was a letter to the editor, a contribution to some discussion of marriage and divorce. It was written in a bold and somewhat jocular tone and contended that many of the couples that the church joined together were never joined together by God. Had not Jesus said that even a lustful look was in itself adultery? Most marriages were therefore already dissolved in the sight of the highest court. As to the story of the Pharisees' question about divorce, anyone with an ounce of understanding could discover that those words about the indissolubility of marriage were wrongly attributed to Jesus. They are, on the contrary, to be attributed to the Pharisees and were typical of their narrow-minded jurisprudence. Rather than feeling oneself restricted by such prejudices, one ought to be guided by one's reason and conscience, and would then arrive at a right solution. The article was signed, "Rector."

Torvik bit his lips together. Now he saw more clearly what was really the gist of the matter.

"This article is either a fake," he said, "or the writer ought to be defrocked—if so be that he really is a pastor. It is not honest to promise at ordination to preach the Word of God as it is given to us in the Scriptures, and then to declare that the very opposite of what Jesus has said is right."

"But Gösta," said Schenstedt, "you know very well that you do not consider yourself bound by the Bible."

Torvik had to admit that his friend was speaking the truth. He had actually said that at times. But tonight he had collided with two altogether new realities and the whole situation was changed. One was his despair about his own salvation, for which he now saw not the least possibility, if he could not rest on the old gospel foundation. No relative or time-conditioned message would now suffice. He needed a word of authority. The other consideration was this hopeless self-will which annulled the clear commandment of Christ while yet claiming the support of his Spirit. And was it not, finally, also the appeal of the religious view of the Bible, made to him, as over against the strictly historical? Was not the view that the Word was such as God wanted it to be after all the faith that best corresponded with the assurance of God as almighty and merciful?

"If I should choose between the Word and my opinion," he said, "I will not hesitate a moment in giving the Word first place. The conscience is a weathercock, but the Word is a solid rock. How can you believe that God is really leading you in the right way when, at the same time, you believe that most of what the apostles and Jesus himself were inspired to say and preach is full of mistakes. I would rather be bound by the Word of God than follow my own feelings."

"I trust more in God himself than in any substitutes."

"The Word is no substitute for God. It is God's way of getting to speak with us."

"Yes, that is *your* view."

"Not mine, but that of Christ and his apostles, and of the whole church."

"The church? How cocksure you have become, Gösta. You surely know that modern faith takes another direction."

"In that case, our modern age is headed for catastrophe. It is certain that no living Christianity wanted to depart from the Bible. Have we not both insisted from the beginning that the guidance we give must be tested by the Bible? Do you still hold that position?"

"I don't know that we can be so cocksure about it. The living Spirit is after all superior to all literalism. True Christianity cannot be bound by any juridical dictates. It is constant creativity and development. Here the conscience alone has jurisdiction. This is the very nerve of all evangelical faith."

"Gunnar," said Torvik, with earnestness and deliberation—as though something suddenly became clear to him, "Do you mean to say that you are breaking directly with that which up to now we have both held sacred? Do you mean that you put that which you believe is guiding you *above* that which is written in God's Word?"

"Without hesitation, if it be granted that the fundamental principle of evangelicalism is development and freedom of conscience."

The pastor held his breath. It was suddenly perfectly clear to him that he and his best friend stood at a parting of the ways, unless one or the other should give up his position. But how had it really come to such a pass? How was it possible that Gunnar had developed in an almost opposite direction from his own?

"Listen, Gunnar," he said. "Have you never had any feeling that you might, in spite of all your obedience, not be a true Christian?"

"What do you mean by that?"

"Don't you feel that you lack something, that after all everything is not right with you down to the smallest detail? I have myself become more and more convinced that, in spite of all my efforts to become a right Christian, I have never really succeeded."

"If you are not a true Christian yourself, you ought not to preach to others."

Torvik kept silent. It was useless to say anything more. The motor droned as they drove up the hill toward the parsonage, and the car swung in between the linden trees. Torvik got out and offered his hand.

"Thank you for tonight, Gunnar. One needs never wonder where you stand. But I can't help feeling that you have entered upon a new road that cannot lead you in the right direction. If we shall be able to work together, we must be sure about the foundation. We must not stand and contradict each other as we did tonight."

"The trouble with you, Torvik, is that you are no longer willing to obey radically and without fear of consequences. Throw your preconceived notions out the window, and God will surely show the way."

"You'll no doubt find out for yourself whether that is valid. A year from now we can perhaps get further in our discussion. It will be a joy to work together with you when you are ready to admit that the Bible transcends us both and all our opinions."

"Do you mean that you refuse to work together with me in the future?" There was something unusually sharp in Schenstedt's look.

"I mean that no one ought to teach the Word of God who does not believe that it is God's Word."

"Then you'll have to undergo a change yourself."

"I intend to do just that."

"Good night, then, Gösta. And good luck!"

"Good night, Gunnar. Don't court disaster on your new way."

The car door slammed shut. Torvik entered the parsonage.

―――――――

Pausing in the hallway, he stroked his forehead as if to wipe away something clammy. He shivered. It was no doubt from the cold and weariness, perhaps also from unhappiness. When he had taken off his overcoat, he caught sight of a little red book that lay on the dresser. On its cover was a picture of Christ as the King of Heaven, and encircling it, the title *The Praying Church.* It was a perfectly new copy, one that had recently come from the book store. Perhaps Bengtsson had put it down, and had then forgotten to take it with him.

He picked up the little volume thoughtfully and began to turn the pages. First there was a lectionary with Scripture selections for all the days of the church year, and then simple suggestions for meditations with themes, these also for the entire year. There was also a list of intercessions with some subjects outlined in part, but also empty spaces to be filled in. Torvik began to be interested. This was just what he might need. He glanced through the various points, the prayers for spouse and children, for relatives and friends, for servants, for the pastor and the congregation, for the worship services, for the preaching, for the young, the homes, the despisers of God and the unconverted, the doubters and the hostile, the sick and the aged. Best of all, he thought, were the empty spaces which, half unconsciously, he began to fill with names and faces and individuals in his own congregation. Mentioned next in turn, were the Church of Sweden, her institutions, the archbishop, the bishops, and fellow pastors. Then there were more white pages that seemed to invite his own additions.

Finally, there were prayers for individual soul needs and for endurance to the end.

This occupied only half of the book. But he put it down. This was enough to think about just now. Should he try it? Was not this the way he must go, if he should get away from this everlasting fluttering between vague feelings and hopeless inertia? If he were faithful in its use, such a framework of intercession would at least keep his prayer life from running dry, as it now so often threatened to do.

He thought about it as he climbed the stairs. Was it not a fixed form, a settled pattern, that his spiritual life needed? Everything tonight had preached to him about the significance of the old heritage, about the external Word and sound doctrine, which were not just a weapon with which orthodox fanatics fought one another, but rather a medicine for tortured souls and an antidote for one's own egoistic inventions. On top of it all, this little prayer book now came with its demand for a self-evident faithfulness and firmness also in prayer.

Suddenly the thought came that Bengtsson had perhaps left the book here intentionally. Was there a suggestion also in this? If so, it was a heart-touching gesture. Even this valiant fighter for the Lord did then have so much compassion with the victims of his solemn strictures, that he would not force upon them all his cures at once, but could leave a bottle on the table with prescription for further use. Be that as it may, a path for the future was opening for him, and he was determined to walk in it.

Everyone, it would seem, was asleep in the house. Torvik took off his shoes and went quietly to his bedroom. The lamp was burning on Britta's night table. She had fallen asleep.

When he had hung up his jacket, it flashed upon him that he had not conducted evening prayers at all tonight. He hesitated a moment. He could of course pray a prayer after getting in bed. But again came the feeling that it was just this lack of order and form that choked his best intentions and let his natural laziness get the upper hand. Was not this the same kind of self-will in respect to prayer that Gunnar was showing in respect to the Word?

It was a perturbing thought that the devil should thus attack him in the very life which he thought he had placed wholly under God's control. But he resolved not to give way to him in the least. From this day he would preach God's Word as he had received it, without excuses or reinterpretations. He would be true to the doctrines of the Church and in employing its prayers and liturgy. "And they devoted themselves to the apostles' teaching and fellowship, to the breaking of bread and the prayers." Thus it was written about the first Christians. That was the whole program!

He was about to put on his jacket again, but stopped resolutely and put on his clerical coat instead. This was to be a rededication. Tonight he had stood at a crossroad and made a decision. The choice was clear. Either he must trust in the Word and the Church, or else believe, as Gunnar did, that he had some higher authority within himself. Since the Word and the inner conviction had this night testified against each other, they could not both be right. Now he must choose. Christendom had surely had to make that choice before. When the Gnostics threatened to spoil genuine Christian faith after the time of the apostles, their defense was the plea for free inspiration. But the church remained steadfast in the apostles' teaching, and so was saved. At the time of the Reformation, the situation was similar. The Anabaptists and the fanatics had urged the Spirit's support for their stand, yet committed all their follies by virtue of their own self-inspired ideas. In his arguments against them, did not Luther insist with great power on the written Word? Might it not be that this was necessary finally in all times of revival? The flood must rise to a certain level, and then possibilities are opened for departure from the old, apostolic channel and a demolition of all the dams. But whenever the development followed this course, nothing but swamps and stagnant pools remained when the flood receded. The deep streams of Christ life flowed on in the apostolic channels of the Church. As for himself, he could not hesitate a moment in choosing his spiritual home and field of activity. He was ordained to serve the apostolic Church, and he would not depart from it.

Just as he snapped on the collar, Britta awakened. She stared at him with amazement.

"Man, what are you intending to do?" she asked.

"Only begin a new life," he answered, and laughed. He went toward the door. She sat up.

"Be careful, then," she said, "that you do not deny Jesus!"

He turned in the doorway, and looked at her, wonderingly.

"I mean the work Jesus has been doing in what He has already let you experience thus far in Ödesjö."

"No danger!" he said with a smile as he left the room. On the stairs he stopped short and remained standing with his hand on the banister. Yes, there was perhaps a danger. There was need for sober thought. There was really no reason for renouncing that which had been. Where would he have been now if this wind of the Spirit had not blown through his parish? He would very likely be sitting in Upsala, a disillusioned former parish minister. And here in Ödesjö, the holy Table of the Lord would have stood as empty as at first, the spiritual inertia would have been unbroken, the many old disputes and offences would be still unsettled. Jonsson would have remained the same inwardly unhappy gambler at cards, and Arvidsson the same respected community leader but, in that case, without the slightest glimpse of the eternal hope he now possessed. No, this work of God was really nothing to pass by with a smile. He needed only to think of Arvidsson, this doughty farmer, genuine through and through, who was now using all his energy and wisdom in helping to make living Christians out of his parish people, to experience a warm glow in his heart. If something had been at fault in all this, he would have to shoulder most of the blame himself, and that because of his spiritual superficiality and his lack of faithfulness toward the Word. But this could be righted.

Now he seemed to see the road of the future quite clearly. The foundation must remain the old and unshakeable one. It rested on the solid rock of the Word, and it bore the ancient road-marks of the church. It led to the same goal as always, passing through the same narrow gate, over the same way of salvation and according to the same order of grace as of old. Nothing of the old was obsolete: the confession remained just as firm, and the answers the church had given through the centuries were just as conclusive against the many enticements of the modern enthusiasts. But through all this that was old and settled blew the Spirit of life and awakening, sweeping away the dust of dead routine and making the miracle of conversion repeatedly as great and new as when it first took place in the early church. The Spirit of revival also belonged to the holy heritage of the Church. If now he would reconsecrate himself to the service of the Church, he would not be untrue to that heritage.

He went into the chamber used for family devotions and knelt on the bare floor before the little home altar. There he prayed first the evening Compline. Then he began to pray for revival, for a salutary unrest among sleeping souls, for real need that would arouse the indifferent, for healing for the bruised and anxious souls, and for strength for everything that had begun to sprout and grow, so that souls might mature and come to secure rest on the Rock of Atonement. For himself, he prayed that he might be given grace to be a true pastor, himself saved for Christ's sake, rooted in the old message, and equipped to care for souls as one rightly handling the unadulterated Word of God. Finally, he prayed for his own Church, as one prays for a beloved mother. He prayed that she might always remain truly apostolic, built on the age-long foundation, and always just as vigorous and youthful, filled with the renewing impulses of the life-giving Spirit.

In the Place
of Sinners

His first sensation was heavy pressure over his chest. The thought which, for a moment, reached the surface of consciousness was confronted by a dark threat, by an unavoidable disastrous fate that already possessed the new day. His will tentatively strained itself to fathom what it could be. Then his whole being became a violent resistance, which spurned against the penetrating darkness. His soul was stretched to the breaking point to embrace a front of sixty miles. He put his shoulder against the bending barrier; he threw the flames of prayer like a burning wall in front of the crack, which was widened and gave in to the black mass. All of a sudden he was wide awake and conscious. There it was: Today again the battle would be all about the Karelian Isthmus. Would the front hold?

As he had done every morning for the last three weeks, Torvik folded his hands and traveled the way of prayer along Suvanto and Taipaleenjoki, through the snowy woods at Loimola and Kuhmo, at Kuusamo and Salla, all the way to Petsamo, beyond the Arctic Circle.

Then again his thoughts began grinding unanswered questions about a fearful future. Today was Sunday. Once again he would celebrate the Mass in Ödesjö church. Once again the bells would chime and be heard over the frozen fields. Yet, for how long? If the inconceivable miracle would not occur—one so inconceivable that no one could fathom how it could happen—if the inevitable would happen, and the lion with the crusaders' straight sword would bleed to death in the snow, if the wave of refugees welled across the border and the dark columns of enemy soldiers followed—now or in a year or so—what would then happen to his own people and his own parish—and his own family? When half awake he had often had horror-filled premonitions of what might happen.

While walking through the quiet rooms on the first floor during late night hours, he could still imagine it all: In the assembly room the foreign commissar had set up his tribunal; the tables were lined up as a bar at the length of the room. The Christ picture in the corner was demolished, at the door soldiers were on guard in their long coats with black spots of melting snow and with dirty straw stuck to their boots. There was the assessor in Eksta, very pale and with a blue spot on his cheek, standing in front of the commissar. An unshaven stranger read the verdict, and the sentence "to be shot" swirled by. Across the parish, the patrols made their nightly house calls in the manner of a frigid pogrom. The church elder from Svenstorp, who had tried to flee, already lay flat on his face behind the tenant's barn; the teachers, the president of the workers trade union, the leaders in the organizations of young farmers and young social democrats were all arrested or deported. Left behind was a frightened, starving and powerless remnant, mostly the elderly—and then the strangers. At school, pale children sang the new songs, and in the church, the pews were thrown together in a corner, and boxes with hand grenades were piled on the floor.

No, what was the good in this! Torvik turned over in bed and folded his hands. After all, they could not shoot God. Temples had been desecrated in times past in Christendom, but the Church remains. The gates of hell would never overcome her. In the final account, all this was only a drop in the cup of suffering that mankind through the millennia again and again had prepared for itself through its disobedience. Was it reasonable to think that our generation, which maybe had been more disobedient than any preceding one, would be spared from it? And had not Christ himself fully drunk the cup to show that the way did not go above a cruel reality but straight through its blood and anguish?

Yet worst was the thought of Britta and Lillan—and the little one whom Britta carried under her heart and whom he himself already had included in his book of intercessions. What would become of them? Would it be their lot to flee with the stream of refugees toward the west? Where could they flee anyway?

And yet—he felt strangely safe. Britta was one of those who could tread on scorpions and serpents without being stung. She would cope with all the misery, warm with prayer and full of love. And as long as she lived, the children would never be raised outside the faith.

The December day had slowly dawned, and the usual Sunday chores began. Torvik prayed Matins and his usual intercessions at the family altar in the parlor. Then followed the family devotions at the same time as the church bells rang for the first time. Since the Feast of St. Michael's he had read Rosenius' daily meditations. Lillan sat on a corner of the sofa with a doll in her arms.

Before the Mass, Torvik never ate anything. Before communion, his wife always fasted as well. She knew that custom already from her devout ancestors in Västergötland, and she adopted it without much deliberation, since she had noticed it as a natural thing with some of Gösta's friends. It rendered a pleasant quietness to these morning hours, when one could devote oneself to getting ready for communion and worship in a way that the "Martha concerns" otherwise would not permit.

The bells had rung the second time. Britta, who had emerged from her sheltered place at the desk in the parlor, tended to the flowers and to Lillan, while her husband finalized his confessional homily. Then he began, in good time, to head to church. He wanted to spend some time alone at the altar before the service. Just as he was putting the announcement book in his briefcase, someone was kicking off snow on the porch, and he heard Arvidsson from the Mansion extending a greeting in his raucous bass voice. Ever since Schenstedt began going his own ways, Arvidsson became the one that was closest to the pastor, an invaluable partner in the care of the parish souls and a truly outstanding example of what kind of fruits the new revival could yield at its best. Torvik suspected that his friend once again came with a matter concerning the cure of souls, and met him with some curiousity in the hallway. Arvidsson wore a grave expression making his way to the pastor's study.

"Is there something of great concern?" Torvik asked.

"You could say that," Arvidsson said, and sat down heavily in the sofa. He was utterly pale. He gathered himself for a moment before he looked straight into the pastor's eyes.

"God have mercy upon us. Agnes at Saleby has reported to the Board of Family and Youth that she is with child, and that Schenstedt is the father."

Torvik had just sat down at the desk and picked up a ruler, an old habit of his. He stiffened like a statue with the ruler lifted halfway from the desk. Then his hand sank down on the desk calendar with a thump.

"Impossible!" was all he said.

"That's what I said, too. She came to me last night. As chairman of the board I had to investigate the matter. Today I made a visit to Saleby . . ."

"Well . . . ?"

Arvidsson's expressionless eyes once again looked into the eyes of the pastor.

"He admits being the father."

There was a long silence. Torvik had an absent gaze. Then he said, "Can you understand a word of this?" He searched his memory. Then he went on fumbling for words. "After all, he has attended church as usual. It can't be more than six weeks since he was away for a speaking engagement. Can you comprehend this?"

"Not in the slightest. Yesterday at this time I would have staked my head that something like this would not be possible—at least not involving Gunnar Schenstedt. The strangest thing is that he does not in any way admit that he has done anything wrong."

Torvik brightened up.

"Are you saying that he intends to marry her?"

"Not at all! Would never occur to him! He promises to pay as required and says that they have nothing to be ashamed of. Through it all they have had everything clear with God. He thinks that since he has not deceived her and will make payments for the child, then everything is clear."

"Isn't he considering her future at all?"

"I never asked him about that. My head was spinning. The worst thing was his amiability. Just as kind and obliging as always. You know, it made me sick. I felt like throwing up."

He was silent for a long while.

"What are we to do now? Where are we to begin with this mess? It has just fallen on me all morning as crumbling scaffolding. Of course, it must be worse for Gunnar himself. Can you imagine his true internal condition?"

Torvik had been sitting with his mouth tightly closed. He clenched his fist.

"If I have not believed that there is a devil, I certainly do now. Here one can see his accomplishments so obviously that one can touch them. I don't want to put the blame on Gunnar alone for this. You see, we live in a poisoned atmosphere. Everything is relative: People consider, opine, hold, feel, and think—right and wrong is a matter of everybody's subjective opinion. Gunnar always had that disposition in his mind. That's why black can become white to him."

Arvidsson returned to his line of thought. "And how about Agnes—and then the child—and then the reaction here in the parish? Since so much evil resulted already from Inger Schenstedt's divorce, then one can only imagine what this will bring about. When someone who has presented himself to be an active Christian without compromising acts in this way, what can you then expect from the young farmhands?"

The pastor brought his fist down on the table.

"But people have to understand that this is not the fault of Christianity or the revival. The fault lies in that he does *not* live as he teaches.

"If people just would grasp it, yes—anyway, I think that he teaches as he lives. That's the most incomprehensible thing in all of this."

He sat quiet and stared ahead with a dead look. Torvik had checked the clock.

"You know, we must leave for church."

They left in silence. The trees were covered with snow and frost. Raw fog hovered over the fields. Along the path in the back yard, they followed the edge of the ditch up to the church. Torvik led the way, his briefcase under his arm.

They talked in broken sentences. First they agreed that Torvik would call on Schenstedt and speak to him in peace and quiet—and that today at communion they would pray God to take away the bitterness and the conceit from their own hearts.

On the hill below the church grounds, Arvidsson stopped. He pointed upward toward the church.

"Torvik, today I thank God that we have her. When things like this happen, the ground shakes beneath you. All that talk about your own conviction, your own opinions, and your beliefs, it's like a swamp where you run the risk of sinking down and disappearing. But up there is a stronghold. If Schenstedt had followed God's Word and the church's teaching as we have it in the catechism and the hymnal, then this would never have happened."

The pastor turned around.

"I have thought of that many times this past year," he said. Then he lifted a finger as if he wanted to admonish himself. "Yet, we have to remember that the stronghold up there won't help us if we don't hold fast to it. What I mean is: We must not forget the personal faith—the faith that believes in the Church's teaching. Without that faith, the Word and the teaching cannot prevent a thing like this."

He was about to add: The same thing has happened even closer to these church walls than today's news. But he kept it to himself, and his thoughts went to the old pastor's snow-covered grave behind the chancel wall, where he had stood so many summer evenings with an unspoken prayer on his lips. Then he continued up toward the church.

When the entrance hymn had been sung and Pastor Torvik, standing at the altar, turned toward the congregation, he suddenly changed color, and his blue eyes intensely became fixed on a certain point on the men's side. Then he focused up toward the organ to steady himself.

Gunnar Schenstedt sat in his usual place, in a middle pew on the men's side. He was well-dressed as always, the one leg placed over the other, with his dark eyes watching the man at the altar with alert and sympathetic attention.

Torvik's eyes were still seeking a focus point at the organ. The balcony railing whirled around for him, the organ front tottered. After all, he had not expected this! And since Schenstedt was here, he might—as usual—come forward for communion. For the first time during his pastoral ministry, Torvik regretted that the custom of registering the communicants before the service had been discontinued long ago in Ödesjö. Then he would have been warned in advance and could have talked to Gunnar for a moment.

His first impulse was now to interrupt the service and rush down to his friend. But that would have been sheer madness and would have made the situation much worse. But how could he now warn him and reach him? If Gunnar's mind was set the way Arvidsson had said, then something terrible could happen today. It was bad enough that he played with religious ideas and found pleasure in turning black into white. Also, his sin was not worse than those of other sinners—there was forgiveness for it. But if he today in defiance intended to commune, to show that he did things his own way, then he came terribly close to committing the sin against the Holy Spirit. No longer was it a matter of just ideas, nor of sinful human beings, but it was about the living Christ himself, the Lord present [in the Sacrament]. If Gunnar dared to treat the Sacrament as a suitable means to vindicate himself and prove his good conscience, then he was dangerously close to that boundary that Judas crossed, when he in stubborn willfulness received the bread from the Savior's hand. "After he received the piece of bread, Satan entered into him." This *must* not happen with Gunnar today!

But how could he reach him?

There was only one chance left. After all, he was standing here and speaking—and Gunnar sat in the pew listening with his big, somewhat dimmed eyes fixed on the ceiling.

As the scripture text for his confessional homily, Torvik had selected a verse from the Epistle, "I am not aware of anything against myself, but I am not thereby acquitted. It is the Lord who judges me." First he talked about those who were aware of something against themselves. He had already addressed those who thought that they could not commune today, and urged them to ask themselves if this was because they were aware of a specific sin, and if so, to repent of this wrongdoing. Then he spoke to those who intended to commune and asked them too, to examine themselves, whether they were aware of any wrongdoing. In his manuscript he had mainly listed a number of economic and social sins, matters concerning income tax returns, employees, work, and property of others. Then he began to talk about sins against the sixth commandment, primarily the obvious sins in deliberation and action. As with all other sins, they must be confessed as sin and be abandoned. The situation must be amended, and this amending could never be just with money, but must always be of a personal kind as well.

While he was speaking, he mustered all his boldness and looked straight at his friend. Schenstedt who had had his eyes fixed on the ceiling, calmly looked back at Torvik. No change was visible in his expression. Torvik took a firm grip on the altar book as if he needed support. He would have liked to grab his friend by the shoulders and shake him. If he could not do it physically, he had to do it with the means of the Spirit. He had learned from Schartau that the binding key could be used also in the confessional address. While feeling how his hands trembled, he said slowly, stressing every word:

"If you are aware that you knowingly and willingly have committed such things that God's Word brands as sin, whether against the Sixth Commandment or against any of the other commandments, then I ask you, in the name of Jesus, for your own sake, to repent. Even if you came here in order to commune, you must not do that unless you confess that your sin is sin, regret it, abandon it, and are prepared to amend, with all that is in your power. In order that you today shall understand how serious this matter is, I remind you of the authority our Lord Jesus Christ has given his servants of his Word when he said, 'If you retain the sins of any, they are retained.' And now I tell you upon the command of our Lord Jesus Christ: As long as you do not repent and believe, your sin is retained. In the name of God, the Father and the Son and the Holy Spirit. Amen."

Torvik felt how Schenstedt, during the last two sentences, had keenly and attentively fixed his eyes on him. He had to mobilize all his strength to overcome his diffidence. He wanted to throw away the book and run away. But he pulled himself together. As a soldier of our Lord he had to stand here pointing the bare edge of the sword against his friend's chest to prevent him from running headlong to perdition. For the remainder of the confessional address, his soul was one great cry for mercy. He knew that he could accomplish nothing by himself but he was hoping for a miracle that would drive his friend to repentance and penance.

He came to the Confession of Sins. In his thoughts he was kneeling at Gunnar's side. He confessed his own lack of love and his laxity. He confessed that he had left his friend adrift in spite of his suspicion that the current was overpowering him. He embraced him in his confession of sin, pulled him with himself before God's throne, carried him like a child to God praying for forgiveness and mercy.

He rose to pronounce the absolution. He didn't dare to look at Gunnar until he concluded with the sign of the cross while saying the name of the Holy Trinity.

Gunnar sat slightly bent forward with his head in his hand. A flame of wild joy shot through Torvik. Maybe after all . . .

When the service had proceeded to the time when the communicants rose in the pews, Torvik stood at the altar and held the chalice in his hand. He again felt how his legs gave way. Gunnar had risen. He came down the aisle. His arms, as usual, were somewhat casually hanging at his sides. When he stepped up into the chancel area, he looked up toward the altar, confident and smiling.

He walked over to the right section of the altar railing and knelt. In the next moment, Torvik saw how Arvidsson came forward and knelt at Gunnar's left side. It was as if he wanted to protect his friend from something and shoulder his portion of a danger that was threatening his friend.

The wide railing was almost filled with communicants at the Lord's Supper. Torvik started to give out the bread. He came to Schenstedt, whose face was as expressionless as Torvik's own voice. He again was hoping that something really had happened. His whole being was a warding-off movement, a shield of prayers that he lifted over Saleby, over his friend, and his parish. When he returned from the sacristy immediately after the service, Schenstedt was already gone. Torvik dared not consider what that might mean, but hurried home after having said good-bye to Arvidsson.

Less than an hour later, he arrived by bicycle through a thin layer of snow on the Saleby front yard. He put the bicycle at the main door, made his way into the cold entrance hall, and took off his coat. He took a couple of deep breaths and knocked on the door to Schenstedt's study. Gunnar's voice answered from inside, and Torvik flung the door open. His friend sat reading at the fireplace. He had his feet placed on a stool. A nice smell of good pipe tobacco filled the room.

Torvik, standing at the door, looked childishly lost. Fumbling with the watch string inside his unbuttoned clergy coat, his big head bent forward, he took a shy glance at his elegant friend, who smiled cheerfully upon him.

"Thank you for the sermon!" Schenstedt said. He did not rise to extend a greeting, since they had already seen each other that day.

Torvik took a few heavy steps forward. He pulled out a chair and sat down closer to the fireplace.

"Gunnar, we need to speak."

In Schenstedt's eyes there was a look that might indicate discomfort, but his tone of voice was as amiable as always.

"Sure, Gösta. What do you have on your mind?"

"Agnes, of course. Through Arvidsson I have learned that you are the father of her child."

"Yes, that's right."

Torvik was leaning forward with his elbows on his knees, his hands clutched together and his eyes fixed on Schenstedt. He was still hoping and yet filled with fear that the last hold of hope would be shattered. He spoke slowly:

"And now, Gunnar, if I correctly understand the way you acted at church today, you want to do what is right and honorable."

"Sure, I will."

Anguish was lurking behind the gleam of hope in Torvik's eyes.

"So you are going to marry her and accept the child as yours."

Schenstedt slightly raised his eyebrows.

"I never said that. I am going to do what is expected of me in every way providing for both Agnes and the child. But marriage—that's unthinkable. You must admit that would be cruel. Agnes could never be happy in such a marriage."

The pastor eyed him with a piercing gaze.

"Did it never occur to you that it was cruel to put her in the situation where she is now?"

"But my dear friend," Schenstedt said reproachfully, "I can assure you that neither she nor the child will lack anything."

"Do you think all needs are met with money? Can you cure bad reputation with money? Can you with money ward off all young men who will be stretching their hands out for her, just because she once strayed? Can you with money get her a man who will sincerely love both her and your child?"

Schenstedt made an averting motion with his hand.

"Dear friend, you don't need to be so reproachful. I understand very well that you with your conception of the church must reason the way you do. But try to understand where I am coming from. To me all that Jesus taught is summed up in the commandment to love. Isolated Bible verses, disconnected commandments and laws, they are all relative and human. Only love is eternal and divine. It may very well appear in a way that seems to be absolutely contrary to the moral concepts of times gone by. And yet it is the love of Jesus that is expressed in the new ways, and if one does not want to act against the love of Jesus, then one must go the new ways. It is my firm conviction that all those old taboos that the church has fenced around marriage now are ready to be dispensed with. Just think about it: They all are based on the idea that the man owns a woman as his property. But now she has fully come of age and can no longer be treated as an investment. She now has her freedom. And a Christian relationship is characterized by love alone. The spirit of Jesus demands that we should be good and considerate, not hurting one another but making each person as happy as we can. Applied to marriage . . ."

Torvik had pulled himself up in his chair. He took a firm grip on the rail.

"Do you really think, Gunnar, that you have been as considerate toward Agnes and given her as much happiness as you can?"

"Absolutely. I can honestly assure you that she has been happy. She hasn't done anything that she herself didn't want to. What do you think of me, anyway? I can assure you that I always treated her with the greatest tenderness and respect. Our relationship has been on a pure and worthy level. We have talked about the highest issues . . ."

Torvik had risen. He paced with long and erratic steps to-and-fro over the floor.

"If you were not my best friend, Gunnar, I would believe you to be a base liar and blasphemer. Instead I believe that you, in some way, have gotten an evil spirit into your body, distorting your views. That's why you cannot see that what you call love is the studied selfishness, a way of swinging along in a sea of amiability while avoiding all real responsibility. All this, which you call love, will cause more suffering and misery for people around you than anything else that you have done. What do you think that you have brought upon your grandmother through all of this?"

Torvik thought he saw a notion of uncertainty in his friend's eyes. But his tone of voice was calm and firm when he answered:

"I am not responsible for the prejudices that the church has put into people. If others would respect my conviction, as I respect theirs, then all such conflicts would be settled once and for all."

"That is just as unrealistic as to say that you have full moral right to drive your car on the left side, because if others would respect your way of driving, there would be no collisions. But if you drive on the left side, when others keep to the right, then you realize, don't you, that you will cause a collision—although it might well be that someone else will get the worst injuries!"

"I don't see how that applies to my situation."

"Don't you see, man, that psychological laws are laws, too! If you do something that cuts a person apart inside, then you are not excused by saying that if a person would just refashion herself, she could very well be able to handle such blows. If in fact the youth in our parish are apt to be influenced by your way of treating Agnes and emulate it in coarser and baser ways, then you are not excused by your never having asked them to do it. And if you behave in such a way that your old grandmother with her whole outlook on life must feel a dagger thrust in her heart, then you are not excused with your not liking her outlook on life. You still put the dagger in her heart. And calling that love and consideration is turning black into white!"

Torvik had stopped at the window. He was facing the fireplace and spoke heatedly.

"Gunnar, you are the one in this world with whom I have had the deepest spiritual fellowship. I am immensely sorry for my leaving you alone so often since that Lenten service last spring. I ask you to forgive me for that. I have been thinking of it today, how much it reveals my selfishness. As soon as I no longer thought that I could use you in the parish work, then I didn't have time for you as a friend and fellow human being. Forgive me for that!"

A light cloud of uneasiness was dimly seen on Schenstedt's forehead, as he made an averting motion with both hands. Torvik had taken a step closer.

"There is nothing on earth, for which I have been longing more than that everything would be as before, Gunnar."

The uneasiness in Schenstedt's face gave way for obvious surprise. He said, "On *my* side there is no hindrance."

"Yes, man, you are not the same as before."

Again Schenstedt looked up with amazement in his big eyes.

"I thought that it was *you* who had changed! Ever since you got caught up in the forms and the traditionalism and all that church stuff, we have drifted away from each other."

Torvik closed his eyes for a moment, as if he were thinking. "Yes, Gunnar, maybe I have become different than before. But I don't want to shorten an inch of the program for which we fought. Just as much as I did then, I still want to make the four demands on me and others—even if I now see that they are not the foundation for our salvation, but goals of our sanctification. There is nothing of the wonderful things that we had in common that I would want to abandon. But I don't think that you today can defend your conduct either as pure or as loving or as honest or as unselfish—in the sense that we then took the words."

Now Schenstedt, too, had risen. He shrugged lightly.

"Gösta, there is no point in our discussing this. I'll follow my free course, and you will follow your bound one. Then God may judge. I hope that you'll respect me as I respect you."

Torvik breathed deeply with his mouth half-open, wheezing his words. He got a pained expression in his face.

"Gunnar, I just cannot do that. If I said that I respected your point of view, I would fail Christ."

Schenstedt smiled.

"I thought I noticed in church today that you dared to brand my way of following my conscience as sin. I am not angry with you for that. But I thought it was too bad that you would have such a hard time to understand a different point of view."

"My *own* point of view I would leave at any time if only we could remain friends, Gunnar. But *Christ's* point of view I can never leave. In the final account, this is not a matter of points of view, but it concerns our eternal salvation!"

"And so you have today bound me to eternal damnation!"

"No, Gunnar, to eternal salvation so that you might not forget that it exists. I will follow you from this day on till you cannot endure any day longer of being bound in sin, as you now have been for several months."

Schenstedt smiled a tired smile.

"Actually, I did realize that your intention was good . . ."

"Gunnar," Torvik said with a harshness that maybe revealed his being more moved than he wanted to show, "even if you yourself totally ignore how your soul will fare, could you not consider your old friends, who would be heartbroken if you gambled away your heart to the devil?"

Schenstedt had turned away and picked at something on the mantle piece. After a while Torvik went on:

"Gunnar, what you have arrived at is not a development, but a falling away. When we fought together, we wanted to obey the God of Scripture. Now you only follow your own conscience."

Schenstedt turned. He had a deep furrow between his eyebrows.

"So what? I have never claimed to represent any movement or confession or sect."

"But you have at least belonged to a living spiritual fellowship!"

"If such a fellowship becomes a constraint for one's conscience, then it must be broken. Nothing must violate freedom of conscience. After all, that is the very basic principle of the Gospel."

"No, brother! The basic principle of the Gospel is to know nothing but Jesus Christ and him crucified. Belonging to him means being a member of his body, joined together with all other Christians in a holy fellowship. One cannot be a Christian for oneself. 'You are all one in Christ Jesus.' The eye cannot say to the hand: I have no need of you. By one Spirit we were all baptized into one body. You, too, Gunnar! You may go your own way. Even so, you can never undo your baptism. And you are baptized in the apostolic Church to the apostolic faith and the apostolic creed. You cannot prevent the Jesus who has forbidden adultery to lay claim to you."

"Leave me alone, Gösta." Shenstedt looked pale and pained. "I have never asked for your advice in this matter. I know your position and respect it. It is painful to me that you cannot respect my position, but that is something that I can do nothing about."

He offered his hand.

"Gunnar," said Torvik quietly and took his hand. "Yet you will not be able to keep kicking against the goads . . ." Then he left.

———————

When he arrived home at the parsonage gates, he continued straight ahead along the road, passing by a couple of sheds that were leaning against each other, shot with gray by frost. Down at the stone bridge over the creek, he turned to the right and followed the narrow road along the shore down toward the church. Steam was rising from the ice holes. A lone crow took off from the trash heap below the church yard wall.

When he stood on the hillside up toward the church yard entrance, he recalled what Arvidsson had said here on their way to the service. He looked up toward the mighty, broad tower and steeple, the tarred shingles of which were white-grained from ice crystals. The church stood there austere and firm, like a veteran at his post with frosty eyebrows and his heavy boots steady on the ground. At the same time there was something motherly in her appearance, a tried and suffering mother's patient look toward the future and her open arms toward her ungrateful children.

He stamped his shoes on the stone slab and took out the keys. Standing there, he could not help but put his hand half caressingly on the wall and swipe it across one of the large cobblestones that showed its contour underneath the liming.

Yes, Arvidsson was right, here was the stronghold. Here was the heavenly city with the firm walls that God had built on the rock Christ, so that it would rise out of the maelstrom of the ages. If one would let go of that stronghold, then one would also be swept away from the rock Christ and be absorbed by the waves. Gunnar's curse was precisely that he thought himself wiser than the Church, that he believed himself having a light superior to that of the Word and a sense for the truth that was sharper than the collected testimony of the prophets, the apostles, and the saints. Was it not altogether the curse of this modern age? Trusting a vague feeling of benevolence and a hazy idea of culture and progress, people let go of the objective and drove away, believing that they are led by the spirit of Jesus or by love or by some inner light, while they—in reality—were victims of their own nature with all its treacherous selfishness.

He had arrived at the aisle and knelt for the entrance prayer. Then he walked slowly up toward the altar. It was already dusk. The purple altar hanging looked almost black.

Purple—it was the Church's color of penance. He had never before experienced Advent as a time of penance as strongly as this year. It was twilight in the world. Old dreams of happiness collapsed as bombed buildings. There was blackout and bitter cold deep inside people in whose minds the very faith in the future was paralyzed. But God's Church stood in the midst of this twilight land observing Advent. She was securely looking forward to a great light that would give light to those who sit in darkness and the shadow of death.

How infinitely wise she was, the Church our Mother! Through the millennia she had seen through all that is wrong and wicked. At all false paths she had built barriers of sound doctrine and wise rules for living. It suddenly struck him that Gunnar's last folly that he contended was a result of recent development, as a matter of fact, had been known almost two thousand years ago. Already in the early Church there were enthusiasts who said that anything was permissible for believers, even adultery and fornication. They were called Nicolaitans; they are mentioned in the beginning of Revelation. There we also find the harsh and yet true designation that the Church already two thousand years ago applied to that kind of wisdom: the depths of Satan. But right in the middle of all this aberration and all its repulsiveness, the Cross with the Redeemer rose then as now, just as once the bronze serpent on its pole in the desert.

He looked up at the Christ picture at the center of the ancient altar retable. Blood gushed from his side in a dark stream. Truly, the stream of the Atonement poured down upon this distorted world. Since God was willing to offer such a precious sacrifice for us his unworthy children, then there was no cause for grumbling lamentation and moaning. He should rather be trustful and thankful that God had not forgotten anybody, including his friend Gunnar.

He was now at the altar rail. This was the place where Gunnar had knelt. Arvidsson had been to his left. Now he himself had proceeded to the right of where his friend had communed, and there he knelt.

———

It was near midnight.

Torvik took the doll that had been left on the couch in the study, after first having mended its broken foot. He was holding some papers in his other hand, his blond hair was very tussled, he was bent forward a little, and he looked absent-mindedly out into the January night. Dry and icy snow was beating against the pane, and the storm was howling.

Now he is lying in his tent, Torvik thought, snow filtering in through an opening in the tent cloth and making a white nib across the sleeping bed. Now it is reaching his head. He wakes up and wipes off the slush from his neck. Or maybe he is on sentry duty—while the cold creeps up from his finger tips to his elbow and tiredness aches under the rifle strap.

Again he breathed heavily, almost groaningly—God alone knows how often this evening. Still holding the doll and the papers, he went over to the large room and turned on the light. The map of Finland was mounted beside the chamber door. Once again he followed the roads and read the names: Joutsijärvi, Pelkosenniemi, Savukoski, Salla. No doubt about it, here was one of the fatal moments where our future now was hanging on a hair over a sword's edge. There was a rumor that the Swedish volunteers would be put in action somewhere up there. If so, Gunnar would be skiing through the woods with the birds of death hovering above.

It was almost three weeks since he left. Everything happened so fast. Torvik barely had had time to grasp it, before Schenstedt came for a good-bye visit, more amiable than ever. The pastor had felt it painful: So aboundingly amiable can only the one be who feels he has got the upper hand.

Ever since the failed attempt at agreement in Advent, Torvik had been determined not to let his friend out of his sight. There were not many opportunities for contact during the holidays. Even when they saw each other, the contact was broken. They avoided talking about what had happened. Neither could they talk about the faith or issues of the soul. They had entered two different worlds without reciprocal communication. So they had to stick to the war and current issues. Their conversation sank down to conventional small talk. It was humbling and bitter. After all, the two of them had once been welded together in a brotherhood of the Spirit, sharing everything in the battle for God's dictatorship.

Once again the pastor's thoughts wandered along that desolate border area where he now was familiar with every place name. Again he was torn inside. Why was he here in his clergy suit, when men in gray uniforms and snow clothing were needed over there? When the war broke out, he had been completely convinced that Sweden would be militarily engaged. He had made sure that papers and documents were in good order, made out powers of attorney, and instructed Britta in the handling of the most urgent parish office business. But the mobilization order was never issued. As week after week passed, the cry from the east became more and more imperative. He had sent everything that he could spare—but what would that accomplish? He had said it himself when he delivered the skis at the bus: there should also have been a man on them.

Britta had sensed how he struggled. The one thing she said was: "You must be certain before you go. Remember that you would be a poor soldier in the field, and that God also needs soldiers at his sparsely manned front at home as well— all the more if the worst would happen and times of martyrdom would become a reality."

He would be a poor soldier, that he knew—clumsy, easily winded, and militarily untrained. But was not that the great thing now, to give one's utmost without weighing its value with cold calculation? When events like this happened in the world, was it not one's duty then to fight against the onslaught of evil, ready to give one's life as a quiet protest?

And on the other hand—if the day now was at hand when the sense of justice no longer could be defended by the sword, because justice for a long time had been trampled underfoot by us ourselves, and our whole culture had become so permeated by moral decay that God had to allow the scourge from the east to come upon us with bloody sentences and martyrdom? What would then become of his parish?

He had slowly crossed the floor and turned off the light again. At that very moment, the moon shone through a rift in the stormy clouds so that its light for a moment played over the varnished floorboards. He proceeded to one of the windows in the large room. Behind the bare fruit trees in the parsonage yard, the grain field slanted down toward the church village. Moon shadows appeared and disappeared over the snowdrifts; the storm drove white snow clouds like hunted spirits across the fields. Farthest down was the church village, a conglomeration of white roofs and black walls.

He leaned his forehead against the icy cold pane. Now if the strangers come? What would they do with his parish? One could very well imagine it: First purge all who had moral courage, leadership experience, or competence to be the backbone in passive resistance—no doubt that all that would be part of the strategy, already carefully applied in Finland under tsarist rule. And then? Most likely an arranged election. He could see what it would look like: A unified ballot composed of a few names from the parish, some pitiable fellows who had been frightened into it or who at last had gotten the chance to come to a level of prominence that the sound judgment of others so far had denied to them—and then only out-of-parish people and strangers, known to nobody here. Then there would be intensive radio propaganda with veiled threats against all who would abstain from voting. On election day there would be a military force at each polling place making sure that the one approved ballot was used. How would the people react? Again he could see it in his mind's eye: The parsonage farmer, that honorable man, took off for the woods in the morning. He has decided not to vote. By evening he returns home, wet and cold. Then a truck comes rattling from the Hyltamåla direction; and it is almost full of people. A soldier steps noisily into the kitchen together with a civilian agent who speaks a different dialect from the one of this province; they have come to pick up Karlsson. He wants to refuse—but then he looks at the children who are clinging together in a corner. He looks at his wife who has understood the threat in the stranger's voice and weeps. He must give in. They also force him to bring the ballot envelope for his wife. At the polling place, a soldier looks over his shoulder, when he puts the ballot in the envelope. He steps forward to the ballot-box. The Commissar with the long mustache nods content-edly. There will be a high level of ballots submitted, maybe the ninety percent he had orders to get.

No, this melancholy was sin, unbelief and ingratitude! Torvik had put the doll and the papers under his arm and folded his hands. The moon was again visible, only thick snow clouds palely illuminated by the shine from above drove across the sky. He prayed for his people and for his parish, prayed for strength to preach the mystery of the Atonement and the joy of the Resurrection, so that here would spring forth wells in the hearts that would continue to sing with quiet happiness and secret strength even behind barbed wire and prison walls.

Again his thoughts wandered out into the night toward the horizon in the east.

How much better Gunnar was than he himself! He had never hesitated. He left—happy and free. Torvik had wanted to order him to stay at home. He had wanted to say, "I will go in your place—you must not die, as your circumstances are now." But he never said it. He had allowed him to leave and he had admired him for it.

Aunt Agneta lived now at Saleby in her solitude. She had arrived there the week after Gunnar left. There was no denying that Gunnar took after his grandmother. In spite of her gray hair, there was still in her appearance much of her dark beauty. She was taller and slimmer than Gunnar. They had the same eyes, though Aunt Agneta's were more serene, in some sense calmer. With Gunnar there was always something volatile that sometimes got a dark tinge of something almost diabolic.

It was during the year of great success for the new revival that he had learned to love Aunt Agneta. She was herself a child of the revival which was a powerful spiritual force in the years around 1880, when they had had a young Rosenian pastor in the parish. Although she always spoke her mind about the shortcomings of the new revival, she still embraced it with such genuine love, that one could always talk to her as with one's most faithful fellow believers.

Now she sat there alone at cold Saleby. It cut Torvik to the quick thinking what she had gone through this Christmas. Inger's divorce had been a hard blow to her. She was completely alone now that Inger had followed Rothman to America and never sent word of her whereabouts.

Slowly he walked into the chamber to the left. At the shorter wall was the altar, where they this evening as usual had said Compline. Still with the doll and the by now crumpled sheets of paper under his arm, he lit the candles in the brass candlesticks and fell down on his knees. He gave thanks for all God's witnesses who had been able to accomplish that which he was unable to do. He gave thanks for the martyrs. He gave thanks for all the storms that God had permitted His church to weather, and for the promise that the gates of Hell would not prevail against her. He gave thanks for her being granted to sing his praise when the Huns were roaming about the walls, and for her having the power to reveal the glory of the redemption even at the age of the last tribulation. He further prayed for a sparkle of that light which the darkness would never overcome. Then his prayer returned to the aching point, where he carried the painful question of his sick heart, and he prayed for full and certain clarity and happy strength to go the way that the Lord of hosts had laid down for him. Finally he commended into God's hands himself and his family, his sleeping parish and his country, his Finnish brothers and his compatriots among the volunteers, and he went upstairs still holding the doll and those crumpled sheets of paper under his arm.

The February day was drawing to an end. The cold was still as intense as before, and a sharp wind swept over the snowy fields. The whirling snow had formed a sharp-edged drift across the road at the entrance gate at Saleby.

When Torvik trudged up toward the mansion, the snowed-over roof standing white against the heavy, gray winter sky, he thought with nostalgia of the many warm summer evenings, remembering how he came here on his bicycle with news from their common crusades, how he was greeted with such warmth by his friends, their laughter echoing between the apple trees.

Now Saleby was deserted. The last snow was not swept away from the steps to the entrance door, and no light shone in the windows. In the grey dusk, Aunt Agneta was walking somewhere in the empty rooms—a thin, silver-haired, and mourning remainder from buried, happy years before the war. It was she he had come to see.

In order to avoid making the maid break open the main entrance door that was frozen shut and to avoid letting in snow and wind there, he opted to enter through the kitchen door. He nodded familiarly to the girl at the sink who had been a confirmand of his. Yes, Mrs. Schenstedt was sitting in the small chamber, she informed.

Torvik remained standing on the threshold of the small green chamber. The old lady was sitting in the semi-dusk thoughtfully leaning back in the white armchair with a long-fringed shawl around her shoulders, her feet on a high stool and with an open book in her lap, her narrow face quietly illuminated in the evening light.

"Good evening, my boy," she greeted. "It was good of you to come."

Torvik moved a taboret forward and sat down next to the old lady. As tall as he was, it seemed to him as if he were sitting at her feet.

"Are you freezing? It's cold here . . ."

"No cause for worrying about me, Ma'am, but you should not be sitting here any longer in the cold of Saleby. You should go back to Linköping."

The old lady just smiled.

"No, my boy, my place is here now."

Torvik addressed with greater energy the concern for which he had come.

"Ma'am, you fare outright badly here! An old mansion like Saleby is not a good winter residence for an old person. First the cold, and then the loneliness . . . We talked about it today again in the parsonage, and I am here to ask you to think of yourself for once."

The old lady just reached out with her hand and placed it lightly on the pastor's sleeve.

"It's so kind of you to think of me. But I'll stay here now. You see, my boy, when an old house where people have lived for more than a hundred years suddenly is allowed to be empty and chilled down, it is as if a heart has stopped. It is not only the water pipes that freeze and the spinet that gets out of tune. It is not only that strangers allow the roses to die and the fence to deteriorate. There is a part of life itself that dies when nobody any longer walks across the rooms, when nobody chats at dusk, and nobody says prayers. Damp and raw air comes in, which is not easy to get rid of again. That's why I'm staying here, tending to the fireplaces. If Gunnar comes back home alive, I'd like him to find Saleby a warm place. It has become cold enough in the world."

Torvik had first put his fingertips against one another, then he slowly folded his hands, sitting with his head bent forward.

"You see, my boy, then you must also think of the temporal things. Gunnar left everything as it was, and there were a few things that needed to be taken care of. Now I have gotten his authority, so I have picked at the papers a little. I am not able to do much, but I can at least sign papers as needed. And just such a thing as my walking across the yard over to the stable once in a while means that the horses get more attention for their grooming. There are a thousand things, you see, that someone should supervise."

Torvik realized that he never could persuade Aunt Agneta to leave this mansion where she had been the matriarch for forty years. He remained silent looking down at her feet. Over her shoes she had slipped on thick socks. He understood why. This ugly arrangement was a matter of necessity. Aunt Agneta was otherwise always very strict with her outward appearance.

The old lady looked out in the blue winter dusk.

"It's windy," she said. "It seems to be a cold and cutting wind, I can feel it all the way in here. I wonder how they are faring up there. I'm thinking of the horses in the snow and of the wounded—and then of Gunnar."

The pastor had placed his folded hands on his forehead. He put his elbows in his lap. Then he looked up.

"Ma'am, you just don't know how much I admire Gunnar—in spite of all that has happened. I think of him every day as I enjoy the warmth of the parsonage. I have not been able to make a sacrifice like his."

The old woman looked sadly out on the sky.

"You should not admire, my boy. Nothing human measures up. Instead you must love. One may always love—also that which is broken and twisted."

She took a deep breath. It was as if the words stuck in her throat. She began talking about something else.

"One Christmas when Gunnar was ten, twelve years old, he broke the big Chinese plate in the living room. He denied it, and I did not bring it up again, but he realized that I knew who had done it. He appeared as if nothing were the matter, he was as happy and kind as ever; but I could see that there was a secret discord in his eyes. Then it happened that on the eve of Epiphany the small table Christmas tree caught fire. It was completely dry and burned like a birch broom. Everybody was screaming that it had to be thrown out, but nobody dared to take hold of it. Then Gunnar sprang forward and, putting his hand straight into the fire, he took hold of the trunk and didn't let go of it until the outside steps. He got some blisters, but otherwise he was fine. Grandfather and everybody else praised him a lot, but I kept silent that time. I understood that he made that sacrifice to justify himself before his conscience, avoiding that way that God had showed him."

Torvik remained silent. He understood what the old woman meant. He also understood that she wanted to let hinting be enough.

He had been sitting for a good while with his head bent down. When he looked up, he saw that she wiped her eyes with her handkerchief.

"Yet, it is harder than one can think," she said. "First to see the last one of your family debase himself in this way, causing so much pain. Everything is so cold at Saleby now. Agnes is crying all the time. After Gunnar left and she no longer has the power of his eyes on her, she does not believe that what she did is right. In a way, that is a good thing because now she comes close to forgiveness. I also pity the other girls. The little one has big, frightened eyes, as if the ground faltered below her. The big one has gotten such hard eyes. It is as if she wanted to say: Say something, if you dare! I had to chase away the farmhands from the kitchen steps a few evenings ago. They looked at me as if they were thinking: We thought everything was permitted here. Well, it may pass. But there is a curse connected with sin. It corrodes as poured acid. A long time afterwards one finds holes where one least would have expected."

"You know," she said suddenly, "I wish I could take upon myself all the consequences of what Gunnar has broken. It is so cruel to see those who have no fault in it. Now I have just my small part that I must carry. And I am happy to do so."

He must have looked astonished, so she explained.

"You see, atonement comes only through suffering. Through suffering our Savior opened the gates of Heaven, through suffering his apostles carried the Gospel out in the world—rejoicing that they were counted worthy to suffer. It is a great favor to bear testimony to Christ by suffering in his fellowship. I believe Scripture calls it bearing in the body the marks of the Lord Jesus. Usually we suffer only for our own sins. But sometimes we are given the favor of suffering for the sins of others. That is part of the mystery of the Atonement: when one is joined to Christ, one is given the task of lifting a portion from a certain sinner and suffering in his stead, so that he does not have to carry alone all the bitterness of his deeds."

She spoke slowly and gently, as if she were afraid to distort a fine and fragile secrecy through clothing it in words.

"There is something wondrous about this power that God has laid in innocent suffering. More than a hundred years ago, they had a pastor here in Ödesjö—I forgot his name: it was my father-in-law who told me about him when I first came to Saleby. He was a hammer of the Lord, a powerful preacher against all evil in the parish. It was not pleasing to the powerful; they conspired together and had him outrageously chased away. The manner in which he handled that injustice in humility and love for all opened the eyes of a twenty-year-old boy, who since that day became a sincere Christian. His name was Eugene Schenstedt. He was the father of my father-in-law."

Torvik was not able to say anything. He felt like a novice, unworthy of uttering a word here. The old lady became silent again looking out through the window.

"I wonder if I shall see him coming back home this time . . ."

Torvik was about to say something, but then he perceived that the old lady did not have the war in mind after all. She went on:

"The first time it took two years. Then he confessed. But he is older now and harder. I am afraid that God must hammer a long time at his heart, before he accepts the truth again. But I'm not letting go of God's hand, I will not leave in peace, not even for a moment. I am displaying all his promises and holding him to all the commitments that he himself has made. Ever since that difficult day before Christmas my heart has been at his feet. And I am not taking it back until he hears me."

Torvik nodded slowly. He and Arvidsson had together committed themselves to prayer as well. They would not cease praying and not allow the lamps to go out, until they would see their friend come loose of the grip of darkness.

"You see," the old lady began again in her soft voice, which although so filled with sadness was yet so soothing, "this whole time I have wanted to do something for Agnes' child. Now I think that I've found the right way. Since Gunnar won't acknowledge his child, who yet is my great grandchild, I'm going to adopt it. That way it will after all carry its father's name and will be an heir of mine together with him. Agnes will stay here as long as I am here at Saleby, then she'll accompany me to Linköping and be there to begin with. After that, we'll see. As long as she wants to, she'll take care of the child. However, I think I've noticed that she prefers to go away, and maybe it would be best that way. Now I'd like you to tell Ernst Arvidsson, that it would be kind of him to stop by when he's coming this way. Then he could help to set up the papers. Of course, it will not be a matter of adoption until the child is born."

Torvik looked firmly at the cabinet in the corner with the Meissener dolls. He dared not to look at Aunt Agneta. This was truly a faith active in love! As a matter of course she was ready to adopt this disdained child to remedy what someone else had neglected.

They conversed quietly yet for a while, until the room became dusky. It was still mostly the old lady that did the talking. In between they were silent for long moments. Then he had to leave and bid farewell.

───────

He stopped for a moment at one of the snow drifts in the main driveway. The wind swept icily cold through the yard; the whirling snow smarted like sharp-pointed grains of sand in his face. It was almost dark. Some fruit trees stretched their frozen branches like praying arms toward heaven. They certainly were blighted with frost long ago. The spruces moved heavily, stiff from cold, rattling with their icy needles.

The words in the Letter to the Romans came to his mind, about how the whole creation is groaning in travail together, because it is subjected to futility and waits with eager longing for the revealing of the sons of God. Yes—the creation is under a curse.

He saw a vision of shivering horses with their tails against the storm and snow under the housing, of sentries with their eyes burning of fever, and of children crying in their half-burned homes. He heard slow tramping of ragged felt shoes and the echo of a softly plaintive Vespers song from the chilled prison barracks among the ices of the White Sea. A wave of infinite suffering drove with the storm through the winter night as if it wanted to drown everything in cold, darkness, and meaninglessness.

"Because of him who subjected it in hope." Again the echo from Romans came to him. Yes—beyond the darkness and the meaninglessness there was burning a love that itself suffered with the fallen creation, and that went in under its suffering and shame, under the curse and the judgment, to atone for all that is broken and save all that is lost to a new world. In his death all woe was turned into blessing. The very suffering became a gate of Heaven, and the cross, that instrument of torture, became a sign of victory and spring of mercy. Walking with him is going to glory through suffering itself and seeing the springs rush forth everywhere through the valley of weeping and the deserts of thistles. Anywhere where someone is suffering undeservedly in His name, new streams are welling up from the depth of His atonement. Now Aunt Agneta through her suffering was ushering in healing and new blessing over Saleby. Thus the Russian martyrs, too, suffered in the cold and misery of the prison camps to open new ways for streams of renewal into their church and among their compatriots. Thus maybe the people of Finland too suffered for the cleansing and purging of their sleeping and secularized fellow Nordic nations.

Maybe life was such in the final account when it was at its deepest and most creative level of blessing. Once baptized into Christ and joined to his life as a member of his body, one also had been consecrated to suffer and die with him—into victory and resurrection. But then the power of horror was broken.

He wiped off the snow from his neck and turned up his coat collar. In the storm and darkness everything melted together in a blue-black whirl of snow and whistling wind. Again he began to wander the long way of prayer from Björkö fort to Samma, across the ice of Ladoga to Mantsinsaari, Suomossalmi and Salla. The wandering ended there. The storm whistled, but beyond the night, the cold and horror, a shining light shone peaceably, as full of sadness and suffering as Aunt Agneta's voice, and yet just as wondrously soothing.

Britta Torvik stood at the kitchen window, ironing some baby clothing. Now and then she glanced toward the Karlsson home, because beyond its gable one could see a portion of the Saleby road right before it merged with the church village road.

The March sun shone in dazzling clarity over the deep snowdrifts. A veil of whirling silver streams rose in the cold, blue air along the ridge of the parsonage barn, because in spite of the cold, the noonday sun was hot on the south side of the roof. Were it not for the harsh peace terms forced on Finland by the Soviet Union, one would have thought that the whole creation was celebrating a day of thanksgiving.

In her thoughts Britta Torvik went through the shocking events of the week. First the rumors of Soviet troops penetrating Finland, then the long night toward Wednesday with anxious waiting for the peace terms and receiving incredible information that the Karelian Isthmus was lost—and finally that terrible morning. Gösta had been weeping like a child. Yet she herself felt a great security after all the heart-rending tension, a security felt all through the agitating emotions caused by this historic tragedy. It was not only her being happy for all the children, who now slowly would be released from the horrible bombing terror, and for all mothers who again could allow their little ones to go outside and play in the sun without fear of hearing the noise of approaching bombers. Neither was it her thinking of all the fighting men who once again would get enough sleep without being interrupted by another enemy attack. Her sense of security was a deeper thing. She understood nothing of politics—and she was not quite convinced that her husband and the other arguing parish leaders understood anything either—but she had a deep and unquestioning trust in God that was proven in the school of prayer. She felt how God lived and was present everywhere, how his rule entwined itself round the most trivial things in the kitchen and the nursery, and in her heart she was certain that it was no different in the puzzling business of the big world. She took it almost as a consolation from God himself that he allowed the great snowfall to happen on this black Wednesday and that he allowed this wonderful sun to shine when every hour was full of suffering, because one knew that the poor people now were packing their belongings and leaving their homes over there in Karelia. It was as if God wanted to say: Yes, my children, that is how evil you have made the world, but now I am spreading the whole cover of the Atonement over the dirt and the bloodspots—as I spread the white clothing of Christ's righteousness over you all in baptism, as I clothe the sinner with the same righteousness, if he believes, and, one hour on your deathbed, shall spread the white burial clothing of the Atonement over your poor heart if you fall asleep believing in the merit of Jesus.

Britta Torvik was, since childhood, brought up in traditional firm and faithful Lutheranism. She had learned to live in the light of Christ's substitutionary suffering. She knew that the whole course of history revolved around a great sacrifice, which God had chosen to be able to satisfy and atone and avoid condemning all the sin that so often sinks the fates of man and the decrees of history into dark night. Thus she never saw only night, but always the light behind it.

She often thought that her husband was a bit theatrical with his violent way of making problems out of everything and his melancholy disposition to wrestle with the windmills. But she noticed how he finally discovered the essential thing, often with a child's enthusiasm, and she thanked God. Lillan crawled from underneath the table where she had been sitting playing with her doll. Without interrupting her work, the pastor's wife kept watching her as she explored the kitchen floor. The afternoon sun shone through the windows painting two yellow squares on the sink. Lillan had found her way there and was completely bathed in sunlight. The mother who saw it with squinting eyes—but just because of that in an almost unreal splendor—thought of it as an image of Holy Baptism. God had drawn a circle of light around her child. She was standing there "in Christ," as the Bible said, within the realm of the atonement and the salvation. She had many times this winter thought of what it meant to her. If the worst should happen and she had to let God take Gösta, if she one day would have to flee in the snow with Lillan on her arm or to sit in a basement and silence her crying child, she would all the time feel God's hand surrounding it firmly with fatherly tenderness. Then she would be able, in spite of all, to give it up, whether it would be she or Lillan who would remain down here. Thus she was also emboldened to feel a bright and serene joy for the child that she had carried under her heart this fatal winter.

A blue shadow had appeared between the snow walls, and when she looked up, her husband came already gliding on his "kicksled" down toward the crossroads. A few minutes later he turned into the driveway. She hurried toward him on the doorsteps. He looked very grave. She asked anxiously:

"Well, how was it?"

He answered short and toneless, "Aunt Agneta left us at half past two."

She bowed her head. He quietly took off his coat. "The doctor did all he could—but there was nothing to do. The death-struggle began as I was arriving . . . and yet this message is one of peace and joy compared with the other that I'm bringing you . . . Agnes is dead."

She cried out and hugged him. He fumblingly stroked her hair.

"They called when I was with Aunt Agneta. The child is alive, it's a boy. She really never regained consciousness. Poor girl . . ."

He held her firmly. His thoughts went reeling in his brain. He was thinking of his own wife who soon would go into the same risk of death, and of the old lady at Saleby, her cheeks blue-black, struggling for air. She had gotten a bad case of the flu a little more than a week ago. It had been overcome with sulfonamid, so she had been up again looking after the house and had then fallen in bed with a violent pneumonia. Simultaneously, Agnes had left for the maternity ward at the hospital. The phone call came as a complete death-blow.

He felt wrath rising within himself. Was he not now a double murderer, Gunnar? This would never have happened to Aunt Agneta, if she could have spent the winter in Linköping. And Agnes . . . he tightened his muscles in exasperation so that Britta noticed it. She looked up at him.

"Don't look back, Gösta—only forward and upward." A moment later she said quietly, "What will happen to the boy?"

"God has now given Gunnar a last chance to make amends," Torvik said with stern solemnity. "Aunt Agneta did not live long enough to adopt him. Now he is just a motherless out-of-wedlock child, whom Gunnar can place in foster care at thirty crowns per month. If he does that, then he's judged. It looks indeed as if God has set up a final great test for Gunnar. He faces now all the evil consequences of his selfishness, which are so horrible that one's heart turns to ice. If he hardens his heart now . . ."

He embraced her firmly. Bursting out crying, he buried his face on her shoulder.

"Britta, Britta, he *must* not harden his heart! You know, sometimes I am scared of Gunnar. I fear him as a willpower; there is something satanic lurking behind his eyes. I could imagine him doing the evil just for its own sake—and then smile amiably talking about Jesus afterward. Antichrist must be precisely such, when he comes!"

"Quiet, quiet, my boy." She gently stroked his head. "You must not speak that way. Sure, I've seen it too. But dear, we are all that way, when one comes to the bottom of our corrupt hearts. With each one of us there is a Yes to the evil that can be held back by God's grace alone. But God is mightier than all evil in the world."

She repeated it slowly emphasizing every word, as if she herself had taken hold on something firm outside of herself: "God is mightier than all evil in the world."

―――――

The ringing in of the Sabbath rose toward the clear sky that had nuances of golden green and pink. The daylight was waning out slowly; it was as if the snowy fields and the high air had gathered in so much light, that they could not cease shining yet for a while.

Between the huge ridges of snow on the parsonage hill, Arvidsson from the Mansion came slowly walking in the loose snow, which constantly caused him to slide. When the ringing of the church bells reached him, he stopped. One could see that he hesitated, then he moved his hand slowly toward the hat brim. He took off his hat, and bowing his head for a moment with calm eyes he stood still with the hat over his chest. Then he quickly put it on again and resumed his heavy walk.

The robust farmer had had his special reasons to emulate his old father's custom today, although he never used to uncover his head when church bells were ringing, and although he could be seen in the church village, right where he was standing on the slope. He had prayed to God for strength to make it all the way to the parsonage.

When he reached the crest, he stopped again and hesitated. He glanced over the village. The snow now showed nuances of blue, the bells were silent and the steeple shutters had been closed. The smoke in the village rose like white ribbons straight toward the sky.

How different everything had become, since he was a boy. At that time none of the stately barns had been built that now were standing everywhere, commanding and massive at due distance from the dwelling houses. At that time there was still a conglomeration of sheds on either side of the parsonage road. And down at the church the stables had formed a semiclosed yard, where there was now just one short range left on the almost empty hill.

If that had been the only change . . . But have not the pews too become almost empty? Has not the old treasure of honor and honesty, of fear of God and sense of what is right been obliterated so that the bare stone foundation of selfishness and lust in our hearts is beginning to show? If anyone in his childhood had said that within forty years those things would occur in the world and in Ödesjö that had occurred this past year, he would certainly have been regarded as crazy.

He breathed heavily and continued walking to the parsonage gate and into the yard, where the parsonage is to the right with its elaborate veranda from the turn of the century.

As usual he entered through the unlocked door without knocking, took off his coat and hung it up, and proceeded toward the door to the left leading to the pastor's study. Before knocking at the door he took two deep breaths.

Torvik, who had heard the slow steps approaching across the hall, had already risen from his desk chair and was walking toward the door. He extended a friendly greeting to Arvidsson, who remained standing at the door, his chest expanded and his arms extended downwards with clenched hands, as if gathering all his strength for ultimate exertion. He looked straight ahead and forced himself to say the words: "Schenstedt has been killed."

The pastor stopped. His arms sank down. He took hold of the desktop. With two heavy steps he returned to his deskchair and fell down on his knees, with his arms resting on books, rough-draft sheets and opened envelopes that were spread over the desk. He folded his hands and bent forward against the desktop.

Arvidsson sat down on the sofa. He leaned forward, covering his face with both hands, as they used to do when praying together. There was total silence.

———

Neither of them was quite sure how long they had been sitting this way. Torvik looked up with dry and expressionless eyes. "Tell me," he said, and sat down heavily in his chair.

Arvidsson started slowly.

"They got a phone call at Saleby after dinner. Karin took it and called me immediately. It was a bomb shell. He died at the hospital two days after the peace agreement."

There was nothing more to say. And yet, all the questions remained. They were heart-rendering to both men. But none of them said anything. The pastor thought of what Lotta of Drängsmarken used to say: We have to leave that. But his heart was still hurting and trembling.

Finally he asked, "What about the boy now?"

"He will get his mother's family name. Since Schenstedt admitted fatherhood we can take out support from his estate. However, he won't have inheritance rights. The childcare board will have to get him a foster home or place him in an orphanage."

Torvik supported his head on his clenched hands nodding it slowly. Hardly audibly he mumbled, "Lord . . . Lord . . . how *could* you?"

They spoke yet for a while, taciturnly and with long heavy pauses. Then Arvidsson rose.

"I'd like to thank you for bringing the news to me in person. Now the road has become even narrower for us. We must learn not to see and yet believe."

They went out to the hallway. The pastor helped his friend with his coat. While shaking hands with him, he said: "Now our prayer guard duty for Gunnar is over." He reflected for a moment. "How long has it been now?"

"Since Third Sunday in Advent," Arvidsson said.

"That's three months," he said slowly. "I have never fought harder in prayer. A three-month struggle, almost as long as the war in Finland, and just as futile."

Arvidsson had put his hand on the door handle. They nodded and bid farewell.

I have to go to Britta, Torvik thought. But first he returned to his study and sat down at his desk. There he broke down, crying vehemently.

————

Palm Sunday had come with beaming sun and also with severe cold. The parsonage was unusually quiet. Since it was a communion day the pastor and his wife did not need to worry about breakfast. A light noise was heard from the kitchen when the maid cleaned up after breakfast for herself and Lillan.

Torvik paced back and forth in the living room. He had in his hand the draft for his communion homily, but it was difficult for him to concentrate. His mind was in an uproar. He was defeated and knocked to the ground. He knew that he must not proceed against God, and yet this question pushed itself to the front again and again: Lord, how could you? Lord, did you not promise that whatever two or three of us would ask in your name, you would do it?

The door to the parlor opened up, and Britta came in. She had her desk in the parlor, where she had just spent some quiet time, as she did every morning.

No one could say that Britta Torvik was beautiful, least of all now when being pregnant. But there was something glowing over her that caused her husband to wonder. He had not seen anything like it since he had seen Aunt Agneta that stormy February day.

"Would you have some time for me?" she asked looking at the draft of his communion homily.

"Certainly, sweetheart. What do you want?"

She stepped forward and taking his arm, she looked almost mischievously at him from the side.

"Promise me that I may have that which I now will ask you for."

Torvik smiled.

"If we can afford it, then . . ."

"If I promise in advance to do it within our household budget—at least for the next three years?" Now a big smile spread over her face.

"In that case you may do what you want."

"Then I decide that we'll adopt Gunnar's son."

Torvik turned around on his heel and took a firm grip around her shoulders.

"God bless you, Britta! But—have you considered what you are doing?"

"Yes, I believe I have."

"Do you realize that there will be no support for a child that one adopts?"

She looked up surprised.

"No I didn't know that—however, I never thought of it anyway."

"But have you thought of what we're taking on? Britta . . . dare you? I am fearful of Gunnar's eyes. He was possessed, Britta. If the boy is the same, consider what you'll get into our home. We might be able to handle it—but what about our own children?"

"Gösta," she said firmly. "God is stronger than all darkness in the world. Jesus has cured the possessed before."

When he still hesitated, she said softly, "Gösta, you said yesterday that God has now set up a great test for Gunnar. Don't you think that he has today set up just as great a test for us?"

He stepped up to the window looking irresolute. For three months he had fought a futile battle for Gunnar's soul! Already these three months had totally drained him. Was he now to struggle long years and maybe decades for Gunnar's son—maybe just as futile? Would he have the strength?

But then he was ashamed of himself. He thought of Britta, realizing what she was ready to take on. Tending to another baby night and day, providing food and clothing, being responsible for countless other things large and small—all this for a child whose father she always had regarded with distrust. Yes, he should truly be ashamed of himself! Here he had proceeded against God, how he could have allowed what had happened. Britta had instead asked God what he wanted her to do.

He turned around.

"My dear Britta, maybe it's foolishness to decide something so important without further deliberation, but if you're willing to accept this sacrifice, then I don't hesitate. If we do something foolish, then I think it's a foolishness according to God's heart."

She kissed him and said, "Thank you!"

He blushed helplessly like a schoolboy. She had quite unconsciously curtsied to him, when expressing her gratitude. He wanted to sink through the floor. But he knew he deserved this humbling experience.

"God bless you, my dear," he said lovingly.

"So you will speak with Arvidsson, then?"

He nodded in affirmation.

———

"In the same manner also, he took the cup, thanked God, and gave it to his disciples."

He lifted his hand in blessing over the old silver chalice, while reading the Words of Institution. The sun hit the gilded brim making a flashing light-spot on the inside of the chalice so that the wine shimmered blood-red with rays of rubies and gold.

". . . saying: Drink ye all of it. This cup is the New Testament in my Blood, which is shed for many, for the remission of sins."

While reading the Words of Institution and making the sign of the cross over the chalice, he noticed that he started to tremble. This mystery always became overwhelming, when he stood next to it. Today he saw almost a revelation. It was as if the shining silver bowl with the wine was transformed into a heart, created out of the shining substance from some celestial glory, filled with a blood that was pure and atoning, eternal and divine—and yet as warm and living as the warmth in a fellow human being's hand.

This shining heart was the center of all life. The sun and the worlds circled around it, the variegated scenarios of all history moved around it in billowing fluctuation, and the seraphs worshiped it in wide shining circles. It had been shining from the beginning of the world, its light penetrated the darkness of the morning of creation, and the trees in Paradise sang its praise with billowing branches. Then darkness came upon the earth, an angry sea of twisted limbs rolled forward with intertwined bodies in violent wrestling, the air shaking from curses and cries of agony. The sky was filled with red, flickering clouds, and the inescapably just retribution appeared like a sword between the clouds.

Then the shining heart descended over the storming sea like a setting sun. Like the sun going down, it was immersed in the black waves, which hissing with rage threw themselves over the bright edge of the chalice. The Holy Blood was poured like streams of gold and ruby over the dirt and the unclean rags in the rolling mass of agonizing humans.

Then the miracle happened. As the wave of a mighty wind washes away the sand from a large stone slab, likewise the blood and the dirt were washed away. Individual people appeared, set free from the rolling mass, and rising slowly they looked in amazement at the chalice that in a new glory had risen out of the black depth, now standing as a bright rock in the midst of the waves. The sky above was high and clear, the sun shone, and the angels sang: It is finished.

The dark mass was still shaking and jerking, but the hopelessness and distortion in its struggle were gone, the powers of the abyss turned away their faces, covering them to avoid seeing the brilliance from the chalice, around which the people streamed together to drink life and atonement from its shimmering depth.

While this was seen flitting past as visions, he had concluded the Words of Institution and knelt to pray the Our Father. He became silent for a moment in mute adoration before the mystery. He felt how everything was spread out as offerings before the altar. It was as if he had put it all down on the old stone slab floor, which was transformed into the Church's everlasting foundations before the heavenly throne. There was the burden of his own incapability, his shrunken heart that had been unable to save Gunnar, and his powerless prayers, which were like plucked-apart flowers. There lay the whole burden of the agony of this Holy Week, the fallen Finns, the abandoned homes, and the scorched farms. There lay his ravaged parish, displayed as on a map, with dark spots of licentiousness and contempt of God's grace. There lay Agnes, bled to death, pale, her eyes shut. And there lay also Gunnar himself, dead, with his white winter uniform as wrapping and with blood spots on his head, which was leaning on the foot of the altar. In the midst of all this failure and brokenness he was kneeling, himself a sinner among sinners. But above, on the altar, where he did not dare to look, shone the light around the chalice, the Atoning Mystery was present, the Lord, the Innocent One, was dead in the place of sinners, he was risen to live as a Savior—and this Sacrifice was the center of life and the beating heart of the universe.

He brought himself and all that lay here of human fragments and mangled lives as an offering, worthless refuse, which here sinking into the great sacrifice on the altar was absorbed by its shining brilliance and united with the blood that cleanses (from all sin).

As he concluded praying the Our Father, he knew that everything was finished. As the Father once had given his Son into an agony that surpassed all that under which the world now is writhing, so he would also in boundless love give all that could be given, day by day. Whatever would happen, it was going to proceed from an overflowing mercy. Even over the deepest enigmas was shining the certainty that the utmost had been done that could be done, and that God was not sparing any means to save all who possibly could be saved of an evil and lost humanity. Was he then to lament? Should he be anxious and ask questions?

Not many people had come to church in the cold, and the altar rail was sparsely filled with communicants. When Torvik distributed the bread, it struck him that the space where Schenstedt had knelt on the Third Sunday in Advent was empty. But right next to it, at the same space as then, Arvidsson was kneeling with his strong hands folded so that his knuckles turned white.

———

Taking Britta's arm he walked slowly homeward after the service. They did not talk much. Because of the deep snow they had to make a detour via the church village, so they stopped by at the post office and got their mail. After having bid Arvidsson farewell, they continued up the parsonage hill, and Britta said, "What would life be without the church?" Torvik nodded quietly. Then nothing else was said between them.

Back home he went to his study to look at the mail, while Britta prepared the coffee. Among the mail there was an Easter greeting from a good friend in Skåne. There was also a gray and creased-up letter which appeared to have been processed by coarse hands. It could be a certificate of registering change of domicile or notification of a new family name. He routinely turned it and became petrified. The cancellation said: Examined by the Military Censoring Authority, and the address, which was written with an aniline pen, was no doubt by Gunnar's hand.

His fingers trembling, he almost dropped the letter. His first thought that he did not dare to finish was that Gunnar was alive. A look at the cancellation date put out the hope. This letter was written before the date of Gunnar's death, but it had been delayed in the censoring process. He was holding in his hands a letter from a dead man.

He sat down. He did not dare to open it. Life and death hung tremulously before him, a scale of balance appeared for a moment, ready to give an eternally valid verdict, weighed down by the infinite future, pointed like a sword against this letter. He did not dare to read it.

Should he go to Britta? No—if this was the worst, then he should take the blow himself.

He folded his hands. Then he recalled the vision at church. Like a quiet melody the mystery of the atonement began singing for him. Without words and without sounds, just as a breath of that Love that had carried the punishment for evildoers and had become the equal of sinners.

He made the sign of the cross over both the letter and over his heart, opened the envelope with a paper knife, unfolded two creased sheets from a notebook and read:

———

"Dear old friend,

"I'm trying to write all that I should write before my fingers go numb in the cold. It's a long story.

"We're now at the front. War is no game. Yesterday we were hit by heavy bomb shells. One of the men lost his foot. I sat with him: A poor wretch who never had seen his father, rootless from the very beginning, at cross purposes with life. Then he ended up here—with his mutilated leg tucked in his trousers.

"Then I loosened up inside. I thought of my own child who might be born today and who would never have a father either. I thought of Agnes who would be lonely in the hospital without having anyone waiting for her at home. I thought of all that I had inflicted on Grandmother. And I thought of Inger whose divorce I encouraged for the joy of being a reformer. I was disgusted with myself. Most of all I was disgusted by my amiability that I had cultivated as a sport. It was the shield, which I held up against all criticism. It was a means I used in order to live without intrusion, without disturbing scenes, well-liked and appreciated—and appeasing my conscience.

"Tears do not come easily in this coarse atmosphere. But my heart has been more torn than anyone can cope with. Now the ache has been cured by Jesus' hand. *He* bound me that time in the church. Now he has loosed me.

"If I'll be granted to return alive, I'm planning on getting a position in the Norrland forests. I'll try to remedy everything with Agnes. But I don't want to be seen in Ödesjö. I think that an evil power would come from the memories.

"Now there is artillery fire again. A satanic whizzing and roaring. But there is peace within me—at last. Forgive me everything. Thanks for everything. God protect you!

"Your old friend,
Gunnar"

———

The sun was shining on the snow, which was glowing with ethereal clarity. All was light; unspeakable hymns of victory sounded beyond the bright blue sky. Torvik saw nothing and heard nothing; all was flaming radiance and music that no longer was expressed through earthly chords. He was not even able to stutter a thanksgiving; he was himself pulled away to a world where everything was boundless jubilation and overwhelming joy, and every fiber of his being became a string that joined the eternal song of praise from the lips of the seraphs.

He returned to his senses. Then he went over to Britta with the letter in his hand. She was the first one with whom he wanted to share this joy. Then he would hurry over to the Manor. Within him was singing an echo of the prophet's words: How beautiful upon the mountains are the feet of him who brings good tidings.

This God's gift of joy was not intended for anyone else. They would only share it with an old woman who already had come forward to the heavenly high altar of the Church Triumphant, and with the angelic host, which bursts out in jubilation every time it sees a little brother on earth lift his face toward heaven and be drawn to God, conquered by the suffering-filled glory of the cross and cleansed by that sacrifice, which is the atonement for the sins of the whole world.

Index

OTHER RESOURCES FROM AUGSBURG

Faith, the Yes of the Heart by Grace Adolphsen Brame
204 pages, 0-8066-3805-2

Drawing on the Bible and the Christian tradition, Brame presents a clear and inspiring study of the Christian life. She explores such vital issues as the relationship between believe and faith, how we live what we believe, finding God in our suffering, and how God lives through us.

Martin Luther: A Life by James A. Nestingen
112 pages, 0-8066-4573-3

A compelling new biography of Martin Luther, featuring eight pages of full-color images from the motion picture. *Martin Luther: A Life* offers the full story behind what the movie dramatizes.

Speaking of Trust by Martin E. Marty
160 pages, 0-8066-4994-1

Brings together passages from Luther's preaching on the Sermon on the Mount and Marty's comments about the place of trust in the life of faith. Marty has arranged Luther's words under three main topics: trust, prayer, and the Beatitudes.

Where God Meets Man by Gerhard O. Forde
128 pages, 0-8066-1235-5

This book about Luther's theology is written out of a two-fold conviction. First, that many of our problems have arisen because we have not really understood our own traditions; and second, that there is still a lot of help for us in someone like Luther if we take the trouble to probe beneath the surface. It is an attempt to interpret Luther's theology for our own day.

Available wherever books are sold.